HIRAETH

JENNIFER LEIGH PEZZANO

Hiraeth

(Hira-eath)
Of Welsh origin.

(n) A deep wistful, nostalgic sense of longing for something;
a home that is no longer, or perhaps never was.

This book goes out to those who dare to reach for more.
May you all find the wild inside yourself.
The heartbeat that calls you home.

PROLOGUE

SPOKANE, WASHINGTON: 2112

A blanket of gray sky stretched above the trees, branches rustling in the chill of the wind that blew against me like a whisper.

The sharp scent of wood smoke and pine, the endless deep green of forest, the gentle pull of his eyes. These were the delicate moments I tucked away inside. Stolen fragments from a life that was not mine but one I had once tried so hard to hold on to.

"It's really nice to see you, Seren." Domine's words were hesitant, as if I was a bird he was afraid to startle, and I shot him a shaky smile as I bent to retrieve the cans of non-perishable food from the back seat of my car.

"It's nice to see you, too." I placed the box into his arms, and a rush of heat skittered through me as our fingers momentarily brushed against each other.

The wind pulled at his hair, tousled strands falling into his face as he glanced down at my left hand, his eyes flickering over the crystal set against a silver band. "What's that?"

My breath caught in my throat, and I took a step back from him, tucking my hands into the pockets of my coat as if it was some shameful secret, a dark stain that would tarnish what was left of us.

1

"Trendon proposed last night." My voice came out fragmented and torn, and I glanced into the sky as images of the night before washed over me. The bottle of wine. Trendon's work promotion. His eyes so eager and hopeful as he slid the small box across the table.

Why had I come up here?

We had closed so many doors, and this was the last one we had left. My marriage to Trendon would be the finality of our story. The closing act. And the thought of that was a sudden howling wind inside me, tearing away at my foundation.

"Wow." Domine placed the box of food on the ground and leaned against the door of his cabin. A stream of faint sunlight momentarily broke through the clouds, casting shadows across his face. "I guess congratulations are in order." He shot me a tense smile, the heaviness in his eyes betraying his words.

"Well, we've been dating for a few years now. It felt like it was time to take the next step. You know how much I've been wanting to have a family." The truth rushed out untethered. A reminder of all the things that now stood between who we once were and who we had now become. I looked down, fiddling with the buttons of my coat, unable to meet the burn of his eyes. I feared if I did, if he stepped closer to me, if he took me into his arms and told me to stay, that I would. I would stay. I would give up everything. And the thought of that terrified me. The power he still had over me was a current I could not seem to shake loose.

"Am I still going to see you?"

His question tore into me, and I forced back the ache in my gut and the abrupt swell of tears that threatened to rise up, leaving me grasping at the threads of my composure.

"Of course. I'll be back next month to drop off more supplies."

He nodded and pushed himself from the door, shoving his hands deep into his pockets, the silence surrounding us a sudden crushing weight.

Say something.

But he just stood there, looking up into the canopy of trees, as if searching for something among the pallor of the winter sky.

"I should probably go. I only have three hours left on my travel pass." My words fell like broken wings, hollow against my lips as I turned toward the car.

He didn't even glance back at me. His face remained impassive, his eyes detached as he continued to stare up at the sky. "Okay, thanks for stopping by."

"No problem. I'll see you in a few weeks." With a sigh, I thrust open the car door and slid into the front seat. My hands trembled as I scanned the key fob over the ignition, the glow of the console lighting up as the motor hummed to life. From the corner of my eye, I saw him turn to me and stride toward the car, and then he was yanking the door open. My heart slammed against my chest as he leaned in so close that I could see the flecks of auburn in his eyes.

"Are you happy, Seren?"

I sucked in a sharp breath, my hands gripping the steering wheel as all the things I longed to say lodged like jagged stones within my throat. The truth was too heavy, an immense wave that would only pull me under. "I'm trying to be."

"Well, I hope you find it with him." His voice came out in a whisper before he took a step back and closed the door, severing the space between us.

A broken sigh escaped me, and I willed my limbs to move, my fingers shaking as I pushed the drive button on the console. The tires crunched along the rutted dirt road, my vision wavering with the release of my tears as I watched him fade slowly from view, until there was nothing left but the outline of him disappearing into the fold of the trees.

CHAPTER ONE

I stood in the kitchen with my coffee cup clenched in my hands. My fingernails set against the glazed ceramic as I stared out at the colorless sky beyond the window.

Late summer had arrived, and with it came the smoke. You could set your clock by it.

For months, the hot, dry weather scorched the hills and surrounding forests until, sunbaked and weary, the land gave up the fight as it did every year.

First came the scent on the wind, then the suffocating ash, until the haze swallowed the sun, and I forgot what blue sky looked like. Nothing but a palette of yellow and gray, faint shadows leaning ominously against the bleached grass of the front yard. A desolate landscape that pressed down on me until I could no longer think.

A stark reminder of the terrain within my own life.

I had become inert. Unmoving. Confined within walls I could not rearrange.

"Mommy, what's this?"

With a sigh, I shifted my gaze from the window and turned to my daughter. Lilica sat at the table, her breakfast barely touched as she swiped through the pages of her interactive textbook. An image hovered in front of her. Leaning closer, I made out the bills and coins depicted in the hologram that revolved in front of us, bathing our skin in a greenish glow. "That's called money."

"Money?" She scrunched up her nose, the haunting gray of her eyes filled with questions.

"Yes." I set my coffee cup on the table and ran my fingers through the silky strands of her hair, the color reminiscent of sunshine against my skin. The same bright hue as mine. "You see, years ago, people used to be able to buy houses and cars, and they had businesses of their very own, like clothing stores and restaurants. Money is what they used to do that."

She stared at the holographic image, her four-year-old mind trying to comprehend the concept of ownership. "Why don't we do that anymore?"

"Well, because we are One now. We don't need things like ownership. Those things only separate us."

I found myself using the regurgitated slogan passed down through the years, displayed on digital billboards throughout towns and cities. They were the same words that slipped from the mouths of high government officials who ran our country. The rhetoric of unity and collective thought.

But the statement felt so hollow to me. It always had. It was nothing but a placating lie. A smokescreen obscuring our sight. We were only renting out our lives, given an elaborate point system tallied on a screen that was exchanged for access to basic services if you complied with all the rules handed to you.

Compliance had become our new currency.

And without it, you had nothing. You became an Outlier, people who refused to adhere to the rules. They were the radical thinkers considered a threat to our society, stripped of their citizenship rights, and forced to live primitively on parcels of allotted land beyond the Grid.

And Domine was one of them.

My heart stumbled as it always did when he filtered into my

thoughts like a hesitant whisper of longing. A reminder of a life I chose not to have. It had been almost six months since I had last driven up to the Compound to drop off pilfered supplies of canned food. I tried to check in as much as I could, but my visits had become less frequent throughout the years, and I never stayed long.

It was another of the many secrets I kept from my husband.

"Hey, honey." I pushed the plate of food in front of Lilica and removed the book from the table, closing the thick polymer pages. "Why don't you finish up your breakfast? Mommy needs to be at the clinic in an hour. And you." I playfully bopped her nose with my finger, eliciting a wide grin from her. "You need to get ready for Learning Group."

* * *

The white cement of the Child Center towered above Lilica's tiny form as I watched her dash down the walkway and then come to a stop, holding up the ID badge she wore around her neck. The red beams of the scanner swept across her, and the doors slid open, swallowing her up into the bowels of the building.

A pressing weight always seemed to accompany these drops offs. A gnawing unease that slunk through the corners of my mind. For the next six hours, she would be lost to me, systematically preened and whittled down to fit into the neat compartments of our society, and I was powerless to stop it.

Taking a deep breath, I tapped the work button located on the screen console and leaned against the sleek leather seat, allowing the car to guide me smoothly back onto the road and toward my office. I shuffled back my thoughts until all that remained was an opaque expanse of detachment. The kind that wove around me and asked no questions. The urgent rush of cars. The grey pallor of the sky. The barren landscape of asphalt and steel buildings. All of this bled out into the background, colorless shapes gliding past me. I couldn't look too close. If I did, I would see the fractures in the pavement.

The stark emptiness we orbited. The revolving doors that went nowhere.

Pulling into the parking lot, my car turned off with a hum, the interior lights softly dimming to black as I grabbed my purse and hurried toward the clinic. The sky hung heavy with heat and smoke, wispy tendrils that clawed at my clothes and stung my nose as I brushed past artificial trees lining the walkway like decorative cartoon cutouts. Simulated grass neatly arranged between the trunks.

Defensible space is what the government called it. This was a place where seasonal fires could not touch us, and no watering was needed. Nature had become an enemy to tame, a concept to manipulate, and the mountains and forest beyond the Grid had become a hostile environment people were discouraged from venturing into. I couldn't even remember the last time my daughter had looked up into the swaying branches of a living tree, ran her hands along the rough woven bark. It had been years.

I scanned my badge at the entrance, and the doors hissed open. My lungs filled with the crisp, cool breeze of the filtered air-conditioned hallway as I stepped inside, the lights blinking to life as I walked past them and opened the door to my office. Enclosed in this brief moment of stillness, I sat down at my desk. Soon, the steady stream of patients would shuffle through the doors. Today was Administration Day.

I stared at the stack of rolling containers EmCorp had dropped off the day before, their large, imposing black logo stamped across each one. Walking to the boxes, I typed in the code that deactivated the seal. With a hiss, the containers sprang open, revealing hundreds of white coated capsules, each one packaged within its own sterilized bag.

I tried to push back the familiar, sinking feeling in my gut as I stared down at the immunity enhancers. Required medicine that fortified us once a month with a synthetic immune system. A once-natural network of biological processes we were now unable to create on our own.

Some had blamed toxins in the environment and smoke in the

air. Others thought it could be the result of genetic mutations. But whatever it was, according to the electronic textbooks I had scoured through during my doctoral residency, the last few decades had shown a consistent decline in our bodies' innate ability to fight off disease, and cancer rates had skyrocketed.

But I knew these pills weren't working. People were still getting sick.

"You in there, Seren?" A gentle knock on the door drew me from my thoughts as my co-worker, Kystina, stepped into the room, her short, dark hair tightly slicked back. This was her warrior look. "You ready for the flood?" She asked with a chuckle as she glanced over at the containers.

I nodded with a wan smile and crossed the room to retrieve a key from the top drawer of my desk. "I think so. I just want to take a quick stock of the herbal medicine we have on hand for today." Sliding the large rolling bookshelf placed against the far wall, I slipped the key into the door hidden behind it. Shelves lined the walls, containing small glass vials of various herbs and tinctures classified by dosage and use. I pulled out the old file folder I kept tucked behind one of the shelves and ran my finger down the list. It was an outdated method of charting, left over from the early twenty-first century, but it was the only way to avoid being tracked.

Kystina rested her back against the wall next to me and crossed her arms. "So, I heard EmCorp may be doing another unannounced sweep next week."

I furrowed my brow, biting the edge of my lip as my eyes scanned the bottles on the shelf, their medicinal properties filtering through my mind like words across a page. "I know."

"Aren't you ever afraid you're going to get caught?"

"Are you afraid?" I turned toward her, fingering the amethyst pendant my mother had given me when I was a child, before she got sick, before my whole family got sick. I knew why I was doing this. These alternative treatments were working. They were helping people. But the guilt of dragging Kystina into this always tugged at the back of my mind.

Kystina sighed and leaned in close to me, her eyes softening. "I know I probably should be, but I'm not."

I squeezed her arm. "Well, if that ever changes, you do know you can transfer to another clinic. I'd understand."

"We've already been through this." She shook her head, a playful grin tugging at the corners of her mouth. "If you're going down, I'm going with you."

I only hoped it would never come to that.

I knew what I was doing was a risk. Herbal medicine had been banned decades ago, and anyone caught practicing it faced imprisonment. But I was doing this for the family I lost, for the voices that could no longer speak, and for all the people who still wanted a choice to find healing in something beyond the pharmaceutical industry running the country. I had to believe one day that could change. The alternative terrified me.

"Okay then, warrior." With a smile, I handed her the patient code sheets discreetly tucked beneath the inventory checklist. "I think we have enough supplies for today."

Closing the door behind us, Kystina helped me roll the bookshelf back and secure it against the wall, shooting me a sly wink. "I'll go unlock the front doors and get the clinic ready."

"Thanks, I'll be there in a minute."

Taking a seat at my desk, I ran my fingers through my shoulder length hair, which I had recently decided to grow out from the tidy angled bob I'd always worn. I longed for something different, a small tear at the structure in my life. A silent revolt from the repetition. As I secured the ends of my hair on top of my head with a clip, my phone buzzed on the desk, alerting me to a message from Trendon.

Don't forget to pick up the items on the grocery list today.

My shoulders tensed as I stared at the holographic text wavering in front of me like a blast of frigid air. So many of our conversations these days had begun to feel that way. Cold, clipped, and devoid of emotion. Two people moving through the motions of a marriage.

"Looks like the patients are here, Seren." Kystina peeked around the doorframe, steam rising from the cup of coffee in her hand. "Are you ready?"

I glanced over at the EmCorp boxes once more, steeling myself for a long day full of sterilized administrations and code scans. People whittled down to nothing more than a check mark in a data system. With a sigh, I grabbed my tablet from the desk, the white glow illuminating the room as I turned it on and stood to adjust my lab coat. "Yes, I'm ready."

* * *

"*Mommy!*" The car door opened, and Lilica climbed into the back seat. She positioned herself on her booster and held her arms still, allowing the seatbelt to automatically slide over her shoulders, locking her securely in place. "We practiced our steps today."

I looked back at her with a smile. "How exciting, hon. Are you ready for the big performance?"

She nodded, her eyes wide. "I get to hold the emblem."

"Oh, wow. That's a very important job."

"Teacher says it's because I'm the best at sitting still and not asking questions."

"Did she, really?" My brow furrowed, and I tried to keep my voice neutral as the car navigated into the stream of late afternoon traffic, the sun a deep orange orb above us.

As a child, I always asked too many questions. So many days spent in the silent room, staring at the blank white wall in front of me, as if its lack of color could cleanse my mind of thought. It never did, though. I just learned over time how to make my voice quieter.

I looked at Lilica through the rearview mirror, watching as her eyes quietly tracked the passing cars, and that sinking feeling inside claimed me once more. *They had already silenced her.*

"Mommy, can we get a treat?"

I punched the grocery icon into the car dashboard and leaned back against my seat. "I don't see why not. We do have to stop and pick up a few things from the warehouse before we head home."

We soon arrived at the parking lot of the food warehouse, our seatbelts releasing us as the soft hum of the electric engine shut down. I stepped out and grabbed my purse, taking Lilica's hand in mine as I weaved us through the maze of cars and over to the queue.

Standing in line, I pulled up my identification badge on my phone while we moved slowly toward the entrance. A loud beep notified acceptance as each person disappeared through the large sliding glass doors, our turn filling the silence that would otherwise be deafening. I held up my badge to the monitor, and its blue light snaked across the front, the numbers on its screen defining who I was, analyzing my data, calculating my worth.

We stepped inside, the dim glow of the solar lights flickering above as if the sun had already grown disillusioned with its struggle to pierce through the smoke of the sky.

"Mommy, can I turn on the store doggy?"

"Sure, love." With a smile, I watched as she grabbed an automated cart and pushed the green button, grinning as it sprang to life and began to glide alongside us like a silent companion.

"When can we go see the real doggies again, Mommy?" She looked up at me as we entered the produce section, her eyes wide and pleading.

"Someday soon, love. I promise." I gave her a tight smile, remembering the last time we had gone to the Animal Facility. Those visits always left me with a feeling of sorrow afterwards. A disconnect that felt unnatural. I knew we once used to have animals as pets, but they were unpredictable and carriers of disease, no longer safe to live with, we were told. So we corralled and caged them, viewing the wild in their eyes from a protected distance.

"Hey, sweetie." I grabbed the food scanner from the side of the cart and placed it in her hands as I typed my personal code into the automated cart display, linking my purchases to the points on my Grid Account. "Would you like to scan some bananas for me?"

With an eager nod, she skipped down the produce aisle, waving the scanner like a sword until it landed on her target.

"What next, Mommy?" She bounded back to me with the package of sealed bananas in hand, her voice echoing through the store like a vibrant splash of color against a sea of gray.

I hated shopping. The endless aisles, the sterile protective packaging, the vacant stares. Nobody smiled, certainly not at each other. We lived surrounded by others but lost in the vacuum of our own impenetrable isolation.

"Um, it looks like we need some milk."

"Milk, milk... where are you?" Lilica chanted as we walked through the dairy section with the cart diligently humming alongside us. Reaching into the cooler, she plunked a jug into the cart.

I glanced down at my phone, scanning through the items on the grocery list. "Okay, now we need to find the bread." Looking up, my heart skipped a beat. Suddenly lost in the blur of bodies, the flash of Lilica's white shirt was nowhere to be seen.

"Lilica!" My voice tore through the muffled buzz of the store, causing people to turn away from me.

A frantic mother was an embarrassment. An untidy display of disorder. Children were supposed to stay quietly beside their parents. Independence was a sign of disobedience, a hazard to their development, a symptom of bad parenting.

My pulse pounded in my ears as I bolted down the aisle and rounded another corner, the sickening grip of dread settling deep in my gut. If someone were to report this, it would be a mark on my file. A warning I was an unfit mother. All it took were three civil notations of concern, and then the State would come in and swoop your child away, tucking them into the folds of the system and stripping you of your parental rights. It was a chilling reminder that nothing was ours, not even our own children.

A wave of panic rose within my throat, a silent strangled plea that sucked the oxygen from my lungs as I spun my gaze around, moving from one aisle to another.

And then I saw her, standing in the candy section, her eyes fixed on the dizzying array of choices in front of her. I released my breath in a long exhale and pulled her close to me, my limbs shaking. "Don't run off like that, okay?"

"But I wanted a lolly." Her eyes were wide and fragile, unaware of the danger that trailed behind her childhood innocence.

I quickly grabbed a lollipop from the shelf and took the scanner from her hand, placing it in the cart as I looked up at the security cameras blinking above us. "Let's get out of here, Lili. Let's go home."

CHAPTER TWO

*T*he shrill pulse of the alarm pulled me from the darkness of sleep, the space beside me an empty expanse of sheets. The blinds drew themselves soundlessly up as I shut off the holographic clock beside the bed, a strange feeling overcoming me. It was reminiscent of Déjà vu mixed with a fleeting impression of tall trees and dense moss beneath my feet.

Images that felt so real, like unbroken memories.

My mother had spoken of dreaming when I was a child. Stories that once visited us as we slept, like a movie played out in our unconscious mind. An endless, alternate reality we could explore. I used to lie in bed at night and wish for one, but they never came. Something had happened a long time ago, a shift in our collective thoughts, a disconnect we could not define, and we had lost our ability to dream.

But I still went to bed every night hoping for one to visit me.

I closed my eyes, willing the visuals to clarify, but like smoke, they drifted through my fingers, intangible and impossible to grasp. What surfaced instead was Domine, and my mind momentarily wandered back to the last time I saw him.

The sun's rays had slanted orange light through the trees, the rustling branches like a whisper, enticing me to stay. His face shrouded in the long shadows of cedar and fern. The harbor of his deep brown eyes, soothing like sun-drenched earth, silently watching me as he stood outside his cabin.

I missed him.

Despite how hard I tried not to. *I always missed him.* I was perpetually caught between the structured layers of the life I chose and the one I had left behind so long ago.

Pushing the thoughts of him from my mind, I rose from the bed and made my way into the bathroom, the tap on the sink springing to life as I ran my hands beneath it and splashed cold water on my face.

"Mommy?"

I turned to see Lilica standing in the doorway of the bathroom, her hair tousled against flushed cheeks.

"Yes, hon?" I bent down and stared into her glassy eyes, my hand instinctively rising to her forehead.

"My throat hurts. I don't feel good."

Heat radiated against my hand, and a sinking weight coiled in my gut as I brushed back the strands of hair that had fallen into her eyes. "Looks like you have a little fever. Why don't we get you back into bed?"

Lilica nodded and slowly shuffled back to her room as I grabbed my phone from the nightstand. Speaking Kystina's name into the receiver, I waited for the connection.

"Seren, what's up?" Her voice came out groggy and muffled.

"Sorry to wake you, but I won't be able to come into the clinic today. Lilica's sick again."

"Oh no. How bad is it?" The heavy tone of concern crept into her voice, mirroring the same sharp apprehension that pierced me like a knife whenever Lilica ran a fever. No matter how hard I tried to push it down, to swim past the fear, it was always there. The enemy we constantly battled. The fragility of living in a world surrounded by invisible threats we no longer had protection from.

"I think she'll be fine. I have some supplies here at the house I can give her."

"Oh, good." There was shuffling on her end, and then the sound of water running as she spoke quietly into the phone, concealing her voice. "Let me know if you need anything specific, and I can drop it off for you."

"Thanks, Kystina. You think you'll be okay without me today?"

"I'll be fine. Go take care of your little girl."

With a sigh, I set the phone on the bedside table and slipped into the walk-in closet. Bending down, I retrieved the medical bag I kept hidden from Trendon, tucked discreetly behind the dresser, its edges worn and frayed. Zipping open the small leather pouch, I rooted through the various bottles, the glass clinking together like the wind chimes that used to hang outside my window as a child. A comforting melody that reminded me of my mother's gentle touch and the herbal remedies she concocted late at night. Salves and tinctures doled out under her quiet and watchful eye. Remedies holding secrets inside.

"The earth will always provide us with the medicine we need."

Her words were a steady drumbeat I carried with me always. Knowledge passed down from the generations of women who once lived among the sprawling green and rugged coastline of Wales.

Medicine was all that was left of my lineage.

I pulled out a small jar of marshmallow root and my bottle of immunity powder, a dehydrated blend of echinacea, black elderberry and ginger root. Noticing my supplies were dwindling, I made a mental note to gather more from work. I had just placed a new order for herbs at the clinic and was glad I would not have to navigate the risky black-market exchange for another year.

Padding into the kitchen, I pressed the hot water button on the brew dispenser. The humming blue light illuminated my skin as I reached up into the cabinet for a cup and my eyes fell to Trendon's empty coffee mug sitting on the counter beside the sink. The only evidence of him these days. His late nights and early mornings at work had reduced us to nothing but a handful of exchanges, like distant planets orbiting the same sun. And the saddest part of all was I had begun to prefer it that way.

Steam rose from the cup, the earthy scent enveloping me as I walked down the hall and poked my head into Lilica's room to find her asleep. Her silken hair spread across the pillow. Sitting on the edge of the bed, I ran my fingers down her cheek. She stirred and opened her eyes, smiling up at me weakly. "Is your mommy tea ready?"

"Yes, love." I lifted her head up against the pillows and handed her the cup. "You drink up all your mommy tea, and you'll feel better soon."

"Will you tell me a story?"

"Of course. What kind of story would you like to hear?" I stretched across the bed beside her, the aroma of soap from last night's bath still lingering on her skin.

"Tell me a story about the time before."

I smiled, remembering my mother's own stories whispered in the quiet of my childhood bedroom.

"Okay. Let's see… once upon a time when the world was full of artists and musicians. There was a little girl-"

"What are artists and musicians, Mommy? I forgot."

I looked down at her, eyes wide and pressing, the past an endless galaxy she wanted to explore. "People who created things from their imagination."

"And what did they create?"

"All sorts of things. They made beautiful paintings and sculptures, words and sounds that made you feel all kinds of emotions."

"Like what I see in my book?"

"Yes. Just like in your book."

"Where are they now?"

My breath stilled, and I glanced out the window into the haze of a scorched sky, remembering the soft, melodic sounds my mother would make when I was a child. Songs she hummed like whispers from a past now faded and lost. "I don't know."

* * *

*T*he glow of Lilica's night globe washed the room in a muted blue light. She lay asleep, limbs tangled in her sheets as I ran the scanner of the thermometer across her forehead, my pulse a rapid thrum within my chest.

18

Please don't let it be too high.

I breathed a sigh of relief as the holographic numbers flashed in front of me. Her fever had finally stabilized. She was going to be okay. Tucking the blankets around her, I placed a gentle kiss on her forehead and quietly closed her bedroom door, retreating into the kitchen.

I stood at the counter, robotically placing the remains of dinner into airlock trays, and watching as the fridge hissed open, its drawers sliding forward like a vacant command awaiting my submission. That feeling hit me again. The same one which had followed me around for years, gnawing at the corners of my mind, poised and ready to strike like a cornered animal.

I was trapped. We all were.

There was no color to paint upon our walls. The world was either black or white, with muted tones that matched the fire-scorched sky. And I longed for color. I longed for sound. I wanted to give my child something more. A song she could sing around herself.

The silence within the house shuffled into the corners as the headlights of Trendon's vehicle spilled through the living room window, casting slanted shadows across the walls, and startling me from my restless thoughts.

The door opened quietly, bringing with it the smell of smoke as Trendon appeared in the entryway to the kitchen, his form swathed in the dark imposing suit of his patrol uniform. Removing his tactical vest, he placed it in the locked closet as he did every night, away from the probing curiosity of Lilica's explorations. She'd seen him in his uniform only once. He had sat her on his lap, trying to explain to her that his uniform was to keep people safe, but the fear in her eyes was evident.

There were only three corporate sectors allotted to us when we entered the workforce. Healthcare, corporate retail, and civil service, all designed to keep the system moving perfectly in place. Trendon had chosen civil service and directed the branch of check points and curfew monitoring. He was the dark knight gliding across streets, his presence keeping us tucked away inside our homes. Reminding us we were protected and looked after, like children seeking solace from lurking shadows. But it was only a thinly veiled illusion. A lie cloaked within the rigid grip of restriction. In the end, it was our own fear that imprisoned us.

"How was work? You're home early." I leaned up against the counter, regarding him with a forced smile.

"We had a new recruit today, so I gave him the rest of my night shift." Trendon ran his hand over his cropped thinning hair, his jet-black eyes flickering across the kitchen. "Where's dinner?"

"I just put it away. But I can warm some up for you in the oven if you like?"

"Thanks." With a nod, he brushed past me, the space around us muted and dull around the edges. Both of us had grown mutually content with the cold as whatever sun that had once sustained us grew further away from our sky, until there was nothing left but the shell of who we used to be. I couldn't even remember the last time we had touched each other.

"How was your day?" The tidiness of his question twisted around the sound of a glass being placed on the counter.

"Lilica had a fever this morning, so I stayed home with her." The beep of the warming oven sounded as it released its doors and awaited the food I had retrieved from the refrigerator. Sliding the plate of food into the oven, I stood back and stared at the glowing red coils that now illuminated the door.

"Oh." He perched himself at the table and pulled out his phone, fingers swiping away at the screen and bringing up the holographic image of the latest EmCorp report. "Please tell me she received her immunity enhancer this month."

"Of course she did." I folded my arms across my chest. "She's fine now. Her fever broke a little while ago."

Trendon didn't look up from the image hovering in front of him, only nodded absentmindedly as the monotone drone of an EmCorp official filled our kitchen.

Food shortages continue on the Eastern Seaboard...

Two underground resisters arrested today on charges of treason...

I bit my lip, trying to block out the words and the chill that always overcame me whenever they sprang onto his screen. I detested the daily EmCorp reports, but Trendon followed them religiously, his eyes glued to the hologram every night.

I slid into the chair next to him, hoping to direct his attention away from the report. "Lilica's asleep, but you can pop your head in and say goodnight if you want."

"No, that's okay."

That sharp sliver of contempt pricked me once more, and I dragged my gaze toward the darkness of the kitchen window. Trendon's lack of interest was a palpable force that swallowed up the air around me. I knew his work consumed so much of him, but whenever I tried to bring it up, he would only give me an irritated look, as if my remarks were only an annoying sound to be easily flung aside.

A memory unearthed like a tarnished artifact. Bitter and sweet. My body resting against a chair in the backyard. Skin warm beneath late summer sunlight and the reprieve of blue sky. My belly ripe, mind in repose. The smile on Trendon's face as he sat beside me.

What happened to those days?

Our marriage had once felt so easy, gliding effortlessly into place with his promise of security and a chance to finally start the family I had always longed for. But over the past few years, as his job stripped more of him away, he had become a stranger in his own house, navigating his parental role with a mixture of reluctance and duty, firmly upholding the rigid rules of the Grid without question. And I found myself drifting further from him until I couldn't even recognize the man I had married anymore.

We had become nothing more than a barren landscape confined within the boundaries of mutual agreement and the constraints of compromise. In the end, had I only been too scared to risk a life with a man who was untamed? A man who made me feel wild?

There was no room for wildness in this world.

"Okay then." I sighed and pushed myself off the chair. "I'm going to bed."

Only silence answered back as I made my way down the hall and into our room. I stared at the bed, my eyes trailing over the immaculately folded corners, the crisp whiteness of the bedcover like a barren field of snow. I had a sudden urge to rip away the sheets and toss them onto the floor. To expose the stains of our marriage buried within the fibers of the mattress. All the secrets I kept. The stifling constriction that screamed inside me.

Gathering my nightgown and toothbrush, I slipped from the room and into Lilica's, closing the door to her bathroom and running the water into the sink. I had been sleeping in her room more and more lately, seeking comfort in the soothing rise and fall of her breath, her tiny body curled against mine, cocooned in a private world composed of only the two of us.

CHAPTER THREE

*M*y breath hitched as I placed the glass slides under the microscope and clicked the objective lens into position. The machine let out a low hum as the light sliced through the slides, analyzing my blood. The seconds ticked by. My entire life perched precariously on the edge while I awaited the results.

The mechanical whirring soon quieted, and a green light flashed onto the screen, the tightness in my chest loosening slightly.

Serum Biochemistry Results:
*Glucose… normal
*Urea… normal
*Sodium… normal
*White Cells (WBC)… normal
*Red Cells (RBC)… normal
*Tumor Protein Markers (TPM) ***NOT DETECTED***

I let out a slow exhale. Relief whispering through my limbs, stilling the frantic pace of my heart. My body was a time bomb waiting to detonate, and for one more month, the bomb lay dormant.

Standing from the desk, I walked to the window and stared out into the gray haze of a summer sky. The mountains stood somewhere out there, encased beneath the layer of acrid smoke from the distant fires, and I longed for rain and blue sky. The caress of sunlight like a blissful pardon, erasing the memory of another long, bleak summer.

Thirty-eight years old. I was a year older than my mother had been when she got sick, ten years older than my brother when he passed, and five years ahead of my father. Terminal cancer statistics were now one in every three people. It had taken my whole family. And it could eventually take me and, one day, possibly my daughter as well. Every month, I diligently ran my bloodwork, and every negative test filled me with a conflicting sense of relief and guilt. Cancer had not touched me yet. Why had *I* been spared? Why was I the lone sapling growing among a forest of fallen trees?

"Seren, your next patient is waiting in the lobby." Kystina stood in the doorway, face solemn as her eyes skirted over to the blood samples that lay on my desk. "Did you already run your results?"

"Yes. They were negative."

"Oh, thank God." She swept through the room, grabbing the glass slides and stacking them neatly onto the cart beside the microscope. "I wish you didn't have to do this every month."

"Me, too." With a sigh, I grabbed my tablet as the name of my next patient wavered in the air in front of me. "Would you let Mr. Candon know I'm ready for him?"

"Sure thing." With a nod, Kystina closed the door behind her, the sound of her footsteps echoing down the long hallway as I whisked away the remaining evidence of my results, tucking them inside my desk drawer.

A gaunt face appeared in my office, eyes glancing nervously around the room as I settled myself at my desk.

"Mr. Candon, please have a seat." I gestured to the chair in front of me, watching as he shuffled over and sank down, arms folded across his chest. I tapped the screen, and his holographic chart sprang up in front of me, causing my breath to still.

A long exhale tumbled from him, his voice barely a whisper. "It's pretty bad, isn't it?"

I looked over at him, his skin sallow and shrunk against bone. Chemo had ravaged him, leaving behind the shell of what I assumed was once a vibrant young man. "How long have you been doing the treatments?"

"Six months."

I quickly scanned his chart, taking note of blood work completed before and after each session. "It looks like you've had three rounds." My finger hovered over the results. "Your tumors are not responding to the treatment. In fact, they appear to be-"

"Growing larger." He jerked forward, resting his hands on his knees. "I know. That's why I'm here."

I swiped his file closed and leaned back in my chair, regarding him with a measured look. "So, what is it you hope I can do for you?" New patients were tricky. There was always the threat of entrapment. Agents of EmCorps were known to appoint cancer patients for the sole purpose of exposing herbal healers. I had never encountered one, but I had heard the stories, and I knew I had to be cautious.

"Well, I've been told you offer *other* treatments." His voice dropped low, and his eyes shifted across the room.

"And who told you that?" I folded my hands on the desk, my words guarded.

"Rederick."

The tension in my shoulders lifted. Rederick was the man who helped me obtain my herbs through the black market and was the main source of my referrals at the clinic.

A beat of silence passed as he shifted uncomfortably in his seat, and when I looked into his eyes, I saw fear. The man was dying and clinging to his one last hope.

"Okay, then. What I can do is set you up with a treatment plan." Reaching down, I pulled some papers from a bottom drawer. "I'll just need you to fill out this additional intake form first. It will keep you out of the system." I slid the papers across the desk and handed him a pen. "I cannot make any promises that what I offer you will work, but with the type of cancer you have, I've seen a high rate of success."

He nodded, awkwardly gripping the pen in his hand as if it were a foreign object, his fingers shaking as he bent to read the text. "Will these treatments be…" He trailed off as if grasping for words, and I knew what he was trying to ask. It was the same question they all asked. Coded language encased in apprehension.

"Discreet? Yes. All the herbal medicine will be in pill form in a standard pharmaceutical bottle. You do not need to worry about someone finding out."

A flicker of relief washed over his face, and in that moment, I saw my brother Elis, sitting across from me. Frail and bent from his failed chemo. A ghost trapped in a cage. While I had been only a med student at the time, helpless and unable to save him.

I reached across the desk and placed my hand on his. "You've made the right choice in coming here. And I'm going to do all I can to help you fight this."

*E*vening crept through the kitchen, activating the solar lights, and bathing the room in a tepid glow. With a sigh, I pulled the packages of freeze-dried carrots and broccoli from the cupboard. I longed for fresh vegetables, but with the continuous fires affecting the growing season, they were a restricted commodity, and I had already gone over my allotted limit for the month.

The weekend loomed ahead of me as Trendon was now home from work and cloistered in his office, hunched over the glowing console of his computer. The silence between us had become perfunctory, my mind in a constant state of numb detachment. That innocuous place where nothing could touch me. At some point, I had stopped trying to salvage who I was beneath the roles of mother and doctor. My apathy had become a chaperone, pulling me soundlessly through the dark.

"Yes. I intend on running an inspection next week."

Trendon's voice drifted through the crack in the office door. He was most likely on the phone with his father. A stern, intruding man I had never warmed to. Seated as head of the board of directors that oversaw the inner workings of the Grid, he wielded his power with a cold precision. And as the years went by, Trendon began to remind me more and more of him. Gone was the soft optimism in his eyes, the ease in which he navigated through a room. He had sharpened his edges, drew within himself. Stretched and shifted his skin until he became nothing more than a mold for his father to pour himself into.

It repulsed me. This transfer of toxicity. His father's legacy etched into the very marrow of his being, like a story played out a thousand times, woven through generations of repression. And I was unable to stop the pull of the current.

"Where's Lilica?"

Trendon's tone was clipped, and I spun around to find him standing beside me. His movements could be stealthy and soundless, an unnerving skill he had acquired from his job.

"I think she's playing in her room." My hand involuntarily tensed up around the spoon I was holding. "Why?"

His face furrowed, a look of disturbance flashing in his eyes before he turned and calmly walked down the hallway. A few seconds later, he was escorting Lilica by the arm past me and into the living room.

"Trendon. What's going on?" The bite of confusion lanced through my words as I strode into the room to find him looming over Lilica, his finger pointing at the toys on the floor.

"I thought I told you to clean this up." His voice was low and flinty, and the look in Lilica's eyes was one I seldom saw.

One I never wanted to see.

Frozen in place, her wide eyes darted between her father and the toys scattered across the living room rug. Trendon bent down and snapped his hand out, clasping her chin firmly and yanking her up to meet his gaze. "Disobedience will not be tolerated. Do you understand me?"

My skin prickled with heat, a simmering anger rising inside me as I watched Lilica nod silently and drop to the floor, her tiny hands frantically grabbing at her toys.

"That's enough, Trendon." I brushed past him and placed my hand on her back. "It's okay, honey. I'll help you with these." I felt

Trendon's taciturn stare like a chill sweeping across my skin as I gathered up the remaining toys and led Lilica back into her room.

"Is Daddy very mad at me?" Lilica's lip quivered as I closed the door to her room and placed her toys in the corner.

My hands trembled, the residue of my emotions longing for release, and I shook my head, slipping on a strained smile. "No, sweetheart. Your Daddy just likes a clean house. You know that. And it's important to remember that when we are asked to do something, we should try and do it as best we can." I knelt beside her and swept a lock of hair out of her eyes.

"I know." She lowered her head in a gesture of compliance, that spark within her already dimming, and my heart constricted. How could I shield her from this slow internal stripping away of the self?

From the moment our children were born, we were expected to cull the wildness, to shrink their spirit down so they would one day comfortably fit inside the roles designed for them. And while I stood here with a painted smile, inside I was screaming.

Have I always been screaming?

And how long did I have until the sound eventually slipped from my mouth?

"I was going to pick up my toys, I promise. I just wanted to finish brushing dolly's hair."

The stormy gray of Lilica's eyes pleaded with me, and I drew her into a hug, feeling the rapid rhythm of her pulse against my chest. "I know, hon. It's okay. You didn't do anything wrong. You just have to try to remember that when your daddy is home, the rules are a little different."

She looked up at me and nodded. It was a silent understanding born from the small secrets we kept. The herbal remedies and whispered stories. The fragments of freedom I tried to give her in the absence of Trendon's rigid hold. But how long would it last? How long did I have until the Grid swallowed her up?

I released a long sigh and placed a lingering kiss on her forehead. "Why don't you play in your room for a bit, and I'll let you know when dinner is ready?"

"Okay, Mommy." She pulled away from me and crawled onto

the bed with her doll, murmuring something in its ear, the heavy moment washed away by the sweetness of her smile.

Closing the door behind me, I made my way back into the kitchen where Trendon was sitting stiffly at the table, his hands folded, jaw firm. "You coddle her."

His words cut through the air like a vague threat, and I clenched my hands, biting back a retort that would only end in more strained silence. We never fought. And in the beginning, I thought that was a good sign. But I suddenly longed for fire and loud words. The kind I once had with Domine. An intensity that would break through the suffocating shell of my life.

I hated the silence.

"You scared her, Trendon. Was that really necessary?"

He leaned back in his chair, his dark eyes fixed on mine. "What is *necessary* is to teach our child to obey. The literature states that we, as a community of One, must nurture collective knowledge while resisting the grievous temptation of self-imposed will-"

"I know what the literature says." I cut him off with a wave of my hand, remembering the digital documents given to me when I was pregnant. Pages upon pages of structured outline, defining what I could and could not do within my role as a parental guardian.

"I've been thinking we should consider sending Lilica to the ameliorate facility."

"What?" I clutched the counter, my breath lodged in my chest. "What are you talking about? She doesn't need to be reformed. She's a *really* good kid."

Trendon tapped his finger against the table, his face impassive. "It would only ensure she is raised correctly. I don't think, with the current demands of your job, that you really have time for it these days."

I shook my head. "What are you talking about? No. Absolutely not. We are *not* sending her away. She is being raised just fine."

"Is she?" He stood from the table and looked at me, his eyes detached. I tried to find the flicker of warmth hidden there, the tenderness that had once been present, but all I saw was a steely reserve, and it terrified me.

Where did you go?

"Look, she's doing really great at the Learning Center. I forgot to tell you her teacher assigned her to hold the emblem at the parade next month. Isn't that good news?"

My pacifying chatter filled the kitchen, sticky and sweet like honey, hoping my desperate act would mollify his resolve. Despite our supposed equality within the home, his choices had always held more sway than mine. His deep connections within the Grid stood like silent shadows around us. While I played with fire.

Something softened in his eyes, my assurances appearing to have placated him, for he moved closer to me and placed his hands gently on my shoulders. "Well, she still has a year until she is even eligible. I suppose we can revisit this conversation at that time."

I nodded, trying to keep my face neutral, as I inwardly recoiled from him. The press of his hands suddenly felt like a cloying serpent constricting my lungs.

Releasing me, he strode down the hallway, his voice echoing off the bare walls. "I'll be in my office for a while. Let me know when dinner is ready."

Shaking, I collapsed onto the kitchen chair, my breath returning to me in short streams of air that trembled against my lips as the hot bile of my anger rose in my chest. He was *not* going to take my daughter away from me.

She was all I had.

CHAPTER FOUR

*H*undreds of masked faces stared ahead, silently watching the procession as it slowly made its way through the streets.

"Sorry I'm late."

A hand fell on my arm, and I turned to see Kystina standing beside me in the smoky haze. She adjusted the straps on her government issued respirator mask. The imposing black apparatus the only defense we had when outside for periods longer than twenty minutes.

I pulled her in for a quick hug. "Don't worry about it. I'm just so glad you were able to come."

"Of course. I wouldn't miss Lilica's parade for the world." Her words came out muffled, trapped between the barrier of the mask, as she threw me a wink and gestured toward the street. "When is she up?"

"I think she's next." I scanned the group of children waiting in line behind a float. Every year at the end of August, we celebrated Restoration Day, a day that observed the changing of the flag. Gone was the old banner of red, white, and blue. The remnants of a freedom we were told had grown too dangerous. We now bore a solid swath of gold, representing triumph over autonomy.

The stifling patriotism and propaganda always pressed against my chest like a stone, a heaviness that paralyzed me. My mother used to speak of the Shift. The time before the changing of the flag.

She had only been a child. But she remembered the round ups and imprisonments plastered across screens. The systematic elimination of people who had dared to rise up against the structure of new government. People who had become threats to the fundamentals of our collective unity. But this wasn't unity. It was nothing but compulsory nationalism, blindfolding us all. And there was my daughter, Lilica, materializing through the crowd with the flag held high, a figurehead of a new generation boldly rushing forth into arms that would only restrain her.

"Mommy!" Lilica's cheerful voice rose above the drumbeats as she enthusiastically waved to me from the edge of the parade, pulling me from the weight of my thoughts.

"Look at her. She's so adorable." Kystina leaned in close to me, her wide smile faintly visible through the transparent screen of her polymer mask. "Where's Trendon?"

I sighed and brushed a strand of hair from my face. "He's at home packing for a convention in DC this afternoon. He said he wouldn't be able to make it."

"Oh, that's too bad."

"Yeah, it is." The lie burned on my tongue. There were some things I could not bring myself to share with Kystina, and this was one of them. I kept the secret of my dying marriage tucked away so tight, as if the very act of my silence could rectify the damage.

The strain around us had grown compressing after our conversation in the kitchen about Lilica, and as the weeks went by, I found myself struggling to even look at him. I had been relieved when he told me he would be gone for the weekend. It would be a reprieve from the tense silence and watchful looks he gave Lilica, as if he was just waiting for her to do something wrong. Waiting for an excuse to send her away.

I was ensnared in a marriage I could not leave. The bindings of a union that locked us in place. The Grid did not support separation, stressing that it went against the fundamental values of unity. Divorce was a fracture of the family unit, a dark stain that would strip us of our parental rights. There was no way out. I was required to play the role of dutiful wife. Forced to live with the choices I had made.

I bit my lip, trying to ignore the feeling of gravity slipping beneath me and the scream lodged in my throat as the parade wound its way through the streets, feet marching in step. The ominous echo of drumbeats the only sound among the stoic silence of the crowd as my daughter's tiny form was swallowed up momentarily by the procession.

* * *

*L*ilica's voice rang out from the backseat as we pulled into the driveway. "Look! Daddy's still here."

Tensing up, I glanced over to see Trendon's jeep still parked on the street and I released a stiff sigh as Lilica hopped out of the car and ran up the walkway, the excitement from the parade still resonating off her like a wave of energy. Following her to the door, I saw Trendon sitting on the couch as Lilica bounded inside. "Daddy, the parade was so fun. I held the flag so good!"

His eyes grew hard as he looked at me. "Lilica, please go to your room."

"But, Daddy. I want to tell you about--"

"Lilica, in your room, *now*."

His voice was stony, and a chill washed through me as I watched Lilica deflate, her eyes brimming with tears of confusion. Placing my hand on her back, I motioned for her to go.

"What's going on, Trendon? I thought you had a plane to catch?"

"I did."

"Well, what happened?"

"I had to cancel it."

"Why?" I set my purse down on the counter beside the door, trying to still the creeping feeling of dread inside me. The look on his face was cold and calculated, as if he were sizing me up, planning his next move.

And then he made it. Bending down, he reached for something

behind him on the floor. In his hands, he held my bag of medical supplies, turning it over slowly as if they contained explosives ready to detonate at any moment. "Would you care to explain to me what this is doing in our house?"

The creeping dread now crashed against me in a dizzying tidal wave. I sucked in a breath, my heart lurching in my chest as I tried to hide the tremble in my voice. "Where did you find that?"

"I was looking for my collapsible suitcase in the closet."

My mind scrambled around, grasping for a cohesive explanation, something that would diminish the consequence of the truth, but I came up blank. Caught in the headlights of Trendon's frigid stare, all that escaped my mouth was a long exhale.

"You know it is my duty to report this."

"Trendon." My voice came out pleading as I gripped the edge of the counter for support. "I'm your wife."

"That is irrelevant." His tone was hollow and composed as he stood from the couch and walked over to me. "You have broken the law. Do you think our marital arrangement has anything to do with that? In fact, *you* assuming I would do anything less than my civil duty tells me you are living in some deep state of delusion."

"Jesus Christ. Are you serious?" A vile loathing slammed into me as I stared at him and his closely cropped hair, his vacant eyes, his complete inability to think beyond the rules handed to him like oppressive scripture. *When had he become so mechanical and unmoving?* I couldn't even remember anymore.

"Yes, Seren. I am *very* serious."

"What are you going to do? Throw me in jail?" I spat my words at him, bitter and mocking, still unable to wrap my mind around what he was saying to me.

"What I am going to do, Seren, is give you a choice. You can either go through the process of a state trial, which might grant you a shorter sentence given that you were caught only in possession of illegal substances and not distributing them." He paused for a moment, his jaw clenched in thought, eyes sharp and boring into me. "You *aren't* distributing them, are you?"

I shook my head vehemently, my breath catching in my throat as my narrative uncurled like a shield, hoping to buffer the damage. "No, of course not. Listen, Trendon. Let me explain. I have those medical supplies for Lilica. They really help her when she gets sick. Do you remember what happened last time she was given antibiotics? She ended up in the hospital. We almost lost her."

That haunting memory from two years ago rushed back. Her lying lifeless and pale, tubes snaking through her body. The crushing helplessness and fear as she drifted further away from me. Had I not, in a state of frantic desperation, slipped her that herbal compound when no one was looking, I don't know what would have happened.

The thought of it still made the earth tilt beneath my feet.

"What… are you talking about… Seren?" His jaw tightened as he glowered down at me, the sharpness of his words slicing through the air.

I bit my lip. I had said too much. My pulse pounded out a desperate rhythm within my chest as I grappled to find some kind of footing. "Trendon." My voice came out in a whispered plea as I placed my hand on his chest, hoping my touch would awaken something inside him, bring him back to me. "These herbs have been helping *her*. Our daughter. Isn't it our job as parents to do everything in our power to keep our children healthy?"

A silence took hold of him as his shoulders slumped, his eyes softening and shifting around, mind locked in some battle I would never be able to understand. "Seren." He spoke my name like a long exhale, a flicker of softness washing across his face. But just as quickly as it came over him, it was gone, and something cold slithered over his gaze once more as he shook his head.

"Like I said, I'm giving you a choice. You know what needs to happen. You can either go to trial, revoke your medical license, and serve your time of five years. Or you can commit yourself to one year at the State Facility, and the charges against you will be expunged."

My heart plummeted, the room growing distorted as I felt my entire world implode around me. The Facility was the place people voluntarily entered but never came out the same. A government-run camp intent on deprogramming those who believed they had fallen prey to the *underground propaganda of dissonant thinkers.* From what I had heard, they pumped you full of psychiatric drugs, isolated you, and exposed you to a battery of tests, performing what they called *therapeutic cleansing.*

A harsh whisper tumbled from my lips. "I'm not going to the Facility."

Trendon took me by the arms. "It would be for your own good, Seren. I'm *worried* about you." His voice grew placating, as if he were speaking to a misguided child. "I don't want to see you spiral into the dangerous mindset of the Outliers. Those people are mentally ill."

I yanked myself away from him as bile rose in the back of my throat. Either choice would strip me of everything that was important to me. My cognitive function, my medical career. My daughter. The sickening weight of defeat crashed into me, choking my breath as hot tears pricked at my eyes. "Trendon, please. Don't do this."

"I'm sorry, Seren. I truly am. This isn't easy for me. You know that. But it's what needs to be done." His voice grew soft, but his eyes betrayed him. I could find no remorse there, only a hardened shell, and the sudden memory of our wedding day struck me with a mocking cruelty. The tender look on his face as he had slid the ring onto my finger. All his lofty promises now withered and unraveling between us.

Where did he go? When had I lost him so completely? When had the man I married become so devoted to a society that only took from him? Did he not see it? Did he not see the cracks in the foundation?

With a sigh, he calmly walked back to the couch and picked up my medical bag, looking at it like it was the closing scene in our last sorrowful act. "You have tonight to decide what you want to do. In the morning, I will have to bring this to the authorities."

CHAPTER FIVE

I lost track of time as night closed in around me. Shadows cast by the glare of the streetlights filtered through the living room in an ominous dance across my skin. Trendon had shut himself in the bedroom hours ago, and I had somehow managed to make dinner for Lilica and get her into bed, my motions fueled by a habitual sense of structure and a desperate anxiety that clawed at me. Nothing inside this house was normal anymore. But the fact that my daughter drifted off to sleep for one last night with the belief everything still was normal gave me a small, fleeting comfort I clung to as I paced alone in the dark.

What am I going to do?

This single, howling thought raced through me like liquid fire, leaving my limbs shaking. Every minute grew closer to an inevitable reality. No matter what choice I made, I would lose my daughter. I bit back the crushing heaviness that pressed into me, my fingernails digging into my skin.

How could Trendon do this? The question rose like a scream inside my head, my anger momentarily blanketing the panic that threatened to consume me.

I knew our marriage had become nothing more than a fiction coated in meaningless platitudes and unspoken conditions. A facade I willingly played out while clinging to the vague hope he was still in there somewhere, buried beneath the compressing layers of indoctrination.

How could I have been such a fool?

There was nothing left for me here. My clinic and the work I did for cancer patients had been the only thing tethering me to this place. And now that was gone.

It was all gone.

With a sudden flash of clarity, I knew what I had to do.

Standing outside our bedroom door, I noticed the light that had spilled beneath it all evening was now extinguished. Trendon must finally be asleep. I quietly cracked the door open and held my breath as my eyes fell to the dim shape of him in bed, motionless and breathing deep, as if completely unaffected by the events of the day. His ability to compartmentalize was mind-boggling, but right now, I was thankful for it.

I stepped into our walk-in closet and closed the door behind me. The overhead light flickered on as I grabbed my empty duffle bag that hung on a hook and began to throw various items of clothing into it. Winter sweaters mixed with summer shirts. An assortment of muted colors, my life now reduced to meaningless fabric and the finality of my decision marked by the slow and deliberate sound of the zipper closing shut.

Quietly closing the closet door, I pulled my phone from my pocket, using the glow of the screen to scan the room. There was only one way I was going to get past the checkpoints in town. I needed Trendon's jeep as well as his ID, which was stored on his phone. The rapid drum of my pulse thundered in my ears as I slowly picked up his ignition fob from the nightstand, the soft jingle of metal causing him to stir and roll over with a grunt. I froze with my hand in mid-air, clenching my eyes shut as if I could will him to stay asleep simply by the force of my desperation. Everything rested on this half-thought-out plan forged from the claws of panic in the darkness of the living room.

The sound of a light snore filled the room, and I let out a shaky breath as I leaned down and grabbed his phone.

I glanced under the bed and cautiously peered into dresser drawers in the hopes I could find where he had hidden my medical bag. If I could remove the evidence, perhaps he wouldn't be able to place a charge against me. But my search turned up empty. With a frustrated sigh, I stared at the outline of Trendon, watching the slow rise and fall of his chest as my fingers twined around the gold band on my left hand, the metal abrasive against my skin. Yanking it off, I placed it on the dresser beside the bed like a silent goodbye, and quietly closed the door behind me.

Making my way to Lilica's room, I opened the door, spotting her learning group pack in the corner. By the dim light of my phone, I picked only the essentials that would fit inside, hastily shoving clothes into the backpack. Holding another small bag I found in the closet, I surveyed her room, grabbing a few of her favorite toys and stuffed animals, trinkets and lifelines that would hopefully give her some sense of security as her world quickly shifted around her.

Lilica slept with her arms splayed out, her face soft with sleep, and I crouched beside her bed, my hand hovering over the covers. I didn't want to wake her. I didn't want to pull her from her blissful state, knowing that once I did, her life would never be the same.

Had I lost my mind? Perhaps I had. The mind I had tried for so long to adapt to this society was unraveling, leaving behind a trail I could no longer follow. Maybe that was what it meant to be free? To no longer care if you fit within the confinements of the world around you.

"Lilica," I whispered in her ear as I bent down and gently took her into my arms. "Wake up, sweetie."

Her eyes fluttered open, and she looked up at me in confusion. "Mommy, what's wrong?"

I slipped on a smile, trying to cloak the fear I knew she could sense in my eyes. "Nothing, hon. We're just going on a little road trip." I smoothed back the tousled hair stuck to her cheeks and wrapped her blanket around her shoulders. "Doesn't that sound like fun? We've never been on a road trip before."

She nodded, rubbing the sleep from her eyes. "Where are we going?"

"You'll see. It's a surprise." Standing from the bed, I picked up her backpack and bag. "We're going to play a little game, okay?"

"Okay, Mommy."

"It's called the *quiet game*. We're going to pretend we are tiny little mice in the forest, and we don't want to wake up the wild kitty cat. So, we're going to tiptoe so silently through the house. Does that sound like fun?"

"Yes." She bounced off the bed and stood beside me, taking my hand in hers. "Is Daddy going to play the game, too?"

My breath caught in my chest, and a tangled guilt seized me. Even though her relationship with her father was strained and he at times scared her, she loved him, and I was stealing her away from that love. But I could no longer allow her to grow up in a world so bleak it extinguished the fire inside her. She was my blood. My oxygen. And leaving without her had never been an option.

"No. Daddy's going to stay here and take care of the house."

She squeezed my hand tighter, a sly grin creeping across her face. "And I'm a mousy."

"Yes, love. You're the quietest mousey ever," I placed my finger to my lips as I opened the door and picked up our bags, quickly ushering us down the hall and through the darkened kitchen with the blue glow of the appliances casting fragmented shadows across the floor.

I typed in the code that disengaged the alarm and opened the door, the acrid scent of smoke filling the air as the automatic lock clicked shut behind us like an ominous farewell. Clasping Lilica's hand, I strode briskly toward Trendon's jeep and opened the back door, lifting her onto the seat.

"But, Mommy. I don't have my booster seat." Her voice grew loud, slicing through the stillness of the night.

"Shhh." I placed my finger to her lips. "We're still quiet mice, remember?" My heart pounded faster, an urgency pressing against me. There was no time to grab the car seat from the other car. A patrol unit could spot us out here. We had to leave. "It's fine. You're a big girl now. You're not going to need your car seat for this trip, okay?" I looked back at the house, my eyes skirting over the darkened windows before I placed our bags beside her and softly closed the door.

The jeep silently sprang to life as I slid into the driver's seat and turned off the navigation tool, allowing me full control of the car. I looked back at Lilica as I placed my foot lightly on the gas pedal, creeping the jeep forward and away from the house, away from the past ten years of my life.

I had loved him once. The kind of love that was quiet and small, like a tiny flame that could warm your hands but never heat a room. Perhaps I couldn't blame him for what he did. The government he so tirelessly worked for had become his only ally, a buoy in his empty waters. He had lost me a long time ago, or perhaps he never really had me at all.

Glancing into the rearview mirror, the encapsulated world that had held me in its orbit grew smaller until I turned the corner and it disappeared from sight.

My hands gripped the wheel, palms sweaty and mouth dry as I navigated the jeep through the empty streets. There were two automated check points through town, and each one would bring me closer to the rush of the highway cradled in the vast stretch of mountain range.

"Mommy, the town's sleeping," Lilica whispered from the back seat.

"I know it is, sweetie."

I had only been out once after dark, back when Trendon and I were dating. He had taken me on his patrol route, and I remember being unnerved by the stillness, as if the curtains had been peeled back on a stage, exposing nothing but an illusion. Paper cut-outs and hollowed-out props now lying lifeless without hands to move them.

Approaching the first automated check point, I scrambled around in my purse for Trendon's phone and pulled up his ID badge. The laser beam traced a harsh line across the car, bathing the interior in red, while my trembling hand placed the phone against the window, praying for the green of the clearance light.

The gate swung open, and I let out a shaky breath as I crept past the metal bars, my eyes scanning the streets ahead of me. The reality of what I was doing now came as a crushing blow to my gut as I drove through the check point, and the anger inside grew stronger than the fear. In the end, Trendon had only been a catalyst for the severance I now realized I had always been longing for, like a heavy secret kept tucked deep inside me, waiting for release.

I bit my lip, my eyes falling momentarily to my phone nestled in my purse. I wanted to call Kystina, to tell her what was happening. I expected Trendon to order a sweep of my medical office in the coming days, but I had no way to warn her; all phone calls were recorded and traced. Any attempt at communication would immediately make her complicit, and I couldn't risk going into the clinic and leaving her a note. I could only hope she would play dumb and that maybe she would be able to continue the alternative treatments on her own. A wave of sorrow washed over me as I thought of all my clients, of the man who had sat across from my desk the other day with pleading eyes.

I couldn't help them anymore.

A bright flash momentarily blinded me as a pair of headlights swept past my window, and my heart stumbled. *Did they see me inside the jeep?* I knew this camouflage could only take me so far. The car slowed, and my pulse sounded in my ears, my chest constricting as I prayed for them to keep driving.

The black patrol vehicle slithered past like a soundless, dark predator, and I held my breath, sinking low into the seat, my eyes trained to the road ahead. And then it was gone, its tail lights like two glowing eyes in my rearview mirror. Relief washed over me. Just one more checkpoint, and then we'd be out of town, toward the safety of the open highway and dense forest. A place we could disappear into.

I glanced over at Lilica, whose eyes were beginning to droop. Reaching back, I positioned the blanket around her. "You go back to sleep, sweetie. We'll be driving for a while."

The sleek, high-rise buildings that neatly lined the interior of the Grid were now behind us, and the sparsely populated stretch of industrial factories slid past like giant steel mountains as we approached the last checkpoint.

I held up the phone to be scanned. A tight band of apprehension constricted my lungs, my pulse growing rapid.

Seconds now stretched between me and the highway, which I could faintly see beyond the gate.

We were so close.

Pale light appeared in the rearview mirror, and I turned around to see the faint glow of approaching headlights sweeping across the darkened landscape.

No.

I clenched the steering wheel, my fingers digging into the leather, lips moving in a silent, panicked plea as I stared at the sleeping form of my daughter.

Please let us through… please let us through.

Green light flooded the car, and with a gasp, I lurched forward as the gate sprang open, my foot pressing down hard on the gas pedal.

CHAPTER SIX

The jeep hummed along the open road as I trained my eyes to the rearview mirror, watching for the flash of trailing headlights. But all I saw was the dim glow of the Grid as it faded behind us.

I shifted in my seat, hands stiff from my unrelenting grip on the steering wheel, but my heart had begun to slow its anxious rhythm.

We had made it out.

We were safe.

But what did that mean?

Like a caged bird thrust into the wilderness, I was untethered and adrift in a landscape I really knew nothing of. The fortress of concrete walls and checkpoints that had been built around our society kept us so far removed from the breath of nature, from the richness of life unfolding from earth.

When had we stopped longing for that innate connection?

The parched hills gave way to towering trees of spruce and pine as I wound deeper into the enclosure of the mountains, the canopy above us an emerald green now obscured in darkness. But it was a color I knew by memory.

So many trips I had taken up this road, shuffling supplies and stealing quick visits with my medical travel pass. But my time had always been rushed. Stolen moments that kept me at a safe distance, always needing to keep the compartments of my life tidy and separate. Terrified of what would happen if I let them get too close.

* * *

*T*ires jostled beneath me as the smooth lines of the paved road now turned to dirt, kicking up dark clouds of dust that obscured my view out the back window. I craned my head to see Lilica still fast asleep, her fist curled around her blanket, cheek resting against the seat. We had been driving for almost three hours now. Just ten more miles to go.

Eventually, the dense grove of trees thinned out, and the hazy outlines of dwellings took shape in the distance. They always gave me a sense of comfort, these tiny shacks and log cabins tucked into the forest, a scattered assortment of ramshackle homes in various states of disrepair. There was a vibrancy and fortitude here, born of people living in pace with the land.

The sharp glare of the headlights swept over the Compound, and I cringed, feeling like a hostile invader with my bright electric beams plucked from a world so far removed from this one. I rolled the car to a stop beside a cabin and turned off the engine. The silence enveloped me like a blanket as I stepped out of the jeep and slowly walked to the front door. The dim glow of the full moon struggled to pierce through the layer of haze, bathing the forest in a foggy blue light. My hand hesitated for a moment, suspended in the space between everything I had just left behind and the unknown future standing in front of me. Adrift with nothing left to hold me in place, my heart trembled against my chest like a hesitant bird. Would he accept me and Lilica? So much time stood between us, and the boundaries we formed had become so vast. But I was here. And there was no turning back.

Taking a deep breath, I knocked softly against the wooden door.

There was the sound of shuffling feet, and then the clicking of a latch as the door opened to reveal the shadowed outline of Domine, his dark, tousled hair falling in waves that brushed against his shoulders.

"Seren?"

The deep, rich tone of his voice filled me with the rush of relief. It had been so long since I had seen him, and suddenly the tight thread of composure I had been clinging to snapped. Tears escaped in a torrid stream down my face, my words tumbling out, breathless and frantic. "I'm so sorry to just show up in the middle of the night like this, but something happened... I had to leave... and I didn't know where else to go."

Warm arms enveloped me, the grounding scent of wood smoke and earth so uniquely his. And that's when I realized my whole body was shaking, the pent-up adrenaline finally releasing against him.

"It's okay... it's okay." He pressed me closer, the feel of his hands on my back like an anchor. "What happened, Seren?"

"Trendon." I choked out. "He found my stash of medical supplies and threatened to turn me over to the authorities if I didn't check myself into the Facility."

"Jesus Christ." He pulled back and grasped my shoulders, his eyes flashing, anger and concern written across the shadowed planes of his face. "Does anyone know you're here?"

I shook my head, wiping away the tears on my cheeks. "No. I don't think anybody knows I'm gone yet."

Domine glanced wearily over at the jeep, raking his hand through his hair. "Well, they will soon." He snapped his head back to me. "Wait. Where's your daughter?"

"I got her out, too. She's in the back, sleeping."

"Oh, thank God." He let out a sigh and motioned for me to step inside the cabin. The flare of a match lit up the darkness as Domine placed the flame against the wick of an oil lamp hanging by the door, illuminating the room in a muted orange glow. He swept his hand toward the small bed in the corner, sheets tossed haphazardly aside. "You can get her settled into the bed over there."

"Where are you going to sleep?"

"I can sleep up in the loft." He crossed the room and knelt down to slide a wooden box from underneath the oak frame, pulling out some wool blankets.

"Are you sure?"

He turned to me, his dark eyes piercing into mine. "Of course."

I wrapped my arms around myself, looking back at the jeep and what was left of my life now thrown into bags. In a matter of hours,

I had become homeless, relying on what little Domine had to offer. The bitter sting of tears rose up once more, obscuring my vision. A mixture of relief and desperation tumbling inside. "I'm so sorry I just showed up like this."

Domine's hand fell to my shoulder. "Seren. You know you've always been welcome here."

"Have I?" I stared up at him, searching for the truth beneath the veil of his words.

"Yes." His voice was gentle, but I could detect a flicker of hesitation hovering behind his eyes. A hidden sadness that matched the outline of my own. How many times had I fantasized about coming here and never leaving? How many times had I longed for a life with him again? A life I had said goodbye to all those years ago.

A trembling sigh escaped me, and I wrenched my gaze from his. "I just don't know what I'm going to do now."

"We'll figure that out in the morning, okay?" He looked over at the jeep parked beside the cabin. "But we do need to get rid of that car. Right now. They *will* track you."

"I know. I'll go get Lilica." I quickly made my way back outside and over to the jeep, gently opening the door. She had shifted in her sleep and now lay across the seat, her head resting against my duffle bag.

"She's so big." Domine stood behind me, his voice a cautious whisper.

"She is, isn't she?" The last time he saw her, she had been a baby. I had stopped taking her up here when she started to talk, afraid certain words would slip from her mouth around Trendon. *Forest. Cabin. Domine.* Those had been my secret words for so many years now. Fragile strands I kept safely folded away from my marriage.

I leaned over the seat and pulled Lilica into my arms. She made a soft, sleepy sound and instinctively clung to me as I carried her into the cabin. Placing her down on the bed, I tucked the blanket around her shoulders. Her eyes fluttered open in confusion for a moment, and I smoothed back the wisps of hair stuck to her cheeks. "Shhh. Go back to sleep, sweetie." With a drowsy nod, she closed her eyes and curled into herself, the blanket clutched in her fist.

What was I going to tell her when she woke in the morning?

The threads of indecision wound through me as I watched her sink back into a deep sleep, giving me a few more hours of reprieve.

"She looks just like you."

I turned to find Domine standing beside the bed with my bags. A smile faltered against my lips as I stood and took them from him. "Thanks for grabbing these."

"Is there anything else you need to get out of the car?" His voice was low, and an urgency lingered in his tone.

I shook my head, placing the bags down beside the bed. "No. What do you think I should do with it?"

"I'm going to get the jeep out of here. Did you bring a cell phone or anything else that could track your location?"

Suddenly remembering Trendon's phone, I bent down and sifted through my purse, pulling out both our phones. I placed them into Domine's open hand, along with the key fob. "Where are you going to take it?"

"Somewhere further up into the woods."

Biting my lip, I stared out into the darkness beyond the window. "How are you going to get back?"

"I'll walk."

"Jesus." I let out a long exhale and ran my fingers through my hair. "I should have thought all this through better." I clenched my hands together, suddenly realizing the heavy implications of being here, of possibly putting Domine at risk as well. "I'm sorry. I really shouldn't have come. I don't want to drag you into this. I just didn't know where else to go."

"Seren. Don't be sorry." His hand wrapped around mine, stilling my words and the churning pace of my thoughts. "You got out. *That's* the important thing right now. The rest are minor details. And don't worry about me, okay?" He grabbed a mask hanging by the door and shoved it into his pocket along with the last remains of what had once been my life. Electrical devices composed of invisible fibers that tethered me to the Grid, connecting me to a world which had now become my enemy.

Or had it always been? Had I always been running from it?

Domine paused at the door and looked back at me. The glow of the oil lamp reflected in the softness of his dark eyes. "Try to relax. Maybe get some sleep. I'll be back in a few hours."

The door closed behind him, leaving me standing in a room of memories I had not looked at in so long. With an unsteady sigh, I sank onto the bed, my hands fidgeting with the edge of the blanket as my eyes swept across the room.

Sparse and simple, the one-room cabin held a kitchen area with a small ice chest, sink, and counter. A handmade pine table stood by the window with a pillared candle resting in the center and four mismatched wooden chairs gathered around it, as if waiting for guests to arrive. Beneath the ladder leading to the small loft above me sat a clawfoot tub and a woodstove with an old woven blanket folded next to it. It was the same blanket we had once lain on beside the fire and made frantic love for the last time. A collision of tears and grappling of hands. A desperate goodbye forever etched against my skin.

I hadn't been inside this cabin in over ten years. My recent visits were always carefully navigated outside, beneath the safety of open sky and trees, reluctant to confront the things that lay within these walls. Afraid that if I did, they would pull me back in.

And now, here I was. My entire world reduced to the bags at my feet and the sleeping form of my child. I was in Domine's world now.

I had become an Outlier.

CHAPTER SEVEN

*D*awn spilled through the curtains of the cabin as I rolled over in the bed beside Lilica. Sleep had come in restless fits. Every sound outside jolted me awake. The call of an owl, the crack of a twig, the rustling of something in the bushes. Life stirred in this darkness, a beckoning wildness I was unaccustomed to. The Grid at night always held a sterile, demanding silence that pressed down on me, fashioned from curfew rules and locked doors. But here there were no rules, no doors that needed to be locked.

I stared out the window, the opening in the thin cotton curtains providing a sliver of early morning sky, a palette of pink and purple washed with a smoky gray. Footsteps sounded from far away, the steady crunch of feet against dry leaves, and my breath instinctively caught in my throat, my heart pounding out a worried rhythm. The door creaked open, and Domine stood in the threshold, his eyes weary and bloodshot.

I scrambled out of bed, relief flooding me as I quickly crossed the room to him, the pungent scent of smoke drifting off his clothes and into the cabin. "How'd it go?"

He grabbed a bucket of water sitting by the ice chest and placed it on the counter, splashing the liquid against his face and clearing out the smoke from his eyes. "I think I got the jeep far enough away, and I was able to rip out the motherboard system, so it shouldn't be traced back here." He took a towel hanging from a hook on the wall. "Did you manage to get any sleep?"

"Not really." I looked over at Lilica, still deep in the hold of her own slumber, oblivious to the swift deconstruction of her life. Her entire foundation had unraveled, and my restless night had failed to provide me with a clear answer as to how I was going to explain all this to her when she awoke.

I watched him sink into the chair and lean forward, drops of water from his hair staining the pine table a dark brown as he toweled himself off. "So, how did this happen?"

I sighed and sat down across from him, my hands tracing along the grain of the smooth wood. "Things have been really strained between me and Trendon for a while now. I guess it was what made it easy for him to do something like this… To want to turn me in."

Domine leaned across the table, his eyes flickering with a sharp anger that pierced into me. "You know, I've never liked that guy."

"You've never even *met* him, Domine." I threw my words at him, trying to defend the last bit of my past. The choices I'd made were now a dark stain on my skin, but they were mine, and without them, I wouldn't have my daughter.

"I don't have to. He's controlling and completely brainwashed. You know just as well as I do that those two traits are a dangerous combination."

Lilica stirred in the bed beside us, and I looked over at her, my voice dropping to a whisper. "I know. But in the beginning, he wasn't like this, and I never thought it would get to this point."

"You were a lamb living in a lion's den. What did you think was going to happen?"

His words lodged in me like a knife, a bitter sting that took root and settled in my gut. We had always grappled with the roads that had pushed us in different directions. The contempt he had for the society I chose to live in without him. Our past now stretched beside us like a question both of us were afraid to answer.

"I'm sorry." Domine's hand slipped over mine. "I know you've been trying to help people at your clinic. I've *always* admired you for that."

"None of that matters anymore." I glanced out the window. The hours of anxiety had turned sour, and a deflated feeling of emptiness gripped me. "It's all gone now."

"It's not gone." His voice grew soft as his thumb slowly swept across my palm, leaving a trail of warmth behind, anchoring me from the rush of my thoughts. "It's just been relocated, that's all."

I looked over at him, momentarily sinking into the harbor of his eyes. Could I somehow make a life for myself out here? Could I cobble together a home and raise my child on the edges of society? And what would that look like? What kind of education could I give her? And what if she got sick? I was a doctor with only basic surgical skills. All these questions tumbled through me like water crashing against stone, leaving me grasping at uncertainty.

"Wait." Domine's eyes captured mine, flickering with the shadows of concern. "Does he know what you've been doing at the clinic?"

I shook my head. "I don't think so. But I'm sure he's going to order another EmCorp sweep, just to be sure." I removed my hand from his, wrapping my arms around myself. "I couldn't contact Kystina last night. She has no idea what happened."

Domine leaned back and ran his fingers through his hair. "I know a guy down the road from here. Before he split from the Grid years ago, he used to be some tech giant for EmCorp." He stared out the window as he spoke, his brow furrowed. "He's found a way to hack into the Grid, and apparently, he's working on some untraceable phone line. Maybe you could try to reach her through him?"

"Really?" A weight lifted off me, and relief flooded in. Kystina had not just been my co-worker, she had become in so many ways the only friend I had. And the possibility of the authorities coming after her because I left caused my chest to constrict. "That would be *so* great. I really need to talk to her."

"Okay, I'll take you over to him today." He ran his hands across his face, his shoulders slumping. "Let me just get a few hours of sleep first. I can barely move right now."

"Of course. Get some rest."

With a nod, he stood from the table and walked over to the large chest by the bed. Quietly opening the latch, he removed his shirt and dug around inside for a new one. Through the pale morning light that spilled through the curtains, his skin was the color of caramel, and the smooth definition of muscle along his back seized me with the flush of memories long buried. It was a landscape I had memorized but hadn't touched in years, and something fluttered within me. Turning around, he caught me staring, his eyes holding a look of faint surprise as I yanked my gaze away, a bloom of heat creeping across my cheeks.

"You know where the outhouse is, and there's food in the ice chest and canned goods on the shelves," he said as he gathered up the blankets and pillow, placing them beside the ladder to the loft. "Feel free to help yourselves if you guys get hungry."

"Thank you." I looked over at him. "Thank you for everything. For dealing with the jeep. For letting us into your home…" I trailed off, seeking solace in the view outside the window, watching as the sun crested over the tops of the trees, casting a hazy orange glow across the branches. "I don't know what I would have done without you."

"Seren." He crossed the room and bent down beside me, taking my hands in his. "I'm glad you're here."

* * *

The hours passed, the shyness of dawn receding into morning, and hazy somber light now spread through the cabin.

"Where are we, Mommy?" Lilica stared wide-eyed into the forest. Her hands pressed against the glass of the window.

"We're in the mountains, love." I smiled at her and removed the kettle from the wood stove, pouring the hot water into a bowl of oatmeal. "Domine is an old friend of mine, and he's letting us visit."

"Is he sleeping inside the roof?" She pointed up at the ceiling with a puzzled look on her face.

"That's called a loft." I placed the bowl of oatmeal on the table and took a seat beside her, running my hands through her tangled hair. "Sweetie, how would you feel if I told you that we will be staying here for a while?"

"Why?"

"Well, because it could be a fun adventure. Living in the woods, away from all the lights and noise of the city. What do you think?"

"What about Daddy?"

My gut clenched, and I struggled for words that would thinly coat the truth. I wasn't ready to tell her just yet. I wanted to introduce her slowly to this new reality before I weighed her down with the permanence of it. "Your daddy will be staying in the city and taking care of the house."

"Okay." She grinned up at me and shoveled a spoonful of oatmeal into her mouth, accepting my veiled story, blissfully unaware of what lurked beneath it.

The creak of the ladder startled me, and I turned to see Domine climbing down, his hair tousled from sleep. "So, you must be Lilica." A wide smile stretched over his face as he crossed the room and took a seat next to us. "I'm Domine."

"I know." Lilica quickly spooned more oatmeal into her mouth. "You sleep inside the roof."

He laughed and glanced over at me while I shrugged my shoulders. "I suppose I do." He gave her a wink and leaned back in the chair. "How does a little walk in the woods sound to you? I think your mom needs to make a quick phone call."

With a nod, she pushed back her bowl and sprang from her seat. "Can we go now?"

"I don't see why not." Domine stood and grabbed his boots beside the door while I scrambled around in our bags, looking for something we could use as a makeshift mask. I realized it had become one of the many things I forgot to pack last night in my rush to get out.

"I can't believe I forgot our respirator masks." I sat back, the tendrils of frustration pulling at me.

"Well, I only have filtered cloth masks. I know they're not as good as the government issued ones you're used to, but they're better than nothing." Domine said as he rooted through a drawer. "Here are some extra ones." He looked over at Lilica with a smile. "What's your favorite color?"

"Blue."

"Well then, you, little lady, are in luck." Pulling out a dark blue cloth mask, he handed it to her with a flourish.

The woods were enshrouded in a hazy mist as we stepped out of the cabin. Faint morning rays broke through the layer of smoke and slanted through trees, casting amber shadows around us as Domine led us through a narrow, winding trail, worn down by the press of feet against dry branches.

Lilica stared up into the dense covering of trees above, her eyes wide as she took in the wilderness around her. "The trees are so tall, Mommy."

"They are, love." I bent beside her and followed her gaze upward, my words momentarily suspended as I viewed the vivid green from her eyes. Except for the brief trips up here when she was a baby, she had never really experienced the forest before, and something stirred within me as I watched her take in a world so vastly different from the one she had grown up in. It was a joy mixed with the bitter sting of sorrow. So much had been kept from her.

We continued walking as her chatter weaved through the branches. "Are there animals in these woods?"

Domine nodded and looked down at her. "Yes. There are all kinds of animals that live here. Squirrels, raccoons, owls, coyotes, wolves."

"Are they in cages?"

"Oh, no. They are all free."

Lilica turned to me, her eyes full of wonder as she grasped my hand. "Mommy, can we see the free animals?"

"Well, they're pretty shy, hon. They usually don't want to be seen."

"If you're really quiet, though…" Domine stopped walking and crouched down low to the ground. "You can hear them."

Transfixed, Lilica copied his movements, placing her hands on the ground as a silence settled over us. Eventually, the faint sound of birds twittered in the distance, and then the raucous call of a crow shattered through the trees. My breath stilled, caught within the echo of its cry. We never heard birds in the city. Maybe that was because we had taken away their canopy of trees so long ago, or perhaps it was the summer fires from the surrounding states that pushed them further away from us. But here was a wildness I wanted to run to, and it made my heart ache for a home I never knew. For a place I had yet to find.

"See." Domine stood, the crinkle of his eyes giving away the smile obscured beneath his mask. "They will speak to us if we want to listen."

"Wow." Lilica looked up into the branches, her gray eyes searching for the source of the calls like a caged bird herself, meeting the forest for the first time.

"Turk's place is just around the bend," Domine said, motioning down the path.

Lilica fell in step with him, looking up at Domine in marvel as if he held all the secrets to the forest. And perhaps he did. Rugged and beautiful with his sun-kissed skin and disheveled hair, he had always reminded me of something untamed.

We approached a small, tidy cabin obscured by trees, branches bowing low over the roof, with a modest garden in the distance. Tomatoes, lettuce, and the trailing vines of squash struggled in the open patch of meager light that filtered through the veil of smoke.

Domine knocked on the door, and it creaked open to reveal a tall man with a long, white beard, glasses perched precariously on the end of his nose.

"Looks like you got some visitors this morning, Turk." Domine swept his hand out toward us.

"Well, it seems I do." The warmth of a wide smile stretched across Turk's wizened face. "Please, come in."

I stepped inside, my eyes falling to a pot which simmered on a woodstove in the kitchen, filling the room with the fragrant scent of cloves, cinnamon, and ginger. His living area was cluttered with papers and books, wooden shelves stuffed with more literature, the spines cracked with age. I stared in awe at the array of words bound and tucked away beneath faded covers, wondering where he had managed to get all these relics from a world so long gone.

"You're admiring my library, eh?" He shot me a knowing look as I removed my mask, his hand reaching out to clasp briefly around mine. "I'm Turk."

"Seren. And this is my daughter, Lilica."

"Very nice to meet both of you."

Domine shut the door behind us and leaned against the frame, slipping his hands into his pockets. "We were hoping Seren could use your phone."

"Of course." Turk adjusted his glasses and shuffled over to a table, rooting through some papers. "I know it's buried somewhere in all this mess."

Lilica stared at the bookshelves towering over her. "What are all these?"

"Those, my dear girl, are stories written a long time ago. Endless worlds for you to discover." Turk gave her a wink as he crossed the room and handed me a square metal device that fit heavily in the palm of my hand. "I know it's not the sleek holographic phones you're used to back in the Grid, but I assure you, it works."

"Thank you." I pressed open a latch on the side, and a rudimentary keyboard revealed itself. "Did you make this?"

Turk nodded. "I did. I used to work for the tech sector at EmCorp years ago. Managed to smuggle out some of their electrical devices before I left." His hand rested on my arm for a moment, giving it a squeeze. "When did you get out?"

"Last night." I glanced over at Lilica, who was running her hands along the spines of books, taking in the alien landscape of paper that surrounded her.

"Well, welcome to our island of misfits." He chuckled and turned toward Lilica. "Why don't we let your mom make a quick call, and we can go explore some of these books? There's one of fairy tales I know is hiding somewhere on this shelf."

I watched Lilica's eyes light up as I slipped outside and shakily dialed Kystina's number on the keypad, grateful for my photographic memory. Static filled the receiver, and then the faint tone of a connection. She picked up on the second ring, her voice low and hesitant. "Hello?"

"It's me."

"Oh my, *God.*" The sound of a door closing, and the hum of the air conditioner vent told me she was at the office. "What happened? Where are you?"

"I can't tell you where I am." Tears stung my eyes, and I blinked them back, knowing this would probably be the last time we would ever speak. Even though this call was apparently undetectable, I knew it was still a risk. The authorities could always confiscate her phone and find some way to trace it back here if they grew suspicious enough. "I just wanted you to know that Lilica and I are out. And we're safe."

"Good. I've been so worried." Her voice choked on the other end, and she drew in a sharp breath. "Trendon showed up at the clinic this morning and said you were gone. He started asking me a bunch of questions. He was so calm and detached about everything. Honestly, it was chilling. What the *hell* happened?"

I stared out into the forest, a stark etching of green against gray. "He found my stash of medical supplies at the house and was going to turn me in." I closed my eyes as the events of the previous night rushed back. The image of Trendon's cold stare, the extreme grip of his unflinching conviction. How long had I been living with the apparition of a man? "I don't think he suspects anything going on at the clinic, but just to be safe, you should probably lie low for a while."

"Of course. Jesus, Seren. I'm so sorry." A long pause filled the receiver, and then she spoke again. "But you know, I'm proud of you for getting out. Maybe one day I will, too."

I sank down onto the ground, clutching the phone tightly to my ear as soft static crackled on the line. "I'm going to miss you, Kystina."

"And I'm going to miss *you*. Take care of yourself out there. You're…"

The static grew louder, scrambling her words into garbled fragments as our connection broke up, and then the phone went silent, leaving me with the remnants of her unfinished sentence.

CHAPTER EIGHT

"Seren. Are you okay?"

Domine's voice pulled me from the buzz of my thoughts as I sat on the ground, fiddling with the phone in my hand. I looked over to see him crouched beside me, his eyes washed in concern.

"I'm fine. Everything's fine." My voice came out forced as I pushed myself to my feet, not sure if I was trying to convince him or myself.

All that was left of the life that defined me were tiny pieces I had to find a way to reassemble into something new. And beneath the fragile cloak of shelter this place provided lay the terrifying possibility of being found, of losing Lilica. It was a thought too large and brutal to sit with, and it closed in around me, stealing my breath.

Domine stood, his hand resting on my shoulder. "You don't have to try to hold it together. I know this isn't easy."

"No, it's not." I stared up at the trees, watching as the branches trembled in a silent dance against the smoky sky, my voice slipping out in a choked whisper. "What if they find us out here?"

"Seren." Domine's voice grew low, his eyes flashing with a momentary unease. "Trendon doesn't know about me... does he?"

I shook my head. My visits up here had always been under the ruse of a medical conference, or a stealthy slipping away with my clearance pass during work hours. It was a secret that always gnawed at me, but one I was now grateful I had never divulged.

"Then you're safe here. They shouldn't be able to trace the jeep back to this place. And they will have no reason to search the Compound." His hand traveled up to my neck, his fingers brushing against my cheek and causing a shiver to wash across my skin. "I'm going to do *everything* in my power to make sure they never find you, okay?"

It was a promise I knew he shouldn't make, but one I so desperately needed to cling to. I closed my eyes for a moment, and drew in a shaky breath, allowing myself to tumble into the shelter of his touch, into the refuge of his words. And for one brief moment, I could remember what it felt like when it was just us, before the world got in the way.

"Mommy?"

Domine dropped his hand, and I quickly pulled away, feeling heat creep over my cheeks as I saw Lilica standing in the open doorway of Turk's cabin with a large book clutched to her chest.

"Hey, sweetheart. What do you have there?"

"Fairytales. Turk said I can have it."

The stretch of her smile softened the edges of my thoughts, and I ran my fingers through her hair, gently untangling the strands. "He did? That's awfully nice of him."

Turk leaned against the side of the open door. "Yep. That book's been sitting lonely on the shelf for years, just waiting for the right kid to come along." He gave us a nod as we stepped back inside the cabin.

I handed the phone to him. "Thank you for all this."

"Not a problem. And feel free to stop by whenever you like. My library is at your disposal."

I looked up at the rows of books on his shelf. "How did you get all these, anyway?"

"I know a guy." He threw another wink my way. "He's a pursuer of the past, so to speak. Every so often, he comes up here, and I help him decode EmCorp files. In return, he leaves me books."

I ran my finger along the spines, an endless array of worlds from which to choose. My pulse quickened as I came to a book the color of night sky. Plucking it from the shelf, my hand traced over the title scrawled in cursive across the cover. *The Secret of Dreams.*

"Are you a dreamer, Seren?"

Turk's question caught me off guard, and I turned to him, the tendrils of my yearning curling around me like faint whispers. "No. I've never dreamed before."

"Most who live in the Grid are unable to." He motioned toward the window. "It's from the Resonance. I've come across some studies on the affects the wireless technology has on our minds." He smiled and folded his hand over mine, pressing it against the book. "Take it. It's yours now. I know one day you'll find your dreams."

* * *

We walked back to Domine's cabin in silence. Lilica clutched her book and skipped ahead of us, bending down occasionally to pick up treasures from the forest floor. An acorn with a cap like a top hat. A stick in the shape of a bird, the feathery tendrils of moss. She deposited these into my pocket for safekeeping, already rebuilding her world from the filaments of earth and wood, harvesting her own landscape.

As the cabin came into view, Domine stopped walking and turned to Lilica with a playful glint in his eyes. "You know, I don't think you've met the chickens yet. Would you like to help me collect the eggs?"

"Chickens?" Lilica looked over at me with confusion.

I gave her a smile. "The eggs we buy in packages at the store. That's where they come from, hon. Chickens."

"Are they alive?"

Domine chuckled and motioned for her to follow. "Yes. They are very much alive."

Lilica caught up to him, and I watched as they disappeared around the back of the cabin. The call of a crow rang out in the distance, and I stood for a moment at the edge of the clearing, bathing in the stillness as my breath moved in time with the branches above. That feeling of longing swept over me again, like a hidden memory that had never been mine, and it filled me with a strange mixture of joy and sorrow.

I found Lilica and Domine behind the cabin, standing beside a small, penned enclosure, her eyes wide and fixed on the four chickens pecking around in the dirt.

"Mommy, can I go inside? Is it okay to touch them?"

"I think so." I turned to Domine as he unlatched the gate with a nod, picking up a small woven basket and handing it to Lilica.

"It sure is. They are very friendly. Would you like to go find their eggs?"

With a smile, she grabbed the basket from him and stepped inside, her hands tentatively reaching out as the chickens gathered around her, the sound of her giggles filling the air.

"When did you get chickens?" I asked, leaning against the wooden frame of the coop.

He shrugged as he grabbed some feed from a bucket and sprinkled it across the ground, causing the chickens to redirect their attention away from Lilica in a sudden flurry. "I've had them for almost half a year now. Made a trade with a guy who lives up the hill."

I stared into the distance, suspended within the thoughts that wove around me. The gentle simplicity of Domine's life was such a stark contrast to the sterile confinements of the Grid, with its walls and checkpoints, digital screens, and devices. It was a breath of fresh air I had almost forgotten the feeling of.

"Has it really been that long since I've been up here?"

"Yes. It has." His eyes flashed with all the unspoken words still hovering between us, bringing me back to the last day I had visited him.

The day that had quickly turned to a late afternoon as we stood outside his cabin, lost in conversation, the kind I never had with Trendon, my mind bursting with the elation of shared thought as we spoke of philosophy, science, and social structures. The way my skin prickled with electricity when my arm brushed against his. The dizzying rush of his eyes on me. The moment when I wanted to lean in closer and feel his lips on mine. I had left in such a hurry after that, the look of sorrow on his face colliding with the tight feeling of guilt that gnawed a hole in my gut.

I had always told myself that my brief trips up here were to help him with supplies he didn't have access to. But beneath that lay the deeper reason.

I had never been able to truly let him go.

I had hoped time would temper the flame that always burned when I was around him, but standing beside him now, I realized it never would. It was always there, smoldering like an ember I could not extinguish, and I didn't know what to do with it. I didn't know how to navigate around it. Guilt was no longer keeping me at a safe distance, for the last threads of my marriage had unraveled, and I was now cut off from the world that bound me to them. It was fear that pressed against me now. I was terrified of the fire. The intensity. I had grown so accustomed to guarding myself, to avoiding the depths of my emotions. It had been the only way to survive living on the Grid. I couldn't feel trapped if I never longed for flight, and I couldn't lose something if I never reached for it.

"Mommy, look! I found eggs in little boxes!"

Lilica's voice pulled me from my thoughts, and I looked over to see her running toward me.

"Oh, wow." I peered into the basket she had clutched to her chest, speckled eggs the color of sand and snow. "Looks like you found them all."

"Almost. I think there's one more." Domine bent down and rustled around in the fallen brush beside my feet, and then something warm and round rested in my hand as he curled his fingers over mine with a faint smile. "Sometimes things are hidden right in front of us."

*T*ime no longer passed by in measured hours. Gone were the days dictated by the constant pulse of ticking clocks and holographic alarms. Here, time took on a leisurely pace, guided by the way the sun hit the trees in the morning, the slant of shadows as they cast their imprint on the ground at dusk. The forest was alive with its own cadence, impervious and resilient, and we were only visitors.

Dry brush crunched beneath my feet. Seeking to replenish my collection of herbs, I scanned the ground for yarrow, bergamot, and mullein, looking for open patches within the trees where wormwood grew. September had crept in, and the faint yellow hue of larches could be seen scattered throughout the forest. We had been here for five days now, sharing a new rhythm within the small space of Domine's cabin, and Lilica had yet to ask me when we were going home. But I knew I needed to tell her soon.

"Mommy, what's this?"

Lilica crouched on the ground, her chin resting against her knees as she stared down at a small, circular grouping of fungus growing among a patch of grass. I reached out to touch the light brown caps, noting the central hump and the pliable flesh, the stem tough and unable to break between my fingers. "These are called fairy ring mushrooms."

She looked up at me. "What's a mushroom?"

I knelt beside her. "Well, they're a type of fungus that grows in the wild. Some of them are very poisonous, and you must *never* touch them without checking with me first. Do you understand?" She nodded vigorously at me with wide eyes. "But these right here are edible." I took from my pocket the small, bone-handled knife I had found in Domine's cabin and sliced off a few caps. "We can fry them up for dinner tonight. I've read that they have a very sweet taste."

"Like candy?"

I smiled and dropped them in my basket. "A little bit, yeah."

Mushrooms were no longer found in the supermarkets of the Grid. Like ginger and garlic, the medicinal properties within them had been banned from public consumption, deemed unclean and possible carriers of disease. It was years ago, before the state had put my childhood home up for auction, that I had stumbled across an old textbook buried beneath some boxes in the attic. *Edible and Medicinal Herbs of The Pacific Northwest.* One of my mother's contraband collections, hidden for safe keeping like trails of breadcrumbs left for me to find. I had memorized the entire text in one night, my mind soaking up the information and storing it away in the private compartments of my photographic memory. This gift allowed me access to information that was untraceable and unable to be erased. It was what had made my knowledge and distribution of herbal medicine at the clinic possible. And it now came in handy as I combed the forest floor.

"What else can we eat from the woods, Mommy?" Lilica sprang to her feet, excitedly looking around.

"Well, I think there might be some salmon berries somewhere around here." I grabbed the basket and took her hand in mine. "Let's see if we can find any."

It didn't take long until my eyes caught the burst of yellow and orange nestled in a patch of leaves. Lilica held out her hands eagerly as I filled her palm with the ripe berries, sun-warmed and sweet like honey.

"It's time to get out of the smoke, love." Knowing the minimal protection of our cloth masks, I quickly retraced our steps, looking for the trail that would lead us back to the cabin.

"But I want to stay and look for more forest treats." Lilica reluctantly followed behind me, her voice tinged with disappointment.

"I wish we could." I looked up into the hazy sunburnt sky as if I could will a patch of blue to appear. "Maybe we'll get some rain soon. That will help clear up all this smoke."

The sound of an ax against wood grew closer as I located the small trail that wound its way back toward the cabin. From the edge of the woods, I saw the shape of Domine in the clearing beside the front door, and my breath hitched in my throat. He had taken his shirt off, and a faint sheen of sweat glinted off his broad shoulders and back, the muscles in his arms rippling with tension as he drove the ax down into a log.

"Domine!" Lilica ran over to him with something clenched in her tiny fist. He set his ax down, shooting her a wide smile as he swept his arm across his forehead and reached for his shirt.

"Hello, wood nymph. What you got there?"

She pulled off her mask and beamed up at him, gleefully taking to this new nickname he had given her. Trendon had never called her anything but Lilica, his interactions always stoic and staunch, believing playful epithets were the language of the ignorant.

"We found forest food. This is for you." She thrust something in his direction, and as I made my way to the door, I could see the orange fruit she had apparently saved for him, now smashed to a sticky pulp in her hand.

"Wow, this looks delicious. Thank you so much." With a chuckle, he scooped the berries into his mouth and glanced over at me with an impish grin as I slipped past him and into the cabin.

I shut the door behind me, feeling vaguely flushed as I rooted around in a drawer, looking for the roll of twine Domine had said would be in there.

The door opened just as I was securing the ends of string into the wall, creating a line across the window to hang the herbs. Lilica bounced onto the bed, her fingers flipping through the pages of her fairytale book, already lost in a world of ink, color, and fantasy.

"Did you find anything good out there?" Domine came up behind me, smelling faintly of sweat mixed with pine sap and woodchips. It was a blend I found alluring, and a wash of desire hesitantly stirred within me.

I turned to him, pulling out my clippings from the basket. "Yeah. I found a few herbs I can use."

He leaned against the sink, watching me as I reached up to tie some mullein onto the string. "I made something for you."

My hands stilled their movement. "You did?"

With a nod, he pulled something from his back pocket and slid it across the table to me. I looked down to see a leather pouch. Picking it up, I ran my fingers over the smooth hide, tracing the tiny intricate designs etched across the front. A sprig of lavender, the leaf of motherwort.

"When did you make this?"

"I started it a couple of days ago." Stepping close to me, he brushed his hand over the basket on the table, gently fingering the delicate white blooms of the yarrow as his voice fell low and close to my ear. "I figured you needed something to keep your medicine in."

"Thank you. It's beautiful." My eyes wavered with the unexpected prick of tears. I had not been able to push away the feeling of being a burden, despite Domine's attempts to tell me otherwise. And his gesture was subtle but direct. He was giving me something I could rebuild with. Something that tethered me to this place, to his world. A gift that told me in a quiet and unassuming way that this was my home now.

CHAPTER NINE

*W*rapped in bed with her blanket and the book of fairytales clutched against her chest, Lilica had finally fallen asleep. I placed the last of the clean dishes from dinner on the drying rack, watching the water swirl down the drain. Evening had crept through the cabin, bringing with it a slight chill as the wind picked up outside, causing a hollow moan to slither through the cracks of the windows.

"That stir fry turned out pretty good. Lilica really seemed to like those mushrooms," Domine said with a soft chuckle as he crouched beside the woodstove, stoking up the embers from the fire, the flames dancing in his dark eyes.

"She did." Placing the dish towel on a hook by the sink, I crossed the room and sat down beside him, hugging my knees against my chest. "Another one of the many things we never had access to in stores."

Domine stared into the fire as it sprang back to life. "You remember that guy Turk mentioned the other day? The one that's been giving him government information to decode?"

I nodded, watching as the hunger of the flames leapt and curled against the sides of the stove.

"Well, according to Turk, all the banned foods are not due to safety concerns."

I looked over at him. "What do you mean?"

"Think about it." He closed the door of the stove and settled beside me. "Any food that has high levels of antioxidants has been banned. And what do antioxidants help protect against?"

"Cancer." The word lodged in my throat, bitter and pungent.

"Exactly. Those foods, among many other things, are a direct threat to EmCorp."

"So Turk is saying that the medical establishment is purposefully keeping us sick?"

"That's what these documents appear to reveal. Don't tell me you haven't thought about this before? You know better than I do that EmCorp is the largest corporate business. They control everything."

I bit my lip, feeling a chill run across my skin despite the warmth radiating from the stove. "I *have* thought about this. But at the end of the day, I've always had to convince myself that they *are* trying to help people."

"But they're not, Seren." His eyes flashed with intensity as he leaned in close to me. "What do you think those immunity enhancers are really about? They aren't providing people with a fortified immune system. They're making people's immune system *dependent* on them."

My jaw clenched, and a sickening weight settled in my gut. I knew he was right. The hissing shadows of doubt had always been there. Questions I never had the courage to turn around and fully confront. For how could I? I had to get up every morning and believe there was some good left in the world.

The truth always took more strength to face than the lie doled out.

But here it now was. The bitter truth. And the sharp talons of anger curled around me at the thought of the Grid potentially being responsible for the death of so many in my life. My mother, my father, my brother Elis. There was nothing left of my family but memories housed within silent walls that were no longer mine.

"But why would they do this?" My voice came out shaky, hands fisted in my lap as I pushed down the strangled scream that wanted to spill from me. The same one I had been stifling for so many years like a ghost buried within a shallow grave. "I just don't understand how the fatalities of cancer would benefit them."

"You know it all comes down to money and resource control." Domine's eyes continued to bore into me, the tendrils of his anger now colliding with mine. "People no longer have power over their own reproductive rights, so they keep churning out babies, new generations that fund the corporations. All while keeping population growth low. It's a tidy little cycle of death and rebirth for them."

His words sliced through the air, and he turned from me, raking his hand through his hair as he stared into the fire, his brow furrowed. "And while the government preaches to the masses about collective unity and living without ownership, they are growing richer by the day. That point system you're given, it's all a ruse to keep everyone enslaved. They *own* us. I mean, do you really think all these forest fires are natural? I don't think they are. I think they are designed to keep us contained and easily tracked within city centers. And living out here on the Compound," he swept his hand toward the window, his voice dropping to a fervent whisper, "doesn't mean we're free. Even if we do manage to get out without a target on our back and revoke our citizenship, we're still enslaved, still bound to their rules, not allowed to leave the borders beyond the land they have provided for us. They think if they keep us in a primitive state of poverty, they keep us silent and disposable. And it works." He stared at me, his eyes like a quiet storm. "As long as we stay voiceless and complacent, they don't bother us out here."

The veracity of what he said sunk deep into me, and a leaden silence washed over the both of us as the crack and hiss of the fire permeated the room, the flames licking across the glass of the stove door as if yearning to be released. When stripped down to the basic elements, everything was the same. The fragility of life always demanded sovereignty. Nothing could flourish in a confined space.

Letting out a sigh, I rested my hand on his arm, feeling the muscles contract and release against my touch. "For what it's worth, Domine. I *do* feel free here. More than I ever have on the Grid."

He looked at me, his eyes softening. "Do you remember that trip we took all those years ago?"

"Yes." I smiled at the faded memory. I had been twenty-seven and fresh out of medical school, and Domine had taken time off from his civil engineering job. To celebrate, we had both splurged on a long-distance travel pass and spent a week driving up the coast. Nothing but sand, sun, and tangled bedsheets in rented rooms, Domine's lips tasting of sea salt. My pulse accelerated as the buried images rose and came into sharp focus. It had been so long since I had thought of that trip. Our last blissful dive into oblivion before everything began to unravel.

"*That* was the last time I felt free, Seren."

Reaching for his hand, I entwined my fingers through his. Despite his fierce independence and ability to find a sense of contentment in the life he had carved out for himself here, there was something hidden beneath the exterior. In the depths of his eyes, I saw shadows, as if all the years of his solitude pressed down on him. "You know, a part of me has never stopped wondering what my life would have looked like if I had chosen to leave with you."

He shook his head, his thumb running a slow circle against the inside of my wrist. "No, you had just started your medical practice. I knew how important it was to you. I should have never asked you to choose."

That night rushed back to me. Him standing in our living room with his bags at his feet. My whole world disintegrating. His eyes pleading. My resolve desperately wanting to crumble. The feel of the door as it closed behind me, leaving nothing but emptiness clawing at a room that no longer held us together.

I sighed and squeezed his hand, feeling the energy between us grow heavy. "The thing is, I don't even recognize myself anymore. I feel like the person I was with you is gone now."

"Seren..." His eyes seared into me as he drew my name out like a question, a long exhale waiting for an in-breath. "I don't believe it's possible for that fire inside you to *ever* die. You were just forced to stop feeling it." He leaned closer to me as his fingers curled around mine, sending sparks of electricity dancing across my skin, drawing me into the depths of a longing I had no raft for.

"I hope you're right," I whispered as my face flushed, my heart a sudden wild drumbeat. Sucking in a breath, I pulled away from him, breaking the intensity of the moment. "I'm pretty tired. I should probably go get some sleep."

He nodded, a dark lock of his hair falling against his forehead as he stared into the fire. "Goodnight, then."

"Goodnight, Domine." Rising to my feet, I made my way over to the bed where Lilica lay sleeping and closed the linen curtains that had been put up for privacy, enshrouding the space around us in fractured patterns of light.

As I quickly slipped on my nightgown, I wondered if Domine could see me through the curtains. The thought of his eyes following the curve of my body sent a rush of heat coursing through me, and my breath hitched in my throat.

I slid beneath the sheets, the rise and fall of Lilica's breath whispering against my cheek as I nestled beside her and watched the shadowed outline of Domine pass by the curtain. I tried to brush aside the thoughts of the way his hand felt in mine, the burn of his eyes on me beside the fire, the closeness of his lips. But I couldn't. Everything inside me ached for him as I watched him make his way up the ladder and disappear into the loft.

"What's this Mommy?" Lilica held the tendrils of a root in her hand as she sat at the table, watching me bundle up herbs and place them into the pockets of my pouch.

"That is called goldenseal." I reached over and fingered the thin yellowed strands of the root. "It's good for things like tummy aches, colds, and infections. And this right here…" I picked up a broad stalk of dark green leaves. "This is called devil's club. It's good for coughs and sore muscles."

"What's this do?" She reached for a dried bundle, its tiny purple flowers now withered and crisp to the touch.

"That's comfrey. It helps heal boo-boos."

Her eyes grew wide with interest, tracking the movements of my hands as I tied up the bundle of devil's club with string. She had never seen me working with plants before. No longer was it a mysterious concoction secretively mixed up in an occasional tea. For the first time, I was able to speak to her openly without worry. I could share with her the same knowledge passed down from my own mother, like a legacy of interwoven threads tethering us all together.

"Where's Domine?" Lilica leaned toward the window and rested her face against the pane, looking out into the gray pallor of the sky.

"He went over to a neighbor's house this morning to gather some vegetables. Apparently, they have a garden that they share."

Her finger touched the window, tracing invisible pictures on the glass. "When's he coming back?"

"I'm not quite sure, hon. Soon."

Lilica had grown quite attached to Domine, spending most of her time following him around with an endless array of questions, fascinated by his world, which she had found herself in. And Domine was always there with answers and playful smiles, welcoming in her endless wonder. But beneath all that lay the truth I could no longer avoid, and the questions she had yet to ask. We had now been here for almost two weeks, and I had yet to talk to Lilica about her father.

A heaviness settled in my chest as I set aside the herbs and turned to her. "Sweetie, can we talk about something?"

She nodded and climbed down from the chair, allowing me to gather her into my arms and settle her on my lap. I smoothed back her hair and leaned down, resting my cheek against hers. "I know you miss Daddy."

"A little bit." Her hands fiddled with the buttons on my shirt. "When am I going to see him?"

I took a deep breath, trying to find the right words. The kind that would softly ease her into a reality no child should ever have to face. But there was no gentle way to put it. No way to smooth the sharp edges. "Well, honey, your daddy is not going to be part of our lives anymore."

She looked up at me, her eyes swimming with confusion. "Why?"

"Well, something happened between your daddy and me, but I want you to know it has nothing to do with you."

"Daddy's not mad at me?"

"No, Lili." I took her hand and gave it a squeeze. "Your Daddy loves you very much. But sometimes, mommies and daddies can't live together anymore, and that's why we had to leave. That's why we're here. We're going to start a new life. Just you and me."

Pursing her lips, she glanced out the window. "What about Domine?"

"Well, I guess he is going to be a part of our new life, too."

"Can *he* be my new daddy?"

Her question threw me off guard, and tears unexpectedly rushed to the surface. There was a sorrow in her words, a bleak acceptance grasping at the strings of some hopeful replacement. Something breaks, you glue it back together. Something tears, and you sew it up. I shook my head. "No, sweetie. It doesn't work like that."

"Why not?" She wriggled off my lap, her eyes brimming with the dark shadows of anger. "Why can't I have a new daddy?"

"Sweetheart." I took her hands in mine and pulled her close to me. "Domine can't be your daddy, but he can be your friend."

As if on cue, the door opened, and Domine walked in, trailing the scent of smoke from outside, his arms full of vegetables. "Who's in the mood for a yummy salad for lunch?" he asked as he looked down at Lilica with a smile.

His sudden presence shifted the mood in the room. The mournful weight collided with his oblivious cheer, and Lilica drew away from me, gravitating toward a horizon that held the promise of color and softness.

Sidling up next to him, she reached up to grab a tomato, deep red cradled in the palm of her hand. "I want some yummy salad."

"Great." He threw her a wide grin as he took a bowl from the cupboard. "Do you want to be my little helper?"

"Yes." Wooden legs scraped against the floor as Lilica grabbed a stool and dragged it to the counter, climbing up beside him.

Domine handed her the bowl and placed some lettuce beside it, which she began to tear into small pieces. "This neighbor friend of mine, the one I got these veggies from, she has a little boy about your age. What do you think about them coming over in a few days for a visit?"

I watched as Lilica nodded, the light in her eyes returning as a smile spread across her face.

Their chatter filled the small space within the kitchen, and I stood from the table, quietly slipping out the door.

Leaning against the side of the cabin, I stared into the haze of the sky, trying to arrange the current of my thoughts. Lilica was too young to fully understand that the changes I made were permanent, but she would in time, and when she did, would she resent me for it?

The sound of the door closing pulled me from my thoughts, and I looked over to see Domine walking toward me. "What's going on? Are you okay?"

I wrapped my arms around myself, the slight breeze in the air nipping at my skin and toying with my hair. "I just told her she wasn't going home. That she wouldn't be seeing her dad again."

"Oh, wow." He furrowed his brow, shoving his hands into his pockets. "How'd she take it?"

I swept my hand toward the window. "Well, she appears to have bounced back from it pretty quickly. I don't know… I don't think she was able to fully process things before you came in."

"I'm sorry I interrupted that. I had no idea."

"How could you? I wasn't planning on telling her in that moment. It just came out. I couldn't dance around it anymore." I brushed back my hair with a sigh. "Do you know what she said to me?"

"What?"

"She said she wanted *you* to be her new daddy." I shook my head, a sad smile pressing against my lips. "I suppose I can't blame her. When he *was* around, Trendon had never been much of a father. And you're so good with her. It makes sense that she would try to cling to something better."

A sorrow seemed to stir in his eyes as I spoke, and I suddenly regretted the words that had spilled out. He had never wanted to be a father. That was one thing he had made very clear when we had been together. He refused to bring a child into a world so bleak.

"I'm sorry. I shouldn't have said that." I ran my hands through my hair and stepped away from him, feeling the threads of our tangled past catch around my heart. "I don't want you to feel like you're under any obligation to fill some role for her."

"Seren." His voice was low and heavy with sentiment as he gently took me by the arms. "I adore your daughter, if you haven't noticed. And while I obviously can't be her dad, I would love nothing more than to be given the opportunity to be a part of her life."

My body began to tremble, and I wasn't sure if it was from the sudden chill of the wind that blew leaves around our feet or from the conviction of his words.

And that's when I felt it. The gentle drop of rain against my skin.

CHAPTER TEN

"*I*t's raining." I looked up into the sky, feeling the cool drops against my cheeks. "It's *finally* raining."

Domine broke into a wide smile and ran his hands through his hair, wet tendrils falling against his brow. "Feels a bit auspicious, don't you think?"

A lightness unfurled within me, as if the rain was rinsing away the residue of the Grid, leaving behind a buoyant feeling of renewal, and I found myself pulling him close, my arms slipping around his neck. "Thank you. For everything."

The rain dripped from our hair, running trails down our cheeks, and the concentrated look of longing Domine gave me sent my pulse racing as his hands slowly slid up my back.

The sound of the door slamming jolted me from our embrace, and Lilica's excited cry rang out through the trees. "Mommy! It's raining!"

"I know, sweetheart. It is." I caught her in my arms as she ran to me, lifting her up and spinning her in a dizzying circle as laughter spilled from my mouth. For a moment, everything else was forgotten. It was just us three in a world surrounded by forest, mountains, and the cleansing shower against our skin, bringing life back to the parched land and washing away all the smoke.

We stood outside, the rain soaking our clothes, as we watched Lilica dance among the puddles, an exuberance radiating off her. For the first time, I noticed how much she had come alive since we had been out here. Gone were the furtive glances, the pensive quiet, as if she needed to constantly curl into herself to avoid detection. She was no longer shrinking herself down. She was uninhibited laughter, the rush of wind through trees, the press of new growth bursting through the underbrush. She was open and wild and free.

* * *

*I*t rained throughout the night, a steady torrent that streamed down the windows and drummed against the roof, enclosing us in the rhythmic sound of water against wood. And when morning came, the rain was gone. In its place were bright beams of sunlight that played with the branches and burst through the trees, filtering into the cabin and teasing us with the promise of a clear blue sky.

Lilica bounded through the cabin while I packed some food into a basket for breakfast. Soft-boiled eggs and crackers, thick slices of tomatoes still holding the faint warmth of yesterday. Gathering up a blanket, I followed Lilica and Domine out the door, filling my lungs with the reprieve of fresh air as we stepped outside.

Finding a patch of sun beside the cabin where the grass was not so wet, I spread out the blanket, watching wisps of steam rise from the ground beside me. Everything was washed in effervescent light, and the sound of Lilica's laughter echoed through the air as she and Domine played hide-and-seek among the trees, flashes of movement among green and brown.

The sun caressed my skin as I sat crossed-legged and stared up into the blue of the sky. I had spent my whole life surrounded by artificial trees and concrete. Pressed and molded into the framework of a society that had lost all connection to nature. But here, life flourished with a resilience that took hold of me. Cradled me. And these past few weeks had been like a slow waking up to a world I never knew I needed until now.

A bloom of happiness stirred within, fluttering against my chest like a bird trying out new wings. It was a feeling I had not held in so long I almost didn't recognize it.

Lilica ran up to me and flopped onto the blanket, rosy-cheeked and breathless. "I'm hungry, Mommy."

"I bet you are." I unwrapped the food from the basket, watching as Domine strolled over to us from the tree line.

"Your little wood nymph happens to be quite an excellent hider." He shot her a wink and settled beside us, unclasping a canister of water and taking a long drink. I watched as a trickle of liquid slid down his neck and beaded against the hairs peeking above his shirt line. He had not shaved in a few days, and the stubble that peppered his face made him look even more rugged, accentuating the deep brown of his eyes. His searing gaze met mine, and this time, I did not look away even though my entire body flushed with adrenaline. I wanted him to know I was staring. I wanted him to know how beautiful he was.

"He could never find me, Mommy!"

Lilica's voice pulled me from the depths of his eyes, and I turned to ruffle her hair. "Wow. You *are* a good hider."

She grinned and stuffed some crackers into her mouth. "And I found him every time. He's not a good hider like me."

"Well, it looks like he could learn a thing or two from you then," I said with a playful smile as I popped a slice of tomato into my mouth, the sweet juice colliding with my tongue.

We ate breakfast together in a silent reverence, listening to the sounds of the woods come alive with the elated cacophony of birdsong, as if they, too, were celebrating the return of the sun, the restoration of fresh air. Domine stretched out on his back, resting his head against the fold of his hands, as Lilica ran off to search for treasures hidden beneath the forest floor.

"Don't go too far, hon." I called after her. "Stay where I can see you." I leaned back onto the blanket with a relaxed sigh and turned to Domine. "You know, I don't think I've ever seen Lilica so happy."

He looked at me, sunlight slanting across his skin. "What about you? Are you happy here?"

That flutter inside me stirred once more, yearning for the words to make it real. To claim this feeling that uncurled within. "Yes. I think I am."

A smile spread across his face, and he reached his arm out to me. "Come here."

I scooted closer and nestled my head in the crook of his shoulder, letting out a sigh as the warmth of him radiated against me, enveloping me in his scent of pine and earth. Lying beside him felt like coming home again. The ache and sweetness of returning to the place that held the soft whisper of long-ago memories.

"I had a dream the other night." Domine ran his hand lightly down my arm, and a flush of heat raced across my skin. "The three of us were planting a garden. Right here. Right where we're lying."

"You never told me you dream."

He shrugged and fingered a strand of my hair while his eyes grew heavy and swooped down the curve of my neck, causing my pulse to quicken and my breath to catch in my throat. "I guess it's never come up, but yes. I've been dreaming for a few years now."

I rested my head on his chest, feeling the steady thrum of his heartbeat against my ear, the rhythm so familiar. "What does it feel like to dream?"

"Like a memory you can reach out and hold. Sometimes the images stay with me for days. Other times, they're fleeting and hard to arrange."

I closed my eyes, trying to imagine a world only I could touch, the colors private and tucked away within my mind, awaiting sleeps gentle stirrings. "And what kind of dreams do you have?"

"I dream a lot about water and places I've never been but feel familiar..." He paused for a moment, and I looked up to see him staring into the arc of the sky. "And sometimes, I dream of you."

"Really?" His confession reached in and tugged me into the depths of something warm and inviting, and my voice came out breathless. "Maybe we *will* plant a garden here together."

"I hope so." He looked at me, his eyes swimming with unspoken words that sent a surge of electricity through me, and then he leaned in close, a smile playing on his lips. "There's actually something I've been wanting to show you."

"What is it?" I asked as he suddenly sat up and took my hand, pulling me to my feet.

"You'll see." He led me to where Lilica was crouched beside a log, her hands stained with earth as she turned over loose stones. "Hey, wood nymph, you want to come with us? There's something I want to show you and your mom."

With a smile, she jumped up and followed behind him, weaving in between the fallen branches on the forest floor. A few feet ahead, Domine stopped in an open space among the trees, where the brush had been cleared away into piles, and the outline of mountains towered in the distance.

He turned to me, his eyes sparkling. "What do you think?"

I looked around in confusion. "What do you mean?"

"I mean, what do you think about this spot for your cabin?"

I stared at him, the tendrils of disbelief curling through me. "You want to build us a cabin?"

"I figure if I start now, I should be done by spring." He walked to one of the brush piles and picked up a long stick, dragging the sharp point along the ground until he had drawn a large square in the dirt, roughly the size of a two-bedroom cabin. "This is where you guys come in." With a smile, he handed the stick to Lilica. "Do you want to draw out your bedroom?"

Her eyes lit up as she took the stick from him and proceeded to sketch out a corner among invisible walls, her imagination growing detailed as she drew out a bed and a dresser, a box to keep her toys in.

Stepping into the middle of the square, I leaned in close to Domine. "You're kicking us out already, huh?" I shot him a playful smile, but beneath my joke lay a twinge of uncertainty.

Why was he doing this?

"No, Seren." He looked at me, his eyes soft and focused. "I just want to give you both a place to call your own."

Bathed in the warmth of his sentiment, I felt the sudden press of tears gather, and for a moment, we just stared at each other. I wondered if he was remembering our own tiny apartment on the edge of town, beyond the tall buildings of the Grid. The refuge we had made together all those years ago. A private world composed of possibility.

"I can't believe you're going to build us a house."

"Believe it." He placed his hands on my shoulders, a slow smile creeping back across his face. "And I was thinking right here," he turned me around and splayed his arms out, cupping the view of the mountains between his hands, "would be a great place for the living room with a big window overlooking the view. And here," he pointed behind me, "could be the extra room for your clinic. We've been needing a doctor here for a while now."

"My clinic, huh?" I knew the growing bundles of herbs drying against the cabin window had begun to take up space in the kitchen, and the idea of my own space to freely practice medicine filled me with a sudden rush, like wings beating against my chest.

Reaching out, I curled my fingers through his. "You're amazing, you know that? I love it. I love *all* of it." The threads of potential tugged at me, tentative at first, and then consuming. I was here with Domine. And although the definitions of *us* were still delicate and unclear, we were building something together.

A home that held the promise of a new beginning.

But beneath this bud of hope lay the furtive grip of unease. The restless apprehension that always lay beside me late at night like a dark shadow when my thoughts had nowhere else to hide.

What if Trendon finds me?

Could we really build a life out here?

CHAPTER ELEVEN

*A*fternoon light flooded through the trees, bringing the last remnants of warmth from a faded summer. Fall was officially here. I could feel it in the slight chill of the breeze that flirted with the sunshine, in the mournful call of geese overhead, in the needles that dropped from the pine, scattering the ground like discarded memories.

Standing with Lilica in the coop, I sprinkled feed to the chickens while she gathered their eggs. In the distance, the rhythmic sound of chopping wood pierced through the air as Domine worked in the small clearing by the tree line, shadows dancing across his skin as he assembled logs for the new cabin.

"Are those going to be for our house, Mommy?" Lilica asked as we made our way back toward the cabin, clutching the basket of eggs in one hand while she pointed to Domine.

"Yes, they will be, sweetie."

The crunch of footsteps startled me, and I turned around to see a woman walking toward us with a basket nestled in the crook of her arm and a little boy trailing behind. She smiled when she drew near, the scent of cedar and rose enveloping the air around me as she set down her basket and took my hands in hers, squeezing tightly. "You must be Seren. Domine has told me so much about you."

I nodded, taking in her flowing waist-length blonde hair and deep blue eyes. She had the kind of beauty that demanded attention. And I suddenly felt self-conscious in my stained blue jeans and t-shirt, unwashed hair tied up into a messy bun.

"My name's River, and this little guy over here." A bushy head of golden curly hair peeked out from behind her legs. "Is Echo." River held her hand over her chest, her voice soft and melodic. "We released our old names when we left the Grid last year. These are our *chosen* names now. Ones that are more in alignment with our life path."

"Well, they are very beautiful." With a smile, I motioned to Lilica, who stood a few feet away, watching them with curious eyes before she came over and leaned against me. "This is my daughter, Lilica."

"It's so wonderful to meet you." River's eyes sparkled with warmth as she bent down and extended her hand, clasping it around Lilica's. "Echo would love to play with you today. Do you feel like playing?"

Nodding slowly, Lilica looked up at me with uncertainty. She had never been allowed to play with the other children at Learning Group. The educational system discouraged any form of unsupervised play, believing it bred dissention and took away from the teaching of valuable knowledge.

"It's okay, love. You can go play." I ran my hands through her hair, watching as she broke out into a wide grin and stepped closer to Echo.

"Do you want to see the chickens?" Her question elicited an enthusiastic nod from him, and just like that, some unspoken agreement was made, and they ran off together, their voices merging effortlessly under a canopy of trees and indigo sky.

"There is nothing more sacred than the pure energy between children, wouldn't you agree?" River smiled as she picked up her basket and handed it to me. "This is for you. I brought you some more vegetables from our garden."

"Thank you so much." With a nod, I took the basket from her as Domine approached us from the clearing.

"Hey, River. Thanks for stopping by." A tentative smile spread across his face as he brushed woodchips off his shirt, sunlight glinting through the dark strands of his tousled hair.

"Any time." She beamed up at him, her hand falling to his arm and gently sweeping downward, the look in her eyes unmistakable. There was an intimacy between them. I could see it. And everything within me deflated as the sharp and unexpected pang of jealousy rose and curled around me.

"Mommy! We're going to look for treasures in the forest!" Lilica's voice cut through the air, and I turned to see her and Echo disappearing into the woods.

"Don't go too far!" I called after her, my words catching in my throat.

"Oh, don't worry, they'll be fine. I'll keep an eye on them for you." River flashed me a warm smile and then leaned closer to Domine, her blonde hair falling against his cheek as she said something to him that I could not hear.

"Thanks." Grasping the handle of the basket, I took the eggs Lilica had left on the ground and brushed past Domine. "I'll just take these into the cabin."

My face burned as I closed the door behind me. *You fool*, the voice inside hissed as I placed the baskets on the counter and turned on the tap to the makeshift faucet, the pipes groaning and sputtering in protest as I filled a small bowl and rinsed off the tomatoes and lettuce in the cold water. All the fear and hesitancy that had been holding me back from diving into my feelings with Domine was now replaced with the crushing weight of disappointment. Here I was, thinking we were making slow steps toward something new together, when apparently there had been someone else this whole time.

Why had he not mentioned her before?

All those moments with him beside the fire. The touch of his hand on mine. The way he looked at me. The tenderness in which he took me in his arms on the grass the other day and told me about his dreams. Had I only been grasping at something that was no longer there?

I closed my eyes and took a deep breath, trying to steady myself as memories of that last night together flooded me. The tears and elevated words, the goodbye we both knew we had to make as we grappled on the floor of the cabin, tearing at our clothes, falling into the sorrow and hunger. We had tried so hard to make it work after he left the Grid. All the weekends I would come to him full of longing, only to leave with a desolate ache in my chest. In the end, the separation of our lives had fractured us.

I took a sharp breath, realizing with sudden clarity why I had chosen Trendon that blustery spring day when he approached me outside a department store with his wide smile and confident swagger. I chose him because I needed a buffer, a way to silence the scream of a life no longer with Domine. I knew I had to be empty inside, so that when I came to him again and stood beside the new boundaries we had erected, it wouldn't tear me apart.

But he always tore me apart.

The door opened, jolting me from the tangle of my thoughts, and I turned to see Domine stroll in and grab the pitcher of water from the counter. "River's taking Lilica and Echo for a little walk in the woods right now."

"Oh, that sounds like fun." I forced out a smile as I placed the washed vegetables on a towel to dry. "She seems really nice."

He nodded as he poured water into a glass, his face impassive.

"Are you guys…" I trailed off and made a circular motion with my hand, letting the question die in the air.

Domine leaned against the counter and regarded me with a look that was open and candid. "You want to know if we're sleeping together?" With a sigh, he set the glass down and folded his arms against his chest. "We have been intimate a few times."

My stomach turned sour, the bitter sting of his admission slamming into me. "So, is that what you were doing when you went to get vegetables the other day?" As soon as the flippant words left my mouth, I flinched. "I'm sorry. Never mind. It's absolutely none of my business." I moved past him and into the living room, gathering up Lilica's toys and placing them beside the bed, hoping movement would still the torrent in my mind.

"Jesus. No." Domine raked his hand through his hair. "I haven't been with her since you got here."

"Well, you don't have to stop because of me." My harsh tone prickled the air, the strands of my composure fracturing. This is what he did to me. What he always did. Yanked out the marrow of my emotions, leaving me flailing and exposed. Scrambling for my bearings, I took a deep breath and tried to still the pounding of my heart. Of course he had found someone. Ten years stretched between us, and I had no claim on him. If there was something between him and River, I had no right to get in the way of that. I took a shaky breath and turned to him. "I don't want you to feel like you have to sneak around with her. I want you to be happy."

"Happy?" His eyes flashed as he stepped closer to me. "You want me to be happy? Dammit, Seren. Don't you get it?"

I threw my hands in the air, as if the motion could create something solid. Something I could grasp onto. "Get what? What am I supposed to get?"

He grabbed me by my shoulders, his voice coming out in a tangled whisper. "That I have *never* been able to let you go. That you have *always* been the only thing in my life that has *ever* made me happy."

The fire in his words hit me, and heat coursed through my limbs. It bloomed and crept upward until it spread across my skin, stealing my breath. I closed my eyes, trying to shield myself from the intensity of his gaze. From the overwhelming current of his confession and the visceral ache he stirred within me. It had been so long since I had stared into the depths of my longing for him, and it felt too vast and encompassing for me to hold.

"Seren. Look at me." He swept his hand up my arm and cupped my face, his thumb gently caressing my cheek as my eyes fluttered open and met his. "I was young and reckless all those years ago. So angry at the world. And I had no idea at the time that leaving you would be a sacrifice I would regret every... single... day."

Tears pricked at my eyes. We had never spoken of these things before, always tiptoeing around our past like it was an unpredictable animal that could tear away at the ground we had so carefully built back up. And now here it was, standing naked in front of us, demanding our attention, and I couldn't run from it anymore. I didn't want to.

"Dom." The name spilled from me like a sigh. The name I used to murmur to him in the darkness as his fingers traced across my skin. The soft language of an intimacy I had not spoken in so long.

I placed my hands on his chest, the fabric of his shirt tangling in my fists as I pulled him closer. I couldn't think. I didn't want to. All I wanted was to feel the fierce rush of his lips against mine. That flame that used to dance so brightly between us.

He hesitated for a moment, his eyes heavy. Then his breath swept across my neck, teasing the delicate lobe of my ear as he drew me against his chest and spoke in a broken whisper that made my core tighten and my limbs grow weak. "If I kiss you right now, I don't think I'm going to be able to stop."

"Then don't stop," I gasped, my words tumbling out unrestrained as I wove my fingers into his hair and met the burn of his eyes.

"Seren." He spoke my name like a plea, a desperate sigh that hovered against my skin, and then his mouth found mine. A surge of pleasure cascaded through me as our lips and tongues collided, feverish and engulfing, sending everything spinning around me.

With a groan, he seized me by the hips, walked me backward, and pressed me firmly against the wall, pinning me to him. Ache and fire tore into me, and I clutched at his back, wrapping my legs around his waist as our kiss grew deeper and devouring. His hands slipped under my shirt, and I sucked in a breath as the familiar warmth of his touch sent desire tearing across my skin.

A sound from outside tumbled through my delirium, and Domine stiffened and abruptly jerked back, his head swiveling toward the window as the distant clang of a bell echoed through the air once more.

"What is that?" I asked breathless, my head swimming as he lowered my legs to the floor and released me.

"It's the warning bell." His voice grew low and timorous, his eyes wide and boring into me as he clasped my wrists. "It means the feds are here."

CHAPTER TWELVE

*P*anic slammed into me, and in a shaky daze, I pushed
past Domine and bolted for the door.

"Lilica!" My voice cried out across the clearing as I frantically
scanned the edges of the woods. The rapid thrashing of my pulse
hammered in my ears as I stumbled through the brush, searching
for the flash of blonde hair, the soft lilt of her voice. *Where was she?*
Was she still on a walk with River? The sharp taste of bile rose in the
back of my throat, and a sickening thought clawed at me,
splintering my world in two. *What if they find her?* My vision
wavered as a heaviness slammed into my chest, choking my
breath.

"Seren!" Domine's voice rose from beyond the trees, and I
turned to see him running toward me with Lilica in his arms. A
strangled sob rushed from my lips, and my knees buckled, hitting
the rocks below.

"You found her. Where was she?" I scrambled to my feet and
picked her up, pressing her tightly against me and reveling in the
solid warmth of her arms wrapped around my neck, the faint scent
of sap trapped in her hair.

"She was on the other side of the clearing with River and
Echo." Domine placed his hands on my shoulders, his eyes glancing
toward the cabin as his voice came out furtive and slow. "You need
to go as deep into the woods as you can. Find a place to hide, and
don't move until I come and get you, okay?"

I nodded as Lilica wriggled in my arms. "Mommy, what are we doing? You're squeezing me too tight."

I set her down, my legs trembling, voice tangled and breathless. "You and I are going to play hide and seek in the woods, sweetheart."

"Go. *Now.*" Domine's voice came out sharp and urgent, and I spun around, grabbing Lilica's hand and plunging us into the forest.

Tires crunched against gravel, and my breath hitched in my throat as the slamming of car doors echoed behind me. *We are not far enough away. We're too close.* My heart played out a furious battle cry against my chest as I weaved us through the trees, the branches a blur of green and brown that slapped against my face and snagged in my hair as I pushed forward, clutching Lilica's hand in mine. "Can you run a little faster for me, hon?"

She picked up her pace, her tiny legs struggling to match my hurried stride as I scanned the trees ahead of me, seeing nothing but tall cedar and ankle-high brush. *There's nowhere to hide.*

"Mommy, where are we going?"

I slowed my pace for a moment and looked down at her, forcing a smile over the strain of my mouth. "We're looking for somewhere to hide."

"What about over there, Mommy?" She pointed her finger toward a patch of blackened trees in the distance, stumps burned out from a long-ago fire. On the ground lay a large cedar, the old bark covered in moss and vines.

"That's perfect, sweetie." I led us quickly toward the fallen tree, hoping it would give us enough cover if we concealed ourselves behind it. As we came closer, I noticed it had been burned through the middle, leaving a wide opening with just enough space for both of us to squeeze into. "I need you to climb inside there, okay, hon?" I murmured as I pulled up handfuls of shrubs and brush from the ground. "We're going to hide ourselves in this tree."

She scrambled inside, and I followed, plugging up the opening with brush, hoping the camouflage would obscure us. It was musty inside, my nose filling with the scent of decay and the remnants of charcoal. Beetles had drilled their way through the tough wood, and faint beams of the sun pierced through the holes, showering our skin in fragments of light. Pressing my back against the rough bark, I curled my legs tightly to my chest and wrapped my arms around Lilica.

The snapping of twigs and the steady crunch of boots from far off jostled the silence, and my grip on her tightened.

"Mommy?" Her voice trembled in my ear.

"Shhh," I whispered over the violent rhythm of my heart as I pressed my finger to her lips. "I know what a good hider you are. And I need you to be *very* still and quiet right now. Can you do that for Mommy?" She nodded, her eyes growing wide. There was no mistaking the shift. This was not a carefree game we were playing together, and she knew it.

I tried to slow the pace of my breath as I closed my eyes and sent out a silent prayer to a God I hardly knew.

Please don't let them find us. Please keep us safe.

Footsteps grew closer, and the high-pitched, discordant beeps of a thermal monitor cut through the air. Through the holes in the wood, the flash of a red light cut through the trees, searching for signs of life, for the pulse of heat hidden beneath the undergrowth. I pulled Lilica closer to me and shrank back, hoping the thermal imaging wouldn't detect us through the log.

I held my breath, limbs shaking as boots dug into the earth, so close now I could hear the thump of weapon against uniform. And then the sound stopped, followed by a series of beeps searching for thermal activity. Lilica clung to me, frozen in place as I stared into her eyes, the pale gray dancing with threads of sunlight. *Is this what facing death felt like?* Everything reduced to one moment, magnified and suspended, as you wonder if this will be the last time you ever see your child?

"Over here! I think I found a trail." A voice called out from somewhere beyond us, and the boots pivoted beside the log before turning back, the snap of branches growing fainter until only a broken silence was left behind.

Gasping for air, I clutched Lilica against my chest, relief flooding my body in waves that trickled down my cheeks and gathered in the tangle of her hair. "That was such good hiding, sweetheart."

* * *

I had no idea how long we remained crouched inside the log, but eventually the sun sank behind the trees, casting us in darkened shadow. I could no longer feel my legs, and a chill had crept through the forest, peppering my skin with goosebumps, and causing Lilica to whimper as she grew colder. "Mommy, I want to go back now. When can we go back to the cabin?"

"Soon, honey. We just have to wait for Domine to come get us." I vigorously rubbed my hands up and down her arms, trying to warm her.

"When is he coming?"

"Any moment now." I bit back the waver in my voice, trying to push away the thoughts that wanted to tear into me like sharp talons. *What if he didn't come? What if they had taken him in for questioning?*

Branches shook and creaked above us, moaning an eerie ballad as a sudden gust of wind slithered through the trees, bringing with it the sound of a faint call.

"Seren!"

Domine's voice was a light yanking me from the darkness, and I called back to him as I scrambled out of the log, pulling Lilica behind. "Domine. We're over here!" I stumbled over brush, legs stiff and unstable as my circulation struggled to reclaim itself. The flame of a kerosene lamp flickered through the trees, and then I saw the outline of him striding toward us.

I sank into his arms, his scent enveloping me like a refuge, momentarily buffering my mind from the events of the day.

"Are you guys okay?"

I nodded as he handed me the lantern and removed his coat. Bending down, he wrapped it around Lilica and hoisted her into his arms.

We walked back to the cabin in silence, the lantern spilling a pallid glow across the forest floor while unspoken questions trailed behind us like urgent ghosts.

Once inside, Domine crouched beside the stove, his movements swift and efficient as he stoked up the coals. The flames cracked and hissed, filling the cabin with warmth as he turned to Lilica with a smile that did not meet his eyes. "I bet you're hungry, huh, little wood nymph?"

She nodded as she stood by the fire, tracking his movements as he placed a pot of last night's soup to warm on the woodstove. "Mommy, did we win the hiding game?"

My breath stilled, and I glanced over at Domine, who shot me a tense look. "Yes, hon. I think we won the hiding game."

As he dished out a bowl, I grabbed my coat and knelt beside her. "Sweetie, you get warmed up by the fire and eat up all your soup, okay?" With a strained smile, I brushed a strand of hair from her cheek. "I'm just going to step outside for a minute and have a little chat with Domine."

My chest constricted as she looked up at me, a heaviness swimming in the depths of her wide eyes. "Okay, Mommy."

I shut the door behind us and leaned against it. The light from the moon struggled to pierce through the gathering clouds, throwing shadows across the stoic plane of Domine's face as I stared up at him. "What happened?"

Balling his hands into fists, his voice came out in a low tremor. "Well, they questioned a bunch of us. And I met Trendon. A *real* piece of work that guy is." His eyes flashed with a malice I had seen before. It was the same sharp anger that used to simmer beneath the surface when he lived on the Grid. "It took *every* ounce of strength I had not to slam my fist in his face."

The potency of his words sent a chill through me, and I wrapped my arms around myself. "I guess I shouldn't be surprised that he's leading the investigation."

"It's bad, Seren."

"How bad?"

"I guess they found the jeep. And they're charging you with possession of stolen property, eluding government authorities, dissension, treason…" He trailed off, his jaw tightly clenched as he stared out into the darkness.

I gripped his shoulders, willing his gaze to meet mine. "What else, Domine? Tell me."

His breath escaped him in a slow sigh. "Child endangerment and kidnapping."

The words hit me like shards of glass. I had known that leaving with Lilica would be a tighter noose around my neck if they ever caught me, but when faced with losing everything important, I had no other choice.

My voice trembled as I dug my nails into the palm of my hand, trying to stifle the fresh wave of panic that threatened to surface. "Do you think it was the jeep that led them here?"

"Could have been. But they also apparently seized Kystina's phone."

"Kystina?" The sickening crash of nausea rolled in my gut. "Do they have her on charges?"

"I don't know. I just overheard them talking about how she had been taken in for questioning."

"Shit." I spun away from the door, my hands trembling, pulse racing as I paced beside Domine. "I should have never called her. I knew it was a risk." The thought of something happening to her was a weight I could not carry, and I squeezed my eyes shut as if I could block out the thrashing inside me. "Did they search any of the cabins?"

"They entered a few of them. But even up here, they know they can't do a full legal search without a warrant. Looks like they were just here to poke around and ask questions." Stepping closer, he took me by the shoulders, the sharp look in his eyes withering away whatever vague hope I still clung to. "But they are going to come back."

The truth crashed into me, sucking the breath from my lungs. All the plans we had been slowly building together, the dreams of something new, a chance to start over… it was gone. It was all gone. "We can't stay here, can we?"

He shook his head, his jaw tensing as his eyes fell heavy on me.

"No. It's not safe anymore."

"What am I going to do?" My question came out like a desperate plea as my mind scrambled around for a safehold. I had been such a fool to think they wouldn't find us here, so caught up in the seductive possibilities of a life that, for the first time, made me feel whole inside.

He folded his arms around me, his voice a fervent whisper against my ear. "I told you I would make sure they never found you." He pulled back, the look on his face determined and resolute. "There's a place we can go."

I shook my head, my voice coming out dry and barren. "What do you mean? There isn't anywhere safe for us here."

"There's a place in Canada. An isolated region in Alberta where a sovereign nation is being formed. We can go there."

CHAPTER THIRTEEN

*D*omine unfolded the map on the floor beside the fire. The light from the flames enclosed the cabin in a soft glow as his finger traced the thin line of ink that snaked alongside the Cascade Mountain range and into Canada. "On foot, it should take us about six or seven days to get to the Canadian border. And then from there, roughly three to four weeks until we reach Alberta. This is not the ideal time to go. Spring would be better." He furrowed his brow as his fingers hovered over the brown ridge on the map that ran up through the western side of Canada. "But as long as we can get over this stretch of the Rocky Mountains before the first snow, we should be fine."

His words stirred the embers of a hope that had been yanked out from under my feet only hours ago. Though seemingly overwhelming, it was a safety net I could grasp onto, a tangible plan that mollified the panic crashing around the darkness of my mind. "When do you think we should leave?"

"Tomorrow." He looked up at me, his eyes obscured in shadow. "I can pack up everything we need and have us ready to go by early afternoon."

The swift finality of this decision hit with a piercing blow, and I glanced over at Lilica, who lay on the bed, the linen curtains drawn around her sleeping form. She had finally adjusted to this new life, and now here I was, forced to rip it away from her again. Caught beneath the burden of circumstances beyond my control, tears stung my eyes.

"How am I going to explain this to her?" I turned to Domine, clenching my fists in my lap as the threads of guilt twisted in my chest, threatening my resolve. "I feel so bad having to do this to her all over again."

"Seren." He placed his hand over mine, the rough edges of his calloused fingers sweeping a comforting trail across my skin. "You're her mom. It's your job to give her the best life possible. And that's what you're doing. You're giving her the opportunity to truly *live*." Leaning in close, he brushed away a tear that had crept down my cheek, the look in his eyes tender and convincing as a small smile tugged at the corners of his lips. "Just tell her we're going on a great adventure. I can *guarantee* you that won't be a lie."

"I guess you're right." A small sigh escaped me, and I sank against him. Resting my head on his shoulder, I breathed in the warmth of his shelter, the scent of forest that always surrounded him, the calm assurance of his sturdy plans, and a tentative feeling of trust stirred inside. "We're really doing this, aren't we?"

He slid his arm around me and pulled me closer. "We are."

I stared at the map beside us, noticing the detailed markings and highlighted areas scrawled across the page, the ink worn around the folded creases. He had taken this map out and marked it many times.

How long had he been thinking about leaving?

I tilted my head up, watching the light from the fire play in his eyes. "How do you know about this place in Canada, anyway?"

His finger tracked across the lines on the map. "Travelers often stop by on their way up to Alberta. We provide them with food and a place to rest when needed. The trail to Canada runs right through the Okanogan National Forest." He circled the dense green patch that marked our location. "They call themselves asylum seekers. Some are escaping government persecution. Others are looking for autonomy and freedom."

"So, I won't be the only one on the run?"

He looked at me, his tone growing somber. "No. There are a lot of people out there like you. All it takes is one wrong step, and they suddenly find themselves running.”

I stared down at the pale line still faintly visible on my ring finger, a mocking reminder of a life that had taken so much from me. “Why hasn’t anyone from here left?”

“Some have. But most of us have grown comfortable here. Though we tend to keep to ourselves most of the time, we’re a family in a way. We look out for each other.”

I placed my hand on his arm, my fingers toying with the fabric of his shirt. “You’ve been wanting to go, haven’t you?”

Something that looked like sorrow flashed within his eyes. “I have, yes.”

“How long?”

“A couple of years.”

“So why haven’t you?”

He bent close to me, his voice an ardent whisper against my ear. “Because every time I thought of leaving, I thought of you. I thought about never seeing you again, and I just couldn’t do it.”

My heart stumbled, the intensity of his disclosure stealing the breath from my lungs and filling me with a painful confliction. How long had we both been living a half-life? Ensnared in the remnants of a past neither of us could let go of, like collateral damage we could not rectify.

“Dom…” My words caught in my throat as his hand slipped over mine and our fingers met, entwining in a slow dance that drew out the ache inside me. Our kiss from earlier today lingered between us, full of an unspent desire that made the air around us thick and languid. The rush of his lips on mine, the feel of him as he pressed me recklessly against the wall. I wanted more. I wanted all of him.

I had never stopped wanting him.

I sucked in a sharp breath as his hand swept up my arm and slid into my hair, his eyes mirroring the rush of heat that tore across my skin.

“Mommy? I can’t sleep.”

Lilica’s voice broke through the moment, and Domine gave me a tired smile, his thumb brushing against my lips before pulling away. "I'll let you guys get some rest. We're going to have a big day ahead of us tomorrow."

With a nod, I reluctantly pulled myself from him and stood, my limbs laden and shaky as I crossed the room to Lilica. Through the curtains, I watched the outline of Domine as he banked the fire and made his way quietly up to the loft.

"Can you read me one more story, Mommy?" She sat up in bed, her hair tousled and cheeks rosy, clutching her book of fairytales.

"Sure thing, love." Bending down, I grabbed my nightgown and shed my clothes in the corner by the bed. "What story do you want me to read?" I slid the fabric over my head and crawled in beside her. But there was no answer. She was fast asleep again, her head cradled against the book. With a smile, I slid the book out from under her arm and placed it on the floor.

Pulling the covers around us, I stared up at the ceiling, my mind spinning as I watched the remnants of light from the fire flicker across the wooden beams. This would be the last night we would spend in this cabin. Tomorrow, we would leave the four walls I had grown so accustomed to over the past few weeks. We would say goodbye to the comforting way the morning light spilled into the kitchen, the sound of birdsong that crept through the windows, the cabin we would never build. And we would trade it all for the unknown, for the shelter of trees and the wildness of mountains, to a place that hesitantly whispered of freedom.

I knew plans were transitory and promises could be ephemeral, but as I lay on the bed beside Lilica, I reached for hope.

The rustle of Domine moving up in the loft stirred me from my thoughts, and a sharp ache tore into me once more. Closing my eyes, I allowed the visual of him to suffuse me, the taste of his mouth, the feel of his hands on my skin. It had been so long since I'd been touched, and even longer since I'd felt that fire beneath my bones. I had not been intimate with Trendon in years, but long before we stopped trying to keep the marriage alive, he'd always been taciturn, his kisses stiff, his hands distant. There was no fierceness, no passion, and I used to think it was because he was being gentle with me. I now knew it was because we had never burned together.

Energy surged through me, the brush of sheets against my skin like a teasing caress, and I sat up, staring at the loft through the sheer fabric. I needed him. I needed his arms around me, the warmth of his breath on my skin, the safety of his eyes that saw me better than anyone. I needed to fall apart. I was so tired of trying to hold together the pieces of myself.

Drawing in a shaky breath, I crept from the bed and padded softly across the floor. Pale threads of moonlight spilled through the curtains and scattered fragmented shadows across the room as my hands rested tentatively on the wooden slats of the ladder.

CHAPTER FOURTEEN

*M*y pulse accelerated as I climbed the ladder to Domine, like a bold offering made in the dark. The glow of the moon illuminated the loft, and I could make out the shape of him as he lay on the mattress beside the window.

"Seren?"

I didn't respond. There were no words. All I had was a longing that had grown acute and pressing, and it dared me to claim it. My hands connected with the wooden floor, the ceiling allowing only enough room for me to bend forward as I made my way toward him.

Shards of light slanted across his face as he sat up, and then he was pulling me into his arms. A sigh spilled from my lips, the sound catching in his mouth as he pressed me against him and finished the kiss we had started in the room that now lay below us.

I glided my hands up the length of muscle along his back, the feel of his bare skin intoxicating, a collision of longing and release, and the tenderness that lay beneath. He was home to me. He always had been. And his kiss was like air rushing back into my lungs.

I gripped his shoulders, pushing him back against the bed as an unrestrained hunger took hold of me, born of fire and ache. He let out a strangled groan as my lips traveled across his chest and down to the valley where his abdomen met the waistline of his pants, reveling in the taste of his skin, a merging of salt... and smoke... and pine.

My name became a broken sigh as he grabbed me by my hips and pulled me to his mouth. His arousal strained against my thigh, the sensation delicious and urgent, causing my core to tighten as he slid his hands beneath the fabric of my nightgown.

A soft moan escaped me as his touch met my skin. His fingers swept up to my breasts, lightly teasing my nipples with the brush of his thumb before he descended lower, running his hands down to my stomach. Instinctively, I tensed and pulled back, suddenly aware of how much the years had shifted my body since we had last been together. The extra weight I carried like a protective barrier. My breasts no longer firm and supple. Belly puckered and ravaged by incision scars and stretch marks.

"Seren." As if he had reached into my thoughts, Domine sat up, his eyes burning into mine while he ran his hands down the curve of my back. "Don't hide from me. I want to see you." He slipped my nightgown over my head, and I yielded to him, my body trembling as I allowed the fabric to fall to the floor beside us.

Rolling me onto my back, his lips brushed against my ear. "You are everything beautiful to me. *Everything.*" His kisses swept down my neck, resting at the slope of my breasts. "My God, Seren. I have waited *so* long for you."

I sucked in a sharp breath, the warmth of his mouth unraveling me, his words a caress that stole away my thoughts while he traveled the length of my body, eyes drinking me in as if I were something exquisite.

Slowly he slid down my underwear, his lips marking my skin and leaving a path of heat that made me dizzy as his fingers ran up my thigh and brushed against my sex.

"Dom." I let out a gasp as he lowered his head and tasted me. Arching myself against him, I clutched at the sheets as a wave of pleasure tore through my body, unveiling all the ache and want and need that had bound me for so long.

With a groan, he grasped me by my hips and drew me deeper against his mouth, his lips and tongue re-discovering me, filling me, finding all the places that had not been touched in years. Unable to contain the sharp intensity building inside, I stifled a cry into the pillow as the sudden hot flash of an orgasm cascaded through me, leaving me undone and shaking against the sheets.

He rose up and took me into his arms, cradling me against his chest, his heartbeat rapid against my ear, his breath matching the labored pace of my own. He held me as I came back to him, his hands sketching my skin, coaxing the fire that smoldered beneath. I found his eyes in the darkness, the light from the moon sweeping across his face, and I reached out to trace the curve of his jaw, the softness of his lips, reveling in the way the silence surrounded us. A surrendering that was tender and forgiving of time.

"I dreamed of this, you know." His voice was a whisper across my fingers as his mouth fell to the inside of my wrist, kissing the pulse that trembled beneath.

"You did?"

"Yes. I was holding you in the darkness, just like this. With the moon and the feel of your skin on mine… It felt so real."

"It is real." I threaded my hands through his hair and rested my forehead against his.

"Is it, though? Is this real?" His voice shook with emotion as he stared at me, his eyes dancing with tears. "I thought you were gone from me."

"I'm right here." My breath caught in my throat as all the years rose and fell away, exposing the bright spark of a connection that had never dimmed. My lips sought his, tasting the salt of his tears as they mingled with mine. "I've always been here."

Domine rolled over, pressing me beneath him as our kiss grew fervent and demanding. I grasped at his back, hands pleading, limbs shaking as I curled myself around him. Breathless and frantic, I tugged at his pants, exposing the pulse of his desire. He shuddered as I ran my fingers down his length, cupping him in the palm of my hand, the feel of him familiar and exhilarating.

With a gasp, I drew him against the slickness of my sex, my entire body crying out for him as he hovered above me, his eyes like fire against moonlight. And then his mouth found mine again in a consuming burst of pleasure as he slid himself into me.

I buried my mouth against his neck, muting the sob that rushed out. *He felt so good.* I had forgotten how perfectly we fit together. Light flashed beneath my eyelids in a cacophony of color and euphoria as he began to move within, slow strokes that filled me and stretched me wide open. My name was a plea that softly tumbled from his lips as his breath tangled in my hair, kisses consuming my skin.

Our eyes locked together, the intensity of his gaze pulling me into the depths of an elation I could not contain. I dug my nails into his back, my mouth lost in his as a fractured cry took flight, and I fell blindly into the oblivion of another orgasm.

Through my euphoric haze, I felt him stiffen against me, and a low growl rumbled deep in his throat as he quickly pulled out and released himself. The heat of him pulsing against my stomach.

Reaching down, I touched the remnants, thick and silky against my fingers, his eyes watching me as I brought it to my lips, tasting the salt of him.

"My God. I will *never* get enough of you." Gripping my hips, he rolled me over onto my stomach, his hair brushing against my skin as his lips swept across my back, exploring the places he had not yet touched. I let out a shuddered exhale into the sheets, pinned beneath his caress as he slid down the slope of my curves, hands snaking up my thighs. With a moan, I lifted my hips upward, a renewed eruption of pleasure blooming within as I felt the gentle press of him from behind.

"Ten years, Seren." His voice was a sigh against my ear, his fingers entwining with mine, bracing me against the bed, and I gasped as he slid himself inside me once more. "Ten years I have wanted to love you like this again, and I'm not going to stop."

"Dom…" I trailed off, already lost in the wilderness of us, in the wide-open sky and rich earth of our bodies finding purchase in each other.

* * *

*S*hadows danced across our skin as I lay spent and entangled in Domine's arms. The moon had shifted in the sky and was now a sliver beyond the window. With my head cradled against his shoulder, I stared up into his eyes, still unable to find the words for what we had just shared. It was more than a reunion of our bodies. Being with him was like walking back into sunlight after so many years of darkness, and the vibrancy of color was blinding.

His fingers traveled across my skin, soft caresses that lulled me into the languid place between sleep. I knew once the sun rose, we would have to release each other, and Lilica would awaken with questions as we once more packed away our lives. But in this moment, it all felt so far away. It was just us, cocooned in a space removed from the reality of tomorrow.

"I think I made a mess of you," he whispered as he shifted beside me and sat up, grabbing his pants from the floor.

Reaching out, I ran my fingers down his arm. "I don't mind. Where are you going?"

He turned to me with a playful smile. "I'll be right back."

I scooted out of bed as he descended the ladder. Peering down into the darkness of the living room, I watched as he crouched beside the stove and stoked up the embers, quietly placing a pan of water on top. With a smile, I slipped back into bed and burrowed beneath the sheets. Love drunk and languid, I breathed in the scent of him lingering against the fabric, the sensation of his hands still imprinted upon me like the ink of a tattoo, the tender burn of him inside me.

I must have dozed off for a moment because I awoke to the feel of warm water caressing my neck. Domine sat above me, his eyes drowsy as he ran a washcloth across my chest and down to my stomach, wiping away the remains of his release. He dipped the cloth into the pan beside the bed and moved to my back. Goosebumps spread across my skin as the warmth of the water met with the cool air, a tantalizing sensation that caused a pull of heat to curl within as I relinquished my body to his gentle touch.

"You don't have to do that, you know."

He looked at me with a small smile, one eyebrow slightly raised as he slid the cloth slowly up my leg. "You don't like sponge baths?"

I walked my fingers across his thigh, playing at the fabric of his pants. "No. I *like* what you're doing. I meant that you don't have to pull out with me anymore."

"What do you mean?" He placed the cloth back into the pan and slid underneath the covers, drawing me into his arms.

I had always followed the rhythm method. Contraception was illegal, and the options available on the black market were far too risky. Ever since I was young, I had learned to track my cycle. The ebb and flow of my blood, the quickened pace of ovulation. But regardless of that, Domine had always pulled out with me, his fear of conceiving a child stronger than the surge of his passion. And I used to feel cheated somehow, as if the rush of his seed inside me was the one thing he wouldn't share. The one wall between us.

Biting my lip, I stared up at the ceiling, following the grooves etched across the wood. "When I had Lilica, there were some complications." I ran my hand over the sheets, teasing the fabric between my fingers. "I ended up with an intrauterine infection."

"Is that what that scar is from?" His eyes rested on my stomach, fingers reaching down to trace the creased line running below my navel.

"Yeah, and it was pretty bad. They had to do surgery and remove all the infected tissue from my uterus." The memory flooded me. Locked in a bed strung with tubes, unable to see my daughter, the detached look in Trendon's eyes. Had he only been trying to hold himself together? Or had he always been so distant, so removed from his own emotions? A sigh wrenched through me. "After the operation, the doctors told me I wouldn't be able to conceive again."

"Seren." Domine reached out and cupped my cheek, his eyes wide and full of a sorrow that reminded me of my own tucked so carefully away. "I'm so sorry. I know how much you wanted a big family."

I stared out the window, watching the tops of the pine trees shiver against the night sky. The fragility of life had always been my companion, the darkness I could never outpace, and I had been foolish to think that having children would have breathed life back into the people I had lost. A tired smile stretched across my face as I turned to him. "Well, it turns out, Lilica is all I need."

Furrowing his brow, he ran his thumb in slow circles against my skin. "Why didn't you tell me this before? I had no idea any of this had happened."

"There were a lot of things we never talked about, Domine." My words rose up like an undercurrent. A stark reminder of all the misplaced years.

"I know. You're right." He shook his head, eyes swimming with a sorrow that tore into me. "You know, every time you'd come up here to visit, a piece of me would come back to life. And then I would watch you drive away, not knowing when you would return, never having a way to reach out to you. It felt like losing you *over and over* again. And it got to the point where I didn't think I could do it anymore."

He pressed his forehead to mine, his voice low and burning with the remnants of a confliction he must have carried for so long, and my lip trembled as I bit back the sting of tears. "I'm sorry." I curled into him, sinking into the anchor of his arms. "It wasn't easy for me either."

Domine brushed a strand of hair from my face, his gaze soft and full of a devotion that stilled my breath. "Don't be sorry. The world got in the way of us, that's all." His lips swept gently against my cheek, leaving a trail of warmth across my skin. "And then it brought us back to each other."

CHAPTER FIFTEEN

*M*orning light streamed through the window, teasing my eyelids open as my mind swam with images from the night before. The feel of Domine's lips on mine. The warmth of his hands as they traced my skin. The rush of our bodies finding each other again. I allowed this sensation of lightness to wash over me like a gentle tonic, bathing my limbs in a euphoric hum.

With a drowsy smile, I rolled over, every muscle deliciously tender as I reached for Domine, but was met with the coolness of sheets. The faint sound of voices drifted from outside, and I sat up, pulling myself from the bed. I crept over to the edge of the loft where Lilica still slept soundly down below, arms and legs splayed across the sheets. Through the living room window, I could see River outside with her boy in her arms. Domine stood a few paces away as she gestured at him, her face tense.

I didn't need to hear them to know what the conversation was about. As she stepped closer and placed her hand on his chest, I saw the flash of sadness in her eyes. She was saying goodbye. We all were. Today would be full of goodbyes, and the harsh reality hit me once more as I glanced back at my sleeping daughter.

We were leaving, and I had no idea what our journey would look like.

The door closed softly below, and the ladder creaked as I threw on my nightgown and fumbled around in the sheets, looking for my underwear. Domine came up from behind and slid his hands around my waist, the chill from outside clinging to his skin as his lips brushed against my neck.

I leaned into him, my eyes falling to the small window of the loft, watching as the trees rustled against the blue sky. "River seemed pretty upset."

"You saw that?"

I turned to him, sweeping away the hair that had fallen loose across his forehead. "You were more than occasionally intimate with her, weren't you?"

He nodded with a sigh, releasing me as he moved to the edge of the bed. "For a while I tried. I really tried with her. I wanted to feel something again. But I just couldn't." He looked at me, his eyes flashing with a heaviness that tore at my breath. "She wasn't you."

Scooting closer, I rested my head on his shoulder, entwining my fingers through his. "Did she know about us?"

"Not really. But she does now."

I bit my lip, feeling the pull of a sorrow that was not mine. The sorrow of trying to love a man who couldn't love you back. "Do you think she'll be okay?"

"I think so. She said she understands." He tilted my head up, his thumb trailing across my cheek. "Sometimes we can't *choose* love. Love chooses us."

"It does, doesn't it?" My pulse accelerated as I ran my hand down his back, caught in the heat of his stare, in the depths of his eyes, which swam with that raw emotion I loved so much about him. He was unfiltered fire, and it was what made him so incredibly beautiful. Sliding onto his lap, I wrapped myself around him, pressing my mouth against his, greedy and aching for the feel of him again.

With a groan, he grasped my shoulders and pulled back. "God, how I wish I could lose myself in you right now." His voice came out breathless as he tangled his fingers in my hair and rested his forehead against mine. "But we need to start packing. It's time for us to go."

"I know."

* * *

I gently ran my hand down Lilica's back, stirring her from sleep. "Morning, sweetheart. It's wake-up time."

She turned to me, rubbing her eyes and glancing down at the bowl of oatmeal in my hand. "What are we doing today, Mommy?" She took the bowl and shoveled a large spoonful into her mouth.

The door sprang open, and Domine stepped into the living room with two large packs slung over his shoulder. Turning back to Lilica, I took her hand in mine. "Lili. We need to talk about some things." Hesitancy hovered against my chest as she stared up at me with wide-open eyes. *How much truth should I give her?* "We're not going to be able to stay in this cabin anymore."

"Are we going back home?"

My heart constricted. Home was a place no longer defined. All she had left to grasp onto were my words, hopeful promises that held no assurance. I stretched a tight smile across my face. "No, sweetie. We're going to find a *new* home in Canada."

She furrowed her brow. "Where's Canada?"

Domine crouched beside the bed, the soft composure in his eyes stilling the restless unease tumbling within me. "It's a place far away. But with mountains and tall trees, just like here at the cabin."

"Are you going to come, too?"

"I am."

A small smile curled around the edges of her mouth, and I noticed a glimmer of relief wash across her face as she stared down into her oatmeal.

I squeezed her hand. "We'll get to camp in the woods and explore all kinds of new things." Reaching out, I brushed back the tangles in her hair. "What do you think about that? Do you want to go on a big adventure?"

Looking up at me, she nodded, a light gathering in her eyes. "When are we going?"

"Today. Once you finish your oatmeal, we can start packing up all your stuff, okay?"

"Okay, Mommy."

Domine stood from the bed and shot Lilica a wide smile. "And I'm going to need your help in the chicken coop. I hear you're the very best at gathering eggs."

"Are we taking the chickens with us?"

He chuckled as he crossed the room and grabbed a nylon tent and three small retractable lanterns stashed within the small cupboard beneath the loft. "No. The chickens will be staying here. River and Echo will take care of them for us."

Lilica scrambled from bed, her bowl of oatmeal forgotten as she shadowed Domine with eager questions, pointing to the various supplies he placed beside the packs. And just like that, she appeared to accept this new reality handed to her as early morning streamed through the windows, bathing them both in light.

* * *

Steam rose from the boiling pot of eggs on the stove as I sat on the kitchen floor, arranging the non-perishable food into our packs. Bags of oatmeal, dried beans, flour, and rice. Dehydrated beets, tomatoes, and zucchini. With a sigh, I stared over at the cupboard of preserved food Domine had been diligently collecting over the years, knowing the cans and glass jars would be too bulky to pack with us.

"Do you think we're going to have enough food?" I looked up at Domine, who stood by the table, running the blade of his knife against a sharpening rod.

"We should. We have roughly five weeks on the trail, so if we ration, it should last us until we get to Alberta. Plus, I'm bringing my crossbow, and I have these snares if we need some fresh protein." Sheathing the knife into a leather pouch, he picked up the handful of wire loops that lay on the table.

"I wasn't aware that you knew how to hunt."

"Of course I know how to hunt." He bent down, a smirk tugging at the corner of his mouth as he slipped the knife and snares into the front pocket of the pack. "How do you think I fed myself during the winter?"

"Oh, right." I stared over at his crossbow leaning against the table, realizing there was so much of his day-to-day life I had never known about. All the long winter nights spent with only the company of his thoughts. Years that ticked by in an intimate rhythm I had never been a part of. The threads of his solitude were like secrets folded away, and a sudden remorse tugged at me. How I wished I could have shared those moments with him.

A knock at the door stilled the movement of my hands, my fingers curling around a bag of rice as my heart leapt into my throat. I glanced across the room to where Lilica was quietly placing her toys inside her backpack. "Who is that?" I whispered to Domine, my voice coming out strained.

He stood and peered out the window, then threw his hand up in a wave. "It's just Turk." Motioning for him to come in, Domine watched as the door opened and Turk stepped through, carrying a large cloth bag in his hand.

"I heard the bell yesterday." His eyes swiveled around the room and fell on the packs beside us. "Had a feeling you were leaving." Setting the bag on the table, he retrieved something from inside and walked over to Lilica. "I brought you a little present to take along on your journey." He crouched down beside her. "It's a compass *and* a nightlight."

She reached out and took the compass, running her fingers down the smooth glass face as Turk pressed a button, and the walls and ceiling around us lit with a shimmering rainbow of color. With a gasp, her eyes grew wide as she looked up. "It's so pretty."

"I thought so, too," Turk said with a chuckle. "It's solar-powered, so if you strap it to your backpack during the day, it will charge up for nighttime." He stood and gave her hair an affectionate tousle. "Now you'll never get lost in the dark."

"Thank you, Turk. That's really sweet of you." I slid my medicinal bag into the side pocket and cinched the top of the pack, securing the food and cooking utensils in place.

"I got a few things for you guys as well." Turk pulled out a rolled-up sleeping bag. "Figured you might need an extra one of these. And this here…" he placed a small glass jar in my hand, "is some medicine for the two of you."

I twisted off the cap, a pungent aroma wafting up to my nose as I looked inside. Nestled beside a small metal pipe lay the greenish-brown hue of tightly woven buds sprinkled with crystals that looked like sugar. "*Cannabis Sativa.*" I looked up at him. "I've read about this herb in a textbook once, but have never been able to locate it. Where did you get this?"

"I happen to grow it out back behind my cabin." Turk leaned up against the counter with a grin as he folded his arms across his chest.

"Thank you." I fingered the sticky leaves, their scent marking my skin. "I've always wanted to try this."

"I think you'll enjoy it," Domine murmured close to my ear as his hand snaked around my waist, causing memories from the night before to disarm me, peppering my cheeks with a rush of heat.

A smile ignited Turk's eyes, accentuating the lines that creased his weathered face. "I can see now what Domine spoke of. You two have a light together."

I raised a playful eyebrow at Domine. "You've been talking about me?"

"Maybe." He drew me closer to him, the look he gave me speaking volumes.

"That light will be your strength." The deep cadence of Turk's voice wove through me, and I turned to him. "No matter what happens, remember that."

His words were simple but profound, and goosebumps prickled along my flesh.

"Mommy!" Lilica ran up to us, crashing against my leg, her nightlight casting pale rainbows across our skin. "I'm all packed up."

"Good job, sweetie." I looked down at her with a smile, taking in her disheveled hair and the excitement dancing in her wide gray eyes.

"Well, I'll let you guys be on your way." Turk moved toward us, placing his hands on both our shoulders.

"I'm going to miss you, old man." Domine clasped Turk's arms and pulled him in for a hug.

"Me, too. A part of me wishes I could come along. But someone has to stick around to make sure these kids behave themselves." He stepped back with a wink and moved toward the door, his hand resting on the knob. "Good luck out there."

* * *

I stood in the living room, surveying the life now tidied from the walls and cabinets, waiting for whoever would come to take our place. For so long, Domine had orbited the simplicity of his own private world. And I wondered, had he found a sense of contentment I was now forcing him to leave behind?

"Are you ready?" Domine stood in the doorway.

"I think so." I crossed the room and grabbed my pack off the kitchen table. "Are you going to miss this place?" I asked as I stepped outside, watching Lilica crouch beside us, tracing pictures on the ground like a farewell message written in the ink of the earth.

"No." He reached out to brush his fingers across my cheek. "Everything I need is right *here*."

My breath hitched in my throat, and I lost myself in the depths of his gaze for a moment before the slivers of worry pushed through. A sigh escaped me as I stared out toward the trees, my voice lowering to a whisper. "Do you think we'll be safe out there? What if they come looking for us?"

He swept his hand down my arm, his touch like an anchor pulling me from claws of apprehension. "They have no concrete evidence you were ever staying here. And when they do come back, we'll be long gone by then."

I nodded and bit the edge of my lip, hoping he was right.

"We going yet?" Lilica bounced on her heels, her eyes wide with impatience.

"Yes. I think we're all ready to go, love." Securing the straps of the pack around my shoulders, I clipped the front buckle in place and closed the door behind us.

"So, Lilica. Have you ever slept in a tent before? Or eaten around a campfire?" Domine looked down at her with a smile as he slung his pack over his shoulders.

She shook her head, a grin sweeping across her face. "Do we get to do all those things?"

"Yes, we do."

She tugged at his hand. "Can I ride on your shoulders?"

"Oh, no, honey." I leaned down to make sure her shoelaces were securely tied. "Domine has a heavy pack to carry."

"It's okay." He grabbed her by the waist and lifted her into the air, planting her on top of his shoulders. "Wood nymphs are surprisingly light."

A giggle tumbled from her as she clutched her arms around the top of his head. "Light like a feather?"

"Light as a leaf," Domine said as I followed behind them, our footsteps crunching against the dry brush of the trail that led into the forest.

"Like a butterfly!" Lilica sang out.

"Like a cloud," he replied with a chuckle.

The exuberant ring of their voices slipped through the trees and echoed around me. Beams of sunlight flickered through the branches while the wind blew a soft song against my skin, and the tight band of unease that had lingered within my chest all morning was replaced with a sudden feeling of hopeful buoyancy.

We were unbound. The forest was our home now.

CHAPTER SIXTEEN

"Let's stop here for a lunch break." Domine stood beside a fallen log, placing his pack against the weathered bark.

We had now been walking for a couple of hours, and Lilica was showing signs of tiring, her steps slowing, her excited chatter ceasing to a quiet murmur. Taking a seat on the log, I pulled out the sandwiches I had made before we left. "Hey, hon. Come have something to eat." I motioned to her as I unwrapped the last of the thick slices of bread Domine had baked on the woodstove a few days ago, slathered with honey and peanut butter.

She leaned against me, stuffing the sandwich eagerly into her mouth while Domine sat beside us, pulling something from the side pocket of his pack. Sunlight caught the glint of metal, and he lifted the thin rectangular shape to his lips. A long, sorrowful note pulsed through the air, causing goosebumps to scatter across my skin.

"What is that?" Lilica reached out her hand, eyes locked on the object.

"This is called a harmonica." He placed it into her open palm, a wide smile stretching across his face.

"What does it do?"

"It makes music, sweetie." I bent down and ran my fingers along the square holes on top. "You blow into these right here, and the sound comes out." I turned to Domine. "Where did you get this?"

He shifted himself onto the ground, resting his back against the log. "Turk gave it to me years ago. I found it when I was cleaning out the cupboards today."

"Make more music." Lilica thrust the harmonica back at him, and he took it from her with a chuckle, raising it to his mouth. "This one's for you, wood nymph. I'm going to call it *Forest Song*."

A low, soft tone spilled from the instrument as he began to play, the sound wrapping around us and slowly building. It reminded me of gentle rain and rich earth, of flowers in spring, and the way the sun danced with a clear sky in the blush of an early morning. I took a deep breath and stared up into the trees, prisms of light catching the leaves and throwing shadows across the forest floor. Captured in this fragile moment, that strange feeling of yearning stole through me again, like a lost memory. A longing I couldn't define. But one I wanted so desperately to reach for.

The notes of the harmonica grew quieter and then faded, leaving the hum of silence behind. Releasing a long sigh, I looked over at Domine. "Why do you think people stopped playing music?"

He turned to me as the breeze teased his hair, blowing dark strands across his eyes. "Maybe because they stopped dreaming. Maybe without dreams, we lose the ability to hear what is inside ourselves."

I stared at him as a sudden current of emotion tumbled inside. For so long, I had buried myself in a dead marriage. In a life that gradually stripped me away. And now I felt like I was standing on the edge of a precipice, looking down at the dizzying rush of a whole new world. Of a voice that longed to be heard. Of a love that turned me inside out.

I just needed to find the courage to leap into my own song. To trust in the fall.

* * *

The last of the sun's rays slanted through the trees, casting the woods in dusky light as we set down our packs in a clearing. A chill had set in, and I crouched down to root through the pack for Lilica's sweater as Domine unrolled the tent beside us.

My feet ached, and my legs burned from our day of walking in a consistent, gradual incline. But beneath my exhaustion lay the thrum of exhilaration. The rains from last week had kept the smoke at bay, and the fresh air and steady movement had loosened something inside me. I looked forward to sleeping beneath the sky, surrounded by the enclosure of forest.

"I'll start a fire for us," I said to Domine as I stood and glanced around, looking for fallen branches and dry brush to use as kindling. I had never started a fire with a flint starter before, but I was determined to try. It couldn't be that difficult.

"Mommy, look what I found." Lilica ran toward me, holding the delicate half shell of an egg in her hand, blue speckles dotted with white.

"Oh, wow. That's from a baby bird."

"It can be a home for the fairies." With a grin, she crouched to place it face down in the earth.

"Well, that's very nice of you to give them a home," I said as I helped her into her sweater.

"They visit me at night."

Her words caused a tremor of surprise to settle against my chest. "The fairies?"

"Yep." She pivoted from me and ran over to Domine, who had managed to raise the walls of the tent and was sliding the last pole through the top. "Can I help?"

"Well, I think I'm all finished up here, wood nymph. Why don't you go help your mom find some firewood?"

Clearing the ground of debris, I arranged rocks in a circle as Lilica added small sticks to the pile of wood beside me. "Sweetheart, what did you mean when you said that the fairies visit you at night?"

She tilted her head at me, as if confused by my questioning. "They visit me when I go to bed."

My breath tangled in my throat, and I stood, gazing into the open expanse of her gray eyes. *Could Lilcia be dreaming?* I reached over to wipe away a smudge of dirt on her cheek. "And how long have they been visiting you?"

"They started visiting me at the cabin." She picked up a stick and broke it into pieces, scattering them onto the pile of wood in front of her, and then bounded back to where Domine was now crouched beside our pack, retrieving the food for dinner.

I stared over at her, my mind whirling. The thought of her dreaming left me with a feeling of wonder, like the flash of light filtering through trees. A whisper of something profound hidden beneath the innocence of her words.

I wrapped my fingers around the amethyst pendant resting against my chest, my thoughts drifting backward for a moment as a memory of my mother awoke within me. The warmth of her hand against mine. Eyes alight with her own rush of yearning. *"Dreams are pieces of the soul. And I believe they have never truly left us. They are only waiting patiently for us to find ourselves again."*

"Mommy, are you going to start the fire?"

Lilica startled me from my reflections, and I turned to her with a smile. "Yes, of course, love."

Kneeling beside the ring of rocks, I stuffed dried leaves beneath the wood and pulled out the flint starter Domine had given me, striking the attached metal piece against the rod. A small spark flew out and died. I struck more vigorously, and a series of sparks landed on the brush before fading away. Bending closer to the leaves, I blew with a steady force as I repeatedly drew the metal across the flint, but all I could achieve were brief flashes of light that yielded no fire.

Flustered, I looked over to find Domine watching me. His lips curled into a faint smile. "You're really cute when you're frustrated, you know that?"

I sat back on my knees with a loud sigh. "I really don't want to be helpless and completely reliant on you out here." I gestured impatiently toward the pile of wood. "I *need* to know how to start a simple fire."

He crouched beside me, a playful grin spreading across his face as he reached out to brush away a strand of hair from my cheek. "Maybe I like the thought of you being helpless. Maybe it appeals to my savior complex."

I rolled my eyes, smacking his hand away with a laugh. "So, is *that* what all this is about?"

He leaned in close, his words a teasing growl in my ear. "Only if you want to do some role playing."

An abrupt rush of heat spread across my skin. "Stop it."

With a chuckle, he took the flint from my hand and held it over the leaves, striking the rod in one fluid motion. "And you're not helpless. I've just had more time to figure all this stuff out." Sparks landed, and smoke rose up as he gently blew on the embers, coaxing them to life and creating a steady flame that grew and coiled around the wood. "It takes practice, that's all." He stood and grabbed his pack beside the tent. "Plus, you have to learn to be patient. Fire is a lot like an animal. If it senses your irritation, it won't come to you."

"Oh really?"

"Yep." He shot me a smile as Lilica came up and threw herself into my lap, burying her face against my shoulder.

"Mommy, when's dinner? I'm hungry."

"I bet you are, hon. You did a lot of walking today." My fingers worked through her hair, removing bits of leaves and twigs as I watched Domine unfold a small portable stand and place it over the fire, resting a metal pan on top. "Dinner will be ready soon."

* * *

The fire crackled and hissed, shooting sparks upward before fading into the darkness. We had finished dinner, and Lilica lay nestled in my arms, the steady rise and fall of her breath alerting me to the fact that she had fallen asleep.

"I'll lay her down for you," Domine whispered as he stood and carefully took her from me. The glow of the nightlight, still clutched in her hand, suffused the walls with a kaleidoscope of color as he disappeared into the tent.

I inched closer to the flames and stared up into the opening of the night sky. Stars winked at me from above, their own light dancing from a faraway place we could never reach. Exploration had been another ambition that had vanished long ago. I had read about people who used to travel beyond our world, knowledge and curiosity guiding them boldly forward into the unknown. But somehow, we stopped looking up, stopped asking questions, and that drive to discover something greater than ourselves eventually died.

A sorrow tugged at me. When had we grown so detached from the very essence of life?

Domine's arms wrapped around me from behind, pulling me from my thoughts, and I leaned against his chest, sinking into the solid warmth of him. "You must be more tired than I am. I think you had Lilica on your shoulders for at least half the day."

"She really isn't that heavy." He scooted closer to the fire, keeping his hold on me as he picked up a stick and shifted the logs around the coals.

I stared into the flames, watching as they collided and merged into fluid shapes that grew in form. A dance of light against the darkness. "Domine. I think Lilica might be dreaming."

He ran his hand through my hair, fingering the strands that fell against my shoulders. "That doesn't surprise me. She's probably able to detox more quickly from all the frequency signals they use on the Grid to numb you down."

I looked up at him. "What do you mean?"

"Turk used to talk about it a lot." Domine glanced up into the sky, his eyes following the expanse of stars that glittered above us. "The Resonance they use on the Grid, according to his studies, they do more than subdue aspects of the mind. It's a form of subtle mass manipulation. Mind control. And some are more susceptible to it than others."

His words were a chill against my skin, and I glanced over to where Lilica lay asleep inside the tent, the threads of her consciousness unraveling into a world of dreams I had yet to touch. "You really think they have been using wireless technology to control us?"

"That was Turk's theory." He poked at the fire again, sending sparks rising into the air. "Historically, governments have used fear to control mass populations of people. But during the Shift, a lot of people began to see through the façade, and it stopped being so effective. So, it would make sense that they would turn to other methods of control."

My thoughts flashed momentarily to Trendon. The empty look in his eyes, which had only grown more acute with every passing year. The unrelenting loyalty he gave to a repressive system. He had become nothing more than a ghost of the man, locked within a cage he would never leave, and an unexpected sorrow swept through me. How many were locked in cages? Locked within a life they could not extract themselves from?

"I wish there was a way to change things."

Domine looked at me, his eyes shimmering against the light of the fire. "Well, if history's any indication of the inevitability of change, I think there will come a time when the Grid begins to fall apart. When people start to wake up. At least I hope so."

"I hope so, too." I bit my lip and stared into the flames that reached upward as if longing to pull back the darkness. Perhaps there was a reason why our society had withered from the inside. Maybe we needed the duality of death to find life again. Maybe in order to find the strength to rise up against something, we needed to have nothing left to lose.

I turned to him. "And what about the fires? Do you really think they've been created by the government to contain us?"

Domine sighed, a long exhalation of air that encased his words in melancholy. "I don't know what they're capable of anymore, Seren."

"I don't know either." I glanced into the forest, the trees obscured in a blanket of darkness my eyes could not penetrate. "I'm so glad we got out. I just hope Kystina is okay." My voice trembled as a heaviness pressed against me, the events of yesterday urgently rushing back.

"Me, too." His voice grew soft as his thumb traced a slow circle across my cheek. "She seems like a fighter, though."

"She is." With a sigh, I nestled my head into the crook of his shoulder, my body spent from the long day of walking. From the high of the night before, and the abrupt upheaval of the feds arrival. So much had shifted in such a short period of time, and my mind scrambled to catch up.

I was here, with Domine, surrounded by a fortress of trees, and the whisperings of the unknown stretched out before us.

Cradled in the safety of his hold, I succumbed to the fatigue and closed my eyes, allowing my thoughts to grow quiet as I drifted off to the sound of the crackling wood and his voice like a comforting blanket enfolding me as he bent down to whisper in my ear.

"Looks like I'm going to have to carry both of you to bed."

CHAPTER SEVENTEEN

Birdsong pulled me from sleep, and I awoke to the tent bathed in the orange glow of early morning. Lilica lay beside me, her eyes still closed, head peeking out from beneath the sleeping bag.

The stillness caught my breath, and I allowed this moment to claim me. We would eventually rise and pack up our tent, continuing our trek into the woods. But for now, I was suspended within the sunlight shifting patterns across the tent walls, the twitter of birds as they swooped between the trees. Everything was unspoiled and alive.

"Morning," Domine murmured, his voice low and sleepy as he draped his arm across me and drew me closer to him. A rush of heat wound through my limbs, my body aching for him as he ran his hand up the length of my stomach, teasing my breast with the pad of his thumb. I sucked in a breath, longing to slip out of the tent and take him among the trees, to feel the heat of his skin against the chill of the ground. But Lilica stirred and opened her eyes, banishing the image from my mind.

"Good morning, sweetie." I reluctantly untangled myself from the intoxicating pull of his touch and sat up, running my fingers through the knots in my hair. "Are you ready for another day of exploring the forest?"

She nodded, her eyes bright and full of wonder for a day not yet formed.

Taking her hand, I helped her out of the tent and past some trees to find a place to relieve ourselves as Domine started a fire for breakfast. The flames were already leaping against the wood as we returned to camp, Lilica dragging a stick behind her.

"Look at my walking stick," she exclaimed, running over to Domine and thrusting the gnarled white oak at him.

"You know what that looks like to me?" His eyes were playful as he turned it slowly around in his hand. "It looks like it may be a *magical* walking stick. In fact, I think it may have come from a wizard."

"Wow." She sat down beside his feet, her wide eyes watching him as he retrieved a small, folded knife from his back pocket and began to chip away at the rough bark.

"Legend says that if you carve your name into the wood of a wizard's staff, you'll be able to find all the magic inside."

A smile bloomed across my face as I stirred oatmeal into the pan of water above the fire. Domine's ability to breathe amusement and enchantment into the things around Lilica filled me with an overwhelming affection. He was wilderness and laughter. The warm cloak obscuring the bleak reality we were running from. And for a moment, he almost made me forget.

"There you go, wood nymph." He handed Lilica the stick, the letters of her name engraved into the wood. "Now you have magic of your very own."

* * *

As we wound our way through the mountains, the terrain began to change. The verdant undergrowth and dense trees were now accompanied by sharp rocky outcroppings and snow-capped glaciers that loomed above us, sunlight glinting off the peaks. The temperature had dropped slightly as well, and the air felt thinner, the tepid warmth from the sun now blanketed by the slight breeze that nipped at my skin. The last remnants of summer had now been replaced with the urgency of winter's approach, and I wondered how much time we had before the snow came.

Lilica walked ahead of us, her walking stick pounding into the dry earth, sending pebbles scattering down the path behind her. As I glanced toward the view of the mountains, a sudden cry splintered the air.

Snapping my head back, I saw Lilica on the ground, having lost her footing among the rocks. My breath seized in my throat as I rushed to her and bent down, gathering her into my lap. A hole had been ripped through her jeans, and blood oozed from a deep laceration on her knee.

"Mommy… it hurts!" she wailed, her gray eyes filling with tears that ran a steady stream down her cheeks.

"I know, hon. Let's get this cleaned up, okay?" Lifting her into my arms, I carried her over to a cluster of rocks on the side of the trail.

"How deep is it?" Domine crouched beside us and ran a soothing hand down her back.

"It's a lot deeper than I'd like it to be." I set my pack down and pulled out a bottle of water and my medicinal pouch, sifting through the side pocket for some rags. "Sweetie, this is going to sting a little, but I need to clean up your ouchie. Can you take a deep breath for me?"

She nodded and sucked in a shuddered breath, then released a sharp cry as I poured the water over her cut.

"You're so brave, Lili." I leaned closer to inspect the wound as I dabbed lightly at it, blood soaking the cloth in my hand. Rooting through the pouch, I searched for some sort of herb I could apply, but everything I had on hand needed to be boiled down and condensed. My mind quickly shifted through the memory of my mom's wilderness book I had read years ago, images arranging themselves like a glossary.

Antiseptic. Astringent. Antibacterial. Wound protectant. Pine Sap.

The information slid into place, and I turned to Domine. "Can you go look for some fresh pine sap?"

With a nod, he stood and strode toward the scattering of pine trees in the distance.

"Mommy," Lilica whimpered, pointing to her stick on the ground. "Can the magic stick make it better?"

I smiled at her, my thumb reaching out to brush away her tears. "You know, the magic stick already told me what I can do to make you better."

Domine returned with a sticky chunk of sap in his hand, and I took it from him, applying it gently over Lilica's wound. "This is going to help stop the bleeding and keep dirt and germs out."

"Like a tree Band-Aid?"

"Yes, exactly like a tree Band-Aid, sweetie." I tore a thin strip of cloth apart and wound it around her knee, tying it securely in place. "There. All done. How do you feel?"

"A little better." She gave me a meek smile and stood, flexing her knee against the bandage.

I looked over to see Domine staring at me, a faint look of wonder dancing in the sharp focus of his gaze. "I just love watching the way that gorgeous mind of yours works."

I brushed away his comment with a wave of my hand. "It's not that special. I just have a good memory, that's all."

"No. It's incredibly special." He leaned forward, the sunlight catching the glint in his eyes. "Did you know that less than a hundred people in the *whole* world have a photographic memory? You're a statistical anomaly, Seren." He swept away a strand of hair from my cheek, his finger lingering against my lips, inducing a rush of warmth that traveled and took root in my core. "I remember med school being a breeze for you."

"Well, not *everything* was easy for me." A smile tugged at the corner of my mouth. "Do you remember how we met?"

"Of course I do." He grinned at me. "I still have the scar."

"Oh, stop." I gave him a playful nudge as I bent down to tuck my medicinal bag back into my pack. "I did not give you a scar."

"Oh, but you did. Right here." He clutched at his chest and fell back onto the ground in a mock swoon, causing Lilica to erupt into a fit of giggles.

My mind flashed back to the day he had walked into our classroom as a volunteer for our clinical practice. I had been so flustered by the intensity of his eyes on me that I had botched the blood draw, puncturing his skin in multiple places before I found the vein.

"I thought you were a masochist." Laughter bubbled up as I shook my head, watching as Lilica bent beside me, suddenly lost to her own world as her hands shifted around in the earth, fingers curling around a small rock. "You kept coming back."

"Maybe I was," he said with a chuckle as he picked himself off the ground. "I think I must have given you at least a pint of my blood before I gathered up the courage to ask you out."

"And I'm so glad you finally did." With a smile, I trailed my hand down past his shoulder, my fingers running along the dark blue vein that snaked up his arm as I recalled our first date. How he had leaned across the table at that tiny restaurant next to my dorm and kissed me like nothing else existed in the world. A kiss that claimed me and challenged me, sending me stumbling back to my room in a daze, wanting more.

"Mommy, what's that sound?"

Lilica's question startled me from my warm reverie, and I looked up, the pines like spires against an empty blue sky as a staccato hum from beyond the trees grew closer. My breath stilled in my throat as I jumped to my feet. The cold rush of fear gripped my limbs as the rhythmic *whup-whup-whup* of helicopter blades sliced through the air.

CHAPTER EIGHTEEN

"*L*ilica. Get over here." I tried to keep my voice steady as I scrambled for my pack, searching frantically around for somewhere we could hide. Through the trees, the ominous red glow of the thermal scanners swept across the forest like fire.

"Over here!" Domine motioned toward a large group of boulders that stood atop a steep incline. "The scanners shouldn't be able to detect us as long as we can stay behind the rocks."

Grabbing Lilica's hand, I clambered up the hill after him, dirt and stone slipping beneath my feet. The weight of my pack pushed down on me as if my limbs were suspended in quicksand.

"Mommy. Wait!" Lilica turned around, tugging on my hand. "I forgot my magic stick!"

"Leave it, honey. We'll get it later, okay? Right now, we need to play the hide-and-seek game again."

"I don't want to play the hide-and-seek game!" She struggled against my hold, her eyes wide and pleading. "I want my magic stick!"

"No, Lilica. You need to come with me right *now*." My words came out clipped and breathless as I pulled her up the hill, panic coursing through my body as the sickening whirr of the rotor chop grew nearer, the vibration an echo in my chest. With the promise of cover now only a few feet away, I tumbled over rocks toward Domine, not daring to look back. I didn't want to know how close they were.

Reaching the outcropping of rocks, Domine grabbed our packs, shoved them beneath some brush and reached for Lilica, lowering her down into a deep crevice hidden between the boulders. Jagged rock scraped against my clothes, my heart beating like a violent drum as I scrambled in after her, watching as Domine squeezed himself into the narrow space beside me.

"I want my stick!" She squirmed in my arms and then suddenly ripped herself away from my grasp, slipping through the opening in the rock.

"Lilica!" The roar of the helicopter muted the scream that tore through me. I lurched after her, my arm slamming into a sharp rock, tearing through skin, the shooting pain now irrelevant as I saw the red beam skim across her body. Marking my child.

A garbled cry spilled from me as Domine grabbed me from behind and said something I couldn't process, his voice tinny and far away as he pressed me back against the rocks and ran after Lilica, scooping her up into his arms. Sprinting up the hill, he dodged the beams that snaked across the ground. And then I was holding her against me, my tears spilling into her hair.

"They got her... they got her," I wailed, desperately curling myself around her as if I could make her disappear back into the safety of my body, where nobody could touch her, where I would never lose her.

"Listen to me." Domine took me by the shoulders. "They are *not* going to take her." He glanced back toward the helicopter, which was now hovering beyond the tree line, obscured in the flush of green. "You both stay here. Do not move away from these rocks." He scrambled for his pack and flung it over his shoulder. "They'll think it was me they caught on the scanner."

"No!" I grabbed his arms, my nails digging desperately into him. "They'll take you in."

"Seren." He clasped my head in his hands, his eyes piercing into mine, fixed and resolute. "It's okay. I'm going to try and deter them. I'll be back."

"Don't go! *Please!*" I clutched at him, all rational thought lost to the chaos of my mind.

He drew his lips to mine, then released me and descended the hill toward the helicopter, the weight on my chest strangling me as I watched him disappear through the trees.

* * *

*T*ime passed in fragments, disjointed shadows that leaned against rock as the sun shifted in the sky. The distant hum of the helicopter had lifted and faded away long ago, leaving a stifling silence behind.

I held Lilica in my arms, her muffled sobs quieting as I slowly rocked her back and forth. Blood still oozed from the wound in my arm, sticky and clinging to the fabric of my shirt, but the pain was tucked away, somewhere far from here.

"Mommy, are they going to take me?" Her voice was a whisper against my ear. A hesitant question that tugged at the threads of my composure as the visceral image of the beams sweeping across her body raced through me.

"No, Lili. Nobody is going to take you." I rested my lips against her forehead, my voice trembling. "You're safe now."

She had seen the edges of fear. Ugly shards warped and twisted, laying bare everything I had so carefully tried to shield from her. There was no going back now. The veil had been lifted. We were running from something, and she knew it.

"Is the big copter coming back?"

"No. It flew away, honey. It's gone now."

"Did Domine go with them?"

I peered over the edge of the boulder we rested against, scanning the trees, praying for a sign of movement, for the flash of his dark hair among the pine. But all I saw was stillness and the rustle of wind as it slithered through the tops of the trees. "He went to talk to the people in the helicopter."

"When is he coming back?"

My throat was dry, the words abrasive against my tongue. "I don't know."

"He'll come back. He *always* comes back, Mommy."

I gave her a thin smile, trying to instill a sense of assurance in my voice as I reached down to wipe away the remnants of her tears. "Yes. You're right, sweetie. He always does."

But the questions tore into me, vicious and consuming. What if they had taken him in for questioning? Or worse, imprisoned him on some fabricated charge? Obstruction of justice. Harboring a fugitive. The list was endless. And the thought of him taking the fall for me, of never seeing him again, stole my breath, stole my thoughts, and I fought back a wave of nausea, digging my nails into the palm of my hand to steady myself.

What am I going to do?

Lilica fidgeted in my lap, curling her finger around a strand of my hair, her eyes puffy and red. "We never had lunch, Mommy."

"I guess we didn't. Are you hungry?"

She nodded sheepishly, and I pulled myself from the ground, my legs shaking as I grabbed the pack Domine had stashed beneath the bushes and slid it quickly into the crevice of the rock. Rummaging through the pack, I handed her some nuts, crackers, and the last of the cherry tomatoes, now partially squashed, the juice staining the bag.

She ate in silence, her eyes gazing up into the blue of the sky, while I tried to compartmentalize the situation. My logical brain stepped forward, holding back the rising panic, fitting things into a series of tasks I could perform. We could set up camp here. Build a fire. Wait for Domine to come back.

But what if he doesn't?

I pushed that last thought from my mind. It was too heavy, too desolate. Too crushing. I had to believe any minute now, I would see him walking toward me.

* * *

The sun now hovered low in the sky, bringing with it a chill as the distant peaks of the mountains held the last slivers of light. Gathering my pack, I took Lilica's hand and slowly helped her down the hill and over to the cover of the forest. My legs were stiff from crouching among the rocks for the past few hours, and I knew I had to address the persistent pain that radiated down my arm, but I needed to get the tent up before we lost the light.

"Sweetie, can you gather a few sticks for a fire while I set up the tent?" I tried to keep my voice light, but it trembled as I spoke. Every hour that had crept by brought me closer to a reality I did not want to accept. Domine still had not returned.

"Okay, Mommy."

Lilica wandered past a grove of trees, her shape disappearing between the shadows, and I lunged after her, grabbing her by the arm. "You need to stay close to me. I need to be able to see you *at all times*. Do you understand?"

My voice came out tangled and gruff, and she looked up at me, startled. "Sorry, Mommy."

I bent down and pressed her to me, her heartbeat fluttering against mine. "It's okay. Just promise me, Lili. *Promise* me you'll never run off like you did today."

"Are you mad at me?" She pulled back, her eyes wide.

"No, honey. I'm not mad. You just *really* scared me." The tears I had been holding back all day slipped through and ran a slow trail down my cheeks.

She reached out and touched one with her finger. "Don't be sad, Mommy."

I gave her a small smile and wiped at my eyes. "How about we gather some wood together, and then you can help me set up the tent?"

"Okay."

She followed behind me, sticks clenched in her tiny hands, while a morose silence crept through the forest. For the first time since we left the cabin, I felt exposed and vulnerable. Without Domine's comforting presence, the woods took on an ominous tone, the trees no longer shelter but a place that lurked with unknown threats.

A shiver ran across my skin, creeping down the back of my neck and settling at the base of my spine as I deposited the pile of wood on the ground next to our packs. Lilica crouched beside me, silently watching as I arranged rocks into a circle and fumbled with the flint starter, desperately trying to coax the sparks to life. The comforting glow of the flames was the promise of an anchor. Something to grasp onto as the darkness edged in.

"Come over here, sweetie." I motioned for Lilica to scoot closer as the flames finally awoke and arched around the wood, bathing our skin in fragments of light. Pulling her into my lap, I wrapped my arms around her. "How is your knee? Does it still hurt?"

She shook her head and ran her hand tentatively across the bandage. "It's all better now."

"Oh, good."

"What about you, Mommy? Does your arm hurt?" Lilica furrowed her brow and brushed her fingers across my wound. I instinctively flinched, waiting for the surge of pain, but there was none. Only a strange, faint warmth that radiated up my arm and then quickly dissipated. Looking down, I noticed the gash was not as deep as I originally thought.

"I think I'll be okay, love."

She nestled into my chest, and I sank into the feel of her against me, like a barricade from my own thoughts. I knew I needed to get up, to put the tent together and unpack something to eat, but I couldn't move. The weight of the day pushed down on me with a sudden force, the course of adrenaline subsiding to exhaustion. Closing my eyes for a moment, I allowed the slow tide of my breath to center me, searching for solace among the crackle of the flames and the whisper of the branches as they danced with the wind. Despite the churning pace of fear and all the tumbling questions that sat beside me, I knew there was a peace to be found here. I just had to reach for it. I could not lose myself in thoughts of *what if*.

The somber call of an owl drifted above us, and I opened my eyes to see Lilica gazing up into the trees. "Do you hear that, Mommy?"

"I do, hon. That's an owl."

"No. Do you hear *that?*" She shifted in my lap and pointed behind me. "That sound."

I grew still, my pulse accelerating as the faint snap of twigs grew louder and the low note of a whistle sounded from somewhere beyond the trees.

CHAPTER NINETEEN

*M*y heart swelled in a furious surge of relief as the shape of Domine materialized through the shadows. With a squeal, Lilica scrambled off my lap and rushed toward him.

"I found your magic stick, wood nymph." Bending down, he lifted her up and twirled her around, her joyful giggles cutting through the air.

"See. I told you he'd come back, Mommy." She looked at me with a wide grin, clutching her stick as he set her back on her feet.

I propelled myself into his arms, breathing in his scent of wind and pine, clinging to him as if he held all the oxygen inside my lungs.

"What happened?" I ran my hands up his chest and over his shoulders, my fingers winding into his hair and then tracing across the stubble on his jaw. Drinking him in. Savoring the wholeness of him standing here with his arms around me.

"Well, I had a little chat with the people in the helicopter. I pretended to be some poor shmuck who had gone hunting and lost his way in the woods." He lifted his mouth into a sardonic smirk as he pointed to the crossbow slung over his pack. "They said I was outside the *designated boundary line* of the Compound and would *happily* escort me back. So, they trailed me for about four miles before they finally took off and I could double back."

"Were they looking for us?"

"Yes." He glanced over at Lilica for a moment, his voice

dropping to a low murmur. "They asked if I had seen a woman and a little girl on the trail, and I told them I had the morning before, and that you appeared to be headed west."

A wave of panic hit me, and I stared up at him in disbelief. "What? Why would you do that?"

"Seren." His hands slid down to my shoulders. "They are now looking for you in the very opposite direction. They won't be back here."

"You don't know that." My pulse thrummed out a desperate rhythm. "They *now* know we're out here. What if they come back?"

Domine shook his head. "I don't think they will anytime soon. They have a lot of ground to cover west of these mountains."

"But how did they know to even search out here?" I bit my lip and stared out into the yawning abyss of darkness beyond the fire. "Do you think someone from the Compound might have tipped them off?"

Tension momentarily flashed across his face as he looked at me. "No. Nobody there would *ever* do that, Seren."

I knew he was probably right, but I could not seem to push away the image of River and the look of hurt in her eyes I had glimpsed through the window the morning we left.

I bit my lip and leaned my head against his chest, the steady rush of his heart beating in my ear like a reprieve, washing away the jagged edges of the day. But beneath the relief lay a doubt that twisted in my gut, and my voice came out shaky. "I was so worried, Dom. The thought of…"

"I'm here. Everything's okay." His words swept across my skin, lips resting against my temple as he ran his hands down my arms, fingers brushing across the dried blood on my shirt. "Jesus. Your arm." He pulled back, his eyes flashing with concern.

"It's fine. I'll deal with it later."

"Mommy has a ouchie just like me." Lilica stood beside us with her hands on her hips, as if she was relieved not to be the only one with a battle wound from the day.

"Well, that's a pretty nice-looking fire you guys got going over

136

there." Domine slid his arm around my waist and shot Lilica a playful wink. "Did you do that all by yourself, wood nymph?"

She nodded as a mischievous smile stretched across her face. "Yes, I made it *all* by myself."

* * *

I sucked in a breath as Domine dabbed at my arm with a wet cloth. Firelight played across his skin while he bent over me, his brow drawn tight in concentration. "Do you want me to find some pine sap for you?"

I shook my head, glancing toward the tent where Lilica lay inside sleeping. "Don't worry about it. It's actually not as bad as I thought it was. Which is weird because I could have sworn the cut was deeper." I stared down at the wound, remembering the strange sensation of warmth that had trickled through my arm after Lilica had brushed her fingers across it. It must have been her touch, triggering some sort of mild paresthesia response.

"Well, I'm glad that it's not deep." Pulling out a long strip of fabric from the pack beside us, Domine wound it around my arm. His hands were gentle and lingering, and I leaned against his shoulder with a sigh, relaxing into the feel of him tending to me. "When you approached the helicopter, how did you know they weren't going to bring you in for questioning?"

"I didn't." He looked at me, his eyes somber as he finished tying off the bandage and grabbed the small blanket beside us, draping it around my shoulders.

A flash of panic tore into me, stilling my breath. The idea of losing him was a crippling thought I could not face. "Don't do that again. Don't leave me like that." I slid onto his lap and wrapped my arms around his neck, pushing him back against the log he sat in front of. My fingers dragged through his hair as my voice came out a strangled whisper. "I can't do this without you."

"Seren." He clasped my wrists. "If you *had* to, I know you *could* do this without me."

"No." I slammed my hands against his chest as tears blurred my

137

vision, the sudden rise of anger colliding with fear. I didn't want to feel this helpless and needy. I didn't want to love him this much. "*Promise* me, Domine. Promise you'll never leave me like that again. I can't... lose you." I knew I was pleading with something I had no control over, my desperation clawing at the fragile threads of reassurance. But it was all I had left to cling to.

He rested his forehead against mine. "I can promise you I'll do everything possible to keep you and Lilica safe."

Tears stained my cheeks, and then he was kissing them away, his lips igniting something primal within me. I clutched at him, finding the heat of his mouth, while my hands grappled with the enclosure of his pants.

"*Seren,*" he groaned into my mouth as I shifted my pants down beneath the blanket and guided him inside me. A choked cry tumbled from my lips as we connected, the feel of him like a freefall, and I rocked against him, frantic and hungry, chasing away all the fear and uncertainty that stood beside us.

The fierce swiftness of my release tore through me, and with a gasp, I fell against his chest. Domine stiffened and gripped my hips to pull himself out, but I held myself against him. "No. Stay with me."

He tilted my head back and found my eyes, his gaze feverish and devouring in the glow of the fire, and then with a sharp inhale, he thrust himself deeper and spilled into me, his essence merging with mine. A delicious rush that settled and took root in my core. The last wall between us obliterated.

"My God, Seren." His voice trembled, breathless against my cheek as he swept his fingers through my hair. "I would do *anything* for you. You know that, right?"

I pressed my lips to his, sheltered in the island of his embrace, the feel of his hands as they held me together. But beneath the euphoric comfort lay the tangled emotions which had always been there with him, following me like a timid ghost.

"I'm scared, Dom. I'm scared of the way you make me feel." I drew back and placed his hand against the thrum of my heart. "It's *always* scared me. I've lost too many people in my life."

"I know." He pulled me close, wrapping the blanket around us. "But nothing is forever, and we love regardless of that. It's what makes life so precious. I think it's what gives us strength when we need it the most."

I closed my eyes, my body shaking from all the emotions churning inside. The ecstasy and intensity he extracted from me. The gentle solace of his words.

"Don't be scared." His voice was a fervent whisper, enfolding me in a warmth that burrowed deep beneath my skin as his lips trailed up to my ear. "*I'm* not."

His eyes locked with mine, and I felt him stir inside me once more. We moved together, this time tender and slow, savoring the ache as we held ourselves back from the edge. Lost in the current of his hold, I unraveled myself, exposing something that felt sacred and larger than both of us while the fire burned low, and the sky spun untethered above.

*T*he last threads of daylight streamed through the thin layer of clouds, and the faint trickle of water drifted from somewhere beyond the trees.

"Let's camp here for the night." Domine shrugged off his pack beside the trail and unfolded the map from his back pocket. "There's a stream close by. We can replenish our water."

I nodded and pulled Lilica close to me. For the past two days, I had been on edge. Every snap of a twig, every distant rumble of a passing plane stilled my breath. And beneath all that lay the haunting image I could not shake of the thermal beam running across my daughter. A brutal reminder of how close I had come to losing her. To losing them both.

"Mommy, can we go see the stream?"

"In a bit, hon." I ruffled her hair and surveyed the clearing in front of us. "How about we set up camp first, and then we can do some exploring?"

We had fallen into a rhythm together as daylight waned and our evenings closed in. Domine would set up the tent, and I would make the fire, my watchful eye on Lilica as she scoured the ground for firewood. Our meals were modest yet filling, and despite the long hours of walking and the apprehension that shadowed me, I felt a sense of contentment in the simplicity of things. The ebb and flow of days that blended into each other. Our entire world whittled down to the trail ahead of us and the quiet evenings spent around the fire with the tent as our makeshift home.

I rummaged through the pack, and retrieved Lilica's coat, helping her with the zipper. "You ready to go down to the stream, Lili?"

She nodded, clutching her walking stick against her chest. She now carried it everywhere with her. The day before, she had left it beside the trail when we stopped for lunch, causing us to double back and lose an hour of the day. I joked to Domine that there was a curse on that thing.

Following Domine through the trees, we weaved in between dense bushes and large rocks. The playful gurgle of running water grew louder, and the terrain began to slope downward, dry brush turning to loose gravel, the air infused with the scent of damp earth. Lilica ran ahead of us toward the stream and then stopped at the edge, watching the water as it gently leaped and twisted over mossy stones.

"Careful, hon. The rocks are slippery," I called out to her as she began to sift through the tiny pebbles along the shoreline, her face drawn in concentration.

I crouched to fill up one of the water bottles, and Domine bent down behind me, leaning in to brush his lips across the nape of my neck, causing a warm tingle to spread through my limbs as his hands settled around the curve of my hips. These were our stolen moments together, little pieces of sweetness plucked from the day.

"I think we have enough water for me to give you a sponge bath tonight." His voice grew low and smokey against my ear, and a tight band of tension fluttered within my core.

"What is it with you and sponge baths?" I asked with a playful smile as I turned to him. "Do you have some fetish I was never aware of?"

"It's not sponge baths I'm *fetishizing*."

His voice was a low murmur, his eyes twinkling mischievously as he raked them down my body. Shaking my head, I capped the bottle and thrust it into his hands. "Why don't you stop teasing me, and focus on filling these up?"

"Oh, this is not a tease. It's a promise."

Stop, I mouthed to him, feeling my cheeks flush with heat as the images of us as we made love beside the fire rose up, filling me with a delicious longing. Something had shifted between us since that night. It was as if we were no longer trying to fill in the gaps of our past. To start where we had left off. We had released it all into the darkness of the night sky, and in its place was now a newness, like lovers discovering each other for the first time.

"Mommy!" Lilica ran toward us and held out her hands. "Look at all the pretty rocks I found."

"Those are beautiful, sweetie." I reached out to touch the tumbled stones, flecks of shimmering green reflecting the last of the light.

"Can I go look for more?"

"Sure, just don't go too far, okay? Stay where I can see you."

"I'll keep an eye on her." With a smile, Domine grabbed a few empty bottles and took off down the streambed with Lilica, her hand reaching out to clasp around his.

I filled the last bottle and then dipped my hands into the current, the shock of the cold an invigorating jolt to my senses as I splashed the icy water against my face, reveling in the caress of the breeze as it met the dampness of my skin. From across the stream, movement flashed through the trees, and my breath stilled as I looked up and locked eyes with a wolf.

It stood there watching me, obscured between shadows and light. Silent and unmoving, like a sentinel of the forest, it was close enough for me to see the markings of gray and brown that curved around the face. With a sharp inhalation, I stood, my feet slipping on the rocks as I glanced over to where Domine and Lilica crouched along the shore. And when I turned back, the wolf was gone, leaving only the whisper of branches rustling in the wind.

* * *

*M*y eyes shot open, darkness obscuring my sight, my heart a wild drumbeat against my chest.

Where am I? Where is Lilica?

My mind scrambled through the disorienting haze of sleep, trying to find my bearings as a crushing panic consumed me. Then my vision adjusted, and I could make out moonlight flickering through the walls of the tent, casting faint impressions across the sleeping form of my daughter like a breath of relief.

We were here with Domine. Far from the Grid.

My heartbeat slowed, returning to its normal rhythm as the residue of the life I had left behind slipped back from me like a nocturnal ghost, tucking itself neatly away into the shadows.

Turning, I curled into the solid comfort of Domine, my finger tracing a line down his cheek, resting on the softness of his bottom lip. He looked so peaceful. Lost within the limitless world of his dreams. A world I only hoped I could one day explore. But I wondered if the darkness ever found him there? If his own apparitions followed him through sleep? The snarled thorns of his past entwining around him.

I shifted onto my back, hoping to relieve the pressure on my bladder. But it was no use. I knew I wouldn't be able to wait until morning.

With a reluctant sigh, I pulled myself from the warmth of the sleeping bag and fumbled around for my shoes. Grabbing a flashlight, I quietly unzipped the door and slipped out. Away from the insulated tent, the cold hit me, and my breath danced between the beams of light that spilled across the forest floor. With chattering teeth, I bent down beside a bush, wincing as I exposed myself to the frigid air.

The snap of a twig startled me, and I whipped the flashlight toward the sound. Two glowing eyes met the light, and with a strangled gasp, I tugged at my pants, falling backward as my feet lost footing in the loose earth. The flashlight slid from my hands and clattered against the rocks, illuminating the darkness beyond me.

I opened my mouth, expecting a cry to tumble out, but there was only silence.

Frozen in place, I stared at the wolf, watching as it crouched low and sniffed at the ground in front of me. The moonlight caught the color of its fur, a deep gray against a band of black and white, the wildness in its eyes penetrating. My breath lodged in my throat, and my mind screamed for me to move, to run. But beneath the fear that thrummed against me like a metronome was a strange and unexpected feeling of awe.

The wolf raised its head toward me, then looked up into the sky before turning around and trotting off in a flash of gray that slunk through the trees. I let out the breath I had been holding, and on shaky legs, I pulled myself off the ground and dashed back to the tent, my fingers fumbling with the zipper.

"Domine." My voice was a hiss as I shook him awake. "I just saw a wolf."

He looked up at me, bleary-eyed. "Where? Where did you see a wolf?"

"It was just outside our tent."

He sprang out of the sleeping bag, throwing on his boots, and I grabbed his arm. "It's gone now. What are you going to do?"

"I'm going to make *sure* it's gone." He picked up the flashlight I had thrown beside the sleeping bags. "Stay here. I'll be right back."

With my eyes trained on the entrance, I sank down onto the bedding and pulled my knees against my chest, my whole body trembling from the cold and adrenaline surging through me. The minutes stretched out, straining against the weight of my apprehension as I waited for him to return.

Finally, the faint crunch of footsteps grew closer, and Domine stepped back inside. "You were right. It's gone."

I let out a long sigh, my pulse slowing its agitated rhythm as I crawled back into the sleeping bag.

"Are you okay?" He slid in beside me and drew me against his chest, his arms an anchor, chasing away the chill that had burrowed into my skin.

I nodded into his shoulder. "I'm fine."

"Do you think it could be the same wolf you saw by the stream today?"

"Maybe." I glanced over at Lilica, watching the steady rise and fall of her breath in sleep. Her tiny body curled beneath the sleeping bag.

He ran his hand through my hair, his voice a whisper. "Don't worry. It's probably just passing through."

"Let's hope so."

CHAPTER TWENTY

The days grew colder as we climbed higher in elevation, the faint breath of winter teasing the air as we replaced our sweaters with jackets. Snowy peaks winked at us between the thinning trees as we wound a steady pace through the mountains. We had now been on the trail for almost a week, and the pressing fear that shadowed me grew farther behind as every step brought us closer to Canada. To a place of refuge and freedom.

One morning, we awoke to rain drumming on the roof of the tent, and we spent the day curled in our sleeping bags, drinking tea made from steeped rose hips I had found along the trail. The soft notes of Domine's harmonica drifted through the tent walls as I read to Lilica from her book of fairy tales, her head nestled in the crook of my arm. It was a cozy and welcomed reprieve from our long days of walking, and I found myself disappointed when the clouds broke the next day.

"Come over here. I want to show you guys something." Faint sunlight skittered through the trees as Domine stood at the edge of the trail and turned to us with a wide smile, slipping the folded map into his back pocket.

We followed him through a break in the pine and came to a wide-open vista. My breath stilled as I stared down at the valley of lush green below. The expanse of towering mountains stretching in an endless jagged line across the horizon. The harsh beauty was commanding, and it reached out and shook me, a humble reminder that I was only a tiny pebble among the vastness of this wilderness.

Something inside of me was slowly loosening. I could feel it as our days on the trail stretched and grew. It was a quiet that gently curled around my thoughts, softening the edges. A shifting in the way I moved, in the way my feet met with the earth. As if I were trying to learn the language. The rhythm of wind and trees. The dance of sky.

I released my breath in a long exhale, watching the clouds as they drifted against an endless canvas of blue. "It's so beautiful."

"It is, isn't it?" Domine wrapped his arms around me from behind, his voice warm against my ear. "And guess what? We're in Canada now."

I turned to him, a current of relief and elation bubbling up inside. "Really? We made it?"

"We did. We just crossed through the border line on the map. We are now officially out of the Grid." He placed his hands on my shoulders, his gaze full of a calm assurance that took hold of me. "We're safe now. They can't touch us out here." With a faint smile, he pointed toward a cluster of peaks in the distance. "And you see that mountain range right over there? Those are the Rockies. Once we get over that first ridge, we'll be a week away from Alberta." His eyes danced with light as he stared off into the distance. "We're halfway there."

We made it. We were in Canada.

The last of the tightness that had lived within my chest now released like a whispered goodbye to all the things I had left behind, and a tender feeling of hope rose within as the vivid images of possibility washed over me. The freedom to practice herbal medicine. A place where we could all live together. A school where Lilica could ask questions.

With a smile, I crouched down beside her. "What do you think, Lili? We're in Canada now."

"It's big."

I pulled her against me, kissing the top of her head. "Yes, hon. It's *very* big."

* * *

I set down an armful of wood beside Domine and bent over the map he had unfolded next to the tent, his finger tracing along the line of the mountain range.

"See how the majority of the Rockies run west of us? All we need to do is get over this small ridge right here, and as long as the weather holds, the rest of the trail should be relatively easy."

I studied the lines on the map. Ridges and borders nestled between mountains and rivers. It was a foreign language I was still learning how to decipher. The language of wilderness imposed upon paper. My hand hovered over the black ink that snaked through the mountain range. "So this northern trail will take us straight to Alberta?"

"That's right." He looked up at me, his hair tousled and falling into his eyes, the slow pull of his smile disarming, causing a flutter to settle deep in my core. Taking the map from his hands, I leaned in and stole a kiss that sent heat racing across my skin as I lost myself momentarily in the scent of wood smoke and the taste of his mouth.

With a soft groan, he pulled me onto his lap. "What was that for?"

"Do I need a reason?"

Taking my hand, he held it up to his chest, his pulse thrumming wildly beneath his jacket. "You see what you do to me? I'm starting to worry you've given me a heart condition."

I buried my laughter against his neck, running a trail of kisses up to his ear. "Well, it's a good thing I'm a doctor."

From the corner of my eye, I noticed Lilica standing beside the tent, staring at us.

"Hey, hon." I untangled myself from Domine's lap. "You want to help me finish gathering the wood?"

With a nod, she followed me through the trees, her brow furrowed. "Mommy, what were you doing with Domine? Is something wrong with his heart?"

I turned toward her, a smile playing at the corners of my mouth. "No, sweetie. Domine's heart is just fine." I stopped walking and crouched down, taking her by the shoulders. I realized that Lilica had never seen intimacy between her father and me. Besides the occasional chaste peck on the cheek, Trendon and I had never shown affection. She had stumbled into unknown territory, touching the surface of a topic she was far too young to fully understand.

"Lili. When grown-ups love each other, sometimes words aren't enough to show the kind of love they feel inside."

She looked up at me, her gray eyes wide and full of questions. "You love Domine?"

"I do, yes."

"What about Daddy? Do you love Daddy?"

The answer caught in my chest, a heaviness that pressed against me. The family I thought I was giving my daughter had shifted so drastically. How could I explain to her the complexities of a love that had gone missing so long ago?

"There are so many different ways to love someone, sweetie. I love your daddy for giving me you. I will always love your daddy for that."

"And what about me?"

"You…" I playfully tapped her nose. "You, I love the *very* most."

A wide smile stretched across her face. "I love *you* the very most, Mommy."

I drew her in for a hug, the prick of tears dancing against my eyelashes as the last of the sunlight spilled through the trees, rinsing the ground beneath us in soft light. I lost myself to the gentle sound of the wind as it leaned against the branches. The feel of Lilica's body curled safely around mine. These were the tiny details that when pieced together created something that felt simple, and clear, and whole. And for a moment, it did not feel like we were adrift in a landscape unknown.

Domine was retrieving food from our pack when we returned to camp, our arms full of firewood.

"Mommy, can I play in the forest before dinner?"

I looked out into the woods as dusky shadows slanted against trees. "No, sweetie, it's getting dark. I need you to stay by the fire."

"*Please*. I want to go build fairy houses." She pulled her face into a pout and pointed to a fallen log just beyond the tent. "I'll stay right there."

With a sigh, I bent down to zip up her coat, clipping the buttons in place. "Okay. But don't go past the log, do you understand? I need to be able to see you."

She nodded, her eyes lighting up as she grabbed her walking stick and ran off.

I took a seat next to Domine, watching as he unfolded the portable cooking stand and placed it over the fire that now crackled and hissed, the flames coming to life and curling upward.

"Have you seen the other flashlight?" I asked, rooting through one of the packs beside him.

"It should be in there somewhere. Check the front pocket."

My fingers grazed across a small wooden box, and I lifted it out. The etchings on the top were faded and worn, as if his hands had run across the wood a hundred times. "What's this?" I held the box up, and Domine looked over at me with a smile.

"Why don't you open it and find out?"

Lifting the lid, my breath caught in my throat as I stared at the familiar leather engraved wrist band I had given him so many years ago. The one he stopped wearing when I married Trendon. "You still have this?"

"Of course I do." His words fell low and heavy as he stared into the fire, his eyes appearing to flicker with all the tangled emotions he had carried around for so long. Emotions we had both carried, tucked away in different etched boxes.

Memories rose up as I traced the inscription I had engraved on the inside of the band. *You will always be my autumn.* Below it was a date: *September fourteenth.* The day we met. The day we had also decided would be his birthday. A celebration of the new life we had been slowly building together, our hearts wide open like hopeful flowers pressing through the rubble of our past.

"Do you still wonder about what happened to your parents?"

Leaning forward, he poked at the fire with a stick, his jaw tense. "I try not to."

The story of his family had always been a difficult topic for him, and he never talked about it much. He would grow cold and distant, his words clipped whenever I used to bring it up. All I really knew was that the state had dropped him off at the Orphanarium when he was two years old. A small child with a history erased. A boy with no memories of his mother's warm smile. His father's laughter. It was the kind of barren loss I could not fathom. I had lost my family, but at least I had images of them to cling to. Colors and textures that formed a pattern that could never be taken from me.

"I've come to the conclusion that they were most likely imprisoned or executed for dissention. But I'll never know the truth, will I?" He looked at me, his eyes full of a fire and sorrow that pierced through the gathering darkness. "I suppose that's why they expunged my birth records. So I wouldn't be able to *ever* find out what really happened."

I stared into the fire, a heaviness resting between us as I remembered the day the call came that the authorities had arrested him. He had gone to the state record branch, trying to extract information about his parents from the data system. The anger that simmered silently beneath the surface had been thick and palpable as I drove him home from the station after they had held him for a week without bail. It was the kind of anger that grew and festered, stripping away the color from the world we had forged together. And he had never been the same after that. The light in him replaced with shadows that grew too large to contain. His silence a weight that crushed the both of us.

Taking his hand, I slipped the band around his wrist. "You don't *ever* have to take this off again."

He swept his fingers up my neck, his gaze piercing mine as his touch hovered against my cheek. "Is that a promise?"

"*Yes.*" I pressed my lips to his palm, caught in the way the flames from the fire surged in his eyes. "You have all of me, Dom."

Lilica scrambled onto my lap, breaking the moment as she threw her arms around my neck. "I made fairy houses by the log, Mommy."

"That's great, sweetie. Thanks for staying close." With a smile, I brushed the loose strands of hair away from her face. "Do you want to help us make some dinner?"

"Okay." She slid off my lap and ran over to where Domine was pouring water into a pan for our dehydrated soup. Taking the wooden spoon from him, she began to stir vigorously, her face scrunched in stoic concentration. "When I grow up, Mommy, I want to be a maker."

"A maker?" I tilted my head at her with a smile. "What kind of things do you want to make?"

She stopped stirring and looked up at me. "I want to make people happy."

I stood and crouched beside her, placing a kiss on her forehead. "Well, in that case, you already are a maker, love. You make *me* happy."

"But I want to make sad people happy."

I stared into the depths of her grey eyes, hues that always seemed to shift with her emotions, like the turbulent beauty of storm clouds over water. "I think that is a wonderful thing to want to do, Lili."

Grabbing some crackers and dishes from our pack, I spread out a blanket and motioned for her to sit beside me as Domine came over with the soup. We ate quietly by the crackling light of the fire, listening to the wind whispering in the trees above us and the gentle call of an owl in the distance. My thoughts momentarily drifted back to the wolf. We had not seen him since the night he showed up at our campsite, but I wondered if he was out there somewhere, hidden between the folds of wild darkness.

Lilica set her bowl down, half-finished, and leaned against me. I pulled back the hair that had fallen into her face, my hand brushing across her forehead now beaded with sweat. "Oh, honey, I think you're sitting too close to the fire." I shifted her back from the flames as she looked up at me with glassy eyes.

"Mommy, I don't feel good."

CHAPTER TWENTY-ONE

a chill sliced through me as I stared into her eyes, which were beginning to leak tears. "What's wrong, sweetheart?"

"My tummy hurts, and everything looks funny."

"What do you mean, everything looks funny?"

"My eyes are blurry." She rubbed at them and burrowed into my shoulder with a whimper.

I glanced at Domine from across the fire and shifted her into my arms, trying to fight back the tide of fear that slammed against my chest. "Okay, hon. Let's get you into the tent so you can lie down, and I'll make some tea for your tummy."

She nodded weakly as Domine came over and lifted her up, carrying her into the tent, his voice soft in her ear. "Your mommy's going to help you feel better, wood nymph."

Grabbing my leather pouch from the pack beside me, I sifted through it, looking for peppermint and chamomile. My hands shook as I poured water into the pan to boil, visuals rushing through my mind as I scrambled to recall information. *Migraine. Low blood sugar. Gastritis. Infection.* The possibilities were endless, and I had limited resources to work with.

I slid into the tent to find Domine crouched over Lilica, running a cloth gently across her forehead. "She's still sweating pretty bad." His eyes were wide as he stared up at me. "Do you think it might be something she ate?"

"I don't know. She didn't eat anything today she hasn't eaten before." I ran my hand over her clammy forehead. Checking her pulse, I found it rapid, her breath slightly labored. "Sweetie," I helped her to a sitting position and held the cup next to her lips, "can you drink this for me?"

She took a few sips, then curled back into the sleeping bag, looking up at me with glazed eyes. And that's when it hit me. *Excessive sweating, nausea. Blurred vision.*

No. No. No.

Panic clenched around my gut, sucking the air from my lungs. "Lili, did you eat something in the forest?"

"Maybe."

Her voice was soft and muffled against the blanket, and I took her by the shoulders, my words coming out strained. "Lilica. What did you eat in the forest?"

"Are you mad at me, Mommy?"

"No, honey." I pressed her against my chest and smoothed back her hair, which was now damp from sweat. "I'm not mad at you. I just need you to tell me what you ate, okay?"

"Mushrooms."

My breath stilled, and I pulled back to look into her eyes. "What kind of mushrooms?"

"The kind we had at the cabin. But they didn't taste good. They were yucky."

The sickening wave of anxiety slammed into me, and I grappled after the blurred edges of my thoughts like broken pages from a book. *Marasmius oreades. Inocybe. Clitocybe dealbata.*

Domine leaned in close to me, his face tense. "What mushrooms is she talking about?"

"The fairy ring mushrooms we had for dinner that one night. But there is another kind that looks a lot like them. The ivory funnel. Also known as the sweating mushroom." I rocked her back and forth, my voice coming out in a frantic whisper. "She has muscarine poisoning, Domine."

Lilica sank against me with a moan. "My tummy hurts, Mommy."

"I know, sweetie. I'm going to try and fix your tummy. Can you tell me how much you had?"

"Just a tiny nibble."

"A tiny nibble. Okay." I closed my eyes, trying to steady my breathing, but the frenzied rhythm of my heart was the only thing I could focus on.

What am I going to do? Is there an antidote? Do I have one in my bag?

I couldn't think straight.

Domine placed his hand on my back, and I found his eyes in the dim light, anchoring the thrashing edges of my panic. "It sounds like she didn't have that much. You'll figure this out."

"I'm going to get my medicine bag and see what I have. I'll be right back, Lili." With a nod, she crawled off my lap and into Domine's as I stood on shaky legs and left the tent.

In the dying embers of the fire, I staggered through the dark, looking for the flashlight and dug through the contents of my medicine bag, my mind racing as I tried to shuffle through all the information I had ever read about muscarine poisoning. I knew atropine was the common antidote, but I didn't have any belladonna, and even if I did, administration would be too risky.

I took a deep breath, trying to still the frenzied pace of my thoughts long enough to pull up the images I needed. And then my hands brushed against an herb, my fingers running over the dried spikes of purple flowers. Milk Thistle. My mind skittered over the memory of long buried words. *Can be used to prevent mushroom amatoxins from reaching and damaging liver cells.*

Retrieving the Milk Thistle from my bag, I placed it into a pan of water and quickly stoked up the fire. Crouched beside the flames, I waited for the herb to boil down so I could extract the silymarin I needed. I only hoped the compound would be enough to aid in the detox process.

Once the water was at a rolling boil, I poured the infusion into a cup, scrambled back to the tent, and ducked inside. Domine had turned on the solar-powered nightlight, and the walls shifted with color as he sat beside Lilica, running his hands in a slow circular motion across her back.

"I think I found something that will help." I bent down and took the cloth from Domine's hand, running it across Lilica's forehead. "Hey, sweetie. Can you sit up for Mommy and drink this?"

She let out a soft whimper and shifted in her sleeping bag, resting against Domine as I held the tea out to her. "Take very tiny sips, okay? It's still a little hot. But I need you to drink it all up for me. It will make you feel better." With a nod, she drew the cup to her mouth, taking a small swallow. "There you go, hon. Good job." Leaning down, I placed a kiss on her forehead, my thoughts tumbling around in a desperate prayer.

Please let this work. Please let her be okay.

* * *

The hour passed in agonizingly slow, drawn-out exhalations while I rocked Lilica in my arms, my lips moving to a quiet chant, an old Welsh lullaby my mother used to whisper to me when I was a child and afraid of the dark. The song that had now cradled my daughter through all her nights of illness and fever. The gentle solace of the words stilling my own anxious thoughts.

"Paid ag ofni, dim ond deilen
Gura, gura ar y ddôr;
Paid ag ofni, ton fach unig
Sua, sua ar lan y môr;
Huna blentyn, nid oes yma
Ddim i roddi iti fraw."
Do not fear, it is nothing but a leaf
Beating, beating on the door;
Do not fear, only a small wave
Murmurs, murmurs on the seashore;
Sleep child, there's nothing here
Nothing to give you fright.

Domine sat beside me, watching as I sang to her, his silent presence tethering my body in place as those haunted memories from two years ago took hold of me once more.

The high fever. The panicked rush to the hospital. The antibiotics that had only made her worse.

Her tiny body had been unrecognizable, concealed by tubes and wires. The harsh and unrelenting sound of the hospital monitors. The bright lights and sterile administrations that only caused her to slip even further from me. The choking fear. The silent pleas. All the nights I spent by her hospital bed, holding her hand, praying for her to wake up. And even when she recovered and was back at home, running around in the backyard, her laughter like sunlight, the fear never left me. It was always there. A dark ghost hovering in the corners of my mind, reminding me of the inherent fragility of life.

Lilica stirred against me and looked up, her eyes sleepy. "My tummy doesn't hurt so much anymore, Mommy."

I placed my hand on her forehead, realizing she had stopped sweating, and a fierce rush of relief coursed through me. The Milk Thistle was working.

She is going to be okay.

"I'm so glad to hear that, honey." I pulled her tightly to me, feeling the thrum of her heart against my chest. All the vibrant life inside her. The perfection of her small body cradled in mine.

"Mommy, you're squishing me."

"Sorry, love. I'm just so happy you're feeling better." I quickly wiped away a tear that had crept down my cheek. "Let's get you back into bed so you can get some sleep."

She nodded and crawled into her sleeping bag as Domine moved to tuck an extra blanket around her. My heart clenched as I watched him. That tension he'd held in his eyes now softening as he smoothed back her hair and bent down to whisper goodnight with the same tenderness as a father with his own child.

I stumbled from the tent, stifling the sob that threatened to spill out. From behind, Domine pulled me against him. "It's okay. She's okay. And that's all because of *you*. Your knowledge of herbs and your ability to retain information. It's incredible, Seren."

I shook my head, staring out into the darkness of the forest. "But what if she had eaten more? Or what if she had found a death cap? There would have been nothing I could have done." I gripped his arms as he held me against his chest, trying to restrain the cry that wanted to pour into the silence of the night. "I could have lost her. I can't keep her safe out here."

He turned me around and took my face in his hands, the moon reflecting the stark intensity in his eyes. "No. She *is* safe with *you*. Not back at the Grid, where they would only pump her full of poison and numb her mind. You got her out of there. *You* saved her from that."

"I know. But at what risk?"

Wiping away my tears with the pad of his thumb, he rested his forehead to mine, his voice an ardent whisper. "Life is full of risk. No matter what choices we make."

With a sigh, I sank into him, my body shaking and hollowed out as he held me, allowing his arms to soothe away the tangled doubt as our breath rose and curled into the darkness like ghosts.

* * *

*M*orning shifted across the length of the sky, throwing soft light into the tent, and erasing the remnants of a restless night. A night spent repeatedly checking Lilica's vitals and staring at the rise and fall of her chest as she slept. So many nights I had sat beside her like this, caught within the tide of a fever or a racking cough that split me in two. There was no language for the feeling of watching a piece of your heart as it navigated itself in another body.

"Did you get *any* sleep?" Domine slid his arms around me, the warmth of him releasing the tension in my limbs and chasing away the shadows of unease that still lingered relentlessly in the corners of my mind.

"No, not really." I sighed and turned toward him, nestling my head into his chest as his hands slid up my back, his fingers slowly working the knots along my shoulders.

"Mommy?"

I looked over to find Lilica sitting up and staring at me with a wide smile. "I'm really hungry."

Her words were a warm burst of light, and I reached out to run my fingers through her hair. "That's so good to hear, sweetie. So, you're feeling better?"

She nodded. "All better."

I rose to get up, but Domine grabbed my arms and gently pressed me back down onto the sleeping bag, his voice soft in my ear. "Why don't you try to get a little more rest, okay? I'll cook us up some breakfast."

Closing my eyes, I listened to the sounds of them moving around. The shuffle of shoes and jackets. The zip of the tent door. The snapping of twigs and the clinking of the cooking pot as it was placed over the fire. Lilica's voice like sweet honey, her chatter filtering in through the walls of the tent.

"The fairies visited me again last night."

"Oh, did they, wood nymph? And what did you do together?"

"They showed me where their magic was."

"Oh yeah, where was it?"

"They said it was inside my mommy."

CHAPTER TWENTY-TWO

I crouched beside the trail, the chill of morning on my fingers as I plucked bright red huckleberries from smooth round leaves. The frost had withered most of the plants by now, the mulch on the ground drawing them back into the darkness until spring's release. But cradled in my hand were the last remnants of summer, sweet and tart against my tongue.

"Lili. Look what I found." She ran up to me, and I popped a berry into her mouth, a smile spreading across her face as she discovered the sweetness hidden beneath the skin.

Retrieving a bag from my pack, I gathered as much as I could, filling the muslin cloth with crimson color.

"The forest suits you." Domine bent down and plucked a leaf from my hair, his eyes flickering with heat as he reached into the bag and popped some berries into his mouth. "You look deliciously wild right now."

The intensity in his gaze sent a rush through me, and I let out a small laugh, brushing back the unruly strands as I raised my eyebrow at him. "Really? You're liking this look?"

"I am. Very much." His fingers trailed up my neck, hovering against my cheek as his mouth found mine in a soft, slow dance that warmed my lips and tasted of sugar. I slid my hand along his back, wanting to dive deeper into his kiss. Our moments together were always furtive and fleeting, a constant ache that left me breathless and dizzy. But I untangled my desire and pulled away, leaving the remnants of my longing on his skin.

With a smile, I glanced over at Lilica, who sat beside a stump. Her eyes focused on the ground as she drew something in the dirt with her stick.

"You ready to hit the trail again, hon?" Walking over, I crouched beside her, staring at the picture she had drawn. A man, woman, and two children deeply etched into the earth.

"What's this picture of, love?"

She turned to me with her wide gray eyes. "It's a family." She then sprang to her feet and ran to Domine as he slung his pack over his shoulder.

With her tiny hand curled around his, warmth bloomed inside me. I could see him as a father. In this wild expanse of forest, nestled in the valley of mountains, we *had* become a family. One that was more real to me than what I had ever tried to fashion together with Trendon.

But beneath that lay the burden of all my fears. The racing thoughts that visited me in the dark. I had thrust my daughter into a world of the unknown, and the night she fell sick still weighed heavy on me, a grappling discomfort I couldn't outpace. I could hold her close, never let her leave my sight, and even then, I couldn't promise she would be safe.

There were no guarantees in life.

I looked back down at Lilica's drawing in the earth, my eyes following the rough sketch marks of a small child holding the hand of a larger one, and a deep sorrow tugged at me like a loss unformed. A yearning for another child I knew I could never have.

* * *

"I dreamed last night that we made it to Alberta." Domine spoke softly as he stared into the fire. The remains of our dinner were now finished, bowls and utensils washed and packed away.

"What did it look like?" Lilica's eyes grew wide as she stared at him, her mouth full of toothpaste.

"Well, it had lots of trees and clear blue sky. Houses with happy people inside them."

"Will we have a house when we get there?"

He bent down with a smile and ruffled her hair. "I think we will, wood nymph."

"I wonder how established this place will be?" I leaned back against a log, wrapping my arms around myself.

"People have spoken of it growing considerably in the last few years." Domine poked at the fire, casting dancing shadows across his face. "When the Canadian government was overthrown five years ago, a new system was created. One that allowed districts to govern independently. Apparently, Alberta's district is run by the Liberation party. I've heard it's a lot like any functioning town. They have their own currency, run their own businesses, but they don't have access to corporate amenities." He looked up at me, his eyes awash in the dancing light. "Which means no digital devices or wireless technology."

"That sounds nice." My heart fluttered at the thought. Just beyond the stretch of mountain range was a home and a new life waiting for us. Images of sun-drenched mornings together and soft words caressed me, days spent slowly forging a world of our own design.

The sweetness of my musings was a gentle tease of anticipation, and I reached out to Domine, entwining my fingers through his as my eyes fell to the engraving on the leather band around his wrist. *You will always be my autumn.* He squeezed back with a look that caused heat to blossom across my skin, a longing hovering between us like an unextinguished flame.

I glanced over at Lilica. "Are you all finished brushing, hon?"

She held up the toothbrush with a wide grin. "I got all the teeth. Can you see them sparkle?"

"Hmm…" I bent down and peered into her mouth. "Yep. They're sparkly, all right." I adjusted the blanket around her shoulders and scooped her into my arms. "Are you ready for bed?"

She fiddled with the zipper on my coat. "Can Domine tell me a story tonight?"

"Of course. Do you want him to put you to bed as well?"

She nodded and slid off my lap, a wide smile stretching across her face as Domine stood and lifted her high into the air before positioning her in his arms.

"Goodnight, sweetheart," I called after her, watching as she nestled against his shoulder, her eyes sleepy.

"Night, Mommy."

I settled close to the fire, sifting the embers around as the deep richness of Domine's voice mingled with Lilica's soft laughter. Then it grew quiet, and all I could hear was the gentle cadence of his words as they drifted through the tent walls.

"And then the fairy queen gave the little girl the gift of light. And everything she touched became beautiful. There was no more sadness or fear. Only love."

My throat constricted as I stared into the flames, listening to the whispers of his story, the tenderness in his voice reminding me of my mother's bedtime tales. My tiny body sheltered against hers. The magic she wove into the darkness of my bedroom. The name she would murmur to me in the rolling lilt of her mother's Welsh dialect.

Gwreichionen llachar. Her bright spark.

Staring into the sky, I watched the stars collide with the night in an effervescent glow I could almost reach out and touch, and I suddenly felt her. I felt all of them. The boisterous laughter of my father in the wind, the kindness of my brother's smile in the flickering light of the fire. They were here, watching over me. They had *always* been here, tucked away beneath my bones. Hidden within the tide of my breath. A firmament of energy that held no borders.

"She's asleep."

Domine's voice startled me from my thoughts, and I turned to him as he sat down and slid his arm around me. Reaching up, I ran my hand through his tousled hair. "I think Lilica loves you."

He smiled, leaning over to place a kiss on my forehead. "And I think I love her, Seren."

"Really?"

"Yes. Really."

A wide smile spread across his face, and a rush of warmth enfolded me. How easily we fit together. The tapestry of our past now a landscape unfurling. And even though Lilica carried questions inside her that she would one day speak out loud, there was comfort in the knowledge that she was now cradled by both of us.

Standing, I took his hand, an ache coiling through me as I led him away from the tent and toward the enclosure of trees. I needed to feel him against rough bark and earth, to merge my body with the pulse of his. I wanted him untamed, like an animal in the forest.

"Where are you taking me?" His voice was low and husky as I leaned up against a tree and pulled him to me.

"Where do you *want* me to take you?" My hands snuck under his jacket and crept past his shirt, running my fingers up the muscles along his back.

"I can think of *several* places you could take me, Seren." His breath was a tantalizing shiver as his lips brushed along the lobe of my ear and down to my neck.

Heat raced across my skin, and I arched myself against him. "How about here?" Taking his hand, I guided him past the waistline of my pants, my breath hitching in my throat as his fingers curled beneath my underwear and slipped into me.

"Right here?" He growled in my ear.

"Yes." Gasping, I clutched his shoulders as he slid his fingers deeper inside and ran his thumb along the folds of my sex, finding all the right places, the ones he had never forgotten. I wrapped my leg around his waist for leverage, my entire body trembling and stretched tight like a band, longing for release.

With a groan, his mouth found mine as he continued his dance inside me, slow strokes of his hand that matched the rhythm of our lips and tongue as he pressed me against the tree, filling all of me, pushing me to the edge. I tensed up, a broken moan spilling out as I bit down on his lip, trying to hold back the current building inside. I wanted it to last. I wanted to draw out every sensation with him, but my body was hungry, and it relinquished control, leaving me whimpering and breathless, my hands grasping at him.

Slipping out of me, his hand traveled underneath my shirt. Goosebumps peppered my skin as his fingers ran up my stomach and grazed across my nipple, his voice a breathy whisper. "Do you remember what I told you the first time we made love?"

Dazed and shaky, I leaned my head against the tree and looked up at him, his eyes wide and burning into me as moonlight scattered across his face. "Of course."

That was the night we had tumbled into his apartment together just before curfew, the streetlights flickering to life and spilling through the windows. Drunk on each other, drunk on the feel of our skin and lips discovering one another for the first time, hands trembling as we peeled away the layers that separated us. He had taken me slow and tender on the couch, and as he watched me release myself beneath him, he spoke softly in my ear. "I think I could spend the rest of my life watching you."

"I want that." His hands spread down to my hips and ran up my back. "I want the rest of my life with you."

"You have it, Dom." I rested my forehead against his, seeking out the warmth of his mouth. "You have *all* of it."

"I love it when you call me that." He threaded his hands into my hair, tilting my head up to meet his gaze. "Don't ever stop."

My legs gave way, and I pulled him to the ground, the feel of him on top of me a delicious weight as I shifted my pants down and unbuttoned his. The sharp sting of the cold merged with the heat of his skin, and I opened myself to him, aching to solidify this promise made in the dark.

A stifled cry took flight from my mouth as his desire plunged into me. Earth and pine filled my senses, surrounding me in a wild and reckless euphoria of pleasure, while gently, he pinned my hands to the forest floor and took me as he did all those years ago. Slow and tender. His eyes never leaving mine.

CHAPTER TWENTY-THREE

Standing beside the cliff's edge, I stared across the vastness of the mountain range. The trees looked so different from this vantage point, blurred and washed out like a watercolor painting, an ethereal mirage of color and light. And that feeling of undefined longing tugged at me once more as a faded image of my mother wound around me, curling against the structure of my memories.

Soft words spoken in the backyard of my childhood. The flush of a dandelion peeking from beneath the blades of grass. Sunlight dancing across the honey strands of her hair. She had spoken to me of her ancestral grief, the loss carried through generations like threads deeply woven into the marrow of bone. *"Everybody has longing inside them. Whether it's for something they have lost, or something they have yet to find."* She had then placed her hand over my heart, her eyes wide and full of love as the warmth of a summer long gone whispered across our skin. *"Hireath is the cry inside us, Seren. Never settle for a life that is not your own."*

I wondered if somehow she knew that one day I would break from the chains I was born into. If she was, in her own way, preparing me for a world I would someday leave.

"Mommy, look." Lilica appeared next to me and slipped her hand in mine, pulling me from my thoughts as she pointed upward. "It's a big birdy."

I glanced up to see a hawk circling above us, its large wings silhouetted against the ink of the blue sky.

"How do they get that high?"

With a smile, I crouched down beside her. "They have wings, sweetie. Wings that allow them to be weightless and glide through the air, kind of like an airplane."

"Why can't we have wings?"

"Well, in a way, we do." I wrapped my arm around her, pulling her close. "Our wings are inside of us." I tapped her forehead lightly. "We can go anywhere in our minds. All we have to do is imagine it."

"Like when I dream?"

"Yes, love. Just like when you dream."

She furrowed her brow. "But the fairies that visit me say they are real."

I smiled, tucking a strand of hair behind her ear. "I'm sure they feel very real to you."

The wind suddenly picked up around us, an urgent tug that sent a chill racing across my skin, and Domine turned from where he had been pensively staring out across the stretch of mountains. "I think we have roughly five days until we reach the Rockies."

I nodded and zipped up Lilica's coat, adjusting the knitted cap over her head. "And do you think the weather will hold?" The thought of crossing the mountains and finally reaching Alberta was a hopeful beacon that propelled me forward, blanketing the effects of our long days of walking and rationing food.

"I hope so." He looked up at the wispy clouds riding high above us, feathered streaks of white snaking across the sky.

Shouldering my pack, I stepped back onto the trail with Lilica while Domine took the lead ahead of us. He had been quiet this morning, his eyes distant, his mood somber, and I wondered if it was the pressure of time that was bothering him. We had been moving at a slower pace than expected, giving room for Lilica to rest, and now there was a persistent bite in the air that hinted of winter.

Would we be able to make it through the mountains before the first snow?

I realized how much I relied on Domine. Depended on the presence of his unwavering optimism, like a cloak shielding us from harm. But now something had shifted within him, and a growing feeling of unease wrenched at me.

Catching up to him, I took his hand. "You're doing it again."

He turned to me, a spark of tension hovering along his jaw. "Doing what?"

"Brooding."

He didn't respond, only slowed his pace slightly, eyes fixed on the trail ahead of us. I was familiar with these moods, though it had been years since I had seen one. He could fill a room with the heaviness, lost to the nagging tide of his thoughts.

"You're worried about the weather, aren't you?"

"Yes. I am."

"Okay, so what would happen if the snow came before we crossed the Rockies?"

He stopped walking and spun toward me, his eyes flashing with a look so piercing it caused my breath to still. "We would be forced to turn back."

"Turn back?" I shook my head, my voice lowering to a frantic whisper. "No. We can't turn back."

"We won't have much of a choice." His words came out clipped as he stared at me, and my breath caught in my throat, struggling to find something solid to cling to.

"Why can't we just keep going through the snow?"

"I don't think you understand. Once the snow hits. That's it. The cold is brutal up here. And staying dry and warm would be a challenge. Not to mention the issue of finding enough food and losing the trail." He glanced back at Lilica, who lagged behind us, her walking stick dragging a long path in the earth. "It's too risky."

I bit my lip, the grip of dread snaking its way through me. I knew he was right. There was no way we could risk trekking through heavy snow with Lilica. There were too many things that could go wrong. Too many uncertainties. My voice dropped to a whisper as I met Domine's stoic gaze. "So, what do you think we should do?"

"We hope to make it through the pass before the snow hits."

* * *

The flames licked around the wood, tendrils of warmth stretching through the cold as I sat close to the fire with Lilica wrapped in my arms.

"I made you something, wood nymph." Domine crouched beside her and placed a small figure in her hand.

She grasped the wooden carving, and a wide smile spread across her face. "It's a fairy."

"Wow, look at that, Lilica. She's so pretty." My fingers ran along the wings, tracing across the etchings on the tiny, engraved face. "When did you manage to make this?" I asked, glancing over at him. "It's really good."

"Well, I can't give *all* my secrets away." He shot Lilica a wink as he bent forward and sifted through the fire's embers.

"You're not trying to have her get rid of that *walking stick*, are you?" I whispered close to his ear with a teasing smile.

He widened his eyes in mock horror as he settled beside me. "Never."

Lilica scrambled out of my lap and began to walk her fairy along a log next to the fire, speaking in words lost to the gentle pattering of her imagination.

Slipping behind him, I ran my hands up his back, kneading the knots along his shoulder blades. Relief washed over me as I noticed the tension he had been carrying all day had eased a bit, the softness returning to his eyes. I needed his calm reassurance, the gentle optimism of his smile. It was the anchor holding me together, holding us all together.

"Oh, that feels good." He leaned into my touch, a deep groan spreading through him as I worked my fingers across his back, releasing the tight muscles.

"Mommy, look. There's a doggy."

My hands stilled, and I looked at Lilica, who was pointing at something from across the fire. Through the flames, on the edge of the tree line, two glowing eyes stared back at us. A familiar dark ring of fur surrounding gray.

Domine stiffened beneath me and reached for a large stick beside him.

In one swift movement, I grabbed Lilica, pulling her close to me as my breath seized within my chest. "That's *not* a doggy, sweetie."

Domine rose slowly, grasping the stick in his hand as he moved toward the animal.

"*What are you doing?*" I hissed at him, my pulse hammering wildly in my chest. "Don't go up to it."

He held his hand up as if to assure me. But I knew a stick was no match for the jaws of a wolf. With one hand holding Lilica, I scrambled around in the pack beside me, fingers shaking as I located the handle of our cooking knife and clasped it firmly.

Domine continued to walk forward, his footsteps crunching against the dry brush of the forest floor. "Get! Go!"

The boom of his voice cut through the air, causing Lilica to startle in my arms and bury her face into my shoulder. I held her tighter against me, my hand grasping the knife so hard my fingers ached.

Please go… please go.

The wolf took a step back, crouching low as if ready to pounce, and all I could hear was the sound of blood rushing in my ears, the frenzied rhythm of my heartbeat colliding with the clutches of fear.

Time suspended itself. I didn't know how long they stood there, locked in some silent challenge. But then the wolf lowered its head as if in submission and retreated, turning around once to look at us before dashing back into the woods. The streak of gray now a whisper against the darkness.

My breath released itself in one long trembling sigh as Domine strode back to the fire, grabbing the pack and unhooking the crossbow attached to the side. "I didn't see any others with him. My guess is that he's a lone wolf."

"A lone wolf?"

"Yeah. Sometimes they are cast out from the pack. Or leave on their own to start a new one." He pulled out his crossbow, notching an arrow against the strings.

My grip on the handle of the knife relaxed, and I set it next to me on the ground. "Its markings looked similar to the wolf I saw the other day. I wonder if it's the same one."

"It could be."

"Do you think it's following us?"

He looked at me, unease flickering across his eyes. "Let's hope not." He positioned the loaded crossbow beside him, the flames from the fire glinting off the metal. "But just in case, Lilica needs to stay by our side at all times."

With a nod, I drew her closer to me, my body pulsing with the flood of adrenaline as I stared off into the woods. The darkness shrouded my sight, but I could feel eyes on me, watching from somewhere, and despite the heat of the fire, goosebumps prickled across my skin.

"Maybe he's lonely, Mommy."

I looked down at her with a faint smile, smoothing back her hair. "I don't know if wolves get lonely, honey."

"Maybe they do." She nestled her head on my shoulder, her fingers curling through mine. "Maybe he just wants a friend."

* * *

*N*ight washed across my skin as I rolled over, extracting my arms from the warmth of the sleeping bag. Domine lay beside me, his eyes open and staring at the shadows above him.

"You should try to get some sleep." I reached out to trace my fingers across the light growth of beard that ran along his jaw.

He turned toward me, his eyes heavy. "I can't sleep right now."

Shifting in the sleeping bag, I slid closer and wrapped my arms around him, resting my head on his chest. "Can you promise me you'll stop *walking* toward things?"

"What do you mean?"

"The helicopter. The wolf…" I trailed off, my hand grasping his arm. "I can't live with the idea of something happening to you."

"Seren." He tilted my head up to his. "My job is to make sure you guys are safe. That is *all* that matters to me."

"But *you* matter to me. And *you* matter to Lilica." My voice came out in a harsh whisper, a broken plea into the darkness. "What if the wolf had attacked you?"

He shook his head. "But it didn't."

"It was reckless, Domine."

"I need you to understand something." He sat up, strands of hair falling into his eyes as he leaned over me. "I'm not afraid of death. What I *am* afraid of is the thought of something happening to you two."

His words hit me like a blast of cold air, and I scrambled to find my footing. "*Stop it.* What do you think would happen to us without you? Huh?" I rose from the sleeping bag and grabbed him by the shoulders. "Do you think we could survive out here on our own? We couldn't, Domine. So just *stop* talking like that."

"You're a fighter." He brushed his thumb across my cheek. "And I know that if something ever happened to me, you would be okay."

"Bullshit." I clenched my teeth, that familiar wound of fear curling within me. I needed him too much. I loved him too sharply. Tears leaked out and stained my skin, leaving behind a trail of tangled emotions too heavy to hold. "You don't know that."

"But I *do*." His eyes burned into me. "You've always been a fighter. That's what I love so much about you. You could have given up when you lost your family. You could have given up when you chose to live in a society that wanted to squeeze every last drop of spirit out of you. To make you nothing but an empty shell. But you didn't. You chose to rise above and find a way to live with what you had left." His hand fell to my chest, resting against the rapid thrum of my heart. "*That* is how I know you're capable of anything."

I rested my forehead against his, breathing in the weight of his statement. "How you do it?"

"Do what?"

I looked up at him, watching moonlight cast gentle patterns across his face. "See the best in everything. Remain so calm all the time."

"It's because I've had years to learn how to sit with my ghosts." Something flickered in his eyes as he spoke. A sorrow that expanded like a gathering storm. "I was in a really dark place for a long time, Seren."

My hand fell to his chest as I met the depths of his gaze. A myriad of emotions that lept and twisted before me. "When was this?"

"It was about a year after we ended things." With a sigh, he rolled onto his back and stared into the space above him, as if the sky could reach through the tent and pull out the marrow of his thoughts. "I had nothing left to hold on to, and there was so much anger eating away at me." A silence burned around the edges of his words for a moment, and then he released them in a long, slow exhale. "There were times when I thought about ending it all."

"Dom." His confession slammed into me, choking the air from my lungs, and I sat up, grasping at his shoulders. "Why didn't you tell me about this?"

He turned to me. "Because you were trying to move on with your life. And then you met Trendon." He shook his head. "I didn't want to pull you down into my shit."

Tears pricked my eyes as the reality of his suffering hit me. All those years I had visited him, and he had seemed content, happy even. But had it all been an act? A desperate mask stifling the scream inside him? How much of his pain had he kept hidden from me?

I threaded my fingers through his hair, pulling him close as if the strength of my arms around him could wash the past away. "You could have told me. I would have been there for you."

"I know. But I needed to go through this alone, Seren."

Reaching out, he wiped away a tear that had crept down my cheek, and I sucked in a sharp breath, clutching at his back. "I can't believe you seriously thought about…"

He drew his finger to my lips, stilling the rush of my words. "But I didn't. Eventually, I decided to stop running. From myself. From my past. And I just let it all take me until I was emptied out. And you know what I realized?"

"What?"

"I realized that the only way to find myself was to get lost in the darkness. I had to walk through the fire. And it was ugly and messy and painful. But it was worth it because I learned to stop fighting. And that was when I was able to find some sense of peace with it all."

I dropped my head to his shoulder, feeling the rush of his breath that entwined with mine, the beautiful complexities that lay beneath the surface, the fumbling journey toward healing. Life was a dance with duality. Darkness collided with light. Fear sat beside strength. And in the center of it was love. The kind that grew patiently beneath the earth, waiting for the rain to awaken the roots.

Taking his hand, I pressed it to my lips. "You don't have to walk through the fire alone anymore, Dom. Because we're a family now. The three of us."

"What did you say?" His voice came out in a choked whisper, and I pulled back to look at him, claiming the words I had been carrying with me for days now. Words I wanted to give him.

"We're a family."

"A family, huh?" The waver of tears danced in his eyes, and a faint smile played at the corner of his mouth. "I've never had one of those before."

"I know. But you have one now." My voice trembled as I ran my hands along his back, along all the years of solitude hidden beneath his skin. In the rubble of his past. In the ache and loneliness. In the rebirth.

Perhaps the roads that led us back to each other had been there for a reason. Maybe time was not something we lost, but something we had to find.

CHAPTER TWENTY-FOUR

*V*igilance now followed us since the wolf's visit to our campfire. Every snap of a twig in the distance had Domine reaching for his crossbow, which he now wore slung across his chest while walking, his eyes pivoting cautiously through the forest. Sometimes, I think I would see a flash of gray between the trees, and my heart would jump, but when I turned to look, there was nothing there.

We were now a day away from the mountain pass, and the grip of cold grew stronger, our water now a thin layer of ice we had to break through every morning.

Long shadows filtered through the undergrowth as Domine leaned against a tree and unfolded the map, the paper crinkling as he smoothed back the creases with his hand and squinted against the waning light. "There should be a river about a mile up from here. I think that will be a good place to stop for the night."

Lilica sat beside me, finishing up her snack of dried nuts, while I rooted around in our pack, taking quick stock of our food provisions. I longed for something fresh to eat, but the frost had killed the last of the wild berries along the trail, and the watercress that grew in the shallow streams was now withered. With a sigh, I looked up at Domine. "We're running low on food."

"I'll set some snares tonight. See if we can catch something." He pocketed the map and bent down to ruffle Lilica's hair playfully. "What do you think the fairies eat out here?"

She beamed up at him, stuffing a peanut into her mouth. "Leaves."

"Okay. Well, I guess we can always try that if we get *really* hungry." With a wink, he picked up his pack and crossbow, slinging them over his shoulder.

"No, silly. We can't eat *leaves!*" She giggled and scrambled to her feet, falling in step beside him.

Despite my apprehension regarding the reality of our dwindling food supplies, a smile pulled at the corners of my lips as I cinched my pack closed and followed behind them, our footfalls leaving a gentle echo that slipped between the trees.

My steps fell in time with the rhythm of my breath as we walked, the deep emerald hues of the forest merging so seamlessly with the placid blue of the sky. It was within these moments on the trail that everything else faded away. My mind no longer crowded with gnawing questions and restless worries. There was a stillness that encompassed me. A weight lifted. A slow unraveling that sharpened my senses. But I could not ignore the caution hidden within Domine's eyes. Winter was closing in. I could feel it. The silence in the forest had now grown more acute. Except for the occasional raucous cry of a crow, the twitter of birds was gone, their wings lifting long ago as they answered the call for warmer weather.

It would take us three days to get through the mountain pass, and I prayed for the skies to remain clear.

* * *

The air hung thick with the scent of moss and damp earth, the rush of the river beyond us a steady drumbeat in my ears. The last rays of sunlight struggled to pierce through the branches as Lilica stood by Domine, diligently holding the tent poles in her hands while he raised the tent between two trees.

"I'm going to fill up our water, Lili." I crouched beside her, sweeping back the loose strands of her hair. "Do you want to come with me?"

She shook her head, eyes fixed on Domine, seeming to take pride in her new role as assistant.

"Why don't you wait for us to finish up here, and then we can all go together?" Domine said as Lilica handed him a pole to loop through the tent.

"It's going to get dark soon, so I'll just go now. I won't be long."

His hand landed on my shoulder as I went to retrieve my pack. "Take this with you." He held out the crossbow.

I waved him off, motioning through the trees. "I'm just going to be down by the river."

"Seren." His voice was low, the outline of worry etched in his eyes. "Please, take it."

"Okay, fine." I took the crossbow from him and slid it between the straps of my pack.

"And you remember how to use it?"

I nodded, recalling the morning our breath had curled around us like mist as he drew himself against my back and whispered to me the specifics of proper bow notching and string placement, his voice a soft shiver in my ear.

"I think I have the basics down." With a smile, I leaned forward and found his mouth for a moment. "I'll be right back."

Snaking through the trees, I quickly made my way down an embankment, following the roar of the river. Earth turned to sand beneath my feet as I pushed through bushes and stepped out onto open shore. The river cut a wide arc through the landscape, a rush of churning serpentine water that careened swiftly past me, hugging a jagged cliff on the other side. Bending down, I pulled out the water canisters, leaving my pack and crossbow behind.

The faint press of sunlight hovered above me, breaking through the clouds, and spilling a tentative warmth across my back as I filled the bottles. The water was surprisingly clear, and flashes of movement and color stirred beneath the surface. The flicking of fins. The blush of pink and red. Moving closer, my feet settled on a perch of rocks protruding from the river, and I leaned over to watch the cluster of salmon as they swam upstream, fighting against the current in the last desperate drive of their migratory journey.

Salmon had hovered on the brink of extinction for years, but here they were, flourishing within the delicate cycle of life and death. It was within this wildness so far removed from our human touch that balance still remained, safely hidden from the clutches of our destruction and left to thrive once more. The resilience of life reclaiming itself.

I dipped my hand into the water, the icy chill tugging at my skin as the fish brushed past my open hand, the light reflecting off their scales. I wondered if somehow they knew this was the end of their lives. That after they spawned, they would die and wash up on the banks of this river, their bodies once more returning to the earth. If only we could live with such boldness, knowing the inevitable outcome of our own lives, but bravely pushing toward it, regardless.

A loud splash jarred me from my thoughts. The glare of sunlight against water momentarily blinding me as I looked up.

My breath stilled.

A large brown bear stood upstream, paws slicing through the current as it sought out the salmon. It was close enough that I could make out the definition of muscle rippling beneath the fur. Dark eyes staring into the water.

Every muscle within me tensed, hands gripping the rock I crouched on, hoping it had not seen me as I glanced toward the shore where my pack and crossbow lay on the sand. When I turned back, my heart slammed against my chest.

The bear was no longer watching the fish. It was watching me.

I don't know when the bear started moving. One moment, it was standing in the current, the next, it was kicking up a spray of water, rushing toward me with a startling velocity.

A cry spilled from my mouth, and a sharp pain lanced through me as my foot slipped and my ankle wedged between the rocks. The shock of the cold stole my breath as I pitched into the water, hands grasping at the bank of the shore.

A loud snarl tore the air, and I whipped my head up. A wolf now stood between me and the bear. And I released a strangled gasp as I saw the familiar markings of its coat, the black etchings around its eyes. The wolf let out another growl and advanced toward the bear with hackles raised, the flash of canine teeth exposed in challenge.

All this unfolded before me in a surreal sense of slow motion as I watched the bear rise to its full height and stand on two legs before dropping back down as if reconsidering the effort. And then, with a loud huff, it turned and ambled out of the water, its powerful form receding into the trees.

I couldn't move. I couldn't breathe. My entire world reduced to the icy tug of the river wrapping around my body and the wild pull of the wolf's eyes as it turned and locked with mine. Some flicker of understanding seemed to pass between us. A silent primal language born from river, earth, and forest. And then the wolf slipped away, disappearing into the woods as quickly as it had appeared.

I remained suspended in the current, hands clutching rock as I stared into the swaying trees, their branches like a dance against the fading daylight.

What just happened?

"Seren." Hands took hold of my arms, lifting me out of the water, Domine's voice in my ear pulling me back to myself. "Are you okay?"

I nodded blankly as Lilica stared at me from the shore, her eyes wide. "Mommy, why are you in the river?"

"I just slipped, sweetie." My voice came out in a rasp, and my limbs churned with adrenaline, blanketing the throbbing ache that shot through my foot.

I winced as Domine helped me onto the sand. Soaking wet and shivering, I struggled with the laces on my boot, pulling down my sock to reveal an ankle already swollen and red.

"Mommy, do you have an ouchie?" She furrowed her brow, the faint lines of unease etched across her face as she leaned against me.

I pulled her into my arms, holding her tightly to me. The warmth of her body soaked through the chill on my skin as I pressed my lips to her forehead. "I do. But don't worry, it's just a tiny one."

"That doesn't look good." Domine's eyes were heavy with concern as he crouched down and draped his coat around me.

"How bad does it hurt?" His hands slid down to my foot, tentatively enfolding my ankle.

"I'll be okay. I'm pretty sure it's just a sprain."

"What happened?"

"There was a bear. Right over there." I pointed up the river, teeth chattering, hand shaking. "It was in the water, and then it started coming toward me."

"You saw a bear?" He abruptly stood and grabbed the crossbow that lay on the sand beside my feet, scanning the trees, his face pinched.

"But it's gone. The wolf…" I trailed off, struggling with my words. "The wolf came."

"The wolf?" Tension flashed across his face as he stared at me. "What are you talking about?"

"The wolf that's been following us. He scared the bear off, Domine."

CHAPTER TWENTY-FIVE

*L*ilica watched me beside the fire as I ground up dried arnica from my medicine pouch, mixing it with warm water to form a paste.

"Mommy, did the wolf doggy save you?"

A faint smile formed on my lips as I leaned close to her. "Well, I think in a way, he might have been protecting me." Applying the paste to my ankle, I tore off a strip of cloth and wound it around my foot, securing the bandage tightly in place. "You see, most of the wild animals out here don't want to hurt us. They're just trying to live their lives like we are."

Lilica scrunched up her face. "But the bear was trying to hurt you."

"We don't know that, sweetie." I pulled her onto my lap. "He could have just been trying to scare me away. Maybe he thought I was stealing his fish."

"Well, I ended up stealing his fish instead." Domine softly chuckled as he bent over the fire to retrieve the salmon from the flames. Steam rose from the meat, the aroma making my mouth water as he broke the fish into pieces and handed us each a plate.

The oily richness of the salmon melted in my mouth like butter, and I closed my eyes for a moment, savoring the new taste. I had never eaten salmon before, and most of the fish that had been available in the food warehouses were considered a rare delicacy, one we had never been able to afford when we lived on the Grid.

Despite the throbbing pain in my ankle, I felt a sense of contentment in this moment, with the warmth of the fire enfolding us, the decadent food, the blanket of stars unraveling across an endless sky. Suddenly, there was no other place I wanted to be, but here. With a smile, I glanced at Domine, who stared into the fire, and I reached over, squeezing his knee as his eyes met mine.

"You know, a few years back, I read in one of Turk's books about the indigenous tribes that used to live in this area hundreds of years ago." He popped a piece of fish into his mouth while he sifted through the coals, sending sparks spiraling into the darkness. "They believed the animals of this land were sacred and that the Creator roamed the earth in the form of a wolf, representing courage, strength, and protection."

"What's the Creator?" Lilica's question rose and curled through the crackle of the flames.

Domine smiled at her and swept his hand through the air. "Well, it's kind of like life. It's everything around us."

Lilica pursed her lips, her grey eyes piercing into him. "Can we be Creators?"

Domine let out a soft chuckle. "You know, I don't see why not, wood nymph. We can be anything we want."

A reverence overcame me as I stared into the woods. Was the wolf out there right now, silent and unseen, watching us? There had been no fear when I locked eyes with it at the river, only a staggering amazement, like when you see a sunset that feels too perfect to be real, or touch the petals of a flower, its delicate flawlessness unfolding between your fingers.

Life was wild and beautiful, and when you took down the walls, stripped away the concrete, what lay beneath could take your breath away.

*G*ray morning light drifted through the walls of the tent as I lay between Lilica and Domine. The warmth from their bodies created a shelter I did not want to leave, but the throbbing ache in my foot had grown more persistent throughout the night, and I could no longer ignore it.

Reluctantly, I pulled myself from the sleeping bag, pain lancing through my ankle as I struggled to stand. I hobbled to the tent door and grabbed my boots, trying to muffle the hiss that threatened to spill from my lips as I peeled back my sock to reveal mottled bruising, my ankle now twice as swollen as it had been the night before. I was looking at a grade three sprain with partial tearing. It would take weeks to heal properly.

Dammit.

Frustration sliced through me. We were so close to the mountain pass, and I didn't want Domine to know how bad this was. I couldn't have this slowing us down.

I bent to my pack beside the door and grabbed the medicinal bag from the front pocket. My fingers fumbled with the herbs inside, looking for the woody stems of devil's claw I had found in the woods and harvested before we left the cabin. I hoped it would relieve the pain long enough for me to at least get through the pass today.

Stepping outside, my breath billowed out like smoke, the grip of the cold clawing at my skin as I limped to the firepit and grabbed some sticks to start a fire.

"Mommy, what's for breakfast?" Lilica stood in the opening to the tent, rubbing the sleep from her eyes.

"Morning, love." I slowly made my way over to our food pack, which had been hung from a nearby tree the night before, and released it from the ropes. Easing myself onto the ground, I bit my lip against the pain as I grabbed a pan and sifted through our food supplies, finding the last bag of flour, along with a small jar of jam. "Well, I think we have enough flour and cornmeal left for one more round of pancakes."

"Yummy!" Her face lit up just as Domine appeared with her shoes and coat, helping her arms through the sleeves.

"How's your ankle?"

His question hung in the air as I dropped the herbs into the pan of water, forcing out a tight smile. "It's better."

"Can I take a look at it?" He sat beside me with his brow furrowed as his hand swept down my leg.

"It's fine. I just checked it when I got up. The swelling has gone down." I dipped my head as I began to vigorously mix water and flour into a bowl for the pancakes, my lie resting like a bitter transgression against my tongue.

* * *

I leaned against a tree, watching Domine and Lilica pack up the tent. The tea I'd made had taken the edge off the pain a little. But applying pressure to my ankle still hurt. I knew I should have fashioned some sort of crutch to use, but it would have only given Domine a reason to delay our hike through the mountains. And I couldn't let him do that.

"Looks like we're all ready to head out, wood nymph." Domine cinched the pack closed and gave Lilica a smile before walking over to me. His eyes flashed with unease as he ran his hand up my arm. "We'll go slow today. And just let me know if you need to stop and rest your ankle."

"Don't worry. I'll be fine. I just have a slight limp." I attempted to causally brush away his concern and stepped onto the trail, taking a deep breath as a fresh wave of pain hit me, my resolve like a stubborn knife I could not retract. *I can do this.* We just needed to get over the mountain pass, then time wouldn't be so pressing.

Lilica's voice rose and fell through the trees as she chattered to Domine, and I tried to focus on anything other than the throbbing pain as we walked. The chill of the morning that rushed into my lungs like an icy kiss. The way the sunlight filtered tentatively through the branches above, showering the forest in iridescent mist. The crunch of the frozen ground beneath my feet. The stillness. But the meditative space I usually found while on the trail was nowhere this morning as my ankle screamed at me in protest, a relentless force that demanded my attention.

I must have stumbled over a rock, my gait grown uneven as I

favored my left foot, because suddenly I found myself crumpled on the ground, the sting of defeat slicing through me.

"Seren." Domine's face was tense as he hurried over and lifted me up.

"I'm fine."

I tried to pull myself out of his arms, but he held on to me, not letting go, his eyes sharp and boring into mine. "You're *not* fine."

With a sigh, I collapsed against him, allowing the pain to claim me as he led me over to a rock on the side of the trail. I sucked in a sharp breath as he lifted my pant leg and pulled down my sock. "Jesus Christ. Why didn't you tell me it was this bad?"

"Because!" I ground out, the sting of desperation coating my words. "I know we have to get through the mountains today. I *can't* have this slowing us down."

He looked up at me, shaking his head. "You're *not* walking on that foot."

I dug my fingers into the palm of my hand, staring up into the wispy blue of the sky. "No. We have to keep going."

"Maybe you can carry Mommy like you do with me?"

Lilica's question broke through the tension, and I turned to her with a wan smile as she crouched down beside me. "No, sweetie, I'm a bit too heavy for Domine to carry."

"Why is it that doctors always make the worst patients?" He shook his head with a sigh and reached out to stroke his finger down the length of my cheek, his eyes softening. "We're not going anywhere until that ankle of yours gets better. So stop being so damn stubborn."

*F*or the next two days, we camped out along the trail. Domine kept Lilica entertained with excursions around the forest, watching him set snares and helping him collect firewood. I spent most of my time lying restless in the tent with my foot elevated, alternating between herbal compresses and heat therapy. Flipping through the pages of the dream book Turk had given me, I drank in the detailed interpretations of the symbolism behind dreams. Trees represent strength. Fire transformation. Water unconscious emotion.

Every so often, I would limp out of the tent and stare up anxiously at the sky as if every cloud drifting by held an ominous threat of snow. And the hours unraveled in a slow, incessant hiss. A relentless reminder of the delicate balance we danced between the weather and our survival. And no matter how hard I tried to cling to the limited threads of choice and thought, we were at the ceaseless mercy of the mountains vacillating mood. We held no power here.

Lilica managed to keep the sharp edges of my apprehension at bay. She would bring me tea and tuck her blanket around me, playing doctor with her gentle touch, her wide gray eyes growing strangely lucid as her fingers swept over the bruising on my ankle.

"Are you all better yet, Mommy?"

"Almost, sweetie."

By the morning of the third day, the pain had eased, and the swelling had surprisingly dissipated. It was still early, and Lilica had not yet awoken from her tangle of sleep in the far corner of the tent.

"How does this feel?" The warmth of Domine's mouth moving down my leg sent goosebumps hurrying across my skin. Reaching for my foot, he trailed his lips across my ankle.

A shiver snaked its way through my limbs and a whisper spilled from me. "That feels good."

"Can you move your ankle for me?"

I rolled my foot in a slow circle, and he tipped his head up at me with a playful grin, morning light glancing across his face. "Good girl." Rising above me, he grasped my hands and gently pinned them beneath his, the weight of him delicious and encompassing. "I was afraid I was going to have to tie you up the other day." His words were a teasing growl against my ear, causing a deep ache of arousal to wash through me. "You put up quite a little fight."

I arched myself against him, my breath uneven. "Tie me up, huh?" A slow smile tugged at the corner of my mouth. "Maybe I would've liked that."

With a chuckle, he slowly released me, and I sat up, reluctantly untangling myself from the warmth of the sleeping bags as Lilica stirred in the corner, her eyes fluttering open.

"Good morning, love." I made my way across the tent and knelt beside her, running my hand down her cheek. "Are you ready to hit the trail again?"

* * *

Our pace was steady but slow as we climbed higher in elevation, the terrain growing rockier as the dense forest gave way to scattered pine. The sun hid behind a blanket of clouds as we walked, our breath curling around our faces like a veil as the bite of the cold pushed us forward, the sound of the river a constant rush below us.

"I'm not liking the look of those clouds. It feels like snow." Domine leaned against a tree, his jaw tense as he stared out across the mountains now obscured in a heavy shroud of gray.

"Finish up your lunch, hon," I said to Lilica as I tucked our bottles of water back into our pack and stood to stretch out my ankle. I was surprised at the speed with which the sprain had healed. The pain was now only a distant murmur. An occasional twinge. I had been expecting at least a week until I would be able to put full pressure on it again.

"Do you think we'll be able to get over most of the ridge today?" I made my way over to Domine and leaned against his back, slipping my arms around his waist. "My ankle isn't bothering me. We can pick up the pace a little."

"Forgive me if I have a hard time believing you." He turned to me with a faint smirk as his hands slid down the curve of my back.

"No. I'm feeling much better now." I leaned in and brushed my lips against his, the coarseness of his beard brushing against my skin. "I *promise.*"

"You do, huh?" He looked at me, his eyes drifting across my face as if gaging the validity of my words.

"To be honest. It's actually a little strange."

"What do you mean?"

I pulled back from him and looked down at my ankle. "It should have taken a lot longer to heal. Maybe it has something to do with the elevation, but the swelling is completely gone."

He cocked his head to the side, raising his eyebrows. "You think the elevation could do that?"

"Mommy, I'm all ready to go." Lilica appeared beside us, clutching her walking stick.

"Sweetie, where are your gloves?" I bent down to zip up her coat, pulling the hood tight over her head.

"I don't know."

"What do you mean you don't know? You had them on when we stopped for lunch."

She scrunched her nose and turned back toward the log we had been sitting by. "I took them off to go potty."

"Okay, let's go find them." With a sigh, I took her hand and trekked through the trees, trying to remember where we had stopped to use the bathroom. Every bush and pine looked the same as I impatiently scanned the forest floor.

"Maybe the fairies took them, Mommy? Maybe they needed them to be warm?"

I smiled and looked down at her as we continued our circle among the trees. "Well, I think the fairies have houses to stay warm in, hon."

From the corner of my eye, I saw a smudge of faded black. Bending down, I reached for the gloves laying beneath a bush as a flake of snow landed on the cloth. My heart stilled as I tilted my head up to see the sky now alive in a wash of white, dozens of snowflakes dancing soundlessly around me.

CHAPTER TWENTY-SIX

*T*he snow now fell fast and continuous, and I tried to stifle the rising dread inside me as our hurried footsteps crunched along the forest floor, silent determination pushing us forward.

"This could just be a small system moving through. As long as the snow doesn't get too deep, we should be fine." Domine glanced furtively toward the sky, his breath billowing out in clouds.

"Let's hope so." I adjusted the hip belt of the pack around my waist as the weight began to dig into my shoulders, the frigid air stinging my eyes and nose.

"It's so pretty, Mommy." Lilica sat perched atop Domine's shoulders, staring up into the sky with wide eyes. Snow landed on her lashes and melted against her lips. With a giggle, she opened her mouth, catching the flakes on her tongue.

"It is pretty, isn't it?" And it was. For a brief moment, all trepidation was muted as I looked around at the trees now dusted with white, the verdant green providing a stark contrast of delicate beauty as snow gently cloaked the woods like a blanket.

Washington used to have regular snowfall years ago. I had a few memories from my own childhood of snowballs tucked in the palm of my hand, my tracks leaving patterns across an expanse of white. But as the western climate continued to shift and winter temperatures warmed in the lower elevations, we were lucky to get a few hesitant flakes that tumbled occasionally from the sky.

We were now in a world Lilica had never seen before.

"When I was a little boy, I used to lie down in the snow and pretend I was surrounded by ice cream." Domine looked up at Lilica with a wide grin as a laugh trickled from her.

"Did you try to eat it?"

"Sometimes."

I smiled at the sudden image of him in the snow, dark strands of hair tangled beneath some woolen hat, his mind far away from the Orphanarium. All the loneliness of the sterile rooms and empty halls of his childhood. The hands that never touched him with tenderness. Perhaps that's what I admired so much about him. His resilience of spirit. His ability to construct beauty from nothing. The fierceness with which he could love, despite never knowing love as a child.

Reaching out, I slipped my arm through his and laced my fingers between his hold on Lilica, tethering us together as we walked steadily through the deepening silence of snow fall, with only the rush of the river running beside us.

* * *

I stood beside Lilica, rubbing her hands vigorously between mine, coaxing the warmth back into her fingers as darkness crept through the branches of the trees now laden and bowing against the burden of snowfall. The snow had not eased, and the vague hope I clung to as we trudged through the mountains had now been replaced with the faint tendrils of fear.

What are we going to do if the snow continues through the night?

"I'm so cold, Mommy."

"I know, sweetie." I pressed her tight against me, running my hands along her back. "Domine is trying to get a fire going for us."

Thick flakes coated Domine's hair and peppered his lashes as he leaned over the pile of wood, breathing life into the smoldering embers.

We crouched beside the flames as they began to curl upward

and embrace the wood, sending a plume of smoke into the air and spilling the relief of heat across our skin.

"It looks like there's still some dry wood past those trees over there." Domine pointed behind him as he stood and pulled the tent out of his pack. "I have a tarp in here somewhere. I'm going to collect as much as I can before it gets dark, and then we'll have some dry wood for tomorrow."

I looked up into the dusky gray of the sky, flakes spinning soundlessly around us. "I hope this snow stops soon."

Tension flashed across his face, eyes bearing the burden of his own unspoken fears. "Me too." Grabbing the tarp, he briskly strode through the trees and disappeared into the snowfall.

I turned toward Lilica. "Okay, sweetie. I want you to keep warm by the fire while I set up the tent, okay?" She nodded as I brushed the snow from her hat and retrieved a blanket from the pack beside me, wrapping it snugly around her.

My fingers were clumsy from the cold, and I struggled with the poles, fumbling to get them through the loops as the tight grip of worry gnawed at me. If the snow didn't stop, getting over the last stretch of mountains would be the least of our concerns. How would we stay warm? How would we feed ourselves from the last of our dwindling supplies?

"Mommy, I can't feel my feet." Lilica's voice rose through the press of my thoughts, and I dropped the pole in my hand, scrambling over to where she sat hunched by the fire.

"Let me take a look, hon." I untied her boots and peeled off the three layers of socks I had insisted she put on that morning. An angry bloom of red traveled up her toes and skirted the edges of her heel. Sucking in a deep breath, I held her feet up to the fire, my fingers gently massaging the circulation back as I tried to conceal the concern in my voice. "Okay, let's warm up these cold little toes of yours, sweetie."

Unfolding the cooking platform over the fire, I grabbed a pan from the pack and filled it with water, placing it over the flames. I pulled her into my lap and draped the blanket around her feet as I waited for the water to warm up. "Do your toes hurt, Lili?"

"No. They just tingle now."

I placed a kiss against her forehead, my gut clenching at the thought of how close she had come to frostbite. Once again, that fear rose inside me like a hiss in the darkness, heavy and consuming.

How am I going to keep her safe?

Domine appeared through the snow, his arms weighed down with wood. Placing the pile beside the fire, he covered it with the tarp before turning to us. "I'm going to grab one more load, okay?"

I nodded blankly as I lifted the pan from the fire and placed it beside Lilica, slowly guiding her feet into the water.

"Is she okay?" He crouched beside me, his face pinched with worry.

"She just has some frostnip." I turned to him, my voice a harsh whisper against his ear. "But it's getting too cold for her, Domine."

"I know." He clenched his jaw, his eyes drifting up to the sky. "We need to find a way to keep the tent warm tonight."

"And how are we going to do that?" I ran my hands down Lilica's arms, wrapping the blanket snugly around her.

"I think I have an idea." Standing, he adjusted the hat on his head, now coated in snow, and began placing large rocks into the fire.

Lilica stirred in my arms. "My feet feel better, Mommy."

"Oh, good, hon." Bending down, I pulled her feet from the water, the tendrils of relief winding through me as I noticed they were now a healthy shade of pink. "Let's get you toweled off and put some dry socks on."

Glancing over, I watched Domine continue to place rocks into the growing bed of coals beneath the fire. "What are you doing?"

He looked up with a smile, the softness in his eyes momentarily soothing back the concern that skirted the edge of my thoughts. "You'll see."

* * *

*W*ith Lilica bundled up in a blanket beside the fire and the remnants of dinner now packed up and stored away, I stared up at the dizzying flakes of snow that still fell around us, coating our clothes and stinging our skin. Domine had finished setting up the tent and was now lugging large stones through the opening.

"Looks like you have some big plans for those rocks?"

He poked his head out of the tent, shooting me a wink. "I do."

"Maybe he's going to build a fire inside the tent, Mommy."

I smiled at her. "That wouldn't be safe, sweetie. All that smoke would hurt our lungs."

Domine returned to the fire and fishing out a pair of metal tongs from our pack, began to retrieve the rocks he had placed in the coals, loading them into the cooking pan.

I looked at Lilica with a grin, my eyes wide and playful. "Oh no. Do you think he's going to make us eat those?"

She giggled and burrowed into my lap, her gloved hands twining through my hair. "You're silly, Mommy."

Leaning down, I nuzzled my nose against hers, generating another round of giggles, the sound of her laughter colliding with the snowfall. And for a moment, there was a fleeting sense of peace that quieted the fear pressing against me. The feel of her body curled around mine, the snow tumbling down, the fire casting wavering shadows across our skin. There was a beauty that danced with the harshness of the land, and I wondered if the wolf was out there somewhere, cloaked in a curtain of snow, watching us.

This time, the thought left me with a strange feeling of solace. As if the wildness of his presence could somehow keep us safe.

"Okay, it's ready."

Domine's voice cut through my thoughts, and I stood, lifting Lilica into my arms. "Let's go see what he made for us," I whispered as I walked toward the tent.

A tentative warmth enfolded me as we entered. Domine had set up a circular base of rocks, the stones he had pulled from the fire now resting in the center. Lilica wiggled out of my arms and ran over to them.

"Careful, hon. Don't touch the ones in the middle, okay?" I

crouched beside her as she carefully held her hands out toward the stones.

"Stones can retain heat for up to seven hours, and the double insulated nylon will help keep the warmth from escaping." He ran his hand along the wall of the tent. "So we should stay relatively warm tonight."

I stood and draped my arms around his shoulders, breathing in the cold crisp scent of snow that lingered on his jacket. "Where did you come up with this idea?"

He shrugged, but a slow smile tugged at the corners of his mouth. "Just a little trick I heard about from a hiker a few years ago."

"Mommy, can I sleep in the middle tonight?"

"Of course, sweetie."

The wind picked up outside, a mournful howl that slithered across the walls and battered the sides of the tent as we unrolled our sleeping bags and nestled Lilica between us. My hands traced circular patterns across her back, watching as her eyelids fluttered and then closed, releasing herself to sleep.

"It's all going to be okay, Seren."

I glanced up, his eyes catching mine in the dim of Lilica's nightlight, washing prisms of color across his face.

"Whatever happens. It's going to be okay."

With a nod, I reached over and wound my fingers through his. Caught in the conviction of his words and now safely tucked away from the cold, I closed my eyes with a sigh, allowing myself to believe him as I burrowed into the sleeping bag and hoped the snow would stop soon.

CHAPTER TWENTY-SEVEN

*M*orning light shifted through the walls of the tent, and I rose from the soft, sleepy warmth of Domine and the tangle of Lilica's limbs.

The stones had managed to keep the cold at bay, and my breath did not linger in the air as I bent to put my shoes on, praying for a clear sky as I quietly unzipped the tent flap.

"Shit." My voice billowed out in a frantic hiss as snow tumbled through the opening, coating my legs, and spilling out onto the floor.

"What is it?" Domine sat up, his voice groggy and eyes growing wide as he took in the snow now covering the entrance to the tent. Thick flakes still swirled down from the sky, slivers of icy cold now drifting into the tent.

Thrusting my hands into the snow, I quickly tried to shovel it back outside before we lost heat. A sinking feeling settled in my gut as I took in the landscape before me. A foreign world of undulating white. The only thing I recognized was the corner of the tarp Domine had used to cover the wood, now peeking out from beneath a drift.

Domine crouched beside me and began scooping up large handfuls of snow until we had managed to remove most of it and zipped the tent door closed. Puddles of water now seeped across the floor, soaking our shoes and running a slow path toward our bedding.

Grabbing a towel from our pack, I bent down to wipe at the floor. "We're not going anywhere, are we?" My question was a deflated whisper that already knew the answer. The snow hadn't stopped. We were stuck here.

He furrowed his brow, frustration etched across the planes of his face as he ran a hand through his tangled hair. "No. It looks like we're not."

"What are we going to do?" My words trembled against my lips as I stared at Lilica, still fast asleep within her sleeping bag.

He looked at me with heavy eyes, his usual calm confidence replaced with the weight of uncertainty. "I don't know."

* * *

The sound of shoveling drifted from outside the tent as I wrapped Lilica's boots with sections of tarp Domine had cut out, securing them in place with twine.

"There you go. This should keep your feet warm and dry, sweetie."

"Can I go play in the snow now?"

"Almost." I buttoned up her coat and helped her into her gloves, positioning the hat over her ears. "Okay, now you're all ready."

Unzipping the tent door, I peeked outside. Domine had managed to clear a narrow path to the firepit, which he was now in the process of uncovering with the entrenching shovel.

"Wow." Lilica stared out into the valley of snow, her feet crunching over the carved path that rose and banked her waist. "There's so much snow, Mommy!" Her gleeful voice cut through the steady rush of the river, the pull of her enthusiasm plucking back the trepidation that had gripped me all morning.

"Sweetie, I'm going to help Domine with the shoveling. You can go play. Just stay where I can see you."

Her lips turned down into a pout as she stared up at me with wide eyes. "But I want to play in the snow with you, Mommy."

"It's okay. You two go have some fun," Domine called out from where he knelt beside the fire pit.

"Are you sure?"

He nodded and stood up, plunging the shovel into the pile of snow beside him. "Yeah. I'm almost done, anyway."

Ice crystals hovered in the air, clinging to our clothes and dancing with our breath as I tamped down a path beyond the firepit and motioned for Lilica to follow. "Okay then, let's go make a snowman."

"Can it be a snow lady?"

"Of course." With a smile, I scooped up a handful of powder and packed it into a ball before handing it to her. "If you roll this in the snow, it will grow bigger."

She nodded and crouched down, her mittened hands coaxing the ball across the snow as I glanced to where Domine now stood beside the cleared firepit with the portable ax, cutting saplings into long poles.

"What are you doing with those?"

"I'm going to make a shelter for the fire." He looked over at me as flakes of snow dusted his jacket and hair, a faint smile resting on his lips. His unwavering composure was a rush of relief. A lifeline I clung to. He was winter and earth. A calm, solid presence propping up the world around us and momentarily pushing back the worries that crowded my mind.

"Mommy, look! I made the biggest snowball."

Lilica's voice pulled me from my thoughts, and I turned to examine the work she proudly displayed in front of me, the flush of her cheeks bright against the white of the snow.

Flakes now fell heavy around us as we finished our creation, gathering sticks and rocks found beneath the base of trees. Fallen pinecones holding next year's growth. There was something deeply grounding in this activity, and it stole away my apprehension as I found solace through the lens of Lilica's eyes. An endless world of snow and imagination.

"She's pretty. I'm going to name her Buttercup." She stood on tiptoes, letting out a giggle as she reached up to place evergreen branches on the top of the head, tendrils of green like flowing hair.

"Buttercup, huh?" Domine strolled up to us, a lightness playing in the corners of his eyes. "I think that's the best snow lady I've ever seen." He swooped Lilica up into his arms, eliciting another giggle from her as she grasped his shoulders. "You hungry, wood nymph? I got a nice warm fire and some breakfast waiting for you."

I followed them back to the firepit, ducking under the shelter Domine had erected.

"This is nice." I took off my gloves and settled myself on one of the upturned logs that stood beside the fire, holding my hands out to the crackling flames. "It's kinda cozy."

"Yeah, it kinda is, isn't it?" He shot me a crooked grin as he dished out some oatmeal for Lilica, pointing up at the pine boughs above us. "I can swap these out if they get too dry, but it'll give us some cover without keeping the smoke in."

I bit my lip and stared out into the snowfall, watching as the blanket of gray grew denser, closing in around us. We were trapped within the mountains unrelenting hold, and no amount of hope could sway the reality that now stood before us.

"So, I've been thinking." Domine settled beside me and handed me a bowl of oatmeal, the warmth curling around my fingers. "What if we stayed?" His voice came out low as he bent close to my ear.

My heart clenched as I turned to him, the finality of his words sending the last of our plans sinking like rocks beneath water. "But how are we going to survive the winter up here? You said it was too risky."

"Well, I could build us a shelter."

"What are you talking about? You don't have any tools to do that."

"I have a hatchet. That's all I really need. I know the basics of primitive building. I think I read every book about it Turk had in his cabin. And we have a river close by. Snares for trapping." He leaned in closer to me, his eyes wide and full of conviction. "We *can* make this work."

I looked at Lilica, who sat across the fire quietly eating her oatmeal, unaware of our hushed conversation that would once again dismantle the trajectory of her world. "We don't have any other options, do we?"

"Not really. No." He looked out into the dense thicket of trees now shrouded in white, his brow furrowing. "The snow has completely buried the trail. Even turning back to lower elevation would be tricky right now."

A sigh traveled through me, and I set the bowl down next to the fire, wrapping my arms around myself. "What are we going to tell Lilica?" My voice spilled out like fog, a frozen whisper that collided with the sky, giving weight to my thoughts.

He reached out to tuck away a strand of hair that had escaped from my hat, his hand sweeping across my cheek. "Tell her I'm finally going to build that house I promised you guys."

I rested my head on his shoulder, entwining my fingers through his as Lilica smiled at us through a mouthful of oatmeal from across the fire, her eyes vibrant and unaware of the potential new dangers that now lurked beside us.

There was the cold, and then there was the bigger concern that rose within me like a sharp hiss every time I opened our pack. What if the snares didn't catch enough? How were we going to survive through the winter on what little food we had left?

* * *

"We're not going to live in the Canada town?" Lilica scrunched up her nose as I helped her out of her coat and mittens and set them by the warming rocks Domine had placed inside the tent.

"We are. But we have to wait until the snow melts. So, we're going to be staying here until spring."

"And Domine's building us a house?"

I pulled out the brush from our pack and motioned for her to sit beside me. "That's the plan." She settled in my lap and leaned her head back as I ran the brush through her knotted hair. "What do you think about all that, sweetie?"

"Can I have my own room?"

"Well, I don't know exactly what kind of house he'll be able to build for us out here, but maybe?"

I stopped brushing and turned her around to face me. "Listen, hon. I know there have been *a lot* of changes in your life lately. A lot of things that you don't fully understand." I reached up to stroke her cheek. "Things that one day I will be able to explain better to you. But I don't want you to hide away any feelings you have right now, okay? I want you to know you can talk to me about anything."

"I know, Mommy." She slithered off my lap and grabbed the book of fairy tales that lay by her sleeping bag, her fingers flipping through the pages. She then looked up, her eyes shifting around the tent as if her thoughts had grown too large for her to hold. "Will I never see my daddy again?"

I sucked in a breath, my heart fumbling for a comforting truth, for words she would be able to carry. "When you are older, Lili, you can make the choice to see him again." Moving close to where she sat, I took her hand in mine. "He will always be your daddy, no matter what. And he will always love you. I want you to know that."

"Okay." She smiled up at me, her innocence like a warm blanket I wanted to curl around, a soft barrier from the clawing thoughts and discomforting questions that always lingered in the back of my mind.

Would Trendon ever stop looking for her? Looking for us?

I knew I could never villainize him. He was just a man lost within the jaws of the Grid, his loyalty the only sense of comfort he had. And there was a part of me that felt a deep sorrow for him. For his loneliness. His anger. His disconnection.

I remember reading once about cognitive dissonance. How a mind under stress will grasp desperately to a belief system, protecting it at all costs. Life was not a fairytale of good versus evil. We were all imperfect creatures clinging to the threads of survival. Thrust into a society that had quietly and systematically stripped us of our ability to think for ourselves. Trading our empathy for collective cohesion. Handing over freedom for communal acceptance. And the fear that had followed me through these mountains like a whisper against my neck was now replaced with a sudden and quiet resolve. A strength that flickered and grew inside me, encompassing us both.

I wasn't running anymore. I was forging a new path for my daughter.

CHAPTER TWENTY-EIGHT

$\mathcal{W}$ e had now cleared a pathway from our tent to the river. Crouching beside the rocks, I leaned forward to dip our thermos into the water that rushed past, swollen and churning from two days of continuous snowfall.

The cold had become a constant presence that stripped everything else down. Food. Water. Warmth. These were the things that now consumed me. Basic primal instincts that stole away all excess thought, the hours bleeding into a series of tasks to perform. Gather wood. Keep the fire going. Check the snares.

And I wondered, would it be enough? Would we be able to make it through the winter out here?

"Be careful, hon." I glanced to where Lilica stood next to me, her boots kicking at the snow. "It's a bit slippery."

"What's that smoke, Mommy?"

Capping the bottle, I turned in the direction of her pointed hand. Wisps of steam curled upward from an outcropping of rocks that hugged the shoreline.

"That's not smoke, sweetie." I stood, a swell of excitement bubbling within me as I made my way cautiously toward the small rock pool. "Stay right where you are, okay?"

The smell of sulfur hit me as I approached. A steady stream of hot water flowed through an opening in the rocks, trickling into a shallow pool below, the overflow eddying past me and merging with the river. Kneeling down, I slipped off my glove and slowly submerged my hand into the water. A delicious warmth enveloped me, the heat slithering through the chill on my skin and settling deep into my bones.

"What is it, Mommy?"

"It's a hot spring, Lili." With a smile, I stood and motioned for her to come closer, reaching out my arms to help her across the snow-covered rocks. Bending down, I removed her glove and dipped her hand in the water. Her eyes grew wide, and she drew back in confusion. "It's okay, love. The water is warm."

Tentatively, she slid her hand back in, her fingers swirling against the faint current, and a wide smile stretched across her face. "It's like a bath."

"Yes, it is, sweetie." Giddy laughter rushed to the surface as I wrapped my arm around her. "It's exactly like a bath."

* * *

"Can you believe that? This changes *everything*." My words spilled breathlessly out into the cold air as Domine stacked split logs into a pile.

He looked at me with a smile, sweeping the hair out of his eyes. "You sure are excited about that hot spring."

"I am. Yes. This means we won't have to worry about freezing this winter." I stepped closer to him and ran my hand down his chest. "And do you know how long it's been since I've had a proper bath? Since any of us have?"

Even back at the cabin, the effort it took to carry pails of heated water into the tub had been a laborious endeavor, which meant Lilica and I often shared our infrequent baths. We had now miraculously stumbled upon a luxury I had never imagined I would find, and I couldn't help but feel like it was a sign from some ever-present force. A gentle hand soothing back my worries. A whisper of affirmation.

Maybe we would be okay.

"Mmm…" Domine slid his hands beneath my coat, the chill of his fingers meeting the warmth of my skin. "Well, all I smell on you is the forest." His lips hovered against my ear, causing goosebumps to travel down my neck. "And I find that *very* alluring."

"That's because you're half-feral." A laugh tumbled from me as I pulled away from his teasing caress and looked over at Lilica, who sat beside the fire finishing her lunch, her steady gaze fixed on us.

With a grin, he picked up his ax and swung it into the log next to him. "I thought that's what you liked about me."

"Can I help?" Lilica ran over to Domine, coming precariously close to the swing of his ax, and I sucked in a hiss of breath, yanking her back.

"*Careful*, Lili."

"But I want to help build the house." Her face scrunched into a pout as she looked up at me, a flash of defiance in her eyes.

"Of course you can, wood nymph." He set down the ax and shot her a warm smile, motioning toward the pile of logs. "You can separate the shorter pieces from the longer ones. We'll use these for the base of the structure."

She bounded toward the pile and began to sort enthusiastically through the wood, her voice rising between the swing of Domine's ax as she called out questions in rapid fire.

"Where's the door going to go?"

"Will there be a window?"

"Mommy said you can build me my own room."

* * *

Steam rose around us, obscuring the landscape in a white haze as I dipped the washcloth into the water and ran it down Lilica's back. The last of the day's light crept through the trees, sending shadows glinting across the rock ledge I sat on, my feet submerged in the soothing warmth of the shallow spring.

"Mommy, are you going to get in?"

Bending her head back, I cupped my hand into the water, letting it trickle through her hair. "You have to get into bed soon, but I might go in later tonight."

"You should. It feels *really* good." She grinned up at me, droplets of water resting against her eyelashes, and I cataloged this moment in my mind. Like the photographic stills of my memory, I captured the snow-covered trees, the smile of my daughter submerged in water, the chill of the air colliding with the warmth of the spring. Just the two of us beneath a wild winter sky.

"You ready to get out, love?" I leaned over and grabbed the blanket I had brought with us, holding it out for her.

She rose from the water, skin pink and glowing. "But I didn't wash yet."

I wrapped the blanket around her. "Oh, we can't use soap in here, hon."

"Why not?"

"Well, it's not good for the fishies. This water flows back into the river, so we'll still have to do sponge baths by the fire. This is more like a little treat." Slipping my boots on, I lifted her up, her body a tiny little furnace in my arms as I carried her back to the tent, my footsteps crunching along the snow-packed trail.

Domine had already placed the warming rocks inside the tent when we entered, and I helped Lilica into the sleeping bag, her eyes growing drowsy as I smoothed back her hair.

"Tell me a story, Mommy."

"What kind of story do you want to hear?"

"The story about the lady of the lake."

"The lady of Llyn y Fan Fach?"

"Yes. That one."

With a smile, I settled beside her. Lying my head in the crook of my arm, I gathered her body against mine as my mind drifted back to the Welsh folktale of my childhood. Bedtime stories spoken softly in dark rooms. Words richly woven together through the generations of women who had come before us. Their blood forever entwined with ours. "Once upon a time, there was a woman who lived between worlds. She was a healer and could see into the future."

"And she lived in a lake."

"She did. Until one day she met a man, and they fell in love. And with that love, they had three sons."

"But she couldn't stay?" Lilica wound her finger through a strand of my hair, the nightlight casting patterns across our skin.

"That's right. One day, she knew it was her time to go back to the water. But she returned once more to teach her sons how to be healers."

"And they learned how to heal with herbs like you, Mommy."

"Yes, they did."

"They learned the magic from the earth."

My eyes fluttered closed, and images danced between the darkness. Color and movement like the wings of a butterfly. An endless lucidity I could almost reach out and touch. "Yes, I suppose it is like magic."

I must have dozed off, because the feel of Domine's hand running down my back stirred me, and I opened my eyes.

"Seren. Are you awake?"

His voice rested soft against my ear, and untangling myself from Lilica's sleeping form, I rolled over to see him crouched beside me. "I am now."

"I have a little surprise for you," he whispered as he reached out to run his fingers down my cheek, a small smile tugging at his lips. "But if you're too tired, I'll let you go back to sleep."

I sat up and stretched out my limbs, curiosity pulling at me. "What kind of surprise?"

"Come outside, and I'll show you."

Slipping on my boots, I followed him quietly out of the tent. The sky had loosened its hold, and a thin sliver of moon peeked through the clouds, casting pale blue light across the snow. With a smile, I looked down at the path that wound to the river. "What's all this about?"

He had placed our four solar powered collapsible lanterns along the trail leading to the spring, flickering light illuminating the rock ledges.

"I thought you would enjoy a nice soak." His hand fell to the small of my back as he led me down the path. When we got to the water, I stopped and turned toward the tent. "It's okay." His words were a reassuring whisper beside me. "We can see from here in case she wakes up. That's why I put out the lanterns."

I looked back at him and took in the blanket and candles placed around the pool, a wide smile stretching across my face. "This is romantic."

"I figured it's been a while since I've wooed you."

I wrapped my arms around his neck, breathing in the scent of him as I pressed my lips against his. "You don't have to woo me, you know."

"But I want to." He crept his hands around my waist, fingers inching beneath my jacket. "Take your clothes off and get in the water." His voice grew soft and seductive against my ear, and a ripple of arousal washed over me.

The chill of the air sent goosebumps racing across my skin as I shed my clothes and scrambled across the frozen rocks, slipping into the pool of water. A shuddered moan spilled from my lips as I submerged myself, feeling the heat permeate through me like a fervent caress, reaching deep into my muscles. "Oh, my God, this feels *so* good."

He sat on the rock ledge, rolled up his pants and dipped his feet into the water, leaning me against his legs. His hands slid up my back, fingers kneading the knots along my shoulders and causing another moan to tumble from me. "Okay, I take it back."

"Take what back?" He continued his slow administrations along my shoulders and down to the ridge of tightness that lay between them.

"You can woo me anytime."

He chuckled and bent his head close to mine, his lips brushing across my cheek. "Then I will."

I closed my eyes and allowed myself to sink into the feel of his hands and the warmth of the water that curled around me, washing away all the tension I'd been carrying with me since we left the cabin. The long days on the trail. The ghost of the Grid following me like a pacing animal. Relentless question that never stopped whispering in my ear.

Domine paused for a moment, and I heard the rustling of something in his jacket. Opening my eyes, I watched him place a small glass jar and a pipe on the rocks beside me. "Is that the medicine Turk gave us?"

"It is." A slow smile crept to the corners of his mouth. "I thought you'd might like to try some tonight."

"I would."

He opened the jar, inserted a small bud in the pipe, and handed it to me. He motioned for me to hold it to my lips as he picked up one of the candles beside him. "Turk's medicine is pretty strong, so you only need to take one inhale." The flame flickered in the darkness, the dancing light hovering over the base of the pipe as I placed my lips around the rim. "Are you ready?"

I nodded, locking eyes with him as I drew the smoke in. The sharp sting hit my lungs, and a hacking cough erupted. "Jesus Christ." I gasped, wiping tears from my eyes.

"Told you it was strong." A plume of smoke slowly drifted from his mouth as he grinned.

"Well, you seem to be doing *just* fine."

He leaned me back against his legs once more, his hands working through the last of my knots. "I've had some time to acclimate to Turk's strain."

As he continued to massage me, my head began to feel light and fuzzy. The steam rising from the water took on form like white brushstrokes against the canvas of night, ethereal shapes that collided with the sky. I let out a long sigh as the medicine crept through my body, rinsing away the last lingering discomfort and replacing it with a giddy euphoria that caused my heart to thrum within my chest.

I ran my hand up Domine's leg, tugging on his jeans. "It feels so amazing in here. You need to come in with me."

"You sure?" He cocked his head toward the tent where the lanterns illuminated the opening. "I was going to stay out in case Lilica wakes up."

"She's conked. I doubt she'll be getting up anytime soon." I pulled him toward me, inching his legs closer to the water with a teasing smile. "Come in with me."

He shrugged off his coat and pulled his shirt over his head, muscle rippling beneath skin as he bent to remove his pants. I realized since that night in his cabin, I had only been with him in darkness or with our limbs tangled around clothing. This was the first time I was able to take him in fully against the glow of candlelight. He reminded me of the river. Sculpted rocks against the powerful rush of something wild and breathtaking.

"You are so beautiful." My voice came out in a reverent whisper as he slid into the water beside me.

"Hmm… sounds like the medicine's kicking in." He shot me a playful smile and wrapped his arms around me, pressing his lips against the top of my head.

"No, you've always been beautiful to me." I swirled my hand through the pool, watching the light from the candles dance across the surface. "Like something magical." I looked up at him, bursting with a feeling I tried to find words for. A gratitude that reached beyond myself. "Like a unicorn." I slid myself against him and wrapped my legs around his waist, my hands gliding down the plane of his back, which felt like silk against my fingers. "You're my unicorn, Dom. And your skin… it's so soft. How did your skin get so soft?"

A chuckle rose from within his chest, the deep rumble vibrating against mine. "I think that's the sulfur water. It makes everything feel slippery."

"Oh, right. I knew that." A giggle tumbled out, the sound bathing me in a rush of exhilaration as I wrapped myself tighter around him. I was buoyant in a current of warmth that contrasted the chill of the air, every sensation deliciously heightened as I tilted my head up, watching the glimmer of stars cascading across the night sky. I couldn't remember the last time I felt so alive. So free. So present within my body.

"You're magic to me, too." Domine wound his fingers into my hair and gently tipped my head down to meet his gaze.

Tears welled up, and I bit my lip, trying to hold back the abrupt flood of emotion that rose to the surface and threatened to silence the current of elation inside me. "Do you know how empty I was when we first met?" I placed my hands on his chest, feeling the strident drum of his heart beneath my palm. "I had lost my entire family. Everybody. And it was you who reminded me how to breathe again. It was you who gave me hope. And then you left."

"Seren." His hands slid up my back, eyes flashing with intensity. "You know I wanted nothing more than for you to leave with me."

I took a deep breath, realizing that beneath all the ache and longing I had carried for him all those years, there was also a deep visceral pain I'd never truly looked at.

I had never forgiven him for leaving.

"The thing is, you didn't have to leave. You *chose* to leave. There were three things in my life that were important to me. Only three things, Domine. You. My career. And having a family. I had already accepted a life with you, knowing you didn't want kids." A slow tear crept down my cheek, staining my skin with the permanence of my words. "But then you asked me to give up my clinic as well. Do you know how much that choice killed me inside?"

"I know. And I'm sorry." He shook his head as he pulled me tight against him. "That has always been my biggest regret, one I've paid for *every day* for ten years. I should have never asked you to sacrifice *anything* for me. It was selfish." He cupped my head in his hands, his eyes trembling with the mirror of my own tears. "But I was suffocating in that place. I was dying inside. You knew that." His thumb traced a line across my jaw, coming to rest on my lips. "I couldn't do it anymore. And I wouldn't have been any good to you if I had stayed."

I jerked away from him and grasped the ledge of the rock wall, my fingers digging into the stone. "I guess I just hoped you would have been able to put down your anger toward the Grid and just be with *me*. I know what happened with your parents was terrible, but I wanted us to be able to grow something beautiful from the wreckage. But you couldn't do that. Not even when you left, and I was *still* coming to you like a fool who thought we could make things work."

"You weren't a fool."

I stared up into the spinning vastness of the sky, the stars now obscured by clouds like far away stories I could never touch. "But I was. I thought our love was strong enough."

"Love is only strong when we are strong enough to carry it. And I wasn't strong." He moved to me, his arms encircling my waist from behind, hand spread across my chest as his voice trembled against my ear. "I was angry, and I got lost in the dark."

"We both did, didn't we?" I released a shaky breath and sank into him, feeling the last bit of our tangled past shift and rearrange itself. "Maybe we both had to get lost before we found each other again."

"Maybe."

I turned to him, resting my forehead against his. "I don't know where all that just came from."

"I do. This medicine can be a truth serum."

I sank deeper into the water, pulling him down with me. "Apparently so."

"Seren." His voice grew low and concentrated as he locked eyes with me, reaching up to sweep away a strand of my hair. "I love you."

My breath caught in my chest. He had never put that emotion into words before. I knew it was there. Our love had always been loud enough to take up the space around us. An act that didn't need language. An unspoken agreement of a truth we never needed to define. But hearing those words broke open something within me, something that gave credence to the conviction in his eyes. A vow that felt deeply sacred.

I found his mouth, my reply a whisper against his lips. "And I love *you*."

His eyes darted over to the tent for a moment before pulling me into a searing kiss that sent my pulse racing, obliterating all thought. I slid my legs around him, feeling him stir against me, and I teased myself along the base of him, reveling in the delicious sensation of his skin and the warm water. The soft buzz that wound its way through my body. My mouth lost in his.

A consuming ache took hold of me, and I curled deeper into him, running my hands along his back, tracing his skin, drinking in the heat between us as my voice slipped out in a broken sigh. "I want all of you, Dom."

Lifting my hips, he spun me around and pressed my back to his chest. His fingers slid down past my stomach and dipped into my center, while his other hand ran a slow pattern across my breasts. His touch was electricity surging through me, every sensation magnified as his lips brushed against my ear. "You *have* all of me."

I reached back to grip his hair, his name tumbling out in a slow moan as I felt the press of him from behind. With my limbs now buoyant, he angled my hips upward and slowly drew himself inside me. Pleasure surged within as he tipped my head back and found my mouth, catching the cry that rushed out. Closing my eyes, I lost myself to the rush of him as he filled me, his fingers curled against my sex, lips drinking mine, every inch of me alive, weightless, and on fire.

Snow began to fall lightly around us, kissing our skin with its slivers of ice, and the swiftness of my release claimed me, an expansive current of euphoria that left me undone and trembling in his hold.

With a groan, he slid out of me, and the glimmer of candlelight caught his eyes as he turned me around to face him. Our labored breath rose above us like smoke as he held me against him for a moment, and then, like a sigh that had been waiting for the urgency of air, he wrapped my legs around his waist and slid into me once more. His movements were slow but fervent, every thrust becoming a wave of renewed pleasure that bloomed and grew until I could no longer contain it. And then, with a strangled cry, the bright flash of another orgasm exploded within as he spilled himself deep into me.

"My God. *Seren.*" His eyes were wide and full of tears as he reached out to cup my face in his hands, his entire body trembling with mine as our release expanded and collided, and I could no longer tell if I was feeling his or my own. Seemingly endless and untethered, we rode the wave together until at last it slowed and softened, leaving us gasping upon the shore of our bodies.

"Did you feel that?" His voice shook as he held me against his chest, his heart a wild drumbeat in my ear.

I clung to him, lost in the aftermath of what we had just shared. In the intensity of our release. In the beautiful unraveling beneath a snowy winter sky.

"Yes. I felt that."

CHAPTER TWENTY-NINE

$\mathcal{I}$t took us two weeks to finish building the cabin. The hours of daylight had now grown short, and the snow fell continuously, casting a gray pallor across the forest as we worked. Days were spent cutting notches into logs until our hands grew numb and we were forced to retreat to the warmth of the fire. Hours of digging through snow and scouring the trees for moss we could use for chinking the cracks in the wood. And then came the laborious process of carting stones from the river for the fireplace and plastering them together with a thick mixture of water and earth.

The work drained every inch of energy from me. The repetition of lifting and carrying, heaving and lugging consumed our days. But it was the kind of labor that filled me with a sense of empowerment as I worked side by side with Domine, watching the shelter slowly take form. It felt deeply rewarding to build something with my own hands, to immerse myself in the sweat and toil of self-sufficiency. It was a skill no one could take from you, and it helped ease the feeling of helplessness that surrounded the unforgiving beauty of the mountains.

Lilica kept herself amused by building her own tiny world out of sticks, moss, and rocks. Houses that grew into towns beside us, her chatter filling up the silence.

Nights left my arms and back aching from the strain of the day's labor, and very often, I went to bed with the twinge of hunger clawing at me. Domine had only managed to catch a few squirrels in his snares so far, and if there were fish still in the river, we could not find them. I carefully rationed what we had left, watching our food pack grow lighter by the day.

"Seren, you need to eat more than that." Domine sat by the fire beside me, a worried look etched across his face as he watched me hand the rest of my beans and rice to Lilica.

"It's fine. I'm not that hungry." I averted my eyes from him and bent to throw another log onto the fire. "She needs it more than I do."

He passed me his plate. "Please, eat some more."

I reluctantly took it from him. I knew Domine had noticed the weight I'd been losing. My pants no longer fit, and I had now resorted to using twine to cinch them up.

"Tomorrow we'll move everything into the shelter, and then I'll finally have time to do some hunting with the crossbow." He ran his hand in slow circles along my back. "I'll find us some food. I promise."

I shot him a wan smile and settled against his shoulder, fatigue pulling at my limbs. It would be nice to finally be able to move out of the tent. Though the stones Domine placed over the fire before bed helped keep the temperature inside from dipping below freezing, and the soaks in the hot spring kept the constant chill at bay. It had grown considerably colder, and I was looking forward to the relief of a warm shelter and the luxury of being able to cook inside.

Lilica crawled onto my lap, and I reached out to dust away the flakes of snow that had fallen onto her hood. "Are you excited about our big move tomorrow?"

"Yes, Mommy. I get my very own room."

"You do, love." I noticed her eyes beginning to droop as I placed a kiss on her forehead.

"Let's get this sleepy wood nymph into bed," Domine whispered as he lifted her from my arms and carried her into the tent.

With a sigh, I leaned back against the log I had helped carve out into a chair the other day, following the arc of the flames as they curled and twisted in a dance against the darkness. A crunching sound, like that of light footfalls on snow, drew my attention away from the fire, and I reached for the flashlight beside me. Clicking it on, I watched as the beam swept a wide arc through the trees, and my breath stilled as almond-shaped eyes met mine.

A tense silence penetrated the air around us as I stared back at the wolf, its familiar gray markings catching the light from the fire. The potency of its gaze was a powerful force that took hold of me. Its presence a wild and expansive song that beat against the cage of my chest. And then it was no more than a flickering shadow against the snow as it turned and disappeared once more into the darkness.

"*D*o you have everything, love?" I shouldered the heavy pack full of our cooking supplies and ducked out of the tent, holding the flap open for Lilica.

"Yep, Mommy." She ran past me with her backpack half unzipped, scattering toys behind her.

"Well, she's sure excited," Domine chuckled as he bent to retrieve the fallen toys along the path, our footsteps crunching in the packed snow as we followed her brisk pace to the shelter.

It had stopped snowing sometime during the night, and wisps of clouds hovered against the faintness of a blue morning sky. It had been over two weeks since I'd seen the sun, and everything seemed to glitter as I tilted my head upward, allowing the pale warmth to touch my skin.

The aroma of cedar and pine hit me as I opened the log door held together by strips of rope knotted around pegs of wood, creating a perfect hinge that allowed for easy entrance. Stepping inside, I surveyed the space that would now be our home for the winter. The only light came from the chimney, a thin stream that spilled down onto the hearth we had made from river rock, casting prisms across the earthen floor.

The structure was simple. A small table and chairs built from the base of old tree stumps sat in the corner by the fireplace, and shelving was cut into the walls, giving us a place to store our supplies. On the other end was a space for our bedding, with fresh pine boughs layered over the floor beside a small enclosure, a room just big enough for Lilica.

"Home sweet home." Domine shot me a grin as he placed our blanket and sleeping bags beside our makeshift bed and turned to me. "And the skies are clear. I couldn't have asked for a better day to head out into the woods." He reached for his pack beside the bed and unlatched his crossbow. Slinging it over his shoulder, he leaned in close and placed a soft kiss on my cheek. "You guys get settled in. I'll be back in a few hours."

"Can I go with you?" Lilica peeked her head out from behind the blanket hung across the entrance to her room.

"Why don't you stay here and help your mom unpack?" He bent down and ruffled her hair. "And when I get back, I'll cook us up a delicious stew. How does that sound?"

She nodded, watching as he opened the door with a smile and stepped out into the snow.

* * *

*Ow*armth spread through the shelter, the fire I started in the hearth now bathing the room in a soft glow. I had finished unpacking and stood surveying the shelves full of cooking supplies and the last of our food. Two bags of rice and beans, a bag of dehydrated tomatoes, a scattering of nuts, crackers, and granola, and one bag left of oatmeal. I tried to press down the anxiety that twisted through me. This would barely last us two weeks. Let alone the rest of winter. And even if Domine managed to bring in more protein, we were still lacking in variety.

"Mommy?"

Lilica's voice pulled me from my gnawing thoughts. "Yes, hon?"

"Come see my room. It's so pretty."

I turned to see a wide smile stretching across her face. Her eyes bright. And I was once again struck by the perfection of her. How the smallest things could fill her with excitement, the tiniest details an endless well of exploration. She had yet to carry the weight of worry against her chest. I was her unwavering presence. Her safe harbor. But I knew I could not promise her that forever. Eventually, she would grow up and cast aside her wings. And the thought filled me with sorrow. How fleeting childhood was. A tiny spark burning bright and fast.

"I would love to see your new room."

I followed her through the doorway and ducked beneath the hanging blanket. She had turned on her solar powered nightlight, and the room danced with color. Settling onto the floor, I glanced around at the small shelves built into the wall beside her bed, the surfaces now lined with the fairy carvings Domine had been making for her during our nights around the fire.

"Wow. It's really nice in here, Lili."

"I love my new room, Mommy." She crawled into my lap, wrapping her arms around my neck, and a wave of gratitude swelled within. Her effortless adaptability through all the changes of the past few months was a gift I continued to hold close to my heart.

"When's Domine coming back?" She twined her finger around a strand of my hair. "I want to show him my room."

"Soon, love." I planted a kiss on her cheek, breathing in the scent of forest which seemed to permeate her now. "Why don't I make you some lunch?"

"Okay, Mommy."

I retreated from her room and stoked up the fire, glancing at the woven blanket that lay across the bed. Picking it up, I spread it out in front of the hearth, creating a carpet over the dirt floor. My hands ran across the blue and green threads, so many long-ago memories embedded within the fabric.

The feel of Domine's arms around me all those years ago as we lay on the bed in our tiny one-room apartment of bare walls and unpacked boxes. The way the afternoon light had filtered through the blanket, bathing our skin in fragmented shadows as his fingers traced patterns across my skin. His voice a delicious whisper against my ear. *"This is where our story begins, Seren."*

And it did. It had begun and ended and then began again. The threads of our history forever entwined, weaving an intricate pattern of color against darkness.

With a smile, I stood and slid on my boots. "I'll be right back, Lili. I'm just going to bring in some more wood from outside.

Thick snowflakes blew in as I opened the door, and my breath stilled. Looking up, the clear sky of this morning had been replaced once more with dark storm clouds. I scanned the line of trees as I hurried to gather wood from the stack beside the firepit, noticing the snow had begun to cover Domine's tracks leading into the woods.

He should have turned back by now. He knows not to get caught in a snowstorm.

My thoughts followed me back into the cabin, bringing with it a rush of cold air that settled around the room like an unsettling presence. I tried to busy myself with the fire, setting a pan of salted beans onto the grate to boil. But with every minute that passed, I grew more restless. My ear trained to the door, listening for the sound of footsteps.

Where was he?

Lilica had now finished her lunch and was sitting beside the fire, flipping through her book of fairy tales and humming softly to herself, lost in her world of imagination and seemingly oblivious to my mounting unease, which now curled within like a tight knot in my gut.

I found myself pacing back and forth, cracking the door open every so often to peer outside, hoping to see the flash of his gray jacket through the trees.

But there was nothing but silence and snowfall.

CHAPTER THIRTY

*N*ight descended like an ominous shroud draped over the forest. And Domine still had not returned.

The snow now fell heavily, obscuring my vision in a blur of white as my flashlight snaked across the trees, my voice cutting through the dark. But no matter how many times I called his name, willing him to appear, only silence answered back.

"Mommy?"

Lilica had peeked her head out of the shelter, the glow of the fire sending fragments of light spilling across the snow. "Is he back yet?"

"No, honey. Not yet." Letting out a deep sigh, I clicked off the flashlight and trudged through the drifts, slipping my boots off at the entrance to the door.

A heaviness pressed into me as I stepped back inside. The warmth that enveloped the room. The coziness of the shelter with the shelves lined with cookware and the blanket spread beneath the hearth. It was weeks of hard labor I could not enjoy. This place didn't feel like a home without Domine. It suddenly felt like a prison.

Lilica stared up at me, her eyes wide. "He'll be okay, right, Mommy? He said he'll come back."

"Of course, Lili. He probably just got a little turned around in the woods. I'm sure he'll find his way back tonight." I drew in a shaky breath and slipped on a smile, trying to push away all the dark, clawing thoughts that threatened to consume me. "Why don't we get you into bed, okay?" My voice came out strained, my hand trembling as I reached out to run my fingers through her hair. "I bet you're excited to sleep in your very own room tonight."

She nodded, a faint smile tugging at the corners of her mouth.

* * *

*J*lay on my back in bed, the fabric of the sleeping bags cold against my skin as I watched dancing shadows from the fire play across the walls. Lilica had fallen asleep an hour ago, and the night stretched out before me with only the whispers of my own desolate worry to keep my company.

What if he doesn't come back tonight?

What if something happened, and he's hurt?

It's too cold. How will he make it through the night?

These thoughts raced through me like adrenaline, loud and uncomfortably close, my mind unable to sit with the bleak reality of Domine lost somewhere in the snow.

Rolling over, I stared into the flames, my stomach in knots as I tried to still the pounding of my heart, remembering the first time I had waited for him like this. It had been the night I picked him up from the police station.

His silence had been so heavy and sharp as we drove home, his eyes miles away from me. And then the crushing emptiness of the apartment as I had stepped out of the shower to find him gone. The confusion and concern that tore at me as the hours crept by, hours that had turned into days, leaving me with nothing but blistering questions that ate away at the threads of my own sanity. And when he finally returned, standing there in the living room as the pale light of a dying day spilled across the floor, and he silently took me up against the wall, his mouth hungry on mine, I'd wept. I wasn't angry at him for leaving, for not answering his phone, for making me ache with worry. I was only relieved he had come back. That he was okay. That I could feel him against me again.

I squeezed my eyes shut, clenching my fists against the sheets. I needed him too much. I always had. My love for him was like a bomb waiting to blow me apart.

Life was too fragile for that kind of love.

I don't know how long I lay there, watching the fire die down to smoldering embers, praying the door would open, that he would be standing there with his wide smile and tousled hair that was always falling into his eyes. But the door never opened, and exhaustion must have eventually claimed me, for the next thing I knew, I was jolted awake by the feel of a hand on my shoulder.

"Wake up, Mommy."

Bleary-eyed, I swept my arm across the sleeping bag, hoping to feel the impression of Domine beside me. But I was only met with emptiness and the chill of air against my fingers. A desperate sort of panic flooded my limbs as I sat up, the reality of yesterday once more crashing down on me.

It's morning now. He's still gone.

"Don't be sad, Mommy." Lilica ran her hand down my arm, as if trying to soothe away my fears. "It's okay. He'll come back. The fairies said he would."

I pulled her close to me, burying my face in her tangled hair, clinging to the innocence of her optimism. It was all I had left to anchor me in this vast wildness of forest and mountains. "Yes, love." I forced a smile across my face as I stroked her hair back, smoothing the tendrils behind her ears. "Everything's going to be okay."

But my gut lurched as I spoke those words. How many lies had I handed her? How many fabrications conjured to buffer the truth while reality loomed around us, harsh and unrelenting?

It was winter. We had little food. And I had no idea where Domine was.

* * *

I stood at the edge of the forest as snowflakes coated my hair in slivers of ice. It was now late afternoon, and the light was beginning to wane, the sky slipping into a deepening gray, casting long shadows that leaned against the snow. Hours had been spent in a restless flurry of pacing around the shelter and stepping outside to scan the tree line. It took every ounce of reserve inside me not to go out into the forest in search of him. But I knew it was a risk not worth taking with Lilica. The snow was too deep and still falling. We could end up lost in it. It was so easy to get disorientated in this kind of snow. It swallowed up everything around you.

But I had to do something. I couldn't stand here helpless anymore.

Doubling back to the shelter, I opened the door to find Lilica by the fire, walking her carved wooden fairies across the hearth.

"Sweetheart. Can you get on your boots and coat for me? We're going to go for a little walk."

I washed all thoughts out of my mind as we bundled up and stepped outside, our breath spiraling up into the winter sky. Focusing on the tree poles Domine had placed into the snow as a guide, we trudged through the drifts, Lilica's mittened hand clasped tightly in mine.

"Where are we going, Mommy?"

"We're going to check on some snares Domine set a few days ago." My eyes flickered across the branches, looking for the flash of red cloth he used to mark the location of his traps. But the snow was so deep, the branches straining with the weight of snowfall, that I couldn't see anything but white. I stopped walking, my pulse thudding in my ears as I looked back toward the shelter, now a faint outline through the trees, a trail of smoke drifting from the chimney.

"Mommy. Look. What's that?" Lilica pointed toward a tree ahead of us, where a bit of red cloth peeked out from beneath the snow.

"Good job, hon. You found one of the snares."

Bending down, I followed the line he had tied to the base of the tree, my hands digging into the deep snow until I felt the metal wire and pulled.

"It's a little squirrelly," Lilica whispered, watching me with wide eyes as I untangled the frozen creature from the snare. "Is it dead?"

"Yes. It is."

She furrowed her brow. "What are we going to do with it?"

I realized she had never watched Domine check his traps before. He had always cleaned and gutted the animals away from camp. This messy part of life and death so neatly compartmentalized and tucked away from her. I stood, slipping the squirrel into the folds of my jacket. "We're going to eat it, sweetie."

Lilica stood next to me in silence as I reset the trap, her lips drawn into a frown. "Lili." I brushed the snow from my gloves and knelt beside her. "You know, death is a natural part of life. And eventually, everything dies."

She looked at me, the deep grey of her eyes swirling with questions. "Everything? Even fairies?"

"Yes, love. Even fairies." I reached out and brushed my thumb across her cheek. "But that's what makes life so special. It's a precious gift we get to carry for a short time."

"Is it lonely when you die?"

I stared at her, trying to retrieve an answer from what little I knew of death. As a doctor, I had extensive knowledge of what happened to the body. The heart rate stilled. Blood no longer pumped through arteries. Brain activity grew quiet. But where exactly did the soul go? Did it live beyond our bodies? Was it an endless energy with no tether?

These concepts of death were not explored living within a culture that had slowly stripped away our connection to spirituality. Silencing our drive to explore the depths of what it meant to be alive. What it meant to be human.

"You, know, love. I don't think so. I think when we die, we become a part of everything. And there is no loneliness. Only peace."

"That sounds nice." A hesitant smile spread across her face, and I realized the persistent grip of anxiety had lessened a bit as I knelt beside her in the snow. It was a gentle reminder of something much bigger than my own fears.

It was surrender.

Taking her hand in mine, I led her back toward the place we would now call home for the next few months, my footsteps quickening with the thought that maybe… maybe Domine would be inside waiting for us.

A rush of warm air hit me as we entered the shelter, and my breath released in a deflated sigh as I glanced around the empty room. The absence of him like a silent scream. I dug my nails into the palm of my hand, the prick of pain momentarily grounding me from the onslaught of panicked thoughts that threatened to rush forward once more.

Where are you?

* * *

I clutched the bone handle knife as I stood staring at the squirrel that now lay like a dark stain on the snow. I had watched Domine skin animals on a few occasions, and it didn't appear too complicated.

Kneeling onto the snow, I rested the blade of the knife against the base of the tail, making a small horizontal incision. Drawing the knife slowly up the squirrel's back, I worked the blade in deeper toward the breastbone, trying to loosen the skin from the meat so I could then separate it by pulling upward as I had seen Domine do. But the pelt was so frozen and my hands already beginning to numb from the cold, that all I managed to do was tear the skin off in small, jagged pieces. Tears of frustration stung my eyes as I threw the knife down, looking at the mangled mess I had made of the animal.

"Domine. Dammit! Please come back. *Please*." My words tumbled out in a desperate plea that collided with the sky as I pulled my gaze toward the forest, willing him to appear like an apparition. Solid form taking shape against the heavy blanket of snow.

But there was nothing but trees and a brutal silence that fell on me like a weight, sucking the oxygen from my lungs.

"Mommy?" Lilica called to me from the shelter, her head peeking out from between the crack in the door. "Are you okay?"

"I'm fine, love." I turned and shot her a stiff smile. "I'm almost done here." Taking a deep breath, I picked up the knife, focusing the blade back beneath the skin.

I can do this.

* * *

I crouched beside the hearth, stirring salt and spices into the pan of meat positioned over the fire. I had managed to separate most of the skin from the squirrel and remove the entrails, depositing them far enough away from the shelter so they wouldn't attract animals.

Lilica sat beside me, a long, high note filling the space around us as she blew through the reed of Domine's harmonica.

"I'm making a song for Domine." She took a deep breath and blew into the instrument once more, releasing a shrill cacophony of sound that pierced my ears. "If he's lost, it will help him find his way home."

I leaned over and ruffled her hair. "Yes. I think Domine will definitely be able to hear your song, love."

Grabbing a plate from the shelf, I dished out the rice and meat and placed it on the table for her.

"Are you going to eat, too, Mommy?" She slid onto one of the carved wooden stools and looked at me with a mixture of confusion and concern.

I shook my head and settled myself on the blanket beside the fire, staring into the crackling flames. "No, I'm okay, love. I'm not really hungry." I closed my eyes, taking a deep, steady breath as the crushing thought of spending another night waiting for him seized me.

I opened my eyes to see Lilica beside me with the plate of food in her hand. "You need to eat, Mommy." She held out a spoonful of meat, her eyes almost pleading.

"Okay, I'll have a few bites." With a smile, I opened my mouth and let her feed me, the rich gamey flavor resting on my tongue.

We sat eating beside the fire, listening to the sound of the wind as it slithered through the chimney and stirred the flames. The last of the light from outside now extinguished and replaced with dancing shadows of amber that leapt across our skin.

The crunch of snow from somewhere outside startled me, and my heart jackknifed in my chest.

"My song worked, Mommy!" Lilica scrambled to her feet, the remains of the food on her plate spilling onto the blanket as she ran toward the door and flung it wide open.

"Lilica. Wait! We don't know what's out there."

But she didn't listen, her form quickly disappearing from my sight as she dashed out into the darkness.

CHAPTER THIRTY-ONE

"*L*ili. Come back inside. Right now!"

I rushed out the door after her, struggling with my boots, realizing she didn't even have hers on.

"Where are you?"

But there was no answer, and a wave of panic crashed against me as I trudged through the snow, frantically grasping for my sight in the dark.

"Lilica!"

My breath clawed at my throat, my pulse a violent drum in my ears as I peered into the depths of the forest. And then the faint sound of giggles and the deep resonance of Domine's voice drifted from beyond the tree line. My knees gave way, relief flooding through me like euphoria.

He's back. He's okay.

He materialized from the trees, a dark shape drawing closer until I could make out the form of Lilica in his arms and two rabbits slung over his shoulder.

"I found a little wood nymph wandering around in the snow. Thought I'd take her home with me." Through the darkness, I could see a wide grin stretched across his face, and then I was crushing my body against his, the past two days rushing forward in a swell of tears.

"Oh my god, Domine. I was so worried."

"I know. I'm sorry. I'm okay, though." He reached out and

cupped my cheek, brushing away a tear, his mittened hand like ice against my skin.

"I told you my song would work, Mommy. I told you!" Lilica looked down at me with a proud smile on her face as I took his hand and quickly led us back toward the warmth of the shelter.

I set some water on the fire to boil, watching Lilica run in excited circles around him as he crouched beside the hearth, removing his coat and boots. "Where did you go, Domine?" she sang out, tugging on his arm, her bright gray eyes locked on his.

He settled onto the blanket and swept her into his lap. "I guess I got a little turned around in the woods."

"And where did you sleep?"

"Well, I made myself a little snow cave."

"Snow cave?" She furrowed her brow, reaching up to brush the ice crystals from his beard. "That sounds cold."

He chuckled and lightly tapped her on the nose. "It was, yes. But my body created enough heat to keep me from getting *really* cold. Did you know that a long time ago in a place far away from here, people used to live in homes made of snow? They called them igloos." Leaning over, he fished something out of the front pocket of his coat. "And look, I made you something." He pulled out a wooden fairy sitting on a mushroom. "Thought you'd might like to add this to your collection."

Taking it from him, she let out a tiny squeal and sprang from his lap, ducking beneath the blanket to her room.

A warm elation wrapped around me as I poured the hot water into a cup of tea for Domine, everything falling back into place as his eyes met mine. There were no words to the gratitude that flourished within me, and I scooted closer to him, resting my head on his shoulder and breathing in the scent of snow and wind that hovered on his skin.

"You're so cold. Let's get you out of these clothes." I ran my hands down his arms and slipped off his gloves, noticing the flash of concern in his eyes as he stared past me and into the fire.

"How bad is it, Seren?"

I looked down and sucked in a sharp breath, my fingers grazing across the tips of his, which were now a deep, mottled blue color, his pinky finger white and curled inward.

"Can you feel that?"

He turned toward me with his jaw tightly clenched. "No. I can't."

* * *

J tried to push back the sinking feeling inside me as I removed Domine's hands from the bowl of warm water. "You have third-degree frostbite. I'm just glad you didn't get it on your feet." I unsheathed the knife beside me and began to cut out long, thin strips from an old shirt I had found in our pack. "If your fingers start to hurt, that's a good sign."

Leaning over, he gripped my arm, his eyes wide and pleading. "I can't lose my fingers."

"I know." My voice came out in a whisper as I began to carefully wrap each of his fingers with strips of cloth, tying them securely in place. I found myself unable to meet his eyes. There was only so much I could do. He needed the kind of medical attention I couldn't provide out here, and the bleak reality of that was a knife in my gut. I finally looked up to see him watching me, his eyes heavy. Reaching out, I drifted my hand along his cheek, my fingers shaking as they rested on his lips. "I'm going to do everything I can, okay?"

With a nod, he looked over at Lilica, who had fallen asleep by the fire, her body nestled beneath a blanket. "I'll go put her into bed."

"No. I'll do it." I ran my hand through his hair, brushing back the unruly strands still damp from the snow. "You stay here and warm up by the fire."

Lilica stirred as I gathered her gently into my arms and carried her into her room, tucking her snugly into the sleeping bag.

"Will his fingers be okay, Mommy?" Her voice was soft and muffled beneath the covers, and I bent to place a kiss on her forehead.

"I hope so, love."

"I knew he'd come back, Mommy. The fairies told me he'd come back."

"The fairies from your dreams?"

She nodded sleepily, her lashes fluttering against her cheeks, and a wave of relief rose up once more. *How close had we come to losing him?*

"Well, I'm so glad you were right, honey."

I returned to find Domine crouched next to the fire, running his hands briskly along his arms. He turned and shot me a wan smile. "I can't seem to get warm."

"You must be experiencing the effects of mild hypothermia." I quickly gathered up our sleeping bags and moved them closer to the fire, watching as he fumbled with the buttons on his shirt.

Bending beside him, I helped him remove his shirt and then unclasped his belt, sliding his pants down to the floor. Quickly shedding my clothes, I drew him into my arms and wrapped my legs around him, pressing my body tightly against his as I slid the sleeping bag over us.

"Mmm…" He sighed deeply into my ear as I began to run my hands along his shoulders and down his back. "You're so warm, Seren. God, you're so warm."

I looked up at him, watching the light from the fire play across the planes of his face, and that rush of elation seized me once more. He was here in my arms. He was okay.

Everything is okay again.

"I was so scared when you didn't come back." My voice wavered as I slid on top of him, my mouth falling to his neck and breathing in the sharp pine scent of him as my lips ran a soft trail across his skin. "What happened out there, Domine?"

He let out a rush of air, his hands snaking to the small of my back. "I was an idiot. That's what happened. I didn't pay attention to my surroundings. I thought I'd be able to follow my tracks back. And then I was so focused on catching those damn rabbits that by the time I realized it was snowing, it was too late. I ended up wandering around for a few hours, getting even more turned around until it grew dark, and I was then forced to make some kind of shelter."

I placed my hand on his chest, feeling the rhythmic beat of his heart, the hard muscle that twitched beneath my touch, the sturdiness of his body against mine. But underneath all that strength was a fragility we all shared. We were exposed out here. At the mercy of the elements. And nothing we could do would change that.

"So, how did you find your way back?"

"That's the crazy thing. You won't believe it. But it was the wolf."

I sat up. "Our wolf?" I had taken to calling him that in my mind, as though he had become an intrinsic part of us somehow. Hiding beyond the shadows, silent and elusive. But always there.

"It was so surreal." He stared up at me, the flames from the fire mirrored in his eyes. "It was the next day that I noticed he was following me. At first, I tried to scare him off. But he wouldn't leave. He kept relentlessly trailing me and then dashing off through the trees. Over and over, he did this until it began to feel like he was trying to get me to follow him. At that point, I was so hopelessly lost, I figured it wouldn't hurt. So I did. I followed him. And he led me back here."

I released my breath as goosebumps prickled along my skin, and I thought back to that day at the river when the wolf had stood between the bear and me. The stoic wildness in his eyes. The whisper of some inherent understanding we now shared. "Wow."

"I know." He reached out for me, burying his face against my neck. "I honestly thought I was going to freeze out there. And the thought of leaving you two alone…" His words stilled, and he looked up at me, the press of tears forming in the corners of his eyes, mirroring the rush of my own.

I pulled him tighter against me, as if I could fuse the pattern of our skin together. To extract all the fear and release it to the snow and cold outside. To never let him go. "But you didn't. You're here. You're here now."

235

*L*ilica's playful chatter filtered softly from beyond the wall of her room as I unwrapped the bandages from Domine's hands. It had been two weeks, and the blisters on his fingers were beginning to heal, revealing a layer of fresh skin underneath. But he still had some pain, and his pinky remained a concerning shade of black. The skin hardened to the touch.

Biting my lip, I gently pressed on the dead tissue. "You still don't feel anything?"

He shook his head, his eyes clouded with a sorrowful resolution as he leaned over me beside the fire. "No. Nothing."

I had been hoping he would regain some nerve response, that the damage hadn't gone too deep. But as the days wore on, it became clear this was not going to happen. He now ran the risk of infection, as the necrotic tissue would eventually start to spread to other parts of his body.

Domine's voice grew low, a resonant tone that hovered against my skin like a chilling verdict. "You know what we have to do."

His words cut into me, and I fumbled with the ties on the bandages, my hands growing unsure and shaky. "Why don't we give it a few more days?"

"No." He leveled me with his gaze, his eyes piercing into mine. "We need to get this over with now."

And he was right. But I still found my mind trying to scramble for another option. A miracle I could cling to. Some small delay in the inevitable.

With a heavy sigh, he stood and walked over to one of the packs that sat in the corner of the room. My breath hitched as I watched him root through the contents and retrieve a needle and thread from a box, setting it calmly on the table before turning back to me. "We'll do it after Lilica goes to sleep. I don't want her to see this."

CHAPTER THIRTY-TWO

$\mathcal{M}$y gut churned as I paced beside the fire. I had done surgical procedures before, but this was different. There always was a clinical disconnect between the patient and me, a razor-sharp focus I could draw upon. But Domine was not a patient. I could not disengage from him. He was a part of me. And the reality of doing this without modern equipment and proper pain medication caused a thin sheen of sweat to break out across my skin.

"She's asleep. Are you ready?" Domine had slipped out of Lilica's room and stood by the door with his jaw tightly clenched.

"I don't know, Domine." I twisted my hands together, noticing they were trembling as I glanced at the implements I had sanitized in boiling water that now lay on the table like instruments of war. "Are you sure you want to do this tonight?"

"I'm sure." He leaned over and grabbed the lantern and ax, and my heart lurched, drawing what oxygen I had left from me. "I'll be outside."

I closed my eyes and took a deep, calming breath, trying to still the racing of my pulse. *I can do this. It's only a finger. It's not a limb.* But the thought of inflicting any level of pain on Domine was a heavy constriction in my chest I could not distance myself from.

The chill hit my skin as I stepped outside and closed the door softly behind me. The light from the lantern Domine placed on a wooden stump spilled across the snow, and I watched as he crouched down, folding his knuckles against the edge and resting his pinky on top.

"Let's get this over with." His voice was hollow, and his eyes stared out into the darkness.

I stepped toward him and picked up the ax, feeling the cold and unyielding weight in my hands. "I wish there was more light." My voice shook as I bent beside him, trailing my fingers along the joint that connected to his knuckle.

"I'm ready. I'm going to count to three, okay?" His words came out stiff as he clasped his other hand tightly around his thigh and closed his eyes. "One... Two... Three."

I knew it would be a fairly clean amputation. The dead tissue had not traveled beyond the fifth metacarpal. So why then could I not raise the ax?

My pulse pounded in my ears, and I just stood there, frozen.

He looked up at me, his gaze sharp against the flickering light of the lamp. "Seren?"

"I'm sorry." The sharp prick of tears obscured my vision, and I clenched my hand tightly around the handle of the ax, frustration slamming into me.

"Give me the ax."

I stared at him. "No. I can do this."

In one fluid motion, he rose and yanked it from my hands, quickly driving the blade down onto his finger.

"Domine." A tight gasp lodged in my throat as I watched the steel cut through him.

There was a dull thud, and then a garbled groan as he threw the ax down and stood with a hiss, momentarily swaying on his feet. I grabbed him by the shoulders to steady him and raised his arm above his head to slow the pool of blood now streaming down his hand and staining the sleeve of his coat.

"Why did you do that?"

"Because I knew you couldn't." His face was ashen, and his eyes unfocused as he tilted toward me.

I realized he must be in some state of mild shock, and I slid my arm around his waist, drawing him against me for support. "Come on. Let's get you stitched up."

* * *

"*Y*ou shouldn't have had to do that." I shook my head as I threaded the needle through his skin, pulling it tight to close the wound.

"It doesn't matter who did it," he said through gritted teeth, his other hand fisted on his lap. "It just needed to be done."

"I know. But that was *my* job. I shouldn't have hesitated." I couldn't chase away the feeling that I had failed him, and a sinking heaviness clawed at me as I pushed the last stitch through and tied off the end.

"Hey. Look at me." His eyes were wide and glassy, and I knew the extent of his pain was only beginning to hit him as the effects of adrenaline wore off. "I should have never asked you. I don't think I could have done it either if I was in your position."

"Maybe not." Reaching up, I smoothed back the hair that had fallen in tangled waves across his face, my thumb running across the sheen of sweat that now gathered on his brow. "How's the pain right now?"

"I'm fine."

"And I don't believe you." I leaned over and pulled the pan from the fire, wringing out the strip of cloth that had been soaking in the infusion of Yarrow and St. John's Wort. Resting his hand in my lap, I gently applied the herbs. "These will help with the pain and fight off any infection." I wrapped the cloth around his hand, covering the wound tightly. "I wish I had more to work with, though." I furrowed my brow, running through my mental list of available herbs, and then quickly stood, remembering Turk's medicine.

Rooting around in the empty pack stashed in the corner, I found the glass jar and pipe. "Here, take some of this."

He winced as he settled himself closer to the fire, his hands fumbling with the pipe. Taking it from him, I held it to his lips and retrieved the small stick I had placed in the coals, creating a flame for him to draw from.

"Thanks." A stream of smoke billowed from his mouth as he leaned forward and blew into the fire, his hand reaching out and curling his fingers tightly around mine.

* * *

The embers from the fire glowed in the darkness, casting lazy patterns across the walls as I opened my eyes. Turning over in bed, I found Domine sitting up, his hand clasped around where his pinky had been, his breath coming out ragged.

"Domine?" I slid closer to him and ran my hand down his back, which was slick with sweat. "How long have you been up?"

"About an hour."

"How bad is the pain?"

"It's bad." His voice came out in a hiss as he clenched his eyes shut.

I scrambled out of bed and grabbed the flashlight, the beam of light spilling across the floor. "I'll get you some more of the cannabis."

"I just took some. It didn't seem to do much."

"Maybe you just need to take more? I can also brew you up some skullcap." I dug through my bag of herbs, trying to locate the thick woody stems.

"Seren. There's nothing you can do. I just have to ride this out."

I looked over at him, his face obscured in shadow, and that feeling of helplessness clawed at me once again. I wanted so badly to take away his pain. To wash away that haunted, faraway look in his eyes.

Moving back to the bed, I slid behind him and wrapped my arms around his chest, my hand falling to the feverish beating of his heart.

"This is nice," he whispered as he leaned against me. "Your touch always feels so good."

"Does it?"

"Yes."

My lips brushed against his ear and to his neck, my kiss sending goosebumps trailing across his skin. "Lie down."

He shifted on the bed, and I gently pressed him onto his back, running my hands along his shoulders and down his arms. "I want you to close your eyes and try to focus on my touch. On the way my hands feel."

"Okay." His breath came out in a shudder, and he closed his eyes, the tense muscles along his chest relaxing as I swept my fingers across them and traveled down to his abdomen, my lips tracing the path left by my hands.

A low moan trembled in his throat, and he reached for me, threading his fingers through my hair as I unbuttoned his pants and pulled them past his legs.

I ran my hands up his thighs, featherlight caresses that teased his skin, paying homage to every dip and curve of muscle. "Does that feel good?"

"Yes." His voice was ragged as I slid my hand over the coils of his pubic hair, cupping the softness of him in my palm, my fingers slowly tracing along the head.

"Seren?" He opened his eyes and looked at me. "What are you doing?"

"I'm taking you somewhere else."

"I don't think I'm able to…" As he spoke, I bent down and ran my tongue along the tip of him. "Oh, god..." With a soft groan he closed his eyes again, growing large in my hand.

I took him into my mouth. Slow strokes that caused a strangled moan to spill from him as he tensed up and reached for me.

"Come here."

I withdrew my mouth, running my lips along his length. "Shhh… let me give you pleasure right now." I placed my hand on his chest, lowering him back onto the sleeping bags.

"Seren." His hand fisted my hair as I took him deeper into my mouth, his breath growing sharp and labored. "My god… oh god… you feel so good."

An ache grew within me, curling through my limbs and

spreading downward as I continued to stroke him with the heat of my mouth, his broken words becoming a tight band of longing that arched through me.

I slowed my pace, savoring the feel of his arousal, my tongue drawing circles across his skin as my hands ran along his thighs.

He jerked beneath me, his entire body now trembling as I placed my lips to his shaft, tasting the salt of him. "I'm so close, Seren... god, I'm so close."

"Not yet." I rose up to find him watching me, his eyes wild in the glow of the dying fire as I trailed kisses up his stomach and then back down, prolonging his pleasure, teasing out his release.

He let out a gasp as I drew him once more into my mouth. His bandaged hand pushed against the blankets while the other one grew urgent, his fingers threading through my hair and tugging lightly as his voice became a low growl. "Oh, fuck... Seren. What are you doing to me?"

I pressed my thighs together, trying to still the intensity of my own arousal. I had never been with him like this before. He was unhinged and carnal, and it made me breathless.

"I'm going to come..."

He sat up and gripped my arm, a stifled moan tumbling from him as he spilled himself deep into my mouth, the salt of his release coating my tongue. And then he was pulling me against his chest, his lips seeking mine.

"My God." His mouth fell to my neck, his voice a throaty whisper against my skin. "That was amazing." He cupped my face in his hands, his eyes burning into me. "And the pain... I can barely feel it anymore. What kind of sorcery was that?"

A soft chuckle escaped me as I ran my hand down his chest, my limbs buzzing with energy. "Orgasms are a natural analgesic."

With a groan, he flipped me onto my back. "I want to taste you."

I grasped his shoulders, my voice coming out shaky as I tried to push back the desire that surged through me. "You should really get some rest while the pain is better."

"I don't want to rest." He breathed into my ear as his hand slid into my pants, his fingers finding the slickness of my sex. "I want to taste you right now. Please, let me taste you."

His fingers curled inside me, and I let out a sharp gasp, no longer able to contain the ache that begged for release. I fumbled with my pants and slipped them off as he grabbed me by the hips and dipped his head down, his mouth falling hungry against my sex, eliciting a sharp wave of pleasure to cascade through my body.

Bathed in the heat of heavy breath and firelight against skin, I rocked against him, wild and reckless, letting myself tumble into the abyss.

*S*now drifted over the fresh mound of earth as Lilica stood beside us, a sprig of evergreen clenched in her fist.

"You want to go first, love?" I placed my hand on her back, staring into her wide gray eyes.

"Goodbye, pinky," she whispered, bending down to place the evergreen beside the small circle of rock. "We'll miss you."

Domine smiled and crouched beside her, his bandaged hand tucked inside his coat.

"Your turn." She watched him as he cleared his throat and stared at the tiny grave.

"Well, we've had some really good times together, pinky. I'll never forget you." He placed his fingers to his lips in a kiss and touched the earth.

"Mommy?"

Lilica turned to me, and I joined them in the snow, bowing my head as if in prayer. "Thank you for being such a great pinky. You will be deeply missed."

As if satisfied with our eulogies, Lilica nodded, her wide eyes focusing on me. "The fairies that visit me at night say that when something goes away, it turns into something new. Do you think that's true, Mommy?"

I stood and wrapped my arm around her shoulder, her words stirring a gentle warmth within me as I thought of my mother, father, and Elis. The family she never had the chance to know. Perhaps they were with her somehow? Hidden within the light that broke through clouds. The caress of wind against skin. "Yes, hon. I like to think that nothing really disappears. It just changes form."

"Maybe Domine's pinky will be a flower one day?"

"Maybe it will be, wood nymph." Domine ruffled her woolen cap and bent to retrieve his crossbow. "You ready to go find some dinner?"

A wide smile spread across her face as she rushed to get her walking stick she had left inside the shelter.

"I think we might have a blossoming funeral director on our hands," Domine said with a chuckle as he slung his bow over his shoulder.

Lilica had insisted upon a burial when she awoke in the morning to find Domine's hand bandaged up once more. She had been the one to dig the small grave with the trowel, scraping through the frozen earth and placing small stones in a circle, her tiny hands rearranging the loss and turning it into something sacred.

"I'm ready!" she called out, bounding through the drifts with her stick held high, cheeks rosy from the cold.

"Okay. Let's go see what we've caught in our snares."

Domine took the lead with Lilica close behind him, their footsteps leaving winding tracks in the freshly fallen snow. And that's when I saw him. A flash of gray and black against white. Eyes full of wild sky and forest, watching me. I stopped and rested my hand to my chest, the silence between us like an unbroken sigh. And then he was gone.

CHAPTER THIRTY-THREE

"We should call him Prince, Mommy."

"Call who Prince?"

"The wolf."

Lilica sat beside me while I stirred the pot of stew over the fire, dropping in the last of the frozen rabbit meat.

"My fairy tale book has stories about princes who save people. And the wolf saved you and Domine."

I looked over at her with a smile. "Yes, I suppose you're right, love. I think that's a perfect name for him."

I shifted myself onto the floor, stifling a yawn. I had been feeling so tired the past few days, the weight of lethargy dragging through my limbs as if I was suspended under water. And all I wanted to do was crawl back into bed and sleep.

The door burst open, bringing with it a gust of frigid wind and swirling flakes of snow that drifted through the air, the last fragments of daylight now swallowed up by the dense gray sky.

"It's getting pretty bad out there." Domine shook the snow off his coat and removed his boots. Slivers of ice clung to his beard and coated the strands of his hair as he knelt beside the fire and held his hands up to the flame. "And nothing in the snares, unfortunately."

I bit my lip, trying to push back that tight feeling in my chest. But it was always there, lingering in the corners like a shadow that changed form with each passing day. A constant reminder that we lived on the edge, the restless animal of hunger always pacing beside us. "Well, this stew should last us at least two days. Hopefully, we'll catch something soon." I tried to keep my voice light, hoping to hide the concern that lingered behind my words as I pulled the pot from the fire and dished out a bowl for Lilica. "Maybe I should be the one to check the snares next time."

"You losing your faith in me?" He shot me a playful grin as he shrugged off his coat and settled beside the fire, removing his gloves.

"No, it's not that. I just worry about your hands." I had grown cautious of him being out in the cold for too long, knowing that his circulation was now compromised. "How is your hand feeling, by the way?"

"Much better." A slow smile spread across his face as his fingers swept up my arm, the light from the fire playing in his eyes.

"Well, I want to check your bandage tonight."

"Yes, doctor." He leaned in close to me, his voice a teasing whisper against my ear that sent a bloom of heat to spread across my skin, gently coaxing me away from my unease.

* * *

I awoke with a start.

Staring up into the darkness of the ceiling, the grip of nausea churned in my gut. It was the kind that demanded my attention. A persistent wave that took hold of me. I untangled myself from Domine's arms and quickly slid out of bed, groping around for the solar powered flashlight. A weak beam of light flickered across the room as I stood and stumbled toward the door, forgoing my boots, hoping I would make it outside in time.

Crouched in the snow, I bent forward and released the contents of my dinner. The wind clawed at my bare skin, burrowing the cold deep into my bones and stinging the soles of my feet as I wretched and heaved what was left inside me.

Then I felt a warm hand on my shoulder. Domine's fingers sweeping back my hair.

"Let's get you inside." He lifted me into his arms, carrying me back to the shelter, and I leaned into him like a child.

Domine stoked up the fire as I crouched beside it. My hands clasped around my belly, the emptiness inside like a dull ache. He draped a blanket over me and grabbed a towel, bending to wrap it around my feet. "Are you okay?" He looked up at me, shadows from the flames slanting across the furrowed lines of his face.

"I don't know. I think I might be coming down with something." My teeth chattered as I drew in a shaky breath. "I've been really tired these last few days."

"Maybe it was just something you ate?" A flash of concern swam in his eyes as he handed me a canister of water, watching as I uncapped it and took a small sip, the refreshing liquid settling my stomach and cleansing my palette.

"Maybe."

"Do you want me to make you some tea?"

"No. I just want to lie down." I crawled back into bed, my entire body trembling and spent as Domine slid in beside me and gathered me into his arms.

"Get some sleep." His voice drifted against my ear, gentle and soothing, as his hand ran down my back, cradling me in the harbor of his touch. The warmth of his body tucked around mine.

* * *

*T*he sounds of crackling flames and whispered voices slowly roused me from the darkness, the blank slate of silence that still remained impenetrable to dreams. And I wondered as I lay there, watching slivers of faint morning light filter through my lids, what bold colors bathed my daughter's mind at night? What dreams did she now dance with? And what was holding me back from discovering my own?

Opening my eyes, I rolled over in bed with a sigh, listening to the hushed conversation between Domine and Lilica as they sat together by the fire.

"How old are the trees?"

"Some are hundreds of years old."

"Why can't we live that long?"

"Because we are like flowers, Lili. Our beauty is not meant to stay forever."

I smiled, a warm affection washing through me as I watched him lean over to ruffle her hair, his eyes soft in the firelight. His tenderness with her never failed to make my heart quicken. The love I felt for him had grown into something larger, something that now encompassed all of us.

"Mommy. You're awake."

Lilica rushed over to the bed, the chill of her feet pressing against me as she slipped beneath the sleeping bag. "Are you feeling better?"

"A little, yeah."

"I made you oatmeal. I made it all by myself for you."

"Did you really, love?" I ran my fingers through her hair, placing a kiss on her forehead. "Well, I can't wait to try it."

I sat up as Domine handed me a bowl. But the moment the aroma reached my nose, another wave of nausea hit me. Trying to fight it, I gave Lilica a wide smile as I shoveled a spoonful into my mouth. "Mmm... it's really good, hon."

After three bites, I could no longer push back the persistent churning in my stomach, and I sprang from the bed, grabbing my boots and coat and rushing out into the snow.

I spent the next three days in bed, drifting between sleep and drinking copious amounts of wild fennel and peppermint tea. It kept the nausea at bay, but I could only consume the blandest of foods. Rice and the last bit of crackers I had managed to stash away had now become my staples. And while I lay there, waiting for the sickness to abate, a tiny thought hovered in the back of my mind, so small and unformed I could barely distinguish it. A whisper of a question that felt so foreign, I brushed it aside.

On the fourth day, I was still struggling with my appetite and fatigue but forced myself out of bed, determined to press through whatever had come over me.

"You're still feeling nauseous?" Domine ran his hand down my back as I pushed around the rabbit meat on my plate, willing myself to eat the protein I knew I so desperately needed. He had managed to catch four in his snares yesterday. A triumphant win that replenished our dwindling food supplies.

"Yeah." With a nod, I set my plate down, watching as he finished threading the needle through the rabbit pelts he had been working on. He was making a coat for Lilica as her other one had grown too small for her, her pale wrists now peeking out from beneath the cuffs of the sleeves.

"I'll be right back." I rose from the fire and slid my boots on by the door before stealing a quick glance into Lilica's room. The colors from her nightlight washed across the walls as her eyes fluttered in sleep, hand fisted against her cheek.

Icy darkness hit me as I tramped through the drifts to relieve myself, making a mental note to suggest to Domine that we build some sort of outhouse enclosure in the coming days. Crouching down, I grimaced as the wind sliced against my bare skin. And then it hit me. The tiny thought that had lingered against me suddenly became a rush of realization, sending my heart racing in my chest.

I had not bled at all since we left the cabin.

I assumed it had been a combination of stress, weight loss, and the rigorous days on the trail, but as my hand crept inside my jacket and felt the notable tenderness of my breasts, it became all too clear. The nausea. The fatigue. They were symptoms so familiar, bringing me back to memories of when I had been pregnant with Lilica.

But how is this possible?

My legs shook as I stumbled back inside, closing the door softly behind me. Domine glanced up and must have noticed the look of shock on my face, for he stood and quickly crossed the room, his hands falling to my shoulders.

"Seren, what's wrong?"

I gripped his arms, my mouth dry as I struggled with the words. "I'm not sick, Domine. I'm pregnant."

"What?" His eyes grew wide, and he took a step back, shaking his head. "But you said…"

"I know. The doctors told me after I had Lilica that my uterine lesions would prevent me from ever being able to conceive again." I drew in a shaky breath, trying to find my bearings beneath the frantic scream of my thoughts. "But all the symptoms are there. I'm just surprised it took me this long to realize it."

Something shifted in his gaze, a joy that sent tears trembling to the surface of his eyes as he cupped my face in his hands, his voice a fervent whisper. "Oh my god. We're going to have a baby?"

A crushing weight slammed into me as I pulled away, my heart constricting in my chest. "We don't know that. There could be complications." I wrapped my arms around myself, my feet treading back and forth across the floor. "With the amount of scarring on my uterus, I run a very high risk of miscarriage, or worse…" I clenched my fists, willing my heart to calm as the clutches of panic rose up and claimed me. "An ectopic pregnancy." My words punctured the air between us, brutal and sharp, and I watched as his face crumpled and grew ashen.

"No."

"Even if this baby is viable, there are so many potential risks. Uterine rupture. Placenta previa." Tears stung my eyes, and I sank down onto the bed, staring blankly into the fire, my mind like a storm, a howling wind that would not still. "I don't know what to do."

"Seren." His voice came out choked as he crossed the room and took me into his arms, holding me tight against his chest. "Do you want this baby?"

My tears released, wracking sobs that soaked his shirt as I allowed myself to fall into the abyss of my own conflicted sorrow. "Yes, I do. I want this baby more than anything. But I'm scared, Domine. I'm so scared something will go wrong."

CHAPTER THIRTY-FOUR

The ticking of time stretched out into days, and the days slowly turned to weeks. Every moment was spent in a constant state of silent vigilance.

We were both waiting.

Waiting for something to happen. Waiting for nothing to happen. Waiting for hope.

There was a heaviness now shared between Domine and me. A dark secret tucked within my body, and at times, I would catch him looking at me, his eyes swimming with an emotion I was too terrified to define.

Every day, I searched for signs. The twinge of pelvic pain. The stain of blood. My heart always perched precariously on the edge. I spent hours scouring through the recesses of my mind for some sort of herb that would help. But there was nothing I had access to. There was nothing I could control. Surrender was all I had left.

"Do you believe in miracles, Seren?"

Domine lay in bed with me, his head nestled on my chest, hand trailing down my stomach as light from the dwindling fire cast shadows across the room.

I stared up at the ceiling, my thoughts turning over the same loose stones. Ones that held no answers, only a yawning abyss of *what ifs* that filled me with a clawing apprehension that took root in my gut. "I don't know."

"Well, I do." His hand slid beneath my shirt and lifted it up, moving downward to press his lips against my belly, his voice a warm whisper that traveled across my skin. "I believe in miracles."

A sharp ache swelled within me. How I wanted to celebrate this. To bathe in the disbelief and joy of another child. But I knew I couldn't. It was too soon.

I ran my hands through his hair, fingering the strands that now brushed against his shoulders. "What was it that made you change your mind? For so long, you were adamant about not wanting kids."

He looked up at me with a flicker of surprise. "Do you really have to ask me this?" He rose and hovered over me, his eyes soft and trembling in the firelight. "Isn't it obvious?"

"I don't know. I never wanted to assume..." I bit my lip, glancing off into the fire, watching as the last of the flames licked against the blackened stones.

"Seren." He tilted my face to meet his. "Your little girl has stolen my heart. And the thought of having another child with you, of us growing together as a family, well, it..." I watched as the shimmer of tears danced in his eyes, a rippling current that caught my reflection. "It hurts how bad I want this."

"Me, too." I pressed my mouth against his, and for a moment, I could almost see it. The boldness of life tumbling within me. The dance of tiny hands and feet. The gentle growth of our family.

Please.

Please, let everything be okay.

"What do you think, love? Do you like your new coat?" I stood back with a smile, watching as Lilica ran her hand along the inside of the coat, her fingers brushing against the soft rabbit fur. I had disassembled her old coat the night before, sewing the zipper and buttons onto the new jacket.

"I love it, Mommy!" She pulled the hood up and began to bounce around the room, twitching her nose at us. "I'm a bunny!"

Domine chuckled from where he sat at the table. "Why don't you check your pockets, little bunny."

She stopped her bouncing and thrust her hands inside the coat, pulling out the small fairy family Domine had spent the last few weeks carving. Her eyes grew wide as her fingers traced over the detailed faces and wings, the set made complete with a tiny mushroom house for her to tuck them into.

"Happy birthday, Lili." A rush of splintered emotion hit me as I bent down and took her into my arms. How I wished I had more for her. A birthday filled with bright color and laughter. A childhood full of safe memories. Promises I could keep.

"I'm five now, Mommy." She grinned up at me, her gray eyes full of pride.

"You are, sweetie. And when we get to Alberta, you'll get to have all the presents and cake you want."

"It's okay." She wrapped her arms around my neck, burying her face in my hair. "I love my birthday right now."

Untangling herself from me, she ran over to Domine and tackled him in a hug before dashing into her room with her new fairies clutched in her hands.

"Where did this child come from?" I shook my head with a small smile as I sank into the chair beside him and ran my hand along the spirals etched into the pine. A silent reminder of the passage of time. A history of growth now intermingled with our own footfalls against the forest.

Leaning over, he swept back a strand of hair from my cheek. "She came from you."

* * *

I stirred the pan of syrup over the flames, watching as it bubbled and rose above the brim. I didn't have anything to make a cake with, but I had stashed away the last bit of pancake mix, and the box elder trees I had come across the other day had given me an idea. Domine had managed to fashion a tap using the ax and trowel, and we were able to siphon a trickle of pale sap from the trees.

Placing a spoon into the pan, I brought it to my lips, a wash of pleasure running through me as the sweetness coated my tongue, tasting almost like butterscotch.

"I think it's ready." I removed the pan and set it to cool beside me as I grabbed the plate with the large pancake on it, inserting the five makeshift candles we had fashioned from sticks and tree resin. "You ready to make a wish, Lili?" I lit the sticks from the fire and placed the cobbled together cake in front of her.

A wide grin spread across her face as she closed her eyes tight and blew furiously on the flames, smoke curling upward like tiny ghosts. My heart clenched as I watched her, and I prayed from a place so deep inside that whatever wish she had made would come true.

I cut the pancake into small pieces and drizzled the syrup over them, handing a plate to Lilica. We sat in a circle beside the fire, quietly enjoying the treat as the crackle of wood sent sparks drifting upwards.

"It's really good, Mommy. I love my cake."

"I'm so glad you like it, hon." I leaned back against Domine, the warmth of his arms curling around me as I took a sip of the peppermint and fennel tea I was now rationing. Though the nausea had settled considerably in the last few weeks, faint twinges still remained. My hand crept to my stomach, fingers tracing the slight rise I had noticed the other day. *How far along could I be?*

We had left the cabin in mid-September, and it was now January. Time had bled into days I struggled to arrange. Calendars and clocks a concept so far removed from our lives. But I could roughly calculate the day Lilica came into the world, and I knew the life inside me was still growing.

I grappled with my breath, the familiar swell of anxiety rising within as I thought of all the things that could still go wrong. All the things I could do nothing about.

Breathe. Just breathe. I closed my eyes, hoping to slow the staccato pace of my heart. Trying to extract the simplistic beauty of this moment. The warmth of the fire. The harbor of Domine's arms. My daughter, healthy and whole beside me.

"Don't worry about your belly, Mommy."

My eyes shot open. Lilica had finished her pancake and was now playing with her fairies beside the hearth, walking their tiny wooden feet along the stones. I slid my hand from my stomach and stared at her. *We hadn't told her yet. She couldn't possibly know. Could she?*

"What are you talking about, love?"

"The magic inside your belly." She looked over at me with a smile. "The fairies told me."

Goosebumps prickled along my skin, and I struggled to make sense of what she was saying, my thoughts wrestling with the threads of logic. "Are these the same fairies that come to you at night when you go to sleep, Lili?"

"Yep."

I sat up, clutching the cup of tea. "What kind of things do they say to you?"

"Lots of things." She shrugged and continued to walk the wooden carvings along the floor. "They said they are protecting the magic inside your belly."

A sharp inhale caught in my throat, and I turned to Domine, who had reached out to clutch my hand, his eyes wide. *Should we tell her?* I mouthed the question to him and was met with a slow nod.

"Sweetie." I crossed the room and knelt beside her, my heart pulsing in my chest. "Do you know what the magic inside my belly is?"

"Uh, huh." She nodded and looked up at me with a grin. "I'm going to have a little brother one day."

Everything stilled, and my mind swam in distorted patterns, my hand grasping at the floor to anchor myself. "Well, we don't know that, Lili."

"It's true, Mommy. The fairies told me."

Her words were so precise. So definitive that they cut right through me, the weight of reality shifting beneath my feet. Could she somehow be dreaming of things not yet formed? How else would she know about my pregnancy? Chills traveled across my skin as I pulled her into my lap, smoothing back her tousled hair. "I was going to wait to tell you about the baby growing inside me because there are still a lot of things that could go wrong... but yes, love, you might be a big sister one day."

My voice trembled as I stared into her eyes, those swirling irises that reminded me of a winter's day. And I suddenly felt as if there were a presence beside us. Something much larger than I could comprehend. Something sacred and powerful. And a question rushed at me like a bud of hope daring to push forth.

What if Lilica's words were true?

* * *

The sound of ax against wood stirred me from the depths of sleep, and I rolled over, my hand meeting the emptiness of sheets. I sat up, adjusting to the darkness of the shelter, the fire now only faded embers stirring restlessly in the hearth.

The chill in the room slithered across my skin as I slipped from the warmth of the sleeping bag. My mind rustled through the disorientating haze of sleep, wondering why Domine was outside chopping wood right now as I made my way to the door and grabbed my boots and coat.

The icy clarity of a night sky winked down at me, stars like glittering silk spreading across a canvas of black ink as I closed the door softly behind me and trudged through the crusted snow. Domine stood by the side of the shelter, his back bent beneath the weight of a log as he positioned it on the ground and swung his ax deep into the wood.

"What are you doing?" My question spilled out like smoke as he turned to me, the light from the lantern casting shadows across his face.

"We're running low on firewood." His voice came out clipped as he drove the ax down into the log once more.

"It's the middle of the night, Domine." I moved closer to him, placing my hand on his back. "Come back to bed."

"I can't sleep." The thwack of the ax echoed through the trees like a sharp crack as he continued his onslaught against the wood.

"Dom."

"What?"

I took his hand and pulled the ax from his grip. "Come to bed. You can do this in the morning."

With a sigh, he stared down at the pile of split wood and ran his hand through his hair, tension flickering across his face.

"Come inside." I gently took his arm and led him back into the shelter, his silence hanging heavy in the air as he stood in the doorway and removed his coat. "Are you okay?" My question spilled out in a tentative whisper as I bent to stoke up the fire.

"I'm fine." He slid into the sleeping bag and rolled away from me onto his side.

I placed a log onto the fire, biting my lip as I stared into the flames that grew and lept, casting a reprieve of warmth and flickering light across the floor. We had spoken earlier in the evening about Lilica's revelations and what they could mean, and he had appeared fervent and hopeful as he trailed his hand across my stomach, eyes soft with possibility. But I knew something else was now on his mind. A nagging weight he was trying to push aside. Pieces he was trying to hold together. And his sudden withdrawal was a cold wind that cut across my skin.

"Will you talk to me, please?"

"What do you want to talk about, Seren?"

His voice came out like a hollow sigh, and I crawled into the bed beside him, resting my hand on his back. "How about we start with what's bothering you."

He turned toward me, his eyes tired. "I told you, I'm fine." He reached out for me, his arms wrapping around my waist as he drew me tightly against his chest, the rhythm of his heart a steady force anchoring me to him, speaking in a language that slipped between the shadows of all the words he would not share.

*W*inter pushed forward, enclosing us in its relentless, frigid grasp. And as the weeks slipped by, I watched my body shift. My breasts were now fuller, belly taking the shape of a small hill hidden beneath the layers of my clothes. I knew I had entered my second trimester, and Lilica's haunting statements still rang in my head like a mantra that managed to muffle the nagging concern that followed me.

"What are we looking for, Mommy?"

We stood beside the rush of the river, frozen snow clinging to the banks. Dropping to the ground, I shoveled through the ice, searching for the flash of deep green. "We're looking for nettles, love."

She scrunched up her nose. "What are those?"

"They're a plant that is very rich in vitamins and minerals."

Though the trips into the forest with the crossbow, and the snares Domine set daily had managed to give us enough protein, I knew our diet was lacking in nutrients. We needed more, and the life tentatively growing within me was a constant reminder of that. Of the fragile balance we walked between starvation and survival.

"Look, Lili. See this right here?" She crouched beside me as I uncovered the hardy, feathered leaves of new growth hidden underneath the snow. "This is a nettle plant. They can survive the cold of winter but have lots of tiny little hairs that will sting if you touch them with your bare hands. So always be careful when you come across them."

She nodded, watching with wide eyes as I plucked off the leaves with a piece of cloth and stuffed them into my medicine pouch. "Are we going to eat them, Mommy?"

"Yes. They are safe to eat when cooked. I've read that they taste a little like spinach."

We spent the next half hour digging together through the snow along the river's edge, Lilica's voice excitedly calling out to me whenever she found a plant. Eventually, the bite of the cold claimed us, and I bundled up the nettles, following our tracks back to the shelter.

Stopping at the edge of the tree line, I plucked a handful of pine needles, adding them to our forage. High in vitamin C and other rich minerals, I knew they would make a good tea.

"He's back!" Lilica sprinted ahead of me, running toward Domine as he materialized through the forest on the other side of the shelter, his arms loaded with firewood. The deep tone of his voice collided with the rise and fall of her chatter as he set down the wood and bent to ruffle her hair.

A flash of gray danced in the corner of my eye, and I turned around to see the faint outline of the wolf among the trees, watching me. My heart tumbled in my chest, and a whisper spilled from me like a long sigh curling into the air. "Hi, Prince." Silent and still, he stood against the forest, his eyes locked with mine. And that's when I felt it.

A flutter, like the delicate wings of butterflies beating against my womb.

I sucked in a sharp breath and placed my hands on my belly. Tears gathered in my eyes as I stood there, sharing stillness with the wolf, while life moved courageously inside me. And I allowed myself to embrace the elation that stirred within, yearning to take shape. To give form to something I could reach out and touch.

All the months of apprehension that had shadowed me like hungry ghosts. The hiding. The running. The memories of Trendon that cut into the corners of my mind like a sharp knife. The wondering if the Grid would ever find us. For a moment, it all dissipated, taking flight like a bird untethered from its cage. If there was magic in this world, it was here. In this moment of snow and cold and the wildness of life. A safety that cradled me.

Tilting my head up to the sky, I allowed this hesitant joy to rush forward.

I was finally ready to bargain with hope.

CHAPTER THIRTY-FIVE

*T*ime was now measured by my body. By the swell of my stomach and the tiny movements within. The rush of life growing stronger.

Snow fell steadily, cloaking the forest in a heavy blanket of white, and every morning, we would shovel a path from our door. The drifts outside the shelter now rolling hills that obscured our sight.

Our days were spent in a quiet rhythm of firelight. A cocoon of warmth that chased away the howl of the wind outside. A tiny world we orbited among the vastness of the mountains. I began to teach Lilica how to read, her finger slowly tracing over the words in her book of fairy tales.

Once. Upon. A. Time.

Domine had made a checkerboard and taught her to play, her face drawn in concentration as she moved the round wooden pieces across the board, the gentle tapping sound like a soothing melody. While I took vigil. My mind a constant expanse of thought that floated between elation and a restless unease. And when Lilica would place her hands on the rise of my belly, bending down to whisper secrets too soft for me to hear, my heart surged and then constricted. I still couldn't get too attached yet. Nothing was guaranteed.

"Seren?"

Late evening had wrapped around us, and the crack and hiss of the fire filled the shelter as Domine brushed his hand across my cheek, drawing my attention away from the flames. I turned to him, watching the light play across his bare chest as he lay next to me in bed, his eyes searching mine.

"You're worrying again, aren't you?"

I nodded, giving him a wan smile as my fingers traced over the puckered scar that now stretched across his knuckle. It had healed well, but the memory of what he had to do that night still tore into me whenever I looked at it, my own guilt reluctant to loosen its hold. "It's hard not to worry."

"I know. But we've made it this far." His hand lightly trailed down my neck, past the slope of my breasts, and stopped at my belly, causing a rush of warmth to travel across my skin. "This baby is a fighter. Just like you."

I pulled him close, my hand clasping his as I met the heat of his mouth. He kissed me back like I was his air. Deep, slow, and hungry, and an urgent flood of longing washed through me, sending my pulse racing. His kisses still took me apart. They had always taken me apart. Words were not needed when he kissed me like this.

Arching myself, I slipped off my shirt and pants, discarding them on the floor, and pushed back the sleeping bag, watching his eyes burn with a concentrated intensity as he drank me in.

"God, you're so beautiful." His breath grew labored as his lips trailed whispers across my skin, against my ear, tracing an aching path to my breasts as his hands wound through my hair. Everywhere he touched, pleasure bloomed, my nerves alive and humming beneath him.

Fumbling with his pants, I slid them down and took him in my hand, a tangled sigh spilling from my lips as I spread my legs and guided him to me.

He hovered above, arms planted beside my shoulders as he drew himself slowly inside, lingering gently on the edge of my depths as his eyes met mine. He had been different with me lately. His fervency held back and replaced with a soft reverence, as if I was something fragile. And while I enjoyed the tenderness, I missed his fire.

"I want you to let go."

He stopped his movements, his voice trembling with a hesitance. "I don't want to hurt you."

"You're not going to." I gripped his hips and pressed my mouth to his, my teeth lightly nipping at his bottom lip. "Just let yourself go."

Something shifted in his eyes, and with a groan, he thrust himself all the way inside me, and I gasped, stifling a cry that begged for release as a sharp wave of pleasure crashed into me. His hands grasped mine, pinning me to the bed, his mouth consuming me until I was breathless. Until I was weightless. Until all I could feel was the pulse of his desire colliding with mine, and the beautiful, reckless heat we shared.

He shuddered against me, his breath a broken rasp, lips seeking my skin, and I joined him in the swift freefall. My limbs entwined around him as an orgasm so acute swelled within me that tears gathered, leaking a slow trail down my cheeks.

Domine lips captured the salt of my tears as I threaded my hands through his hair, losing myself in the depths of his eyes. In the perfection of this moment, with the glow of the fire dancing across our skin. The gentle out-breath of our release.

Pulling him into my arms, I traced my fingers across his back as the life inside me fluttered, tiny arms and legs dancing within.

"Dom." I took his hand and placed it over my stomach. "Can you feel that?"

He looked up at me, his eyes growing wide and full of wonder as his hand swept across the rise of my belly, his voice a shuddered whisper. "Oh my, God. *I felt that*. I just felt our baby."

*S*taring into the fire, I watched the flames lick over the coals, illuminating the walls in soft amber light. Domine had left to check the traps well over an hour ago, and I tried to still the impatient worry that paced beside me.

"Lili, I'll be right back. I'm going to get some more wood."

She nodded from where she sat crossed legged beside the fire, her book of fairy tales open on her lap, brow furrowed in concentration as she ran her finger across the words on the page. "Okay, Mommy."

I threw on my coat and closed the door behind me, the bite of the wind slicing across my skin as I trudged through the drifts toward the woodpile. Lifting the tarp now laden with wet snow, I bent over, the gentle rise of my belly jutting forward as I gathered up a small bundle of wood into my arms.

From the corner of my eye, I saw the flash of Domine's black coat obscured between the trees, and I sighed in relief, squinting into the growing dusk with my breath held, hoping he had brought back something. The last few days, our traps had yielded nothing, and we were now dancing around the sharp edges of hunger, carefully rationing for Lilica what was left of our meager food supplies. But as my vision sought him out through the gloom, I saw that his hands were empty, and he was not making his way toward the shelter. He stood there among the trees with his back to me, hands fisted at his sides.

"Domine?" I dropped the pile of wood and made my way over to him, following the winding trail of tracks that led into the woods. He didn't appear to hear me, and it wasn't until I grew close enough to touch him that he turned in my direction.

His face was a mask. A vacancy that had fallen across his features, his eyes leaden with shadows as if some silent battle raged inside him.

"What's wrong?" I ran my hands down his arms, my heart quickening. He looked so far away, and it sent a chill racing across my skin. "What happened?"

"Nothing." He pulled away from me and yanked off his hat,

raking his hands vigorously through his hair. "I just need to be alone right now."

"Domine." I reached out and grabbed his arm, drawing him close, searching for him beneath the somber veil of his eyes. "Talk to me. Don't shut me out."

He stiffened beneath my hold, shaking his head as he stared up into the trees. "What if I can't do this, Seren?"

My breath tangled in my throat. "What do mean? What are you talking about?"

He looked at me, his jaw tightly clenched. "What if I can't keep you two safe?" He gestured into the woods, a flash of anger gathering in his eyes. "I mean, I can't even provide us with enough *god damn* food. And you're pregnant. We could starve out here." His words came out clipped, like daggers piercing the air, and a heaviness pushed against my chest, sucking the oxygen from me.

We were solely dependent on him. I knew that. I had always leaned on his experience of living in the woods. His innate knowledge of survival skills. His unwavering resilience and optimism. I clung to it like a comforting blanket. But I could see the burden of responsibility was crushing him.

"Listen to me. We're not going to starve. We're going to be okay. We'll find food. We always do." I grabbed his shoulders, willing myself to believe my own words. "It's not *your* job to keep us safe. It's not your job to always hold it together."

He let out a shaky exhale, his voice trembling in the air. "I can't fall apart on you, Seren."

"Dom." I stepped closer to him, staring into the swirling depths of his eyes, the dark edges that danced between his fire. The silent footsteps of his ghosts. "You don't have to be strong all the time. You *can* let go. You *can* fall apart." I placed my hand on his chest, feeling the steady rise and fall of his breath, the desperate rhythm of his pulse. "Because I'm here. I can pick up the pieces. I'm strong enough to hold you, too."

A light flurry of snow began to fall around us as the shadows in his eyes softened and shifted, revealing a naked fragility that trembled beneath his gaze. "Then hold me, Seren." His voice came out in a fractured whisper as he grasped me by the arms. "I need you to hold me right now."

I wrapped myself around him, and he sank into me, his breath a slow sigh against my neck, his hands clutching my back. We stood there in silence as the snow dusted our hair and kissed our skin with its delicate chill. But I did not feel the cold. Only the beating of his heart against my chest. The release of his exhale. The way he held onto me as if I were his gravity. The way he needed me. The way we needed each other.

"Mommy?" Lilica's voice cut through the growing dark, her silhouette framed against the open doorway. "Mommy, where are you?"

"I'm over here, love."

Domine sucked in a breath and loosened his grip, releasing me with a tired smile, but as I turned toward Lilica and the faint light of the shelter, he grabbed my hand and quickly pulled me against him, his fingers reaching out to cup my face, eyes burning into me. "You know I'm only strong because of you."

CHAPTER THIRTY-SIX

*T*he wolf watched us from the trees as I sat in the hot spring with Lilica, steam rising from the water, obscuring the landscape in a fine mist.

"Do you think Prince wants to come in, Mommy?"

I ran the washcloth down her back. "No, sweetie. I don't think wolves like water very much."

"Why not?"

"I don't really know. I've just never heard of them swimming before."

"Maybe they swim when no one's looking?"

Bending down with a smile, I kissed the top of her head. "Maybe you're right." I leaned back against the rock ledge with a sigh, my body blissfully weightless as the warmth of the water sank deep into my muscles, washing away the nagging discomfort I had begun to feel in my hips and back as the child within me continued to grow, my belly now a large orb holding secrets inside.

Glancing back at the tree line, I saw that Prince was now gone, slipping back into the folds of the wilderness. His brief visits had begun to feel so comforting to me, like a kindred spirit keeping vigil over the three of us. A gentle presence I had begun to rely on.

"What are we going to name the baby, Mommy?" Lilica's hands fell to my stomach as it peeked above the water.

"I don't know, love. I think we should wait until we meet the baby." Those words caused a flutter of joy to percolate through me, an elation I was still hesitant to fully embrace. But I was now approaching my third trimester with no signs of complications, and the child felt strong inside me, which brought new questions to the surface.

When would this baby come? How many weeks did I have left? And could I risk a potential delivery out here in the woods?

These hesitant questions had pressed against me with each passing day, growing larger and taking on solidity as the pulse of time breathed against us.

"I'm ready to get out, Mommy."

With a nod, I pushed away my thoughts and stood from the water, the rush of gravity yanking me from my buoyant state as I made my way carefully across the rocks and gathered up our towels and clothes.

Slipping on our boots, we walked back toward the shelter, the curl of smoke rising from the chimney like a welcoming beacon. Leaden clouds had given way to patches of blue sky, and the teasing warmth of sunlight filtered through the trees. I could feel winter loosening its hold around us, the snow softening, no longer as dense and packed with ice as we plodded through it, the chill of the air less biting.

As we approached the shelter, a flash of bright color caught my eye, and my breath hitched in my throat as I bent down, cradling my belly.

"Lilica, look."

She crouched beside me as I reached out and brushed back the snow, my fingers revealing slender purple petals, their centers dusted with gold. "Crocuses." I smiled at her, watching as she gently ran her hand along the flowers. "Spring is almost here, Lili."

* * *

*D*omine spread out the map beside the fire, his finger tracing the trail that snaked across the mountain range.

"From where we are right now, it looks like it would take us about five days to get over the rest of these mountains." He looked up at me, his eyes flashing with anticipation. "And then another five days or so until we reach Alberta."

"Really? Just ten days. That's all?" My heart stirred at the thought. We were so close. We had been so close this whole time.

"There is a river, though, that cuts off our trail right here." His brow furrowed as he pointed to a blue line running beside the base of the mountains. "This is what I'm concerned about. It could be a bit tricky to cross this time of year. But we'll just have to figure that out when we get there."

"So, when do you think we should leave?" My hands drifted to the swell of my belly. I felt the baby tumble and kick within, my fingers running across the fabric of Domine's shirt I wore, as my own clothes had now grown too tight.

"Well, if the skies remain clear, and enough of the snow melts for us to find the trail again, I'd say we could be leaving as soon as two weeks."

"That soon?" My voice faltered as my eyes trailed around the room. For the last six months, this place had been our home. Our shelter from the cold. A haven of safety we curled into. And the thought of leaving it behind and exposing ourselves to the elements once more left a press of uncertainty that hovered against my chest. "Couldn't we wait a little longer?"

"We could. But with this river ahead of us," his hand splayed out along the map, "I don't think it would be a good idea. The longer we wait, the worse the spring melt will become. We have a very small window where we'll be able to cross. And this is it. This is our window. Right now." He looked at me, his eyes growing heavy as his voice dropped to a whisper. "And then there's your third trimester we need to consider."

I bit my lip, trying to push back the sudden, growing unease as I stared down at the lines etched across the map. I knew he was right. I knew we needed to get to Alberta before the baby came. Letting out a shaky sigh, I sought solace in Domine's steady gaze, my words like slivers of resolve taking form. "Okay, then. We'll leave in two weeks."

"Seren." Appearing to sense my apprehension, he leaned over

and pulled me into his arms, his hand falling to my belly as his lips hovered against my ear. "Don't worry. Everything's going to be all right."

$\mathcal{I}$ stood beside our shelter, watching as Domine placed the last of our belongings into the pack and adjusted the straps over the top.

"I'm going to miss this place." I squeezed Lilica's hand as I stared at the structure we had spent so many hours building. Months of our lives embedded in the wood and stone within. It had become more than a shelter to me. It had become our home. The place where life patiently grew. The place where love lived tucked beneath blankets and warmth.

"I'm going to miss it, too." Domine slid his arm around me and stared up into the trees, where wisps of clouds caressed the blue of the sky. "I hope whoever finds this place next will enjoy it as much as we did."

Something stirred within me. A bittersweet longing that wanted to cling to all the cherished things but knowing that moments always moved forward. The beauty of life suspended in impermanence, leaving only the memories behind.

"You ready to say goodbye, Lili?" I bent down and ran my hand through her hair, noticing how long it had become, the ends curling in tendrils that now tumbled down her back.

"Goodbye, house. Goodbye, room." She looked up at me as she clenched her walking stick in her hand. "Will Prince stay here?"

"I don't know, hon." My eyes drifted toward the trees that had now shaken off their heavy coat of snow, revealing the bright green of new growth on the ends of branches. "Maybe he will. Or maybe he'll decide to join us on the trail."

"I hope he follows us."

I smiled at her and picked up my pack, the familiar weight settling over my shoulders. "I hope he does, too, love."

* * *

*O*ur pace was now much slower on the trail. Snow still clung in icy patches, and drifts obscured the base of trees. Domine stopped every so often to check on me and insisted on taking my pack halfway through the day as my breathing grew labored from the steep incline that rose and sloped as we traversed deeper through the mountain range.

The air was cold, the vapor of our breath spiraling into the air, but the sunlight that filtered through the trees rested warm on my back, creating an invigorating contrast that energized me. It suddenly felt good to be moving again, and the lingering unease of leaving the shelter fell behind me as every step took us closer to Alberta.

"Will they have school there, Mommy?"

Lilica looked up at me as we sat together finishing our lunch, which consisted of stewed rabbit meat and the last of the rice I had stored away through winter, using it to break up the monotony of our meals. Now that spring was here, I looked forward to finding a wider variety to forage on the trail. The tender oval leaves of chickweed. The curled fronds of fiddle heads. Wild leeks and watercress. We had carefully rationed out what food we had stored in the shelter, and if Domine managed a few catches on the trail, we had just enough to last the ten days it would take us to get through the mountains and into Alberta.

I shifted myself onto the ground, supporting my belly in my hands as I leaned against a fallen log, hoping to ease the dull ache in my lower back. "Well, I assume they will have school there, Lili. And now that you're five, you might be starting Level One this spring."

"It probably won't be called that, though." Domine uncapped his bottle of water and took a swig from it. "I'm assuming the education system will be a bit different outside of the Grid."

"Will there be toys and games to play with?" Lilica's eyes grew wide.

"I hope so, love." I stared up into the trees, watching the branches gently bow against the breeze. The thought of my daughter in a classroom full of color and exploration filled me with a hopeful elation. A classroom void of sterile walls and white, silent rooms designed to cleanse the mind of individual thought. A place where knowledge was not information forced into her, but a source of wonder to be gathered.

A place where Lilica could grow untamed.

"How are you feeling? We have about two more hours of daylight ahead of us. Do you want to keep going, or call it a day?" Domine crouched beside me, his eyes soft as his hand rested against my back, his fingers gently kneading out the tension in my muscles. I wanted to set up camp and curl into his touch, to wash away the fatigue that had settled in my limbs. But the growing urge to keep moving tugged at me.

"Let's keep walking."

The hours on the trail soon blended into days, and as we slowly descended from the steep ridge of the mountains, the air around us grew warmer. The winter silence now replaced with the faint call of birds and the trickle of snow melt running from the crevices of rocks. The forest was waking up. And so was I. Something had shifted and grown within me since I left the Grid. No longer did I view the world through a tight lens. It was as if a curtain had been drawn back, revealing prisms of color and light I had never seen before. An unfurling that washed away the shadowed edges of my sight. The way the sun hit the trees in the morning. The color that spilled across the sky at dusk.

Everything was now viewed with a sharp clarity that left me buoyant.

The warmth and crackle of the fire lulled me into a dreamy state as I rested my head against Domine's shoulder, watching the last of the sun's rays dip behind the trees, hoping to see a familiar flash of gray between the green. Prince had not shown himself to us since we left the shelter, and a disjointed feeling of loss tugged at me. He had become an extension of us somehow, his presence slipping so gracefully in and out of the trees like a silent sentinel among the forest, and the lack of his presence now felt like a somber vacancy.

"Is Mommy sleepy?" Lilica whispered in my ear as she crawled onto what was left of my lap, her fingers playing through my hair.

"Yes, love. I think Mommy is ready for bed." With a smile, I wrapped my arms around her, breathing in that comforting smell of earth and trees that always seemed to permeate her skin. I knew I was going to miss this when we left the forest and washed away the wildness, replacing the scent of pine and wood smoke with detergent and store-bought soap. I had grown so accustomed to the earth beneath my feet, I wondered what it would feel like to touch pavement again.

"So, now that we are officially through the mountain pass, it looks like we have about six days until we reach Alberta." Domine had unfolded the map beside us and was studying it intently, tendrils of hair falling into his eyes as the shadows of firelight played across his skin. "We should be hitting the river by tomorrow."

"Well, let's hope it's crossable." I stared into the flames, pulling Lilica tighter against me. "What are we going to do if it's not?"

He looked up at me, his eyes momentarily flickering with concern. "We'll just have to figure that out when we get there. It's still early, though. I don't think the spring melt will be that bad yet." With a smile, he rose and took Lilica from my arms, helping me to my feet. "Let's get you sleepy girls into bed."

Domine brought in some heated rocks from the fire as I unrolled our sleeping bags inside the tent and helped Lilica into her pajamas, the chill of the evening sending goosebumps skittering across her skin.

"Mommy, when are we going to get to the Canada town?"

"Soon, sweetheart. Very soon." Wrapping a blanket around her, I tucked her into her sleeping bag as that whisper of restless unease skirted the edges of my thoughts once more. I clutched my belly as the life inside me shifted and stretched. "You get some sleep, love. We have a big day ahead of us tomorrow."

* * *

a gentle hand moved over my stomach, and I opened my eyes to the tent bathed in early morning light. Domine watched me from across the blankets, his fingers now lightly trailing up my arm.

Stretching, I rolled myself against him. The rise of my belly cradled between us. "Morning."

He leaned in close, his gaze wide and penetrating as he cupped my cheek in his hand, his voice an ardent whisper. "I love you, Seren."

His words caused a deep flutter to surge within my chest, washing my limbs with a delicious warmth. This sentiment that he used so sparingly always broke me wide open. There was a power behind it, a force that took claim of me, like something singular and sacred. A language reserved for me alone.

Entwining my hand through his, a teasing smile blossomed across my lips. "What's the occasion?"

"You are." He swept my hair back, his eyes swimming with a fierce longing that caught my breath. "You're the occasion."

My heart trembled and swelled with the thought of all the mornings to come with him. A lifetime of memories not yet made. Moments held together by time and fortitude. I rested my forehead against his, lost in the sudden rush of my gratitude. "I love you, too, Dom."

We lay there together, suspended in tender stillness and soft light, until Lilica stirred and awoke beside us, bringing movement and sound back into the tent.

The snares Domine had set the night before were empty, so I

heated up the last of the porridge I had boiled down a few days ago, made from acorns gathered on the trail.

Lilica scrunched up her face when I handed her the bowl. "I don't like this stuff, Mommy."

"I know, hon. I'm sorry. We'll get some meat soon. I promise." Our food supplies had now dwindled to only what we could catch and gather, and I pushed back the concern that gnawed at the edges of my thoughts. It would be okay. We were so close. Once we reached the river, we only had five more days left on the trail.

* * *

"*Y*ou ready?" Domine had shouldered his pack and was standing with Lilica on the trail, her walking stick thrust proudly forward.

"Come on, Mommy!"

With a smile, I joined them, threading between the patches of snow with the wash of a bright blue sky above us. A lightness unfolded within as I followed the rise and fall of their voices that wove through the trees, taking in the vibrant beauty of the forest now stripped of its harsh winter song.

As we continued along the trail, our steps now leading us further from the mountains and down into the lush undergrowth of the valley, the day grew warmer, and we shrugged off our coats. The feel of sunlight on my skin was a delicious reprieve, and the air smelled rich with life teeming from the moist soil. Brown-capped mushrooms and skunk cabbage. The white petals of bloodroot nestled between broad green leaves.

Bending down, I brushed aside some leaves on the forest floor, my fingers running over the cream-colored caps of the morel mushroom, the firm texture like honeycomb as I plucked them from the earth.

By mid-afternoon, we heard it. The faint rush of water that grew louder as we walked. A soothing hush that soon turned into a thundering roar. Picking up our pace, we slipped through the trees, coming to a stop as we reached a steep ridge that plunged abruptly downward.

My breath stilled, and a crushing weight pressed down on me as I stared into the swirling river churning below us. There was no sandy beach, no rocks. Just angry water, consuming everything in its wake.

There was no way we were going to be able to cross this.

CHAPTER THIRTY-SEVEN

"Shit." Domine hissed under his breath, raking his hand through his hair as I grabbed Lilica's shoulders and pulled her close to me.

"Be careful, Lili. I want you to stay away from the edge, okay?" I tried to hide the tremble in my voice and the sudden wash of dread that clawed to the surface, demanding my attention.

"Where'd the trail go, Mommy?"

"We have to find a way to cross this river to get back to it, hon."

Domine had begun to pace, his eyes scanning the swollen expanse of water, jaw tense. "I want you guys to stay here. I'm going to hike along the ridge and see if I can find a calmer spot." Dropping his pack beside us, he shot me a tight smile. "I'll be back in a bit."

I stood there watching as he disappeared through the trees, my hands clenched tightly around Lilica's shoulders.

"Mommy, let go." She looked up at me with wide eyes. "You're squeezing me too tight."

"Sorry, love." I loosened my grip and kissed the top of her head, releasing a long breath. "Why don't we make some lunch while we wait for Domine to get back? How does that sound, Lili?"

"What are we going to eat?"

"Well, I picked us a bunch of mushrooms today, and we have some nettles."

She just stared at me, her lips turning into a frown. I knew she was growing tired of our limited food, and a wave of guilt lurched within me. How many times had she felt the press of hunger? Sensed the weight of our collective worry? Buried her own needs beneath a smile? She was too young to have already learned the kind of resilience that left scars behind.

"You know, Lili." I bent beside her, wiping a smudge of dirt from her cheek. "We are just a few days away from Alberta, and when we get there, we are going to have so much yummy food to eat."

A small smile crept over her face, her eyes lighting up. "You promise?"

"I promise." With a smile, I ushered her away from the roar of the river and back into the fold of trees, setting our packs beside a fallen log. "How about you gather some sticks so we can build a little fire for lunch?"

With a nod, she began to collect twigs from the forest floor as I cradled my belly and eased myself down onto the ground, opening my pack to retrieve the food.

"Daddy came to visit me last night."

My hands stilled their movement, and I looked up at her. "He visited you in your dreams?"

"Yep." She deposited a pile of sticks and plopped down beside me. "He said he's looking for me."

My breath stilled. We didn't speak of him often. He had become something we tip-toed around, like a ghost we were afraid to startle. But he was always there, a silent presence lurking in the recesses of my mind, reminding me of all the things I had left behind. All the things left undone. And I wondered, now that we were in Canada and away from the claws of the Grid, could he still come after me and press charges somehow? Would he find a way to take Lilica?

Pushing back the unease, I pulled her into my lap, running my fingers through the tangles of her hair. "You know your daddy loves you very much."

"I know. But he looked so mad, Mommy."

"He looked mad when you saw him in your dream?"

"Yes."

So many questions hovered in the depths of her eyes as she stared up at me. The complexities of why he was no longer in her life was a story I would one day sit down with her and tell. But until then, I wanted to shield her from the grit of the truth.

"Your daddy's not mad at you, Lili. He's just sad because he misses you."

"Sometimes I miss him, too."

"Of course you do, love." I placed a kiss on her forehead, trying to fight back the rising ache in my chest. The tangled confliction I could never seem to fully outpace. "But you get to visit him in your dreams. How special is that?"

A gentle breeze swept through the forest, sending the branches swaying above us, and Lilica placed her hand to my belly, her stormy grey eyes flickering with an acute intensity that sent my pulse racing as her words spilled out in a whisper. "The baby visits me, too, Mommy."

* * *

*D*omine did not return until long after we had finished lunch. The sun now slanted low in the sky, the light waning as he made his way toward us through the trees, his face drawn.

"You didn't find a safe place to cross, did you?" My voice was a deflated sigh as he drew near. I already knew the answer.

He shook his head, eyes clouded with worry. "No. But I did manage to find a spot where the current isn't quite as strong and the bank is more accessible. It's still pretty deep, though." His jaw clenched as he stared at the churning water beyond us. "We'll camp here tonight. I'll figure out what to do in the morning."

"Why don't you build a boat?" Lilica stared up at him from where she had assembled her fairy carvings along the fallen log.

"I don't think we have the right supplies to build a safe enough boat, love." I crouched beside her, fingering the fairy house she had nestled between some moss.

"Why not? You built a house."

"Well, even if we could build a boat, it would be a bit tricky to get across the strong current." Domine looked up, his eyes tracking the branches as a small smile broke out across his face. "But you know what, wood nymph? You just gave me a really great idea. I can't do a boat, but I think I can do a bridge."

"What are you talking about?" I followed his line of sight as he pointed up into the trees.

"A lot of these are long enough to reach across the river. If I lash a few of them together, we should be able to cross at the place I found upstream."

"Are you sure it will be stable enough?" A tight band of worry scrambled to the surface once more. The same feeling that had paced beside me before we left the shelter, slipping in-between the trees like whispered words I could not define.

He took me by the shoulders and placed a lingering kiss on my forehead. "Yes. I promise I will get you two safely across this river."

*M*orning light glinted through the branches of trees as we stood along the sandy bank of the river. We had walked a mile upstream to the place Domine had found the day before, and the rhythmic thwack of his ax against wood now called out like a drumbeat through the forest.

"Be careful, hon. Don't get too close." I glanced over at Lilica as she threw stones into the water, watching the churning current swallow them up.

"I know, Mommy."

The warmth of the sun stole across my skin like a caress as I crouched along the rocky ground, gathering fiddleheads and miner's lettuce, yarrow, and mullein, and tucking them into the pouch of my medicine bag.

Domine appeared from the tree line, dragging three large saplings in his arms and setting them on the bank. "We're almost ready. I just need to tie these together." Retrieving a long cord of rope from one of the packs, I watched as he began to slice it into sections. He worked quickly and efficiently, connecting each pole with individual knots before lashing them tightly together with the rest of the rope.

"I think this is pretty stable, but I want to test it out first." He turned to me, the breeze gently blowing his hair into his face, and I had a sudden urge to wrap my arms around him. To hold him tight against me and not let go. I couldn't seem to shake the unease that had now lodged itself like a heavy stone inside my chest.

Lilica skipped over to me and took my hand as Domine carried the poles to the edge of where the river was less wide, and the embankment jutted slightly downward. Setting them on the ground, he slid them slowly over the current, the weight of the poles bending and swaying above the water until they hit the rise of the sandy bank on the other side, the makeshift bridge now resting roughly two feet above the depth of the river.

"Perfect." He shot us a wide grin. "I'm going to cross first, to see how well it holds."

"Domine. Wait." I lurched forward, clutching my belly.

"It's okay. I'll be right back."

My hand squeezed Lilica's, watching as he stepped onto the logs and began to inch over the river. Halfway across, the poles began to bow, and my breath caught in my throat, my pulse hammering out a frantic rhythm. "Domine!"

"I'm okay." He looked over at me with a smile as he lightly bounced his weight on the logs before continuing on, his feet landing safely on the other side. I let out a rush of air as he threw two thumbs up and turned to make his way back.

"It feels pretty stable." He picked up the two packs beside us and threw them over his shoulders. "I'm going to take these across first, and then I'll carry Lilica over." The roar of the river quickly snatched away his words, and my mouth grew dry, hands trembling as he stepped back onto the bridge once more, crossing over the swell of water churning below.

"Don't be scared, Mommy." Lilica must have sensed my apprehension in the unrelenting grip around her hand, for she looked up at me with bright, reassuring eyes. "Domine will get us over the water. He promised."

"Of course, love. Everything will be fine." I gave her a strained smile as Domine returned from depositing the packs on the other side of the river.

He bent down and ruffled her hair. "Are you ready to cross, wood nymph?" With a nod, she slid into his arms, wrapping her legs tightly around his waist.

I grabbed his hand and leaned in close to him, my voice coming out in a shaky whisper against his ear. "Are you sure it's stable enough?"

"Of course." He looked at me, his gaze solemn. "I wouldn't take her across if I felt it wasn't. You know that."

"I know." Letting out a sigh, I brushed back Lilica's hair and placed a kiss on her forehead. "I'll see you on the other side, okay, sweetie?"

"Okay, Mommy." She shot me a smile as Domine positioned her in his arms and stepped onto the bridge.

"Here we go. Hang on tight to me, okay?"

I stood there with my breath held, watching as the two most important things in my life traversed over the river. Lilica clung to his shoulders, her hands holding tight to his shirt as he slowly inched across the logs, the added weight causing them to shift slightly beneath his feet. My heart jerked in my chest as he paused for a moment, regaining his balance. And then they were on the other side. A wide grin splashed across Lilica's face as she called out to me across the roar of the water.

"Mommy, we made it!"

My legs buckled, relief washing through me as Domine made his way back over the river and took my hand. "Are you ready?"

"I guess so." I stepped onto the logs, my legs shaking as I stared down into the swirling water. I had never known myself to be afraid of heights, but now that I was precariously perched above the rush of the river, fear took hold of me with a convincing force.

"Don't look down." His hands fell to my waist, breath warm against my ear, soothing the frayed edges of my nerves. "I'm going to be right behind you the whole time."

"Are you sure it's safe with both of us?"

"Yes. It's sturdy."

I nodded and took the first step forward, feeling the poles shift slightly beneath us while my belly jutted forward, creating a feeling of imbalance.

"It's okay. I got you." His hands remained on my waist, a stable anchor guiding me forward as we inched across the expanse of water, the spray licking at my shoes.

I trained my eyes across the river to where Lilica sat perched on top of our packs, drawing large circles in the sand with her walking stick. I took a deep breath and focused on the way the sunlight glinted off her hair as I continued to creep forward, my feet taking cautious steps on the logs, which were now wet and faintly slick from the churning water below.

I don't know how it happened. My foot must have slipped. The tremble in my legs leaving me unsteady. For one moment I was walking, and the next moment I was grasping at air, my knees crashing against the wooden poles as I pitched forward and felt the rush of the river grab me.

CHAPTER THIRTY-EIGHT

The shock of the cold hit me, and for a moment, I couldn't move. I couldn't think. My mind momentarily suspended in animation as I sank beneath the dark, frigid grasp of the current.

Is this what drowning feels like?

My limbs began to thrash, tearing through the churning water, lungs screaming as I desperately scrambled for the surface. And then hands were grabbing my waist, pulling me upward.

I gasped in air, my heart pounding in my chest, the blue of the sky blinding as Domine clutched me tight against him, the rush of the river quickly pushing us downstream.

"I got you!" His voice was garbled and choked as he held onto me, and then I saw Lilica running alongside the bank, her eyes wide with terror, mouth open in a scream I could not hear over the roar of the water.

This isn't happening. This can't be happening.

Lilica.

My girl.

I can't leave my girl.

"There's a tree over there! See if you can grab it, Seren!"

Domine's voice broke the surface of my swirling mind, and through my haze, I could make out a dead tree leaning precariously on the side of the bank, its bare, weathered branches dipping low into the water. I reached out my arms as we tumbled closer, hands clawing, breath tangled, a prayer caught in my throat.

Please.

Please, get us out of here.

I grabbed onto a large branch, and with a cry of relief, grasped it tightly, my limbs like laden weights as I struggled to wrap my right arm around the rough bark. The force of the current slammed against me, icy tendrils tugging at my limbs, and that's when I felt Domine's grip on me loosen.

I shot my arm out, grasping at his shirt, only our hands now linked together as the water surged around us, the strength of the river unrelenting as I tried to pull him closer.

"Can you reach the branch?" My voice was a rasp as I clutched desperately to his hand, my eyes fixed on his.

"I think so."

And then I heard it. A sharp crack as part of the branch gave way, and I was violently tugged forward, my leg slamming against a rock below the water.

"Mommy!"

I whipped my head to see Lilica now standing on the edge of the bank, eyes pleading and full of terror.

"I'm okay, love." I tried to call out to her, but my words were lost to the thunder of water. Lost to the shock and panic that screamed inside me.

"Seren! Let me go."

"No!" I clutched his hand tighter, but my fingers were growing numb, the strength in my grasp quickly diminishing.

"That branch is not going to hold both of us! You need to get to shore now!"

"I'm not letting you go!" But the sound of Lilica's cries tore into my chest, and everything within me split in two.

"I'll be okay. I can grab onto this other branch over here. Just let me go." There was a strange calm in his eyes as he relaxed his fingers around my hold.

"No! What if you can't reach it?" My words spilled out in a shattered cry, a broken plea that fractured against my bones.

No. No. No.

"I can reach it. Let me go."

And then he slipped from me. My hand no longer in his. My fingers grasping at air.

Everything froze as his eyes met mine, awash with sorrow and a fierce resolve before the river took him, swallowing him up into its churning depths, and all I could see was the rush of water. His name spilled out in an anguished whisper trapped in my throat, a soundless scream that stole my breath as I realized he had been nowhere near the branch.

And he had known that the whole time.

"Mommy. Mommy!"

Lilica's cries jolted me back to myself, and I grabbed onto the rough bark with my other hand. Summoning what strength I had left, I pulled myself through the current and inched my body across the branch until I felt the relief of solid rocks beneath my feet.

My entire body shook as I scrambled onto the shore, my knees weak and my breath a ragged gasp as I collapsed to the ground.

"Mommy, I'm scared. Mommy, are you okay?"

Lilica's hands tugged at me, her voice a broken sob, and I gathered her into my arms, burying my face in the tangle of her hair. "I'm okay, love. I'm okay."

But I wasn't okay. Nothing was okay. My world had suddenly folded in on itself, and I couldn't get up. I couldn't move. All I could do was hold on tight to Lilica as a silent wail ruptured inside me and tears streamed down my face.

I don't know how long I lay there holding Lilica, but eventually I felt the baby shift inside, tiny flutters and kicks that pressed urgently against me.

I need to get up. I need to find him.

"You're so cold, Mommy."

Lilica's voice fell against my ear, and I wiped the tears from my cheeks, staring into the stormy expanse of her wide gray eyes. "I know, sweetie."

I forced my trembling body up from the ground, wincing as a tight band of pain shot through my leg. I knew I needed to get out of my wet clothes before the effects of hypothermia set in, but all I wanted to do was close my eyes. To will myself back to a tent bathed in early morning sunlight with the warmth of Domine's arms around me. As if this was nothing more than a cruel dream, and all I had to do was wake up.

"Mommy, is he gone?" She stood by the river's edge, staring into the wild stretch of water, her eyes full of confusion and a tangled sadness that ripped me wide open.

"I don't know." I crouched beside her, my voice a shaky whisper as I pulled her to me. I didn't have any answers for her. All I had was a blind hope that he had somehow found a way out of the river. That he was safe. That he was making his way back to us.

It was a desperate prayer that I clung to. It was all I had.

I swept my hand along her cheek, wiping away the salty stain of her tears. "What I do know is that Domine is very strong. We're going to try and find him, okay?"

"Okay, Mommy."

I took her hand, forcing myself to breathe, forcing my feet to slowly guide us upriver and back to where our packs were, back to where the log bridge still sat over the water.

"*D*omine!"

My cry cut across the rush of the river. My feet slipped on rocks, dry brush clawing at my clothes as I stumbled along the bank with Lilica, her somber eyes and heavy silence a mournful weight beside me.

Every breath, every moment, had now become a desperate mantra pounding against my chest.

He's alive. We'll find him. We have to.

The alternative was too paralyzing. A brutal possibility that threatened to destroy me. All I had was a relentless drive to keep looking. To keep hoping that, somehow, he was okay.

These hours of frenzied searching had now bled into days. The deep bruising on my leg a constant ache while my mind swam in a state of silent hysteria as we walked up and down the edge of the river, scouring every rock, bush, and log along the bank, combing for a sign of him until my voice grew hoarse, my body trembled from exhaustion, and I would have to force myself to turn around and retreat back to our camp along the shore.

"Mommy, my feet hurt, and my belly feels yucky." Lilica had stopped walking, her face pinched as she stared into the sky now streaked with color, the last of the day fading from my grasp.

"Come here, love." I bent and took her into my arms as a wave of sickening guilt tore into me. She was hungry and tired. I couldn't keep doing this to her. Brushing back her hair, I placed a soft kiss on her forehead. "Let's head back to the tent and see if we caught anything to eat in the snares."

But when we returned to camp, just as the last of the sun's rays slanted across the sky, the traps were as empty as they had been the day before, and the day before that.

I dug my fists into the ground, staring at the tangle of wires placed among the brush, defeat carving a hole into me. We couldn't survive off nettles and mushrooms. We needed more. And while I knew there were fish in the river, I couldn't find a way to catch them. I had nothing to make a basket or gill net with. My hand rose to my belly, searching for the signs of movement within, the gentle dance I was now so accustomed to, the silent exchange that tethered us together. But the baby had grown quiet the last few days, and I tried to fight the rising panic and grief that threatened to devour me.

What if something is wrong with the baby?

What if we starved out here?

What if Domine is dead?

I closed my eyes and took slow, deep breaths. I wanted to crumple onto the ground. I wanted to scream. To cry. I wanted someone to pick me up and save me. But there was no one to save me. I had to somehow find a way to keep the pieces of myself together.

* * *

J lay there as the faint light of morning crept across the walls of the tent, which now felt too large without Domine, too empty, too cold. His absence was an open wound that would not stop bleeding, and sleep could not find me. There was nothing to chase away the emptiness that howled inside. There was no blessed reprieve into oblivion. My nights had become an unforgiving landscape of darkness and deafening thoughts I was unable to silence, and I would spend hours tossing and turning, clinging to the warm body of Lilica, waiting for the relief of daybreak.

I slid my arm out from underneath her, watching the gentle rise and fall of her breath. Her eyes fluttered behind her lids as she surrendered to dreams, and a sharp wave of anguish hit me, fierce and consuming.

We weren't going to find him.

We had been here for four days now. Four days of searching for him along the river. Of clutching to a desperate hope that was now fading with each passing day. And I knew we couldn't stay here forever. We had to keep going somehow. We had to get to Alberta.

I have to say goodbye.

Scrambling from the sleeping bag, I grasped at the zipper of the tent flap, my lungs struggling for breath as a choking sob built within me. I staggered to the edge of the bank, hands and knees hitting the ground as I pressed my face into the cool sand and let out a muffled scream that shook my whole body. Tears rushed forth, brutal and overpowering as I wailed into the earth. Into the depths of a grief I could not hold back any longer.

You're gone.

And all I had left was the memory of his hand as it slipped from mine. The look in his eyes as the river took him from me. Took him from us.

I can't breathe without you.

My fingers clawed at the ground as if I could rip it open and place all the pain inside. Give it back to the water, back to the trees and rocks. Back to the turbulent and cruel beauty of this place. How could I go on without him? How could I pick up the pieces of myself and say goodbye?

Turk's voice suddenly crept in between the fissures of my sorrow. A faded memory of him as he stood in the sunlit kitchen of the cabin all those months ago.

"You two have a light together. That light will be your strength. No matter what happens, remember that."

But where was my strength? I couldn't find it. The river had taken it from me.

Another strangled sob poured out from the depths, and then something cold and wet nudged my arm. With a gasp, I jerked my head and looked up into the deep amber eyes of the wolf.

He had never been this close before. He'd always skirted beyond the trees, hiding in the folds of shadows like a phantom that would dissipate if I came to near. But here he was, standing beside me, and there was something so gentle and soothing in his eyes that, without thinking, I reached my hand out.

My breath hitched in my throat as I brushed my fingers across the coarse hair on his back, his fur faintly warmed by the morning sun. "Where have you been, Prince?" My words were a tattered whisper as I leaned closer and curled my hands into the fur around his neck, feeling the thick, soft undercoat beneath. "Where have you been?"

He lowered onto his haunches beside me, like an old friend giving comfort to the wreckage of my sorrow, and I rested my head on his back, breathing in the musky wildness of him. The consoling scent of earth and wind. The sudden naked trust between us.

Tears leaked onto his fur as I broke apart against him, giving myself up fully to the deafening grief that pounded within. And then, I felt it. A low, deep rumble that grew and expanded in his chest as he tilted his head back and let out a long, mournful howl that spread over me and spilled across the churning water.

It was a cry that spoke of goodbyes. Of loneliness and ache. Of darkness and light.

Of searching for a home that was lost.

CHAPTER THIRTY-NINE

*L*ilica stood next to me in silence, watching as I took down the tent. I was empty inside. A hollow shell. The pain I had released beside the river this morning was now a dull ache that muddled my thoughts and clawed at my insides. But the memory of the wolf was a beacon of comfort I clung to. He had sat beside me, lending his voice to my grief until I had nothing left, and Lilica had stirred from sleep, causing him to retreat, his form slipping silently back into the enclosure of the forest.

"Mommy. Will Domine be waiting for us in Alberta?"

Her question crashed into me, and the tent poles slid from my hands. I closed my eyes for a moment, summoning the words trapped within my chest. I couldn't cloak my answer in a fairy tale. I couldn't shield her from the truth any longer. She needed to understand.

"Sweetie." I crouched beside her and rested my hand on her shoulder, the ground beneath me appearing to tilt as the truth stumbled out. "Domine... He won't be in Alberta."

"Why not?"

"Because." I took a shaky breath as my throat constricted and a wave of fresh grief rushed to the surface, fracturing my vision. "He's gone."

"No, he's not." She stared at me, her brow furrowed. "He's not gone, Mommy. The fairies told me so."

How I wanted so desperately to believe her. To believe that her dreams were in fact premonitions I could peer into like a crystal ball. That magic was more than a story told to chase away the darkness. But reality was too cruel. And I was too lost within the depths of my grief to grasp at hopeful fantasies.

He was gone. And I had to somehow find a way to keep breathing.

"Honey. Those fairies that visit you. They're just dreams. Part of your imagination. They're not real."

"No! They *are* real, Mommy! Dreams are real." She clenched her fists, eyes swimming with tears. "Why don't you believe me?"

"Sweetie, it's not that I don't believe you. It's just that I need you to understand something." I tried to pull her into the harbor of my arms, as if the strength of my hold could diminish the loss, but she jerked away from me, her eyes flashing as she shook her head.

"No! *You* don't understand!" Her voice was a broken cry as she turned from me and ran, disappearing through the trees.

"Lilica! Come back here!" I lurched after her, my steps faltering on the uneven ground, sending a renewed surge of pain to radiate down my bruised leg. "Lilica!" I swept my gaze across the forest, my heart a wounded bird flailing against my chest as I searched for her among the dense undergrowth. "Lilica, where are you!" But there was no reply, only the roar of the river and the sharp intake of my breath.

A sickening panic coursed through me as I pushed deeper into the forest, searching for the bright flash of her hair, the dark blue of her sweater.

Where is she? Where did she go?

I screamed her name, blindly grabbing at branches, tripping over roots, until my legs gave way against a log and my knees hit damp earth. Branches swayed above me like hands clawing at the sky, and I let out a strangled wail as I sank to the ground.

Lili, please. Where are you?

"Mommy?"

A furious surge of relief tore into me as I looked up into her gray eyes.

"Mommy, don't cry. I'm sorry, Mommy."

Reaching for her, I clutched her against me, breathing in all the vibrant life that tumbled within her. The perfection and fire. The ferocity of my love held within her bones. "No. *I'm sorry*, Lili. I'm so sorry."

She climbed into my lap, curling her hands around me and burying her face against my neck, and I rocked her back and forth as I used to do when she was small enough to fit in the cradle of my arms. When she had yet to know of loss, and fear, and hunger. When it was just me and her enclosed in a world of soft words and warm blankets. How I wished I could take her back to that place of comfort. To shield her from every unforgiving reality. But I couldn't. One day, she would slip from me, and I wouldn't be able to hold her anymore.

Eventually, she untangled herself from my arms, and we stood, her hand clasped tightly around mine as we made our way through the trees and back to what was left of our camp.

Lilica went to gather her belongings while I finished putting away the tent and approached our packs sitting beside the river. My heart stilled as I stared at them.

I knew I could carry only one.

With trembling hands, I crouched onto the sand and opened Domine's pack, retrieving his bone knife, harmonica, flint starter, and the engraved box he had once kept my bracelet in. My fingers brushed against one of his shirts, and my throat constricted as I lifted it out, remnants of his scent still clinging to the fabric. All I had left of him were pieces. Fragments now trapped beneath the crushing weight of his absence. Closing my eyes, I pressed my face against the cloth, stifling a sob as the rush of agony slammed into me once more, stealing away all my breath.

This was all my fault. He would still be here if it weren't for me.

The warmth of Lilica's hand rested on my arm, wrenching me back from the urgency of my sorrow. I quickly stuffed his shirt into the recess of my pack, my voice coming out in a shaky whisper. "Are you ready to go?"

She nodded, staring into the churning depths of the water. "He'll come back to us, Mommy. He *always* comes back."

I pulled her close to me, sweeping away a strand of hair from her cheek. The stoic hope that blazed within her eyes was an unbroken beacon I longed for. If only I could find the strength to hold it with her.

"I hope you're right, sweetie."

The heaviness of the pack bore down on me as I stood and slung it over my shoulders, securing the cross bow on top before placing Domine's pack beside some bushes. Perhaps someone would find it and make use of what was left inside. Various pots and pans we no longer needed. A tarp and some winter clothing.

A life that had quickly unraveled.

I stepped away from the pack, the hot sting of tears obscuring my vision as the finality of it all hit me with a brutal force. How could I say goodbye when every breath was a plea for him? Every muscle and sinew in my body a reverberating cry? How was I supposed to stand among the rubble of loss and find the strength to move again?

We walked in silence, the trail stretching ahead of us in an endless swath of green bathed in mottled sunlight. But the beauty of spring did not touch me. Every step I took was like a knife carving the hole inside me a little deeper.

I just had to keep walking. To will my legs to carry me forward, focusing on the soft rhythm of my feet as they hit the forest floor.

As I navigated over a fallen log, I felt the faintest of kicks inside me. The gentle beating of wings that stretched and unfurled within. My breath hitched, and I slowed my pace, clasping my hands to my belly. This was the first time I had felt movement in almost two days, and a tumbling rush of relief coursed through me. The life within was still fighting.

Please be okay. Please be strong. You are all I have left of him.

"Mommy?" Lilica stood ahead of me on the path, her face drawn in a stoic line as she clutched her walking stick. "Are you talking to the baby?"

"Yes, love." I looked over at her with a faint smile. "I am talking to the baby."

"We should name him Forest." She fell in step beside me, our feet crunching against the undergrowth as we walked.

"Forest?"

"Yeah. Because he came from the forest."

I bit back the ache that twisted inside me. "And what if the baby is a girl?"

She frowned and shook her head. "No. The baby is a boy. I already told you that, Mommy."

I stared up into the trees and watched as the branches whispered their ancient secrets to the sky, remembering her birthday, the feel of Domine's arms around me, the dreams we had so quietly woven together, the hope I had dared to reach for. "I think Forest is a perfect name."

* * *

We made camp beside the trail as the last of the light winked through the trees, casting our skin in disjointed shadows. I sat hunched beside the fire, bleary-eyed and staring at the map, trying to force my brain to focus on the lines that snaked across the paper. From what it looked like, we had five more days of walking until we reached Alberta.

Five days. We were so close.

But all the anticipation of finally reaching our destination had been snuffed out. The light inside me dimmed to a faint flicker I could not draw from, leaving me clawing at nothing but darkness.

"Mommy, I'm still hungry." Lilica stared at me, her empty plate resting on her lap.

I set the map down and drew her into my arms. "I know, hon. I'm so sorry. That's all the food we have right now." I had given her the last of the mushrooms and nettles foraged on the trail, and my own hunger hissed sharply at me. We needed food, and I could not sacrifice my own intake. I had not put on much weight with this pregnancy. Every trace of nourishment went to the child growing within me. And I knew it wasn't enough.

"I'll find us something to eat tomorrow, Lili. I promise." I glanced over at Domine's crossbow leaning against the pack. I wasn't confident in my ability to use it successfully, and leaving the trail to try and hunt would be a risk that could potentially set us back days.

Precious days we didn't have.

"Why don't we get some sleep, and tomorrow we'll wake up bright and early and go find some food. How does that sound, love?" I kissed the top of her head and pushed myself to my feet. The day on the trail had left me exhausted and weak, the weight of my own grief pressing against my chest, and my entire body trembled as I made my way over to the tent.

Crawling into our sleeping bags, I wrapped my arms around Lilica, anchoring the warmth of her body against mine, steeling myself for another long, sleepless night. A night full of screaming thoughts I could not silence. The crushing emptiness that held me hostage. The bleeding inside I could not stop. But when I closed my eyes, the reprieve of sleep finally pulled me close, and I fell into the silence of oblivion.

* * *

"*Mommy!*"

Hands roused me from the tangle of blankets, and I shot my arm out, searching for the feel of Domine beside me. My heart stumbled as reality came crashing back, and I opened my bleary eyes to see morning light spilling in through the tent.

"Mommy. Come look! There's a bunny outside." Lilica hovered over me, her hands gripping my shoulders.

"A bunny?" I sat up and followed her through the open tent flap, streams of sunlight skittering across the floor. On the ground beside the tent lay a dead rabbit. I bent and picked it up, its body limp and still warm in my hands. "Where did this come from?"

"Prince brought it to us." Lilica pointed toward the trees, and I looked up to see the wolf standing there between the shadows of the forest. "I went to go potty, and I saw him with the bunny in his mouth. Then he dropped it by the tent."

My breath stilled, and something took hold of me, a reverence born of wonder as I stared into the depths of his eyes. "Thank you, Prince," I whispered, caught within a gratitude I could barely define. A soft, quiet magic born of wilderness and spirit.

"He let me pet him, Mommy."

Concern shifted against me as I looked at her. "He did?"

"Yes." A smile tugged at the corners of her mouth. "You want to see?"

"Lilica! Wait." I stood and grabbed her arm as she began to move toward him. "I know he may seem friendly, but he's still a wild animal. I don't want you just walking up to him."

"It's okay, Mommy. He's our friend." She held her hand out and made a gentle cooing noise, and I watched with a mixture of unease and amazement as he crept forward, crouching low to the ground until his muzzle met the palm of Lilica's open hand. His tail wagged in a wide circle as she ran her fingers across his back. "See. He likes it. You want to pet him too, Mommy?"

"I actually have pet him before, love."

Her eyes grew wide. "When?"

"Yesterday morning, beside the river." I threaded my fingers through his coat, remembering the delicate moment we had shared. The gentle ache of his song. The unfurling of my grief.

We stood there beside the wildness of the wolf, our hands resting on his back, and a sudden stillness washed through me, like arms holding together the fractured places inside. Beside the fragility of life, existed strength. It had always been there. It was the heartbeat hidden beneath the earth. The breath that slipped between the trees. The darkness colliding with light.

It was the fierce cry of a longing to survive.

CHAPTER FORTY

*T*he wolf now walked beside us. It was as if he knew it was his place, his footsteps filling a space where Domine's should have been. I found solace in his presence. In the silence he carried, the gentle wisdom in his eyes. There was a knowledge that ran deep in his blood. He knew how to survive. To live in harmony with the earth.

Nights no longer felt so unrelenting and bleak with him by our side. Though Prince appeared to be wary of the fire, he was always close, his body curled beside a log or resting next to the tent. And in the morning, he would leave us gifts of food we so desperately needed.

Morning stretched across the forest as I bent to pick up the partridge Prince had caught and left beside the tent, the feathers shimmering in the hesitant dewy light, black and tan plumage against gray. This would be his last gift to us. Alberta was now only ten miles away. We would be able to reach it before dark.

Stoking up the coals of the fire, I sat down and began to pluck the bird, my stomach responding to the thought of the rich meat we would have for breakfast. Protein that would fuel us for the last push forward. The final day spent here in the forest. I tried to summon some impression of relief as the reality of civilization loomed so close. But all I felt was a crushing sorrow. Soon, we would be starting a new life in Alberta. A life without Domine.

I set the bird down, willing myself to breathe. To find the

strength to keep putting one foot in front of the other and not turn back to the river and lay myself beside it like an offering. Like a plea to bring him back.

"Mommy?"

"Yes, love." I wiped at the tears on my cheeks and turned to see her standing beside me.

"Don't be sad. Domine's not gone. He'll come back to us. I saw him in my dream."

"You did?"

She nodded, and crawled into my lap, resting her head on my chest, and I clasped her tightly. The feel of her body against mine was an anchor holding me back from the fierce current of my thoughts. A placeholder for my grief. And for a moment, I clung to her words as if they could wash all the truth away.

* * *

*A*fternoon light flooded through the trees, bathing the forest in long shadows that danced across the trail. Lilica walked with Prince at her side, reaching out every so often to run her fingers through his coat.

A child and a wolf. There was something that felt so inherently natural between them. Between us. We were no longer a part of the outside world. We had blended into the trees, cast our nets upon the earth. And I wondered how we would be able to fit back into the framework of society once more. And did I even want to? Would a part of me always long to slip away again? To shed my skin against the forest floor.

"Mommy, will Prince come with us when we get to Alberta?"

I stopped walking as her wide gray eyes looked up at me. "No, Lili. Prince can't come with us."

"Why not?" Her brow furrowed as she ran her hand across his back. And my heart constricted.

There have been too many goodbyes in her life.

"Honey. I don't think Prince would be very happy living with us. He wouldn't be able to run free. His home is here in the forest."

"Can we visit him?"

I bent down beside her, resting my hand against the warmth of Prince's coat, the deep pull of his eyes meeting mine. So wild and full of secrets. "Maybe."

We continued walking in silence, the swell of birdsong filling the space around us as the trail dipped downward and the trees began to thin out. And then I heard it. A whoosh that intensified and then faded, reminding me of the way ocean waves crashed against the shore. The steady pulse of the highway growing closer.

We were here. We had made it.

"It's a road, Mommy. Look!" Lilica bounded ahead of me, her body flashing between the beams of sunlight as trees gave way to open sky. Standing there on the edge of the trail, she stared at the highway that stretched out to the horizon like an unbroken river. "Is this Alberta?"

A car rushed past us, the sound raucous and foreign to my ears, jolting me from the stillness of the forest. "I think so, love." I placed my hands on her shoulders and drew her close, suddenly unsure of what to do next. All I could see was endless road. Where was the town?

I stared at the small cracks in the pavement, noticing the fervency of wild grass pushing through despite the unyielding density of civilization's insistence to dominate. Turning to the right, something caught my eye, a small wooden sign hidden between two trees. Approaching it, I bent down to read the carved inscription.

Canmore, Canada. 1 mile west.

An arrow pointed across the highway to where the trail continued. Canmore. That was the small town circled on the map. I stood and turned to Lilica. "We're close, hon. We're really close. We just need to cross this road."

"Come on, Prince!" Lilica called for him as she clutched her walking stick.

I looked back at the wolf, who stood watching us. This was it. This was where we had to say goodbye.

"No, Lili. Prince can't come with us."

"Why?"

"Because the road isn't safe for him to cross. He needs to stay here in the forest, where his home is." I crouched down, placing my hand on her shoulder. "We have to say goodbye to him now."

She glanced over at him, her lip trembling. "But I don't want to, Mommy. He's my friend."

"I know, love. I don't want to, either." Sorrow pulled at me as I ran my fingers through her hair. "But sometimes, we have to say goodbye to our friends. Sometimes life takes us places where they can't follow. But he will always be a part of your heart. No matter what."

As if in slow motion, she broke away from me and walked over to Prince. Wrapping her arms around his neck, she buried her face into his fur and whispered something to him. A secret only he could hear.

I knelt beside him and placed my hand on his back, staring into those deep amber eyes that had begun to feel so familiar, as if I had been looking into those eyes my whole life. "Goodbye, Prince. I'm going to miss you."

Taking Lilica's hand, I turned with her toward the road. I didn't want to look back, but as my foot touched the pavement, I felt the wolf gently nudge my arm with his nose. "No, Prince. You have to stay here." He cocked his head at me as I pointed to the trail. "Go." My voice came out choked, tears welling in the corners of my eyes. "You have to go now."

He crouched low, dropping his head in what felt like the finality of a goodbye, as if he understood. As if he knew that our story together was ending. And then he turned and trotted away from us, his form slipping silently back into the woods.

My breath hitched in my throat as I stood there watching him disappear through the trees. He had saved us in so many ways, and I suddenly wanted to rush back into the enfolding shadows. To walk beside the wolf. I wanted to climb into the heart of the mountains and return to the shelter we had built, with the walls that forever held the memory of Domine's touch. I wanted to give birth on deep green moss and raise our child among the trees.

How could I go back to a world without Domine in it? He had always been my wild forest. My home.

"I'm ready, Mommy." Lilica looked up at me, her eyes sorrowful and resolute as she gripped my hand tightly in hers, and a part of me wanted her to cry and stamp her feet. To refuse to leave Prince behind. To be a child throwing her weight against the world.

Her stoic silence felt like a wound I could not heal.

* * *

The trail beyond the road grew narrow and groomed as we walked. Tall cedar and spruce gave way to scattered birch and oak, and the rich scent of moss and earth retreated. The forest had now softened itself, trading the wilderness for a cultivated landscape. A place for visitors to view nature from the safety of signposts and marked pathways.

My body habitually pulled me forward without thought, my feet against gravel a numbing cadence until I found myself stopped at one of the signs that loomed above us with a large arrow pointing north.

Canmore. 0.2 miles.

"Are we there yet, Mommy?"

"Almost, Lili."

The trail soon opened up to reveal the remains of a late afternoon. A wash of blue sky with faint streaks of pink and purple growing deeper against the backdrop of the mountains. We crossed a small footbridge beside tall whispering grass, our shoes making a hollow sound against the wooden planks, and then we were standing on a street lined with storefronts. The air around us now pulsed with a steady hum as cars slowly rolled past, and Lilica stared wide eyed and silent.

There was too much color and movement, and I found myself recoiling from it. So many months I had spent enclosed in earth tones and birdsong, with only the gentle sway of branches. And now we stood beside the loud chaos of life, like aliens thrust into a foreign land.

Someone brushed past us, and I pressed Lilica tight against me, stepping away from the sidewalk. I realized how much we stood out with our large packs and dirt-stained clothes, and I didn't want to stand out. I wanted to blend back into the trees. I wanted to hide beneath the enclosure of rustling branches and rich earth. I wanted to run back to the silence.

Everything felt wrong.

Disjointed.

Empty.

Domine was supposed to be here.

I stood there, trying to fight the growing panic. *What was I going to do now?* We had nowhere to go. No currency. No plan beyond reaching this town. Domine had mentioned a place where refugees could go for assistance. But I had no idea where it was or what it was called.

We were adrift with no anchor to grab onto.

CHAPTER FORTY-ONE

*W*ith a shaky sigh, I shrugged off my pack and placed it on the ground, trying to still my racing heart and find my bearings.

"Hello there."

Someone gently touched my shoulder, and I whipped around to see a woman standing next to me. Soft, dark eyes meeting mine.

"It looks like you two just got off the trail?"

Her smile was warm and inviting, but I couldn't seem to find my words. I nodded blankly at her, clutching Lilica's hand tightly in mine.

"Why don't you two come with me." She motioned for us to follow her down the sidewalk, and I quickly picked up my pack as she strode toward a red painted door with *Intake Office* inscribed on the front.

She ushered us into an office smelling faintly of coffee. A bell above the door sang quietly as she closed it behind her. "My name's Meladia, and that lady over there." She pointed to a woman with glasses, sitting at a desk by a window, her long blond hair tied up into a messy bun. "That's Betha. She will be the one to help you with intake."

The room was small and cramped with overflowing file cabinets and shelves lined with books, the walls holding framed photos of Canada. White-capped mountains and flowing streams. Meadows full of bright flowers. Sunlight delicately bending through trees.

With Lilica's hand still clasped in mine, I walked toward the desk. Betha looked up as we approached, a wide smile creasing the edges of her blue eyes.

"Hello you two. Please, take a seat." She stood as I fumbled with my pack, unsure where to place it. "You can just set that down anywhere." She thrust her hand out and enclosed mine in a firm handshake. "I'm Betha. The one who does all the paperwork around here." She threw me a friendly wink as she settled herself back in her chair and pulled some papers from a drawer. "So, you're seeking asylum here in Canada?"

I nodded. My words still lodged in my throat as I sat stiffly on one of the metal folding chairs beside her desk. Lilica scrambled onto my lap, burying her head against my shoulder.

"Okay. I'm just going to need some information from you." She pushed her glasses up the bridge of her nose and grabbed a pen from a small ceramic jar. It appeared to be something a child had made. Bold colors splashed across the surface of the glaze, and a tiny handprint stared back at me. "Can I get your full names, please?"

"Seren Gallo." My married name slipped from my tongue, foreign and tainted with a life that was no longer mine. A person I no longer was. "No. I'm sorry. I meant Maddocks. Seren Maddocks. And this is my daughter, Lilica Maddocks."

She looked up at me with a flicker of confusion before quickly replacing it with an understanding nod. "I see."

She jotted our names down, and a sudden wave of panic crashed against me as I realized I was no longer invisible. No longer hidden beneath the cloak of trees and sky. I had become a name on a piece of paper. A possible way for Trendon and the authorities to find me. "Wait." I lunged forward, gripping the corner of the desk. "Will this be made public information?"

Setting her pen down, she leaned back in her chair. "No. All personal documentation is kept strictly confidential." Her tone shifted, and she looked at me with concern etched across her face. "Are you running from something?"

I nodded, my gaze shifting to Lilica, who still sat curled in my lap.

"Hey, sweetie?" Betha stood and crouched beside Lilica. "There's some stuff for you to play with over there." She pointed to a corner of the room where a couch and toys were scattered across the floor. "Do you want to go check them out while your mommy and I talk for a little bit?"

Lilica looked up at me with wide eyes.

"It's okay, love. Why don't you go play? I'll be right here."

She slid off my lap and made her way slowly toward the couch, glancing back at me with a look of hesitancy.

"I was caught in possession of illegal herbal medicine." My voice was a hurried whisper as I fiddled with the buttons of my shirt.

Betha returned to her chair. "I see. And where are you coming from?"

"Washington."

"The Grid?"

"Yes."

She sighed and took off her glasses, placing them on the desk beside her. "The Grid has no legal jurisdiction here in Canada."

"So you're saying there's no way they can find us? There's no way they can take my daughter from me?" My voice was a soft murmur as I spoke, but desperation trembled at the surface like a sigh that could find no air.

She leaned across the desk and placed her hand on mine, her eyes warm and gentle. "No. You're both safe here. You guys made it, Seren. You're free."

Those words hit me. All the months of running. Of trying to survive through the harsh winter. The hunger and fear that constantly sat beside me. It all led to this moment. To these words.

I'm free.

But I didn't feel free. I felt bruised and broken, lost without Domine. The fragments of myself rearranged into a pattern I could not recognize. The rush of tears gathered, and I tried to brush them back, but they crept down my cheeks, staining my skin.

"How long have you been out there on the trail, Seren?"

"A long time." I looked over at Lilicia, who was now sitting on the carpet playing quietly with a doll she had found, cradling it in her arms like a baby, her hand sweeping back the silky hair.

Betha opened a drawer and slid something toward me. "These are vouchers for food and clothes." I stared at the slips of paper, the colors blurring together. "And you will be provided with some temporary housing. We had an opening last week, so there is a unit available for you now."

My hands fell to my belly. "I need to see a doctor for an ultrasound."

"Of course. We can get you an appointment first thing tomorrow morning." She placed a key beside the vouchers. "Do you know how far along you are?"

I bit my lip and stared out the window at the mountain range towering against the darkening sky. "I'm not sure. I think I'm almost seven months."

"Listen." She took my hand again, the warmth of her fingers curling around mine. "Transitioning can be a bit of a challenge. Things are very different here. But we have people who can help you adjust. I'm going to set you up with Vanisha." Releasing my hand, she placed a business card beside me with a phone number printed across it and a picture of a tree, its delicate branches reaching outward. "She'll help you get settled in."

"Okay." My head spun, and my limbs felt weak as I picked up the vouchers with shaky hands and crouched to place them in the front pocket of my pack. "Thank you for all of this. For everything."

"Not a problem." She finished writing something on my intake form and then stood, placing a hand on my shoulder. "You guys must be hungry. I have some food bags in the back I can get you, and then I can take you over to your unit."

I nodded as Lilica appeared at my side, tugging on my shirt. "Mommy, what's a unit?"

With a small smile, I bent down and swept back her hair. "It's our new home, Lili."

* * *

*W*e sat in the back of Betha's car as she drove us to the edge of town. The rumble of the engine beneath me felt strange, and there were no electric seatbelts or glowing screens on her console. Lilica had opened her bag of food, and apparently unable to decide what to eat first, was now simultaneously stuffing a turkey sandwich and muffin into her mouth.

"Slow down, sweetie." I placed my hand on her arm. "I don't want you to choke."

"But it's so good, Mommy," she mumbled through a mouthful of food.

Betha caught my eye in the rearview mirror and smiled. "So, this unit you'll be staying in is fully furnished with everything you need." She fiddled with a knob on the dashboard, and a swell of sound filled the interior of the car. It was melodic and haunting, reminding me of the notes Domine used to play on his harmonica by the fire.

"What's that sound, Mommy?" Lilica stared at the car dashboard, her eyes wide.

My throat tightened, and a sharp feeling of yearning rose inside me. "That's music, Lili."

"It's pretty, Mommy."

"It *is* pretty." I stared out the window as the music drifted through the car, filling me with an emotion both sorrowful and light. I watched the houses slip past. Streets with trees that were real and alive with the brilliant burst of spring color, and I suddenly felt like a small child viewing the world for the very first time.

"What did you do when you lived on the Grid, Seren?"

Betha's voice stirred me from my thoughts, and I glanced in her direction, momentarily confused by the question.

"What did I do?"

"Your occupation? You mentioned herbal medicine."

"Oh. Yes" I sought solace in the dusky view of the mountains in the distance, remembering all the patients I had left behind so long ago. The steady support of Kystina. The job that had been my identity for so much of my life. "I was a doctor."

"That's so great." She turned on a blinker and navigated the car onto a narrow street. "We are in need of more doctors here. We have one clinic in town but would love to be able to expand at some point." She looked back at me with a wide smile. "We have a hospital, but the majority of our primary care is, in fact, holistic." With a lurch, the car shuddered to a stop beside a row of multi-colored houses. "We're here."

Dazed, I stepped from the car with Lilica, clutching our packs and staring at the houses pressed closely together. They all looked the same. Boxes with windows and doors. Walls that shut out the light. And there it was again. That urge to step away from all the lines and edges. To retreat back into the soft whisper of the trees.

"Which one's our new home, Mommy?"

"I don't know, love."

"It's right over here. Follow me." Betha motioned us over to a house on the far corner of the lot, slipped a key inside the door handle, and pushed it open. "Home sweet home." She placed the key in my hand with a smile.

I clenched the strange metal key in my palm, feeling the rough grooves dig into my skin as I looked around the space. It held a kitchen and living room with a matching green corduroy couch and two chairs beside a wooden coffee table.

"It's not much. But it has everything you need to be comfortable. There are two bedrooms and a bathroom down the hall."

"What's this?" Lilica approached a large black box with a glass screen.

Betha crouched beside her. "That is a television."

Confusion washed across Lilica's face as she looked at her. "Why doesn't it come out of the ceiling?"

Betha chuckled. "We don't have the same kind of modern things here that you're probably used to. But it works and has a few local channels on it." She pushed a button on the front, and the screen sprang to life with movement, spilling colored light across the carpeted floor.

Lilica clutched the remains of her sandwich in her hand while she stared at the images, transfixed.

"Well, I'll let you guys get settled in. I'm sure you're both exhausted." Betha stood and threw me a warm smile. "Vanisha will be in touch with you tomorrow morning."

The door closed softly behind her, leaving us confined in a room that suddenly felt too loud. I walked to the television and turned it off. The assault of sound blessedly fading into silence.

Lilica wandered past me and down the hall, her voice echoing off the walls. "Mommy, there's a bathtub!"

I stared into the kitchen. Knobs and handles in place of sleek automated screens. I flipped a switch on the wall beside me and watched as a light turned on. Everything had to be touched and turned, moved and pushed, and I found a strange comfort in this. As if for the first time in my life, I had control. An intimate relationship with the objects around me, a physical connection.

"Mommy. Can I take a bath?" Lilica appeared next to me, her face smeared with food.

"Of course, sweetie. A bath sounds like a really great idea."

* * *

I folded back the bedcovers to reveal crisp, white sheets. Lilica jumped onto the bed, her hair wet from the bath and still smelling of the fruity shampoo I had found in one of the bathroom cupboards.

"Mommy, where are you going to sleep?"

"In the other room down the hall. Unless you want me to sleep in here with you tonight?" I positioned her in front of me and began to brush out the tangles in her hair, trying to focus on the task at hand. On the way the mattress sank underneath my weight. The silence that buffered the empty ache screaming inside me.

"No, Mommy. I'm a big girl now. I want to sleep in my own room."

With a smile, I tucked her into the covers and smoothed back her hair, placing a kiss on her forehead. "Okay, then. You get some sleep, love. I'll see you in the morning."

"Goodnight, Mommy." She nodded and rolled over, clasping her fists around the tiny wooden fairies Domine had carved. And the shattered pieces within myself throbbed against my chest as I stared at them.

All we had left of him were memories.

I closed the door halfway, leaving a crack of light from the hallway to filter across her bed, and made my way into the bathroom. Shedding my clothes on the floor, I turned on the shower, allowing the steam to billow out and surround me like smoke as I stared at myself in the mirror. I had not looked into a mirror in so long that the image in front of me felt unrecognizable. Stringy blond hair hung loose and tangled at my shoulders. My cheeks sunken. I reached my hand out, touching the cool glass with my fingers, as if solidity of form could give way and shatter the haunted gaze that stared back at me. I squeezed my eyes shut, hoping the darkness of sight could block out the truth they revealed beneath the reflection.

The child within me fluttered faintly, and my hands fell to my belly, imagining it was Domine's hands that were sweeping across my skin. His arms that cradled me. The depths of his eyes finding mine with all the love the river had taken.

God, I miss you.

How am I supposed to go on without you?

I stifled a sob and stumbled into the shower, hoping to mask the sound of my grief as the hot spray pummeled against my back.

CHAPTER FORTY-TWO

*T*he sound of knocking jolted me awake. Bleary-eyed, I groped at the sheets and untangled myself from Lilica, who must have crawled into bed with me sometime during the night.

"Who is it?" My voice came out shaky as I crept to the door, placing my hand against the painted wood.

"Vanisha."

I opened the door to bright morning sunlight and a woman's smile. She was striking, with hazel eyes set against deep brown skin, and long dark hair dusted with threads of gray that fell in coils down her back.

"I'm so terribly sorry to wake you. But I am to take you to your doctor appointment very soon." She spoke with a thick accent that sounded French, the words flowing past her lips like something rich and melodic.

"Oh, okay." I opened the door for her to enter. "Just let me get ready real quick."

"Well, hello there." Vanisha bent down to Lilica, who had appeared in the doorway beside me. "What is your name?"

"Lilica."

"Oh, my… Your eyes." She stared at Lilica with a sudden look of surprise that flashed across her face before she quickly concealed it with a wide smile. "You are very beautiful."

Lilica tentatively pointed at Vanisha's hair. "What are these?"

"These, my dear, are my locks. You can touch them if you'd like." With a wink, she pulled her hair forward, allowing Lilica to run her fingers through the coiled strands.

"I like them."

"Why thank you. I like them as well." Vanisha stepped into the living room with a large bag I only now noticed was slung over her shoulder. "I brought breakfast and some clothes. I thought you two might like to wear something clean and nice." She opened the bag and handed me black pants and a loose blouse with a delicate pattern of flowers, the fabric soft and almost silky against my fingers. "And these are for you, Lilica." She placed a pink ruffled shirt and matching skirt into her open arms. "I hope you like pink."

A wide smile stretched across Lilica's face as she stared at the outfit. The Grid never had bold colors to wear. Clothing had always been a palette of muted shades that blended together so that we all looked the same. Nondescript and devoid of individual expression. A blank slate to draw upon.

"Thank you so much. You really didn't have to do all this."

"But it is my pleasure." Her eyes sparkled as she breezed past me, trailing the faint scent of lavender. "Betha forgot to show you the phone for making calls." She bent down to a low cupboard hidden in the wall beside the couch and retrieved a thick rectangular-shaped device with a long cord attached to it. Plugging it into a small square hole in the wall, she turned to me with a smile. "Do you know how to use this kind of phone?"

I shook my head, clutching the clothing against my chest.

"It is very easy." She detached the top portion to reveal a series of large glowing buttons. "You just push the numbers and listen for the ring tone." She made a gesturing motion of placing it to her ear before setting the device down on the coffee table.

With a nod, I looked over at Lilica, who was still gazing at her ruffled skirt and shirt as if in a trance. "Sweetie, can you go and get changed for me? I need to head over to the hospital for an appointment."

"Why, Mommy?"

I looked out the window, watching as the morning sun painted faint streaks of pink across the sky. "So they can take a look at the baby."

* * *

*T*lay on the exam table, staring up at the white ceiling, my pulse pounding in my ears. Lilica sat on a chair beside me, running her hands along her new pink skirt.

"I'm so pretty, Mommy."

"You are, sweetheart. You are very pretty." I gave a strained smile and took her hand, clasping it tightly in mine.

The door opened, and a young-looking nurse walked in, her blond hair tied up into a high ponytail. "I'm just here to do some bloodwork." She pulled a tray from the corner and took a seat next to me. "The doctor will be in shortly to do your ultrasound."

Rolling up my sleeve, I placed my arm against the table and leaned in close to her, my voice coming out in a harsh whisper. "I need you to do a cancer screening as well."

She looked up at me. "Well, we usually don't with standard bloodwork."

"Please."

She nodded and slid a disinfectant wipe across the vein of my inner arm. "Do you have any specific concerns or risk factors?"

I glanced over at Lilica, watching as she ran her finger along a stack of brochures, glossy faces with painted smiles staring back at her. "We're from the Grid."

"Oh, I see." She furrowed her brow and inserted the needle into my arm. "Yes, of course. We'll run a cancer screen for you."

Taking a deep breath, I closed my eyes as the needle drew out my blood, my pulse rapidly accelerating. It had been so long since I had tested myself, and the hiss of anxiety awoke inside of me.

What if they find something?

The nurse finished and slipped out of the room, only to be replaced by a tall older woman with a smile that widened as she breezed past us and over to a machine standing against the far wall.

"Hello, Seren. I am Doctor Pendell. I will be doing your ultrasound today."

She moved efficiently as she retrieved a bottle from a drawer and flipped a switch on the machine, illuminating the screen in front of her. "How far along did you say you are?"

"Seven months, I think."

She lifted my shirt and applied a warm gel onto my stomach. "And have you had any spotting or cramping at all?"

"No. But I have uterine adhesions." I twisted my hands together and tried to focus on my breathing, on the way the light filtered in from a crack in the closed blinds. "And I've been worried about complications."

"Well, let's take a look at the baby and see what's going on." Her soft brown eyes rested on mine for a moment as she placed the transducer against my belly and slid it around in slow circles before glancing up at the screen. She stared at the monitor, adjusting the image, and then typed something onto the keyboard.

Lilica began to bang her feet against the chair legs, the rhythmic thumping causing me to reflexively flinch as the residual demands from the Grid took hold of me. "Lili, hon. You need to be quiet."

"Oh, she's okay." The doctor looked over at her with a warm smile. "Hey, sweetie. You want to come and have a look at the baby?"

My heart fluttered, bone and breath colliding in my chest, and I tilted my head up to see a grainy black-and-white image moving on the monitor.

"Would you like to know the sex?"

"Yes." My voice came out in a plea as I stared at the screen.

"It's a boy."

"I told you, Mommy." Lilica grinned at me and peered at the screen, her eyes growing wide as she watched the tiny, jerking movements of an arm and leg, the hazy profile of a head.

"Is he healthy? Is he okay?"

"Yes. I see no signs of any abnormalities or areas of concern. It looks like you have yourself a perfectly healthy baby boy."

"I do?" A surge of relief overcame me, and the sting of tears gathered in my eyes.

We're having a boy, Domine.

She clicked a button on the monitor and enlarged the screen. "You said you had uterine scarring?"

"Yes."

She shook her head and looked over at me. "There appears to be no scarring on your uterus."

My head swam in confusion, the room suddenly seeming to tilt at an odd angle. I had seen the scans the doctors had shown me. The 3D images of my uterus riddled with lesions. "Wait. I don't understand. How is that possible?"

She furrowed her brow, staring at the enlarged image on the screen. "I'm not entirely sure. But I see no lesions or scarring detected on the ultrasound."

Just then, the nurse breezed back into the room and handed the doctor a slip of paper. She stared at it for a moment and then bent down close to my ear. "All your bloodwork is within normal range."

"Even…"

"Yes." She smiled at me and placed a warm hand on my shoulder. "All of it."

* * *

*D*azed, I found myself standing in the waiting room with Lilica, watching as Vanisha stood from one of the seats and walked over to us.

"How did it go?"

"I got to see my baby brother!" Lilica bounced on the balls of her feet as she looked up at Vanisha with a wide smile.

"That is so wonderful." Vanisha turned to me, meeting my eyes as her voice dropped to a low whisper. "Is everything okay?"

"Yes. I think so." I bit my lip and fiddled with the prescription for pre-natal supplements I had clenched in my hand. The baby was healthy. I was healthy. My lesions had somehow miraculously disappeared. But nothing could silence the scream inside me.

You're supposed to be here.

"Well, how about we head on over to the market and pick up some food for your apartment?" Vanisha's hand fell to my back, stirring me from the deafening roar of my thoughts.

With a nod, I followed her out the door and toward the car, my hand wrapped tightly around Lilica's, as if her touch could anchor this feeling of falling inside me.

The car hummed along the road, passing houses and trees that blended into a blur of color as I stared blankly out the window.

"Mommy, what's that?" Lilica pressed her face against the glass as we passed a long stretch of green grass with a jumble of equipment in the middle.

"That is a playground." Vanisha looked back at us with a smile. "Would you like to check it out?"

"Mommy, can we?" Her eyes grew wide and imploring as she stared at the park where a few children climbed along some low bars, their hair ruffling in the breeze.

"Sure, hon."

The car came to a stop, and we stepped out. Lilica ran ahead of me, a bright flash of pink against rich green, her sneakers squeaking in the dewy grass.

"What are these?" She halted beside some plastic seats suspended by long chains.

"These are swings." Vanisha bent beside her, her eyes twinkling. "You want to try them out?"

She nodded eagerly and allowed Vanisha to help her onto the seat, her hands wrapping around the metal chains.

"Okay, are you ready? Hold on tight."

A high-pitched shriek erupted from her as she propelled through the air, and my heart stumbled in my chest until I saw the smile. Her eyes alight with a joy I had not seen in so long.

"Mommy, look! I'm flying!" Laughter bubbled from her, an infectious sound that sent tendrils of warmth curling through me.

"You *are* flying, Lili."

I sat down on a bench, watching while Vanisha continued to

push Lilica, showing her how to pump her legs back and forth until she had managed a rhythm on her own.

"Well, she's having fun." Vanisha appeared beside me and took a seat, her gentle hazel eyes meeting mine. "I know all this is a lot to take in right now. You've spent your whole life living in a world that has constricted you and your child."

"I know." I watched as a bird took flight from a tree, its wings colliding with the clouds as it soared upward, and then I felt her hand curl over mine.

"You lost someone, didn't you?"

My breath stilled, and I turned to her. "Yes. How did you know?"

"I can see it in your eyes. There's deep loss there. And it is not the kind we learn to gently bury with time. It is fresh."

I yanked my gaze away, allowing the grief within me to rise into tears that slipped down my cheeks. "His name was Domine."

She squeezed my hand tightly, her voice a note of sorrow. "I'm so very sorry, Seren."

I sucked in a trembling breath, watching as Lilica soared through the air on the swing, sunlight catching the strands of her hair. "The thing is, I know I should be grateful for this place, for everything that it's offering us. But I don't want it. *I just want him back.*" My words came out broken as the sob trapped beneath my chest struggled to free itself. "I don't know how I'm going to find the strength to do this without him."

She slid her arm around me, her touch like a veil of comfort I found myself sinking into. "To feel *everything* is the only way to live. When you embrace the pain, that is when you find strength inside. That is where healing is found."

Biting my lip, I stared into the blue above me, watching the wisps of clouds float past like graceful hands holding up the arc of the sky. How much pain had I pushed down through the years? The loss of my family I carried with me had only furthered the fear of more. But loss was a part of life. And Domine was right. *"Nothing is forever. But we love regardless of that. It's what makes life so precious. It's what gives us strength when we need it the most."*

Releasing a sigh, I brushed away my tears and glanced back at Lilica, who had jumped off the swing and was now climbing one of the structures. Her face pinched in concentration. "Lilica still thinks he's coming back."

"Lilica is a *very* special child, Seren." She leaned forward and took my hand again, her eyes now piercing into me. "How long has she been dreaming?"

I stared at her, goosebumps prickling across my skin. "She started soon after we left the Grid. How do you know that?"

"Her eyes." She looked over at Lilica for a moment and then turned back toward me. "There are children being born with gray eyes like hers. We call them Dream Walkers. Ones who possess the power to connect to the Source through dreams. The essence of life. Some believe they are here to bring balance back to the world."

An inexplicable feeling grabbed hold of me. The same impression I had on Lilica's birthday when she told me about the baby. It was disbelief mixed with wonderment. As if the threads connecting me to reality were loosening to reveal something larger than I could possibly comprehend. "And you think Lilica is one of them?"

"I think she could be. Yes."

I stared at Lilica, who now sat perched atop a slide, her cheeks rosy from the slight chill of the spring wind. "She always talks about the fairies in her dreams."

Vanisha leaned in closer to me with a smile. "Those are not fairies, Seren. They are spirits she is communicating with. Beings that exist between the veil of this reality."

"How do you know all this?"

She sighed and leaned back against the bench, her eyes glancing toward the sky. "Scientists have been studying the subtle shifts in humanity for quite a while now. We are slowly evolving beyond this three-dimensional world, as we were always meant to. And those in power know it. That is why they have been holding so tight to control by numbing us down with complacency and disrupting our energies with illness."

My head began to swim, and I grappled with my breath, trying to wrap my mind around what she was saying to me.

"I believe when you left the Grid, these abilities within your daughter were activated." She looked at me with an intensity like an endless sea I could feel myself tumbling into. "Why do you think we have no modern electronics here? No access to wireless technology?" She swept her hand through the air. "It is because those things disconnect us from the Source. From the earth. They keep us chained from our own inherent power. You see, we *all* have power inside us. But these children. These Dream Walkers. Your daughter." She smiled, the edges of her eyes flashing with warmth. "They are very special. Not only do they possess the ability to reach beyond this veil of reality, but some of them even have the power to heal with touch."

"The scars I had on my uterus…" My breath came out tangled as my hands fell to my belly, carrying me back to memories of Lilica running her fingers across my stomach, her eyes fixed with a focused stare as she whispered secrets to the child inside.

Was she a healer? Was it her touch that had healed the lesions inside me?

Vanisha tilted her head at me, a knowing smile pulling at the corners of her mouth. "Perhaps Lilica is one of the healers."

It was all too much to take in, and I bent forward, trying to still the sudden spinning in my head. My daughter was a Dream Walker. What was I supposed to do with this information? What compartment could I place it inside?

As if reading my mind, Vanisha placed her hand gently on the small of my back. "There is nothing you need to do but be her mom right now. It is within that place of love that all answers are found."

319

CHAPTER FORTY-THREE

A light rain pattered softly upon the roof as I stood in the kitchen, packing up a sandwich into Lilica's new lunch box. She stood beside me, her fingers tracing over the bright yellow sunflowers on the front.

"Are you excited about your first day of preschool?"

"I thought I was going to kindergarten?"

"You will, sweetie. But because you're starting so late, the teachers thought it would be a good idea to wait until next year."

She furrowed her brow at me. "I'm smart enough for kindergarten."

"Of course you are, love. This has nothing to do with how smart you are." I crouched down and placed my hands on her shoulders. "It's just that school here is very different, and this way you'll have a chance to get settled in better." I looked into the gray of her eyes, and I suddenly wanted to burrow back into the covers with her. To let the day drift around us. To hold her close and never let go. "You know, you don't have to go today if you don't want to. You can stay home with me."

"No. I want to go." Her eyes flashed with a steely resolve, and I drew back with a small smile before leaning in to place a lingering kiss on her forehead. "Okay then. I guess you should go get ready so we can head out."

"Is Vanisha picking us up?"

"No, we're going to walk. It's only a few blocks from here, remember?"

With a nod, she padded down the hall and disappeared into her room, which was now in a state of chaos, with clothing and toys strewn across the floor. I couldn't seem to bring myself to make her clean it. Perhaps it was too much of a reminder of the Grid. I didn't want sterile order and neat boxes to fit everything in. I wanted the mess and disarray of living a life that was finally our own, even though the sacrifice felt too heavy and consuming to hold.

I stared out the window at the rain trickling down the glass. We had been here for six days now. Six sunrises and sunsets against the backdrop of the mountains. And every hour that rushed past me was another moment, another breath without him. Sometimes I would pretend he was here with us. Sitting on the faded green corduroy chair whittling something with his bone knife. Reading a bedtime story to Lilica, with the gentle rise and fall of his voice filtering down the hallway. His arms holding me in the darkness of the bedroom, hands silently tracing the contours of my skin, chasing away all the ache inside me for one brief moment. And if I closed my eyes long enough, it almost felt real.

"I'm ready, Mommy."

I turned to her and wiped at a tear that had crept down my cheek as I picked up the lunchbox from the counter and headed into the living room. We slid on our coats and shiny new rain boots bought with our vouchers at the department store, grabbed our matching umbrellas with the brightly colored polka dots, and opened the door to a morning washed in a misty spring rain.

Lilica chattered excitedly as we walked the three blocks to her preschool, pointing out tiny details to me. The color of the roses in someone's yard. The way the air smelled sweet like honey. The patter of the rain as it hit our umbrellas.

She was vibrancy, the warmth of sunlight pulling back the clouds around me, and I couldn't stop thinking about my conversation with Vanisha. Words that shook my foundation and forced me to reframe everything I thought I knew about this world and the doled-out reality I had clung to my whole life. Our language was too limited at times to explain the depths of an existence that traveled beyond our scope of understanding. Magic was the only thing I could think of to describe it.

My daughter was magic.

The kind that would bloom and flourish now that we no longer lived within the clutches of the Grid. And whatever kind of life she had ahead of her, I felt honored to be able to watch it unfold.

"We're here, Mommy."

Lilica stirred me from my thoughts, and I looked up at the cheerful yellow painted building in front of us. Daffodils peppered the walkway, and the sounds of children drifted toward us as we approached and pushed open the door.

"Welcome." A soft female voice greeted us as we stepped inside a large room full of bright color and the chatter of children.

I looked around at the walls adorned with artwork. The patterned rug strewn with pillows, the floor scattered with wooden blocks. It was so different from the Learning Center at the Grid, with its blank walls and neat rows of metal desks.

"You must be Lilica." A woman with long dark hair bent beside her, a wide friendly smile stretching across her face. "My name is Miss Denya, and I will be your new teacher."

"Hello." Lilica clutched her backpack and stared at the children moving around the room.

"We are just about to do some painting. Do you like to paint, Lilica?"

She looked up at me, her eyes flickering with uncertainty, and I placed my hand on her back, leaning in close to her ear. "Remember those drawings you like to do in the dirt sometimes? It's like that, but on paper with fun colors."

"Okay." Her eyes lit up, and she nodded at the teacher.

"Great, why don't we get your backpack into one of these cubbies over here, and then I can show you around." She guided Lilica over to a corner and helped her remove her boots and coat, placing her backpack onto a brightly painted shelf.

"Lili." I crouched down and smoothed back her hair. "I can stay for a bit if you want me to."

"No. I'm fine, Mommy."

"Are you sure?"

"Yes." Her eyes bounced around the room, a smile tugging at the corners of her mouth as she drank in this new world around her.

"Okay, love. Well, you're going to have so much fun." I pulled her in for a hug I found myself reluctant to release. "And I'll be back in a few hours to pick you up."

My heart clenched as I stood and watched her walk off with the teacher. It had been so long since she had been separate from me. I had grown so accustomed to her constant presence, like a lifeline guiding me forward, and the idea of spending the next four hours without her felt abrupt and daunting.

I closed the door behind me and made my way down the sidewalk, passing the puddles now collecting on the concrete. Shimmering reflections caught the gray of the sky as I squinted into the rain, allowing the drops to fall on my cheeks like tears. The cold sting was a welcome distraction, and all I wanted to do was crawl back into bed. To shut out the light and burrow beneath the covers. To no longer muffle the tangled threads of my grief as they spilled out onto the sheets.

A harsh ringing sound filled the living room as I stepped inside our unit and set down the umbrella in a corner. For a moment, I just stood there, staring at the phone, forgetting momentarily what its purpose was. Fumbling with the bulky receiver, I lifted it to my ear. "Hello?"

"Is this Seren Maddocks?" The voice on the other end sounded tinny and far away.

"Yes. This is her."

"This is Grenda from the hospital."

"The hospital?" My heart slammed against my chest, and I gripped the cord in my hand. "Is this something to do with my bloodwork, or the baby?"

"Oh, no. Nothing like that." There was a pause on the other end before she continued. "There is someone here who's looking for you. She says her name is Kystina."

A wave of confusion slammed into me, and I sank onto the couch, my hands grasping at the fabric for support. "Kystina?"

* * *

J pushed open the doors of the hospital, glancing wildly around. And then I saw her. She was sitting on one of the cushioned chairs in the lobby with a large pack at her feet, her short, cropped hair now loose and wavy against her shoulders. Our eyes met from across the room, and a rush of exhilaration spread through me.

She was here. How was she here?

Kystina pulled me into a crushing hug, and I held her tightly against me, sinking into the solidity of her arms. She smelled of forest and wood smoke, and the familiar scent felt like home. "Oh my God, Seren. Look at you." Her eyes traveled down to my belly, an elated smile unfurling across her face. "I knew you'd made it."

"How did you get here? How did you get out?" My words came out rapid and breathless as I clutched her arms. "I was worried about you."

"I'm fine. I managed to get out through the underground. They're rising up, Seren. A group of them helped me and a few others. They're over at the intake office right now."

My gaze bounced around the room as my thoughts struggled to arrange themselves. "Why are you at the hospital, then? Is everything okay?"

"Seren." Her voice grew low, and she placed her hands on my shoulders as if to steady me, her eyes locking onto mine. "It's Domine. He's here."

"What?" The room grew fuzzy, my legs suddenly unable to bear the weight of my own body as gravity collided with the urgency of my pulse. "How do you know about him… what do you mean he's here… he was-" The words lodged in my throat, my head swimming.

"We found him by the river."

"He's alive?"

"Yes." She kept a firm hold on my shoulders, anchoring me. "He's alive."

For a moment, I couldn't breathe. Everything inside me was suspended in disbelief. The hum of voices and the movement of people around me muted.

Domine was alive.

"Is he okay? I need to see him. Right now!" A loud, frantic sob tumbled from me as I grasped at Kystina. "Where is he?"

"They just took him in for surgery."

"Surgery?"

"Yes." Her face grew solemn as she nodded. "He has a pretty bad infection in his leg, and it's broken in two places. But the surgeons are confident they should be able to save it."

"His leg?" My lip trembled, and that's when I realized tears were streaming down my face. The rush of joy and relief mixed with a terrible sorrow at the thought of all he must have gone through. "How did you find him?"

"Let's go sit down. You look like you're about to pass out." She slid her arm around me, and I crumpled against her as she guided me toward one of the empty chairs in the lobby.

I sank onto the chair and grasped my knees, trying to still the racing of my heart and the flood of emotions that spun like a storm within me, tangling my breath.

Kystina took my hand and squeezed tight, her eyes resting gently on mine. "We found him on the bank about five miles downriver from the trail. We had been looking for a place to cross."

"Five miles?" I pressed my hands to my head and bent over, my voice coming out choked. "I walked up and down that riverbank for days looking for him. How could I have passed him? How did I not see him?" I clenched my hands together, fingernails digging into my skin as a sickening rush of guilt crashed against my chest. "He was so close the whole time. This is all my fault. *Everything* has been my fault. If I had not slipped…"

"No, Seren, none of this is your fault." She placed a steadying hand on my back, her touch pulling me from the wreckage of my thoughts. "He was wedged underneath a log and delirious from infection. *We* almost didn't see him."

A moment of silence punctuated the air around us. Kystina's hand remained on my back while I stared at the floor, watching faint shadows flicker across the black and white tile as people strolled past. If Kystina hadn't been a few days behind me on the trail, if they had gone upriver to find a place to cross instead, Domine would have never been found. Life was a series of accidental miracles, and I suddenly felt cradled by something so large and encompassing it stilled my breath. Turning to her, I clasped her hand in mine. "Thank you. I can't believe you found him, Kystina. You saved his life."

"He's a fighter, that one." She brushed back a strand of my hair, her fingers softly wiping away the tears on my cheek. "Why didn't you ever tell me about him?"

A smile washed across my face. The first smile in two weeks that felt truly real. "Because he was my beautiful secret."

She nodded, and I saw tears of her own gathering in the corners of her eyes. "Sometimes we need beautiful secrets in our life." She stared out the window, watching the rain as it now fell steady upon the sidewalk. "The first few days after we found him, before I managed to get his infection somewhat under control, he was pretty incoherent, but he kept repeating your and Lilica's names over and over again. I could tell how much he loves the two of you." She turned toward me with a wistful smile and motioned toward my belly. "The three of you, I should say."

I spread my hands across my stomach as the gentle stirrings of the child moved within, and the emotions that had been trapped in my chest released in a long sigh. The thought of seeing him again, of feeling his warmth against my skin, the soft cadence of his voice, the rush of his eyes, filled me with an overwhelming elation I could barely contain. "How long will the surgery be? When can I see him?"

"The doctor said she would give me an update soon."

I bit my lip, my fingers restlessly twining together. "How bad is his leg?"

She sighed and leaned back against the seat, running her hands through her hair. "Pretty bad. He had two compound fractures. But I was able to stabilize the break on the tibia, and we made a stretcher and took turns carrying him. It was slow going, but we managed to make it into town early this morning."

I closed my eyes, trying to block out the images that rushed at me. Him lying broken beside the river. The pain and fear that must have consumed him. I felt it all with a visceral ache that tore into me. "But he's going to be okay?"

"That's what the surgeon said."

I stared at the clock, watching as the seconds ticked by, each one bringing me closer to him, and the shock that had stilled my mind lifted, leaving questions tumbling to the surface.

"Kystina." I leaned closer to her and grasped her arm. "What happened at the Grid? What made you leave?"

She glanced out the window again, her hands clenched in her lap. "Well, a few days after you left, they took me in for questioning. They couldn't find any solid evidence to incriminate me, but it didn't stop them from putting me on surveillance and revoking all my travel passports." She shook her head, her eyes flashing with a resolute anger. "For months, those fuckers followed me everywhere. Unmarked cars outside my house. Men in suits trailing me at the store. That's when I made contact with the underground." Her voice lowered to a whisper. "There are people inside the civil service branch who are part of the underground. They were able to smuggle me and a few others out one night in patrol cars."

My breath hitched in my throat, imagining what could have happened if they had been caught. If any of us had been caught. I looked down at my hands, fingers gripping the edge of the upholstered seat as a question hesitantly slipped from my lips. "Did you ever hear from Trendon again? Do you know if he's still looking for us?"

"Oh, yes. He's still looking." She turned to me, a small smile twitching in the corners of her mouth. "But he won't find you. He thinks you're somewhere down in California."

I clasped her hand in mine, so grateful for her solid presence beside me. For the gift she had brought back into my life. "I can't believe you're here. I thought I would never see you again."

"You can't get rid of me that easy," she said with a chuckle, the deep blue of her eyes twinkling with a mirth I realized I had missed so much. She had been my pillar for all those years while everything inside me was crumbling. She had always been there. Strong and unwavering.

"Are you Kystina?"

A voice from behind us startled me, and we both turned to see a woman in scrubs standing beside us.

"Yes." Kystina nodded and gave my hand a tight squeeze.

"Domine is out of surgery now."

CHAPTER FORTY-FOUR

My heart leapt in my throat, and I scrambled to my feet. "How is he? Were you able to save his leg?"

"And you are?" The woman looked at me quizzically before glancing down at a clipboard in front of her.

Kystina stood and placed a hand on my back. "She is-"

"His wife. I'm his wife." The words tumbled from me before I even had a chance to think.

The woman jotted something down and looked up at me with a smile. "Yes. We were able to reset his compound fractures and remove the infected tissue. We're hoping with some physical therapy, he should be able to make a full recovery."

"Thank you." The flood of relief washed over me, and I resisted the urge to throw my arms around her. To tell her how much we had been through. How much I had lost and found again. "Can I see him?"

"Well, he's still coming off the anesthesia and will be a bit groggy, but yes, you can see him." She motioned for us to follow her down the hallway, her shoes squeaking on the shiny tile floor. Every step bringing me closer to him.

She stopped at a door within the post-surgical unit, her hand resting on the knob. "The doctor should be in shortly to talk with you."

"Okay." My voice trembled as I stepped into the room, my eyes falling to a hospital bed in the center of the room. Domine lay shrouded by a stiff white sheet, wires snaking across his chest, eyes closed. My breath caught in my throat as I crept closer to him and reached for his hand. The feel of his skin, warm against mine, was a shock to my system, and the swell of gratitude burst within me as I watched his chest rise and fall, the machine beside him monitoring his heart rate. His breath. The delicate rush of life inside him. "Dom. It's me. I'm here."

"He's still asleep. He should be waking up soon, though. His vitals look great."

I turned to see a nurse I had not noticed when I came in. She now stood next to me, adjusting the sheets over the cast that covered his lower right leg. He looked so fragile and out of place among the sterile equipment and blank walls. I knew him strong against snow fall and green trees. Endless sky and mountains. He was the force that stood beside my heart, and I just wanted him to wake up. To see those deep brown eyes on me again.

Sweeping back his hair, I gently traced over a mottled bruise on his forehead, noticing a small laceration along his cheekbone and another above his eye. I leaned close and pressed my lips to his temple, breathing in the scent of forest that faintly hovered beneath the disinfectant.

You're here.

The sound of a chair sliding across the room startled me, and Kystina's hand rested on my back, motioning for me to sit. I sank into the chair, clutching his hand tightly in mine as I jerked my eyes to the clock above my head. "Oh my god. Lilica. She gets out of preschool soon. I need to pick her up."

"Don't worry. I can get her for you."

I looked up at Kystina. "Are you sure?"

"Of course. Just let me know where she is."

I fished out a crumpled map from my back pocket, noticing my hands were shaking as I unfolded the creases. "I walked here, but it's not too far." I pointed to a circle on the map. "The preschool is called Growing Tree. And you'll probably need a note or something." My eyes fell to a pen and note pad sitting on the counter. Jotting down a hasty message for the teacher, I signed my name and handed it to Kystina.

"Okay, I'll be back in a bit." She took the piece of paper and map from my hand with a smile and headed toward the door.

"Kystina."

"Yes?" She turned toward me.

"Thank you. Lilica will be so happy to see you."

Her eyes grew soft as she opened the door. "I'm going to be really happy to see her, too."

I slid my chair closer to the bed as the nurse brushed past me and stood at the monitor, writing something down on a clipboard before glancing back at me. "I need to go check on another patient, but I'll be back soon."

I nodded as the sound of the door closing wrapped the room in silence, leaving me with only the steady beeping of the monitor and my unraveled exhale. I ran my hand down Domine's arm, fingering the leather bracelet, which still remained intact around his wrist, hoping my touch would stir him from sleep, but his eyes remained closed, body unresponsive. Leaning over, I rested my cheek against his. "Wake up, Dom." My voice was a whisper in his ear as I closed my eyes and felt the shiver of his breath against my skin.

I lost track of time as I sat there with my hand clasped around his, my head on his chest, listening to the rhythmic anchor of his pulse. But suddenly, I felt his fingers twitch and then take hold of mine with a strength that made me sit up with a gasp.

He stared at me, his eyes wide and locked with mine, and for a moment, I couldn't breathe as my heart swelled and took my words.

Reaching out to me, his fingers lightly touched my cheek. "Seren?" His eyes flooded with confusion, sparks of amber colliding with the glare of the overhead light. "Is that you?"

I took his hand, bringing it to my lips. "Yes. It's me. You're in the hospital. You just got out of surgery. They were able to save your leg."

He glanced wildly around the room, trying to sit up, his words faintly slurred. "Where's Lilica?"

I placed my hand on his chest, trying to still his momentary disorientation as his heart rate spiked on the machine. "Lilica is okay. She's safe. Kystina is picking her up from preschool right now."

He sank back onto the pillows, and that's when clarity seemed to wash over him, for he suddenly gripped my arm, the solidity of him piercing into me. "Seren." His voice came out choked as he pulled me close and slid his hands into my hair, resting his forehead to mine. "You're here."

"I am." A sob rushed from me, and I clutched at his back. All the days of my grief and the fractured anguish that had clawed a hole so deep inside me now dissolved against him. "I thought you were gone. I thought I had to do this without you."

"I know." His voice was a soft murmur as he brushed back my hair, his thumb sweeping away the tears on my cheek. "I'm so sorry."

Taking his hand, I placed it over my heart, which thrummed desperately inside the cage of my chest, emotion tearing into the root of my composure. "And I *can't*. I can't do this without you."

He shook his head, threading his fingers through mine. "But you already did. You got here on your own. I knew you would."

The swell of tears streamed down my face as memories I had been unable to sit with now engulfed me. The icy chill of the water. The pull of the current. The look on his face as his hand slipped from mine. "Why did you tell me to let go when you knew--"

He placed his finger to my lips, stilling the words that frantically spilled out. "Because I love you."

The door opened, and the doctor walked in, but Domine didn't break his gaze from me. His eyes spoke with a silence that needed no language, like an embrace without touch, and everything fell away as I lost myself to it. To the visceral elation of him alive and here beside me.

"It's good to see you up."

The soft cadence of the doctor's voice broke the moment. Taking a shuddered breath, I hastily wiped away the tears from my cheeks as Domine finally looked over at the woman who now stood beside us, her salt and pepper hair pulled into a loose braid that hung down her back.

The doctor slid a chair over to the bed and took a seat, her clipboard resting on her folded knee. "How are you feeling?"

"I feel better now." He squeezed my hand and looked down at his cast, which peeked beneath the sheet. "And I'm glad to see my leg is still intact."

"Yes." She jotted something on her clipboard. "As the nurse explained to your wife, we were able to remove the infected tissue and repair the fractures."

Domine turned to me as she spoke, a small smile stretching across his face, and warmth rushed through me as his thumb ran a slow circle along my wrist.

"With some physical therapy, you should be able to regain full mobility." She leaned over and detached the wires from his chest, flicking the monitor off. "We're going to prescribe you some antibiotics and medication for pain, and we'd like to keep you a few nights for observation. But after that, you should be good to go." I nodded at the doctor, watching as she stood and made her way toward the door. "I'll let the nurse know you're awake."

"My wife?" Domine looked at me as she left the room, his eyes flashing with intensity as he reached out to stroke my cheek. "I like the sound of that."

"Me, too." I leaned into him, brushing my lips across his fingers. There were no labels between us. There never had been. But I knew I had given myself to him the moment I climbed that ladder up to his loft. The moment I opened my heart to him once more. We had married beneath the trees, under starry night skies. In all the days spent together. He was my forever. He always had been.

"Seren." His voice was a hesitant whisper as he searched my eyes. "Is the baby okay?"

"Yes." My lip trembled as I took his hand and placed it on my belly. "It's a boy."

"A boy?" His eyes grew wide, and he let out a long sigh, cupping the taut rise of my stomach. "Lili was right."

"She was." I squeezed his hand, wanting to tell him about

Vanisha and the Dream Walkers, about Lilica's gifts. But the door suddenly flew open, and Lilica ran into the room in a flurry of excitement.

"You're back! I knew you'd come back!"

"There you are." His eyes lit up, and he broke into a wide smile as Lilica tumbled into his arms. "I missed you so much, wood nymph."

"And I missed *you*." She clung to him, her tiny fists clenching his shoulders, and a buoyancy swelled within as I watched them. Their bond a resilient thread woven gently together.

Releasing him, she stared down at his leg, her face growing somber as she tentatively touched his cast. "You have a big ouchie."

"I do. But the doctors were able to fix it, and I'm feeling much better now."

"That's good." She traced her fingers along the sheets. "I tried to tell Mommy that you'd come back, but she wouldn't believe me."

"She wouldn't, huh?" He swept his hand through her hair. "Well, I think your mommy was just *really* sad. Sometimes sadness makes it hard for us to believe in something better."

"You're not sad anymore, are you, Mommy?" She looked up at me, her eyes wide and full of hope as everything in her world slid delicately back into place.

"No, hon." I drew her close to me, placing a kiss on her forehead. "I'm not sad anymore."

Kystina appeared beside me and nodded at Domine with a smile. "You're looking better."

"Well, I have you to thank for that," he chuckled as Lilica began to chatter to him about her first day at preschool.

"I got to paint pictures and play with so many toys. And we sang songs."

"Really, wood nymph? What kind of songs did you sing?"

I slid my arm around Kystina as Lilica took a deep breath, her voice sharp and clear, filling the room with a haunting, buoyant light.

"You are my sunshine... my only sunshine. You make me happy... when skies are gray."

CHAPTER FORTY-FIVE

*C*ar headlights sliced through the rain as Vanisha drove us down darkened streets and past neighborhoods now growing familiar. We came to a stop in front of our unit, and I released my hold on Domine's hand as I helped him out. He grimaced as he slid from the seat, navigating the awkward crutches in front of him.

Soft light streamed from the windows, bathing the sidewalk in fragments of shimmering orange as we made our way to the front door. A flood of warmth and the comforting aroma of basil and rosemary hit me as we entered. And for the first time since we arrived here, this place felt like home.

"Hey, guys." Kystina greeted us from the kitchen, her hands submerged in soapy water as Lilica bounded down the hallway.

"You're here!" She rushed at Domine in a tangle of arms and legs.

"Careful, hon." I placed a steadying hand on her shoulder. "Watch his leg, okay?"

"Okay." She stared up at him starry-eyed, clutching his arms. "I'm supposed to be in bed, but I'm waiting for you to read me a story."

With a smile, Domine leaned on his good leg and bent to ruffle her hair. "I would love to read you a bedtime story, wood nymph."

"Pajamas and teeth brushed was as far as I got with that one." Kystina dried her hands on a dish towel and went to grab her coat, sliding it over her shoulders. "She's been waiting by that window for him all night."

"Thanks for watching her and for making dinner." I motioned toward the pot of soup on the stove. "It smells amazing."

"Not a problem." She placed a quick kiss on my cheek. "I don't think I'm ever going to get used to the variety of food available here."

"Me neither." My recent trip to the grocery store with Vanisha had been like walking through an exotic landscape. The plethora of fresh vegetables and herbs on display had overwhelmed me, and I had found myself frozen with indecision, wanting to buy them all.

"Kystina." Domine reached out his hand as she stood beside us, his eyes searching hers. "Thank you. For *everything*."

"You're welcome." Her tone grew somber for a moment as she placed her hand on the door, looking at us with tenderness before drawing her face into a playful grin. "Hopefully, the guys haven't trashed our new unit yet." She let out a chuckle. "I swear, it feels like I'm living in a college dorm again with those three. But we're kind of a strange, misfit family now. I don't mind all the space they take up." She gave me a soft smile and opened the door, shooting a quick wave to Vanisha, who was still parked outside with the car engine idling, streams of exhaust drifting into the night air.

She stood in the doorway for a moment, looking up into the rain falling against her hair in droplets that caught the light from inside. "This is it, Seren. Our new chapter."

Hope stirred within my chest, full of promise, and I pulled her into a hug, the swell of my belly jutting between us. "I'm so happy you're here."

"Me, too." She squeezed my hand before dashing toward the car, her raincoat a vivid splash of color against the darkness.

Closing the door behind me, I turned to see Domine settling himself onto the couch as Lilica curled beside him. In her hand she clutched her book of fairy tales, now worn and tattered from all the months of flipping through the pages.

"Read this one." She leaned her head on his shoulder, the light from the lamp beside them casting gentle shadows across their skin as Domine looked over at me and mouthed, *come here.*

I slid off my coat and sank onto the couch, which fit the three of us so perfectly together. Resting my head on his chest, I closed my eyes and listened to the rhythmic cadence of his voice as he began to read, the rise and fall of his breath, the steady beat of his heart.

* * *

*T*he feel of a hand sweeping back my hair woke me, and my eyes fluttered open to meet Domine's.

"Looks like I put you both to sleep," he whispered, nodding toward Lilica, who lay nestled beside him, an arm sprawled over his chest.

"I guess you did." A smile washed across my face as I glanced around the room, noticing the open book on his lap and the soup still on the stove. "Are you hungry?"

"Not really." He traced his thumb lazily along my bottom lip, and I shifted against him, the sudden look of heat in his eyes causing a sharp ache of longing to coil through me. The past two days had been spent with a hospital bed between us. Bright lights and doors opening and closing. Nurses and doctors checking vitals and making notes on clipboards. And I wanted him alone, among tangled sheets in a darkened room. His hands covering every inch of my skin. His arms surrounding me.

"I'll get Lili into bed." My words came out breathless, and I pulled myself from the couch as Domine gently lifted her up, helping position her against my hip.

She barely stirred, her body limp and heavy in my arms as I made my way down the hall and flicked on her bedroom light. Lowering her onto the bed, I drew the covers around her, noticing for the first time the shrine she had erected on her nightstand. Various rocks and acorn tops, dried leaves, and tiny twigs were neatly arranged in intricate patterns that spiraled around her collection of Domine's carved fairy statues. It was art. A story told of deep forests and rushing rivers, the chill of snowfall, and the gentle eyes of a wolf. A journey now over but forever tucked away in the endless space of her mind.

"I love you, Lili," I whispered as I bent and placed a kiss on her forehead, watching her eyelids flutter in sleep, her breath falling soft against the pillow.

The sound of water running through pipes stirred me from my thoughts, and I quietly slipped from her room, my eyes falling to the trail of light slanting from beneath the bathroom door. Placing my hand on the knob, I tentatively cracked it open. "Domine? Do you need any help in there?"

He stood with his shirt off, his good leg propped against the sink, hair wet and falling into his eyes as he bent close to the mirror with a razor poised in his hand. "I was going to shave for you." He turned to me with a sheepish smile. "But I'm realizing it's a bit more work than I thought."

Walking up to him, I slid my arms around his neck, resting my cheek against his. "I like the beard."

He set the razor down and dipped his head close to mine, his breath a whisper against my ear. "Then I'll keep it."

I trailed my hands down his chest, across sinewy muscle and warm skin, stopping at the now yellowed bruising on his rib cage. "How is the pain right now?"

"All I feel are your hands on me, Seren." His voice was throaty as he bent and brushed his lips against my neck, sending goosebumps racing across my skin. I tilted my head back, letting out a gasp as he gently pressed me against the sink and found my mouth in an explosion of heat that sent my pulse racing.

His kiss was like the release of a breath I had been holding, the caress of his lips hungry but slow, and I grasped his shoulders, wove my hands into his hair, curled around his body as I fell into the abyss of him. He was fire on my skin, a reckless urgency to reach into the center of myself. The place where his heart rested with mine.

With a groan, he gripped the edge of the counter for balance and pulled back to look at me, his eyes swimming with intensity as his voice came out in a broken whisper that caused my core to tighten and ache. "Should we get out of this bathroom?"

"Yes." I let out a breathless chuckle, my limbs buzzing as I detached myself from his arms and handed him the crutches he had leaned against the wall.

The hallway was dark as we made our way to the bedroom and closed the door. The silence was like a sharp thrum of energy humming between us as he lowered himself onto the edge of the bed and turned on the lamp, the light throwing shadows across the room. "I want to see you."

I found my hands trembling as I reached to unclasp the buttons on my shirt. There was a shyness that hovered within me, as if I were revealing myself for the first time, breathless with the possibilities, the rush of him like a delicious promise. Sliding the fabric down past my arms, I removed the last of my layers and stood there naked before him.

His eyes burned into me as he drew me close and placed his hands on the rise of my belly, his touch so soft and tender that tears gathered in my eyes. "I can't believe you're here." My words came out in a choked whisper as his lips met my skin, drawing slow kisses along my neck, trailing across the slope of my breasts.

"I can't either." His hands slid up my back as his mouth continued to explore me, moving from my breasts down to my stomach, his lips leaving an aching path of heat behind. "You feel like a beautiful dream." His eyes traced the contours of my body, drinking me in, and there was something different in the way he looked at me. It was with a reverence but also a disbelief. As if he feared I would fade away and disappear beneath his touch.

On shaky legs, I knelt beside him and wove my hands through his hair, my lips finding his in a dance that stripped me of thought until all that remained was the taste of his mouth. The way his breath teased my skin. The feel of his arms as they anchored me.

Unhooking the buckle on his pants, I slid them down his hips and past his cast.

"Seren." His voice was a shudder as I ran my hands up his thighs, my fingers brushing across his length, the pulse of his desire like a silent language that sent a rush of longing to curl through me.

A fervency that took root in my center. A yearning to reach out and fall with him.

I leaned him against the bed, the expanse of my belly pressing against him as I positioned myself on top and guided him inside me. I let out a disjointed cry as he touched my depths, and I tilted my head back, giving myself over to the overwhelming surge of pleasure that cascaded through me, the endless burning song between us.

"My God. *Seren.*" He sat up, hands now urgent and ravenous, pulling me closer, his eyes feverish and brimming with tears as I slowly rocked against him. Lost in the fire. Lost in the feeling of him surrounding me. A feeling I thought I would never have again.

He was gone, and now he was back.

The wonder of that was a rush of emotion that erupted within. An answered prayer that pulled back the dark, and my tears mixed with his as I found his mouth, tumbling blindly into the euphoria.

"Dom." I spoke his name like a plea. A wild whisper in the gentle light surrounding us. I ran my fingers across his lips, breathing him into my skin, aching to go deeper, to crawl into the depths of him as we continued to move in a rhythm slow and tender, his eyes searing through me, extracting a language that needed no words. And he held me, putting back together all the pieces I thought had been lost.

* * *

*E*vening spilled patterns across the sheets, Domine's fingers lightly tracing the shadows that danced across my skin as our labored breath grew fluid and soft. Lying beside him with our limbs entangled, I listened to the stillness surrounding us. The icy whisper of winter nights and swaying trees was now replaced with the hum of appliances and the gentle swish of cars passing on the rain-soaked road. It was different, but it was still ours. It was our silence.

Domine cupped the swell of my belly, his hand following the undulating movements. The kicks and thrusts of life inside me. "I don't think I'll ever find the right words to express how amazing this is." His voice grew choked as he stared at me from across the pillow. "I'm going to be a father."

I reached out and slid my hand over his. "You already are."

He smiled, his gaze languid in the dim light, and I closed my eyes for a moment, sinking into the harbor of his touch as he continued to brush his fingers across my stomach. "There's something I haven't told you." My voice was a whisper as I opened my eyes and looked at him. "When I had that ultrasound, the doctor couldn't find any lesions."

"What do you mean?"

"I mean they're gone."

His eyes grew wide as he propped himself up on his elbow. "How is that possible?"

"I don't know." I stared out the window into the darkness as I plucked the truth I had been holding close to my chest. "But Vanisha told me something about Lilica. About children being born with gray eyes. Dream Walkers, they're called. Those who have the power to communicate through dreams, and some of them have the ability to heal." I turned to look at him, the magnitude of everything suddenly hitting me with a vastness I feared my hands were too small to hold. "She has gifts, Domine."

He swept back a strand of hair that had fallen across my face, his voice soft. "Honestly, I'm not surprised to hear this. I don't know anything about gray-eyed children, but I *know* Lilica. And I've always felt she has something magical inside her."

Tears gathered in my eyes as the thrum of his words reached deep into me, the breadth of his love for her so palpable. "I just don't know what to do with this information. How do I guide her through all this when I barely understand it myself?"

"I don't think it's your job to guide her."

I shook my head, wiping away a tear that had crept down my cheek. "What do you mean?"

"I mean, there are things that will always be beyond our understanding. But I think Lilica was given this gift because she has the strength to carry it. She'll let you know what she needs from you. From both of us."

"I hope so." I released a sigh and found his hand, tracing over the scar on the joint of his pinky. The remnants of what the wild took from him. The fractures and wounds that still needed to be healed. "This whole time she knew you were alive, that you were coming back. I wish I had been able to believe her."

He nodded, sorrow tracing the lines of his face. "She came to me in a dream, you know."

I looked up at him, watching as the light in his eyes flashed with sudden shadows. "When was this?"

"When I thought I was dying."

His words were a punch in my gut, and I sucked in a sharp breath. He had barely spoken of what happened out there on the river. As if the details were a dark stain he was not yet ready to release.

He shifted onto his side, tendrils of hair falling into his eyes as he stared at me with such burning affliction it stilled my heart. "I had been lying there on the riverbank for about four days. The pain in my leg was so unbearable. I could barely move to drink water. And it reached the point where I didn't even want to anymore. I was ready to give up."

"Dom." I stretched out my hand, running my fingers down his cheek, across his lips, as if I could erase the memories of his suffering. Take all the damage away.

He grasped my hand, his eyes burning into me as he threaded his fingers through mine. "But then she came to me. She said the fairies were going to help me. That I was going to see both of you again. And the next morning Kystina found me."

Goosebumps raced across my skin, and my breath lodged within my chest. I realized that Kystina finding him was not just a miraculous coincidence, a random stumbling past a bend in the river where he happened to be. But something more. Something powerful. A force that had propelled her to him. Propelled us all back together.

Life could be brutal and full of loss, but it was also magic. A bright spark of beauty waiting to enfold us. The delicate dance between darkness and light.

Emotion took hold of me, born of a fervent gratitude, and I reached out to him, my fingers brushing across the plane of his face, outlining the contours of skin and bone, the resilient etchings of all we had been through. "We made it, Dom. We finally made it."

"We did." He drew his lips to mine, his hands cradling the edges of my elation, arms holding me in a quiet room with empty walls that awaited a new story. Our story.

This was where I could uncurl myself. *This was a life of my own.* The place I had been longing for. The heartbeat within. And suddenly, the intensity of love didn't feel so terrifying anymore. It was no longer something that could be taken away, for I knew it lived fiercely inside me, and it always would.

Love was not something given to us. It was something we grew.

I sank into the refuge of his skin against mine, his hands sweeping back my hair, and I closed my eyes, allowing the gentle tendrils of sleep to untether me. And then I slipped away, not into darkness, but into a place wild and full of color.

A place of dreams.

* * *

rees whispered softly, the air warm with the scent of wildflowers and earth as I walked across a forest floor. Moss beneath my bare feet like velvet, my hands trailing over branches that bent and swayed with my touch.

"Where are you?" I spoke to the wind, to the trees, to the sky unfolding before me like a brilliant canvas. "Where are you?"

"I'm right here, gwreichionen llachar."

I turned around and looked into the deep sapphire eyes of my mother, her soothing gaze like a water's embrace I had not felt in so long, and my words unfurled around her like hesitant wings. "Where have you been?"

"I've always been right here." As she spoke, a bright light the color of pine branches rinsed in morning sun shimmered across her skin. Her voice now rested deep inside my mind as her form slowly fell away to reveal that of a wolf.

"Run with me. You're home now."

And I did. My limbs burst with an energy I had never experienced before. It spiraled around me like an intoxicating liquid as I followed her through the trees. My mind unbound. My steps effortless and buoyant as if gravity no longer held weight.

As if I could fly.

As if I had always been able to.

EPILOGUE

I stood in my clinic as early afternoon streamed through the open windows, bathing the floor in prisms of warm light. My eyes ran across the herbs and tinctures neatly labeled along the shelves. Echinacea, goldenseal, feverfew, and milk thistle. Herbs I no longer had to hide away, concealed behind shelves and buried within closets.

I had no more secrets to keep.

But beneath this freedom lay a furtive unease I could not seem to shake. As if at any moment, this life I had built back together would come crashing down. Sometimes I thought I would see the flash of steely dark eyes and Trendon's tall, thin frame lurking in a grocery store aisle or walking behind me on the sidewalk. But when I turned around, it was always someone else. It was never him.

How long would I live with this muffled fear tucked against me?

Turning toward the window, I stared off into the distant mountains, the peaks jutting upward against the wash of the sky. Vanisha had spoken of the trauma that living within a controlled society can bring. *"It will take time until you are fully healed,"* she had said. *"The human mind is a trained creature. It does not yet know that you are safe."*

But what did safety really mean? So many of us spent our whole lives running from our own shadows. Terrified of the screaming silence inside. The emptiness. The loneliness. The losses. The wounds that would not heal. But safety was not a refuge from threats. It was finding the courage to tend to your scars. The healing no one could take from you. It was finding home inside yourself. I knew that now. And I could feel myself stretch and shift with this knowledge. I was not safe because I was here in Canada. I was safe because I was learning to walk softly with my own ghosts.

The sound of a door opening stirred me from my thoughts, and I turned to see Kystina stroll in with a wide smile, bouncing Forest against her hip. "You ready to go?"

"Yeah, I'm ready." I grabbed the patient file sitting on our desk and placed it inside the wooden cabinet, sliding the drawer closed. "Thanks for watching him."

"Always a pleasure, you know that." She winked and attempted to pull back her long hair that Forest now clenched in his chubby fists.

"Momma." Forest reached for me, his dark hair tousled against rosy cheeks, and I swooped him up into my arms, peppering his face with kisses.

"How's my sweet boy? Did you have fun with Auntie Kystina?"

He squealed, a toothy grin erupting across his face as he stared up at me with the same haunting gray eyes as his sister.

Kystina flipped the *Open* sign hanging in the window and turned off the lights, holding the door for me. "The van's all packed. I figure we can just head over to the site and pick up Domine and Lilica."

"Sounds good." I took a deep breath, the scent in the air fresh and sweet as I stepped out into the warmth of a clear summer sky, wisps of clouds lazily drifting above us. "I still can't believe there's no smoke here."

Kystina smiled and slid open the van door. "I know. It's amazing, isn't it? Someone in town was telling me it had something to do with the mountains. They affect the direction of wind patterns and jet streams or something." She rearranged the packs in the back seat. "Whatever it is, I'm not complaining."

"I'm not either." My mind tumbled back to something Domine had said when we had been on the trail. And I wondered if we had no smoke here simply because we were far enough away from the Grid. Far from the intentional burns that had so effectively pushed us from nature.

Leaning in, I buckled Forest into his car seat and handed him the stuffed bear Lilica had given him, which he had now taken to carrying everywhere.

"Ba Ba!" He wrapped his arms around the bear and buried his face into the worn fabric as I slipped into the front seat beside Kystina.

"Where's Jaze?"

She turned to me with a chuckle. "Where do you think? I can't seem to get a hammer out of that man's hand."

"Oh, right. Why did I even ask?" I shot her a playful smile and glanced out the window as the van pulled out onto the road. Jaze had been one of the travelers with Kystina during their trek to Canada, and over the past year, their relationship had bloomed into something deeper. Our small family entwining like roots as Domine became the new manager of the construction company here in Canmore, and Jaze now worked alongside him as an assistant.

"Do you think we'll be able to pry them away from the house?"

"Let's hope so." She flicked on her blinker and took the road out of town, leading up toward the enclosure of trees that hugged the mountain range. "If not, we can always hide their tools."

Letting out a laugh, I glanced back at Forest, who was staring out the window as the landscape turned to grassland, the waving meadows now a golden brown kissed from the heat of the summer sun.

The van bumped along the dirt road and came to a stop beside the edge of the tree line. The sound of hammering echoed through the air as I stepped out and saw Domine perched on the topmost beam of the house, installing plywood onto the roof. Turning in my direction, he spread out his hand in a wave before making his way down the ladder.

"Mommy!"

Lilica ran toward me with a wide grin, sunlight glinting off her hair, cheeks smudged with sawdust.

"Hey there, hon. You've been helping with the house?"

"Yep!" She unbuckled Forest from his car seat and lifted him into her arms, his legs dangling awkwardly against her small frame. "I got to hammer walls."

"That's great, sweetie." I bent and placed a kiss on her forehead, sweeping back her hair with a smile. "Are you ready to go camping?"

"Yep." Forest wiggled in her grasp, and she set him down, taking his hand as he tottered through the tall grass.

Walking behind them, I watched as Domine made his way across the field toward us, the limp in his right leg only slightly noticeable as he lifted Forest high into the air, causing a swell of laughter to take flight.

I stood and stared up at the house. It had been a week since I had last been here, and it looked like Domine and Jaze had made considerable progress. It was an expansive single story nestled against the mountains, with large windows that would let the light in. I closed my eyes for a moment, envisioning the way the sun would fall through the glass in the morning, washing the oak floors in soft shadows. The way the trees would enclose us as we sat in the living room, their branches swaying in a silent dance that whispered of wildness.

A smile crept across my face. When we had put our names in for the property draw six months ago, I was not expecting us to get it. It had been a hopeful dream, a fantasy of living so close to the woods yet still connected to the pulse of this town. And now, here I was, standing in front of our home.

"It's coming along nicely, don't you think?" Domine slid his arm around my waist and brushed his lips across my neck, his beard tickling my cheek, causing a rush of warmth to thread through me.

He smelled of lumber and sun-drenched skin, and I leaned into him as he cradled Forest in the crook of his arm.

"Yes. It really is."

"All right, you guys, let's get a move on." Kystina leaned lightly on the horn with a playful smile as Jaze slipped his lanky form into the passenger seat beside her.

Beneath a swath of blue sky, Lilica bounded through the grass toward the van, the long stalks swishing against her legs, leaving behind a trail for us to follow.

* * *

The trees grew thicker as we wound our way deeper into the mountains, filtered sunlight casting beams along the forest floor. I stared out into the endless expanse of green, my breath rising in my throat like a silent plea for a lost lover. I had taken walks along the trails outside Canmore. I had stood beneath the canopy of trees and listened to their gentle song. But I had not ventured deep into the pulse of the wild. Not since Lilica and I had crossed that road, leaving everything I thought I had lost behind me.

I entwined my hand through Domine's, watching as the light caught his profile. The angled sweep of his brow, the curve of his cheekbone, the way his eyes danced with softness as he turned to look at me. I would never grow tired of looking into those eyes. They were my refuge. My anchor. The place I could always fall into.

"Oh, this looks like a good spot." Kystina slowed the van and pointed toward an old logging road, the gate now sagging with the weight of vines that crept along the rusted metal. "You guys want to check it out?"

"I do!" Lilica called out from the back seat where she sat beside Forest, her trusty walking stick clutched in her hand, eyes wide with eagerness.

"Well, let's go exploring then." I looked back at her with a smile and ran my hand through the mass of Forest's curly dark hair. Except for the piercing gray eyes he shared with his sister, and the gifts he would one day discover, he looked so much like Domine, it never failed to still my breath. He was the thread that connected Domine to his own lineage. To the family he lost. Their story now woven together with ours.

Kystina and Jaze chatted quietly in the front seat while the van bumped along the rutted dirt road, taking us into the fold of the mountains, into the hidden places untouched by trails and signposts.

We drove until the road narrowed and was swallowed by the forest floor. Bringing the van to a stop, we climbed out, twigs crunching beneath our feet as the sound of birdsong saturated the air.

"God, I've missed this." Domine thrust his hands into his pockets, the wind tossing strands of hair into his face as he looked up into the dense enclosure of trees with a sigh, his eyes following the gentle sway of the branches.

"Me, too." My voice came out in a whisper as I stood beside him, remembering the dream I had the night before. The rush of cool wind on my skin. The flush of elation. The stillness that always came when I went to the places my mind longed for. My dreams were always full of wilderness. A vastness I would never grow tired of exploring.

"You know, I never thought I would grow so fond of all this nature stuff." Jaze broke the silence as he leaned against the door with a grin, sweeping his hand across the expanse of trees. "But this is where I fell in love with Kystina." He reached out to encircle her waist as she grabbed a pack from the back of the van.

"Oh, stop." She playfully batted him away, a flush peppering her cheeks.

I let out a laugh, watching Kystina's hard exterior crumble as he pulled her in for a quick kiss.

"Mommy, can I look for the fairies with Forest?"

"Let's find a place to set up camp first, okay, Lili?" I slid the baby carrier over my chest and unbuckled Forest from his car seat, nestling him snugly against me, his legs tucked around my waist.

"He's almost getting too big for that thing." Domine chuckled as he shouldered both our packs and grabbed one of the coolers.

"I know." I swept my hand through the threads of Forest's curls, breathing in his warm scent and the steady rise and fall of his breath against my skin as the memory of his birth washed through me.

Vanisha had been there, her calm green eyes holding space, stilling my unease as I had labored for hours with Domine in the pool of warm water she had set up in our living room. I had been reluctant at first to do a home birth. Children had always been born under the bright lights of hospitals back at the Grid, attached to machines and prodded by sterile hands and masked faces. I had known no other way. But Vanisha was skilled in midwifery, and the intimacy of the experience had been innate and profound. Forest was born healthy, and in the same way he was conceived, with the buoyant arms of water cradling him. For I now knew that the night we made love in the hot spring beneath the snow flecked sky, we had created something beautiful, something that went far beyond the connection of our bodies.

Shafts of light spilled through the branches as we walked deeper into the woods. Lilica ran ahead of us, weaving between the trees, her hair catching the sun. She was in her element here. She always had been. The thrum of her heart intrinsically dancing with the breath of the earth.

The trees suddenly thinned out, and Lilica stood in a clearing of dry grass that still held the faint impressions of what I imagined had been a family of deer resting among scattered morning sunlight.

"It's a fairy ring, Mommy." She skipped around the circular space. "Can we camp here?"

"I don't see why not. This looks like a great place, Lili."

I turned to Domine, who had deposited the packs on the ground with a smile. "I think this is perfect, wood nymph."

We set up camp, falling into a fluid rhythm together as Domine and Jaze went to gather wood to make a fire and Kystina helped put up the tents. Lilica watched Forest beside the clearing, showing him treasures found among moss and earth, her chatter rising and falling between the trees.

The sound of the crackling fire drifted through the tent as I stood inside, drinking in the gentle whisper of memories. All the nights we had spent within these walls, nestled against the rustling of trees and star-soaked skies. Despite all the obstacles we faced and the fear that had trailed me, I had never felt so alive. So connected to the very essence of my own presence.

"There you are."

Domine's arms encircled me from behind, his voice a soft murmur against my ear, and I sank into the feel of him as the last of the sun's rays shone through the tent, caressing the walls with light. I turned to him, placing my hand on his chest. "Thank you."

With a smile, he tilted my chin up to meet his eyes, resting his forehead against mine. "For what?"

"For saving my life."

His thumb swept across my cheek, his eyes wide and dancing with emotion. "Thank you for saving mine."

I brushed my lips across his and descended into the freefall of his kiss as he slid his hands through my hair and pulled me against him. None of us knew what the future would bring. Life was delicate and unpredictable. Maybe one day, Trendon would find us. Maybe one day, the Grid would come back like a ghost to haunt me. But for now, we were tucked beneath the shelter of trees and sky. And that was all that mattered. This moment held together by the resilience we had forged.

A blush of pink washed across the sky as we stepped out of the tent. Kystina and Jaze sat beside the fire, the melodic sound of strings against wood drifting through the air as Jaze softly plucked on his guitar. Lilica sat off in the tall grass with Forest, humming a song as she wove wildflowers into the dark curls of his hair.

Making my way over to them, I crouched next to Lilica, fingering the white trumpet-shaped petals in her hand as Forest scrambled into my arms, smelling of honeysuckle.

"Mommy!" Her eyes grew wide, the flowers tumbling from between her fingers as she abruptly stood and pointed toward the trees. "It's Prince! He came back. He came to visit us."

In the distance, light and shadows etched across the familiar markings of the wolf, and my heart stumbled and swelled as we locked eyes in a silent greeting born of time and growth. Of paths ending and merging once more.

I noticed movement in the corner of my eye, and my breath stilled as another wolf slipped through the trees to stand beside him with two pups crouching low in the undergrowth.

"Oh, Lili. Look." Holding Forest against me, I leaned in close to her. "I think that's his mate and their puppies."

"He's a daddy now, Mommy."

"He is, love."

Prince and I stared at each other, the stillness within his eyes speaking of all the moments we had shared beneath wild sky and lush forest. Our story now forever entwined, caught within the filaments of sunlight that shimmered between us. And then he bowed his head low to the ground and turned from us, disappearing back into the fold of the trees with the others following close behind.

I released my breath in a long, slow sigh. He had found his family. His home. The gentle heartbeat that tethered him to the earth.

Just as I had.

Milton Keynes UK
Ingram Content Group UK Ltd.
UKHW010734231023
431165UK00004B/300

9 798223 048077